PASSION'S REALM

Enticing, entrancing April Danby had given her heart to one man when she was little more than a girl. Then she lost him and vowed never to feel that way for another.

Noah McCloud had been madly in love with a bewitching temptress who had betrayed him. Now he knew better than ever to put his happiness and dreams into the hands of a woman again.

Noah told himself to be wary of April from the moment he met her. For her part, April drew back from the fierce response rising within her at Noah's gaze, his touch, his lips on hers.

But this was Albuquerque, where men and women left their pasts far behind . . . and let the passionate present rule. . . . .

Debra Adler

ALBUQUERQUE

Sara Orwig

AN ONYX BOOK

NEW AMERICAN LIBRARY

A DIVISION OF PENGUIN BOOKS USA INC.

PUBLISHER'S NOTE

This is a work of fiction. Names, characters, places, and incidents either are the product of the author's imagination or are used fictitiously, and any resemblance to actual persons, living or dead, events, or locales is entirely coincidental.

Copyright © 1990 by Sara Orwig

ONYX TRADEMARK REG. U.S. PAT OFF. AND FOREIGN COUNTRIES REGISTERED TRADEMARK—MARCA REGISTRADA
HECHO EN DRESDEN, TN U.S.A.

SIGNET, SIGNET CLASSIC, MENTOR, ONYX, PLUME, MERIDIAN and NAL BOOKS are published by New American Library, a division of Penguin Books USA Inc., 1633 Broadway, New York, New York 10019

First Printing, January, 1990

1 2 3 4 5 6 7 8 9

PRINTED IN THE UNITED STATES OF AMERICA

To Jan and Mike for their courage.
Words are inadequate.

PROLOGUE

Battle of Vicksburg
1863

The rain fell steadily as the soldiers continued to battle in the fading light. Captain Noah McCloud of the Alabama Twentieth Regiment rode through the trees. Before him, his line of men were holding a ridge against a Yankee attack. Two cannon blasted and recoiled, muzzles smoking. Noah knew they wouldn't be able to last much longer.

"Captain!"

He shifted in the saddle to see a mud-spattered soldier ride up. "Orders from Lieutenant General Pemberton, sir. Also, there's a letter he said to give to you."

Fleetingly Noah wondered how long ago the letter had been written. He saw the fancy scrawl and knew it was from Fanchette Viguerie. He pushed it aside and began reading the general's message. "Retreat at once! Move your men back to Stouts Bayou and wait for further orders. Lieutenant General John Pemberton."

Noah swore and stuffed the orders in his pocket along with his letter, which he had already forgotten. Suddenly a shot flew overhead, tearing off leaves and branches as it sailed through the trees. He quickly began calling orders to his men.

"Beaufort, move the cannon back. Stouts Bayou. Pass the word. Now!" he shouted, riding up and down the line. His horse stumbled, and Noah soon realized it had been shot. He flung himself off and landed in the mud as cold rain spattered his face. He commandeered another mount quickly and continued organizing the retreat.

"Move out!" he shouted.

As the last stragglers began to retreat, the Yankees crept forward on the ridge, steadily gaining on them.

One of his men, young Private Mark O'Neill, suddenly screamed and fell over, writhing on the ground. Noah galloped to him.

"Get on my horse," he shouted, leaning down to give a hand. O'Neill clasped Noah's arm and climbed on behind him. They rode south, and Noah noticed another private stretched on the ground. As he dismounted, he saw it was young Luther Wilbanks, who had lied about his age in order to join the army. He had been shot in the thigh, and had another wound in his side.

Noah lifted Luther to the back of the horse and helped him clamp his hands on the pommel. Then Noah took the reins and began to plod swiftly through the mud, catching up with the line of men in retreat. He handed the reins to a soldier. "Get these men to safety. I'm going back."

"Yes, sir."

With his prize rifle, a .44-caliber Henry, in hand, Noah hurried to join the last few soldiers holding the Yankees back. Aided by the cover of darkness, the group retreated safely, wading through the mud to catch up with the others.

Two days later they reached Lieutenant General Pemberton's troops, and that night, for the first time in months, Noah stretched out on a blanket to sleep. Remembering his letter, he pulled it from his pocket. It was wrinkled and torn, but the delicate slanting letters made his heart jump.

"Dear Noah—" he read.

"Letter from Miss Viguerie, Cap'n?" came a question, interrupting him. He looked up to see one of his men, Dick Waltingham, from a neighboring plantation back in Alabama. Dick warmed his hands, smiling, with a wistful expression on his face as he glanced at the paper in Noah's hands.

"Yep. From Fanchette," Noah answered, bending his head over the letter as the flames highlighted his thin, straight nose and prominent cheekbones. As he began reading, he could imagine Fanchette's black eyes, hear her high voice tinged with a thick French accent.

Dear Noah:

It gives me much pain to write this letter, but I must be truthful to you. My life passes too swiftly, and I cannot wait for you any longer. Samuel Craddock has asked me to be his wife, and I have accepted. I am truly sorry, Noah. I hope you will understand.

C'est difficile. *We remain* deux amis. I—

Filled with pain, Noah crumpled the letter. He stared at the dancing flames as he remembered Fanchette lying in his arms, Fanchette yielding to him.

Samuel Craddock was old enough to be her father. And rich as Croesus. Noah swore softly, knowing full well Fanchette's love of fancy dresses and elegant things, knowing only the wealthiest men in Baldwin County had been allowed to court her. He tossed the letter into the fire, watching it curl and blacken, his hopes and love curling and dying with it. He turned to face Dick, then rose abruptly and strode away into the darkness to be alone. He swore that never again would he give his heart so swiftly and easily as he had to Fanchette.

1

1865

Beneath the snow-covered western slopes of the great Sandia peaks lay the town of Albuquerque, the heart of the New Mexico Territory. Its lights glowed through the falling snow, which blanketed the town, while in the El Paraíso saloon, smoke hung like a cloud over the noisy patrons. Potbellied stoves glowed warmly as whiskey heated the men. Candles burned along the edge of the stage, where a slender golden-haired singer in a bright green dress moved forward, giving her audience a glimpse of long, shapely legs through the slit in her tight skirt.

As her haunting, vibrant voice came across the stage, men became silent, all of them, soldiers, gamblers, and drifters. They all stared hungrily at her. April Danby's voice dropped, and a throaty rasp enhanced her velvety tone. She could see the upturned eyes, the looks of lust and longing, but it was merely a sea of faceless, nameless men. Always in her heart she sang to a dark-eyed, black-haired man who had died years ago in a gun battle.

She glanced down and saw a handsome blond soldier, who must have been about seventeen years old. His eyes held a wistful longing as he watched her with openmouthed awe. She suspected that he, as well as so many others present, was a long way from home tonight.

There were wild rumors that the war would end

soon; after the battles of Valverde and Glorietta Pass,
the Union Army in New Mexico Territory had turned
its attention to fighting the Indians. So as remote as
Albuquerque was from most of the war, the fighting
had come here as well, and soldiers overran the town.

Slowly, kneeling so her skirt fell open to reveal her
shapely legs, she withdrew a lace handkerchief from
the deep décolletage of her silk dress. The stillness in
the room was broken. With each inch of lace that
slipped into sight, the noise grew. Men whistled and
cheered and called to her, but she ignored them. She
watched only the blond, who stared at her with wide
blue eyes while perspiration popped out on his brow.
She smiled at him and tossed her handkerchief across
the candles. He was on his feet in an instant to catch
the handkerchief, while men yelled and clapped their
hands.

She stood up, twitching her hips as she strode swiftly
back to center stage, and the piano player switched to
a rowdier tune. She smiled at the blur of pale faces
beyond the bright candles as she belted out another
song. Her strong, clear voice made the men listen and
stomp their feet in time to the music, cheering when
she was finished. Then she was gone, striding offstage
for her dressing room.

She headed straight for her tiny room, passing the
women in the chorus line. When the other women finished performing, they would mingle with the crowd,
but it was part of April's agreement with Rigo Werner,
the owner, that she didn't have to sell drinks, or her
body.

She was nineteen now, and drew a crowd on the
nights she sang. The war had added to the number of
men in town and to her popularity. She closed the
door, shutting out the noise while she gave the room
a cursory glance. She was no longer aware of the
cracked window, the rough wooden walls and dusty
plank floor. She was fortunate to have a tiny room to
herself. She had a dressing table covered in pots of
rouge and powder. A red satin dress was tossed over
the only wooden chair, and a battered screen stood at

one corner of the room. She reached up to unfasten the hooks that ran down the back of her dress.

"Ma'am—" came a deep voice.

April whirled around, and a soldier appeared from behind the screen. He wore a butternut linsey-woolsey frock coat with the two gold-braid bars of a first lieutenant of the confederacy, and he was covered in blood.

April gasped, staring at him as he leaned against the wall. Golden hair fell over his deep blue eyes. He held a rag to his shoulder, and she could see the spread of bright crimson beneath it. His trouser leg was also soaked in blood from a wound in his thigh. For the first time she noticed the blood on the floor. As they stared at each other, she heard a commotion in the hall.

"Hide me, please," he gasped.

Stunned, she answered, "You need a doctor."

"Hide me! Bluebellies are after me. They'll take me to prison. Hide me, please . . ."

Moving instinctively, she turned the key in the lock. Still in shock she repeated over and over, "I have to get you to a doctor!" She was afraid he would bleed to death in the next few seconds.

"No, ma'am. Have to get home to Noah. Have to get home . . . to Laura Lee."

For just a moment April remembered how deeply she had loved Emilio Piedra.

"Hide me. Bluebellies will hang me."

Someone pounded on the door. "U.S. Cavalry, ma'am. Open the door!"

April made her decision. "Get behind the screen." She went to help him, and as he dropped to the floor, she almost went down with him. She wiped the blood off her hands and glanced down briefly at him. His eyes were squeezed shut in pain, long, thick golden lashes covering his cheek. The thumping on the door galvanized her into action. She stepped out of her dress and held it to her chin, then yanked down a twist of hair, sending pins flying. She shook her head as she unlocked the door and opened it a fraction.

Two uniformed men faced her. The scowl on the officer's face vanished instantly as his hazel eyes swept over her bare shoulders.

"I'm dressing," she said firmly.

"Sorry, ma'am, but we're hunting a dangerous man. He killed a man."

"That describes two-thirds of the soldiers here tonight," she retorted.

"No, ma'am. This is different. He killed a U.S. Army captain, and it wasn't in the line of duty. He's here in the El Paraíso."

"Well, he's not here with me, I can promise you! I'm changing clothes, and soldiers aren't allowed in my dressing room." She let her dress slip enough to reveal the shapely contours of her high, full breasts. His gaze swept over her, and he licked his lips.

"Good night," she said firmly, smiling at him.

"Sorry to have bothered you, ma'am," he whispered, while the other one stared and barely nodded. The silence continued until, with reluctance, they both walked away.

As April started to close the door, she glanced down. A smear of blood darkened the plank floor. She noticed another, both clearly leading to her dressing room. She locked the door quickly.

The Rebel was propped against the wall again, his face ashen, but he gave her a lopsided grin. "Good girl!"

"You have to get out of here. There's blood in the hall."

His blue eyes seemed to focus on her. "Just for a few hours, can I go home with you? Please."

"You'll bleed to death if you move around that much."

"You change clothes. I won't look. I have a horse outside. Please let me go home with you."

"I have a buggy," she said, dropping the dress. He leaned back against the wall with his eyes closed, and she changed swiftly, yanking on her woolen dress and heavy cape, unmindful of her disheveled hair.

She hunted behind the screen and held up a cape. "Stand up and let me put this around you."

He opened his eyes and swayed as he tried to straighten up. Grimacing with pain, he was silent while she flung the cape around his shoulders. As she put a wide-brimmed hat on his head, pulling down the veil, he gave her another cocky grin that made her heart lurch. She didn't see how he could survive the next hour.

"I'll help you to the buggy."

Afraid she would hurt him, she put her arm around him, and together they struggled into the hall. With her heart pounding in fear, she glanced back at the two officers as they stood facing the small stage. If either of them turned, she would be caught, and the Rebel would hang.

"Keep moving!" she whispered, feeling his weight sag. Her back tingled, and she curbed the urge to glance over her shoulder. "Keep walking," she whispered. "We're almost to the door."

She glanced back to see the men laughing as they watched the dancers on the stage. One looked at her, and she waved; to her relief, the Rebel was already outside, leaning against the wall.

She slipped her arm around him, looking at the height of the buggy and wondering how he could possibly manage to climb up. "I can't lift you."

"No trouble," he murmured, and pulled himself up, gasping with pain. As he collapsed in the seat, he groaned. "Bring my horse," he said in a rasping voice.

Obeying him, she quickly tethered his horse to the back of the buggy. To her horror, she saw a dark trail of blood that led from the door to the carriage, but snow fell thickly, obliterating it. She sprang up, flicking the reins.

"They'll find the blood in the dressing room, but I left the door ajar and the lamps out. They'll think you were in there after I left."

When he didn't answer, she assumed he had passed out. Through the empty, snowy street, they drove in

silence. The only sounds were the creak of her buggy
and the steady plodding of the horses. Usually she enjoyed the ride home after work, the solitude, the qui-
etness of the town with the adobe buildings and dark
silhouettes against the snow, but tonight she felt as if
she were being watched. She tried to keep from constantly looking over her shoulder as she headed up the
lane to her small frame house on the edge of town.
Empty fields flanked her yard and there were four
houses across the street. It was the house directly
across that worried April, because the elderly widows,
twin sisters Lesta and Vesta Dodworth, constantly
watched their neighbors. To April's relief, no light
burned at their home, and she didn't see the blurred
oval of a Dodworth face at the window.

April opened her back door before going back to
gently shake the soldier. She helped him through her
tiny kitchen to the parlor. Wood still glowed in the
stone fireplace, and she hurried to place another piñon
log on the dying embers. As soon as it was blazing
again, she knelt beside the wounded man.

"I'm going for a doctor."

"No!" He reached out to clamp his fingers in a
steely grip around her wrist. "No! I'll hang! Promise
me. No doctor! Please."

"Shh," she said, afraid that his agitation would
make him worse. She nodded reluctantly, knowing she
was running a terrible risk in giving him shelter. "I'll
turn down my bed." She left him alone, going to her
bedroom to pull back the pink coverlet and fluff up the
feather comforter. A crash came from the front, and
she dashed back to the parlor to find him slumped in
a chair. Fear gripped her as she ran to him. He stirred
and sat up, smiling weakly at her.

"Come to bed," she said, helping him up. Once he
was stretched in her bed, she began to peel away his
bloody clothes, dropping them in a heap on the floor.
She was shaking with fear, but she still managed to
bind his deadly wounds.

Afterward, as she picked up his discarded clothes

to wash them, he opened his eyes. "Ma'am. What's your name?"

"April Danby," she said, thinking he looked unnatural in her pink bedroom. He lay propped against a mound of pillows and in spite of his weakness, he was very masculine, very out-of-place in her bed.

"April. Real pretty."

"What's your name?"

"Ralph. I need to write a letter."

"Just a minute," she said, amazed that he had rallied sufficiently to request pen and paper. She brought them to the bedside. "If you'll tell me what you want to write, I'll do it for you."

"Sit down . . . here," he said slowly with effort.

She placed the paper and pen and ink on the table beside her bed and sat down.

"April. It's been . . . a long time since I touched a pretty woman. May I just touch you?"

She studied him in the soft yellow glow of the lamp. He seemed so brave and young, and so terribly injured. She stiffened at his request, but managed to respond. "Of course."

His hand moved slowly to cover hers in her lap. Then he reached up to touch her cheek.

"I don't mind if you touch me," she whispered, placing his hand against her heart. She suspected he wouldn't last through the night.

"Oh, April, what an angel you are! I don't want to bring you trouble."

"You won't."

"Will you do one more thing?"

"Certainly."

"Can you get me some more clothes for travel? I have to get home."

She was torn between arguing with him that it would be certain death if he tried to travel, and cooperating so he wouldn't waste his strength arguing. He seemed inordinately determined, so she muttered, "I'll try."

"Tonight?"

Her mind raced. She knew where she could go to

get some, but she couldn't imagine his being able to travel for weeks. "I'll do it, but you can't travel."

"Promise me!" he gasped, attempting to sit up.

"I promise!" she replied quickly in alarm. "I will. I'll go in a few minutes."

He relaxed, and his hand moved lightly over her breast. The touch was gentle, impersonal to April, and she stroked his hair off his forehead.

"April," he murmured. "Go get me those clothes."

She stood up, and his hand dropped to the bed. He looked as if he were asleep when she shut the door quietly behind her. It seemed ridiculous to get clothing immediately, yet if it made him rest easier to know she had it, it would be better. She wanted to get the doctor, but that might also alert the soldiers, and she couldn't bear to see him hang. So she rode straight to the Golden Pleasure Palace and went in the back door. In minutes she had a bundle of clothes under her arm. Several of the girls who danced at the El Paraíso worked at Miss Hannah's, and April knew all the girls well. She rode home in the swirling snow, thinking about the wounded young soldier in her bed.

He lay sleeping with the pen, paper, and ink still on the table. She dropped her cape on a chair and laid out trousers, shirt, coat, and boots, hoping if he stirred and saw them he would rest easier. She took her flannel gown out of a drawer and left to get a blanket so she could sleep on the settee in the parlor.

Before she closed her eyes, she gazed at the white flakes tumbling silently against the window and prayed the Rebel would be better tomorrow.

Hours later she opened her eyes and stretched, almost falling off the settee, as the first faint rays of dawn lit the windows. Remembering Ralph, she sat up swiftly and hurried to the bedroom, where she expected to find him sleeping. She prayed he was still alive.

The bed was empty, covers thrown back. Crimson spots of blood soaked the sheets. Shocked, she blinked her eyes. The floor was streaked with blood, and the clothing was gone. Then she noticed the letter on the pillow. She crossed the room to pick it up, and held it to the window to read. The handwriting was shaky and uneven, almost too wobbly to be legible, but she could make out some words:

"April:

Thank you. I'm leav . . . don't want to cause trouble. . . . an angel . . . hope we meet in heaven."

The last line was impossible to decipher and she stared at it for a while, before finally she decided it might read: ". . . take care. No . . ." She couldn't be sure, and it didn't make sense. She stared at the empty bed. Ralph would die if he tried to travel. Her mind raced over what to do, and finally she rushed outside and hitched the horse to the buggy. She drove straight to Dr. Yishay's sprawling adobe house.

Running his fingers through his tangled black-and-gray curls, he ushered her into his office and sat down with a kindly smile that faded swiftly as she told her story.

"Oh, dear, Miss April, you'll get yourself into a peck of trouble. You don't hide murderers from the United States Army, and that's a fact!"

"Doctor, he won't live if he travels. He's bleeding badly. I can see the path of blood from my house leading out of town. Please go after him."

"And if I don't, I suppose you will!"

"Yes, I will. He's just a young man. He's brave, but hurt badly."

Suddenly the doctor's features softened. "Miss April, is this the one?"

It was an old joke between them. Aaron and Gerta Yishay had tried for the past two years to interest April in some of the nice young men they knew. If she ever showed the faintest interest in one of them, Dr. Yishay would always ask, "Is this the one?" because they openly told her they wanted to see her happily married.

Unable to smile this time, she shook her head. "Doc, he's hurt badly."

Aaron Yishay's smile faded. "Ah, little one. You

have a soft heart. We should turn him over to the authorities.''

"It's wartime. What soldier hasn't killed in the past four years? Please!''

"All right! I'll go. But you tell those Bluebel—those soldiers you haven't seen the man, you hear? And you go home now. Scrub away the blood, burn his old clothes, and say no more to anyone. Promise me, Miss April," he said, his thick black beard doing little to hide the stubborn set to his jaw.

"I'll promise if you'll put your coat on and go!"

"Yes. Right now."

"Thanks, Doc! Oh, thanks!"

"You're too tenderhearted, Miss April."

She laughed for the first time since she had discovered Ralph in her dressing room. "No one else in town would say that."

Aaron grinned as he wrapped a muffler around his neck and pulled on his heavy greatcoat. "Not those rascals at the saloon. You just stay hard-hearted where they're concerned. Mama and me, we worry about you living all alone the way you do. It just isn't right!"

The argument was an old one that she no longer heeded. She pulled her cape tight under her chin. "Hurry! Please take care of him."

"I go, I go," he mumbled.

They parted and April rode home bathed in the first slanting rays of sunshine. The blue clouds to the north portended more snow, and she said a long, silent prayer for the Rebel. When she arrived at her home, she burned his bloody clothes, scrubbing away the last traces of blood from her pine floors. She also removed the bed linens and washed them. To her relief, a light snow had commenced again. She knew before long it would obliterate the bloody tracks, yet Aaron Yishay had already had time to leave town on Ralph's trail.

It was two hours later when she heard hoofbeats and went to the front to see three soldiers dismount. With a pounding heart she opened the door, facing the same officer who had come to her dressing room, a tall lieutenant with thick blond hair.

" 'Morning, ma'am," he said grimly, and her heart skipped with fright that she hoped she could conceal.

"Good morning. Won't you come inside?"

They filed past her. "I'm Lieutenant Ferguson," he said with a clipped accent that reminded her of northerners she had met. "This is Lieutenant Taylor and Sergeant Paterson."

"May I get you some hot cider?"

"No, thank you, Miss Danby. If you'll just sit down a moment, we have some questions we'd like answered."

"Of course," she said, sitting on the rocker and hoping she sounded calm and puzzled. The three soldiers made her cozy room with its braided oval rug and calico curtains seem small and cramped.

"Ma'am. Have you harbored a Rebel here during the past hours?"

She laughed. "Whatever gave you that idea! Does it look like I have a Rebel here?"

"I'd like to look around and see, if you don't mind," he replied solemnly, his hazel eyes bright with curiosity.

"No, I don't care," she said, sobering, praying she had eliminated all the bloodstains. Lieutenant Ferguson was a broad-shouldered man, over six feet tall, and his masculine presence seemed to dominate her tiny parlor.

"Has he stayed with you?"

"Sir! I'm not accustomed to having men callers, much less a soldier I don't know at all. Last night you asked me to tell you if I saw him. Don't you think I would have done so?" she asked indignantly, and his face flushed.

"We heard someone say they saw a man here at your house this morning."

"I do not have a suitor and I've never entertained one overnight!"

'That's your own fault, Miss Danby!" he snapped, and then his face turned a deeper crimson. "Begging your pardon, ma'am, but it's a well-known fact you discourage men."

She laughed, and when she did, the angry look on his face dissipated. "Look the place over to your heart's content, and I'll fix us some hot cider. You can look in the attic. Look on top of the roof if you want!"

"This man is injured. He can't climb to an attic or roof. How in hell—pardon me. How he got away from us, I don't know. He was in your dressing room after you left last night."

"In my dressing room? How do you know that?"

"He left a bloody trail. I don't know why we can't find him. He should have bled to death at the El Paraíso, not still be hiding somewhere. If you'll excuse me, ma'am, we'll look around."

"Of course." She went to the kitchen to get cider and cups. Her hands were ice cold with fear, and she prayed the soldiers wouldn't detect anything amiss. By the time they finished searching the house, she had poured steaming cups of tangy cider.

When they finally left, she stood in the doorway watching them. As Lieutenant Ferguson mounted, April noticed his hazel eyes sweeping over the house, and she suspected she hadn't fooled him at all. There was nothing he could do, however, unless he found some evidence that she harbored the Rebel. "Sorry we troubled you, Miss Danby."

She nodded coolly and shut the door.

Shortly after noon she heard a knock on the door, and opened it to face Dr. Yishay. One look at the scowl on his face, and she knew his news was bad.

"Come inside." She stepped aside and followed him into the parlor, taking his hat and coat. He crossed the room to warm his hands at the fire. "I'm sorry, Miss April. I have bad news. The Rebel died before I found him."

"Oh, no! I wanted to get you last night, but he wouldn't allow it." She sank down on the sofa, remembering the soldier's gentle touch and soft voice, his cocky grin in spite of his wounds.

"I'm sorry. And, to make matters worse, Vesta Dodworth has told everyone in town, including the

U.S. Army, that she saw someone riding with you in
your buggy last night."

"They can't do anything to me now, and they can't
hurt him either," she said, feeling forlorn and saddened in spite of having known him for such a brief
period of time.

"I'm sorry, Miss April," Aaron repeated, his brown
eyes filled with kindness. "I had to notify the army
and answer their questions. I told them I had been up
early hunting deer and I found him. The Rebel was
holding something in his hand, and I brought it to
you," Dr. Yishay said, and crossed the room to hand
her a gold band. She stared at it as it gleamed dully
in the light.

"We don't know who that ring belongs to, so you
keep it. He might be happy if he knew you had it."

She closed her palm around the ring and nodded.
"Did the army know his last name or how to notify
his family?"

"Nope, he didn't have any identification, so all they
know is Ralph M. but they'll work on it. Too many
good boys died in this senseless war." He walked over
to squeeze her shoulder. "Don't look so downhearted,
honey. You did your best for him, and he didn't hang.
He died a brave soldier's death from wounds in battle."

She nodded and went to the door with him.

"Take my advice. Don't ever admit he stayed here.
It won't do you any good."

"Thanks, Doc." She squeezed his wrist and stood
in the doorway as he mounted up for home. To her
amazement, hot tears stung her eyes as she gazed at
the gold wedding band in her hand. It fitted her finger
and she wondered if he had left a wife behind. Inside
were the initials M.M. She went inside, and that night
when she sang, she put heart and soul into her song,
remembering the Rebel and his determination.

With the arrival of 1866 in New Mexico Territory,
soldiers still abounded. Some men came home from
war, while others left to join it. Meanwhile, the Union

was supplying more and more soldiers to the frontier forts to combat the Indians, and the Apache fled their Bosque Redondo Reservation, spreading fear throughout the territory.

In Albuquerque, April was now at the Brown Owl Saloon, where she still sang nightly except Sundays, and she received better pay for her performances than ever before. She seldom thought of the night she had found the Rebel, and she still refused all offers to be squired by any of the local men. Willowy and golden-haired, she would be twenty this year.

One night in March she awoke to hear pebbles hitting her window. She opened the window wide, the cold night air making her shiver.

"April!" came a call.

She peered into the darkness, then recognized her friend Melissa Hatfield. Melissa knew April because they attended the same church. April played the piano on Sunday mornings, a fact that redeemed her from the tarnish of her singing at the Brown Owl in the eyes of the ladies of the town.

"Melissa!" April exclaimed, seeing her best friend standing in the darkness outside. "What on earth? Come around to the door and I'll let you in." She closed the window and yanked on her cotton wrapper, aware that something must be terribly awry for Melissa to be out all alone at night.

The moment the diminutive five-foot-tall Melissa stepped through the door, she gripped April's hand tightly. Her black curls tumbled in disarray, and her brown eyes were round with fright. "I need your help."

"You will if you keep wandering around in the dark alone!"

"Patrick is in trouble."

"Oh, Melissa," April said, fearful for Patrick O'Flynn, who was hated by Melissa's father.

Her words tumbled out so swiftly that April barely understood what Melissa said. Her high-pitched voice rose higher with nervousness. "I overheard Pa telling Mama to keep checking on me while he rides out to the river to see if Patrick is waiting to meet me. If he finds Patrick, he is going to teach him a lesson.''

"Is Patrick waiting?''

"Yes,'' she cried in anguish. "I was going to slip out and meet him.''

"You shouldn't! If you're caught, you'll be compromised. Your father would kill Patrick.''

"You know that's the only way we can see each other! April, I'm ahead of Pa. He hasn't left the house yet. If you'll slip into my bed while I ride out to warn Patrick, he can get away before Pa gets there. Will you do it?''

"Lordy, how can I convince your Mother I'm you?''

"The window is open. Just climb up the tree and into my room. Get in my bed and pull the covers high. Will you, April?''

"I don't think you ought to be out alone.''

"April, Pa will beat Patrick to a pulp!''

Or worse, April thought. "All right,'' she said, relenting against her good judgment. "I'll do it.'' All too well she knew Ned Hatfield's vile temper, and his hatred of the Irish, Patrick in particular.

"Thanks, April! I knew you would.'' Melissa fled, galloping out of the yard while April rushed to throw a cape around her shoulders. She picked up her small derringer and slipped on moccasins to hurry across the yard. She raced along the deserted streets, avoiding the raucous saloons until she reached a quiet block of two-story houses built by three of the town's wealthiest men.

The largest and most ornate was Ned Hatfield's house, often called "Ned's Castle" to his face, and "Ned's Folly" behind his back. It seemed an extension of his character as far as April was concerned. Owner of the general store and one of the town's leading citizens, he was as pretentious as his house, never satisfied with life around him. How he had a daughter as sweet and fun-loving as Melissa, April didn't know. How he had won the favor of his wife, Selma, who was generous, tolerant, and good-natured, was another mystery.

So different from frontier architecture and the town's usual adobe-and-jacal construction, the Hatfield's ornate house was painted blue and yellow, and decorated with spindles and molding. It had a mansard roof, a second story of half-timbered gables, scrollwork over the porch, and two turrets corbeled from the corners. A tall cottonwood flanked the west side, and April scrambled up to an open window. As her foot touched the floor, the doorknob turned.

April made a dive for the bed and pulled the covers high. She heard footsteps in the room, and then the window was lowered a fraction. Next the door closed, and the steps faded away. As soon as it was quiet, she sat up and unfastened her cape, dropping it down on the opposite side of the bed. She stretched out again, pulled up the covers, and lay waiting, studying the large bedroom, so different from her own, with Melissa's china dolls, the carved four-poster bed. It seemed like hours before April finally heard Melissa climbing into the room.

"April!"

April was on her feet instantly. As she swirled the cape around her shoulders, Melissa hugged her lightly. Silvery moonlight splashed through the open window, illuminating Melissa's turned-up nose and heart-shaped face. "Thank you! I got there just in time to warn Patrick. I hid when I saw Papa coming, and then rode like the devil to beat him back here. I waited and watched him come in. He's gone to bed now, so you're safe. Thank you! Thank you forever!"

"That's fine, Melissa," April said, biting back her laughter. When Melissa was happy her enthusiasm bubbled over and the whole world became rosy. When she was frightened or sad, her spirits plummeted accordingly. "I'll see you Sunday morning."

"Are you scared to go home alone?"

"No," April said, not altogether truthfully. She actually dreaded the walk home across town at such a late hour. "I have my derringer."

"Thanks again," Melissa said as April climbed out the window onto the nearest tree. Melissa lowered the window behind her, and April cautiously stepped down to the next limb, clinging to the rough bark. Somewhere in the distance a coyote howled, a lonesome, forlorn wail that sent a chill down April's spine. The empty night was eerie, and she wanted to be home. As she descended to the next limb, her cape caught on a branch. She struggled, trying to reach up and free her cape, aware her white nightgown was showing and her bare legs were revealed from her thighs down to her moccasins.

"May I be of service?" came a deep voice filled with amusement. She turned so quickly she lost her balance and fell.

A man on horseback moved swiftly, reaching out to catch her. Strong arms banded her to halt her fall while she was pulled against a solid chest, her legs harmlessly hitting the horse. As her hat toppled off, golden hair cascaded over her shoulders. Her gown had flown up above her pale knees, and the arms around her tightened noticeably.

"Hurrying away from a tryst?" came the deep voice again. The combination of the darkness and the man's broad-brimmed hat hid his features, but nothing could hide the obvious amusement tinging his deep voice.

"Will you put me down now!" she snapped struggling in vain.

"You'd be safer if you'd let me escort you home. Unless you're seeking more male companionship."

She burned with anger at his assumption that she had climbed out of the window after an assignation. "I'm not hunting male companionship, least of all yours! I wasn't slipping away from a tryst!"

"Of course you weren't," he mocked, laughter sounding in his words.

She struggled in his arms. Her side was pressed to his chest, and with her wiggles, her thighs pressed against him, her legs dangled over his, and to her embarrassment and horror, she felt his swift, throbbing response. Her cheeks flamed as she became still.

"Put me down!" she gasped, looking up. His face was inches away, discernible now in the moonlight, handsome and commanding, with a thin, straight nose, prominent cheekbones, and a firm jaw. He smelled fresh, his shirt had a cottony smell, and she was aware of every inch of her flesh pressed against his.

"I'm Noah McCloud, and you're . . . ?"

"Never mind! Put me down!"

"Tell me your name, Goldie."

As she fumbled in the inner pocket of her cape, she realized she had dropped the derringer. She struggled uselessly in his arms. He laughed and leaned down to set her on her feet. Swinging his foot over the horse's withers, Noah McCloud dismounted, picking up the derringer to hand it to her with a flourish. "You'd be safer if you'd let me take you home."

"I'll be safe, thank you. Just leave me alone!" she said as she grabbed her derringer and marched away. At the corner of the block she looked back to be sure he hadn't followed her.

It was the dead of night, and the fall had jolted her nerves. She was frightened, so she skirted the Plaza carefully, crossing and recrossing the wide dusty streets to avoid passing a lighted saloon. Suddenly a man stepped out of a darkened doorway in front of her.

"Ahh, what have we here? A little pigeon out at night!"

2

April jumped with fright, then lifted her chin, her hand tightening on the derringer as she withdrew it from the folds of her cape. "I'll shoot if you don't move out of the way."

He chuckled and waved his hands. "Ayee! A pigeon with a pistol!" He had a drooping black mustache and wore a wide sombrero, and his thick body blocked her path. "I can accompany you home, *pichón,* and keep you safe from all danger."

She walked backward carefully, keeping the derringer aimed at him as she slowly widened the distance between them. She glanced over her shoulder, and out of the corner of her eye glimpsed a dark figure. Two men stepped out of an alleyway and grabbed her before she could do anything. One struck her hand.

The derringer fired harmlessly before she dropped it with a yelp of pain. Arms clamped around her waist, and a hand clamped over her mouth.

"Ah, *pichón,* we will take you home with us now," the man said, his voice growing thick with lust while he retrieved her derringer.

A fetid odor of garlic, whiskey, and tobacco assailed her as the arm tightened painfully around her waist, lifting her off the ground. The man chuckled in her ear while another reached out to stroke her throat, his hand drifting down over her breast.

"Ayee! This one wears nothing but her cape and nightgown!" he whispered exultantly.

The click of the hammer of a pistol cut into the night, a slight sound, yet everyone stiffened, and the deep voice of Noah McCloud spoke. "Release her and put your hands in the air!'' She was free. She ran the short distance to get behind Noah McCloud, thinking no man had ever looked so solid, so tall, or so commanding.

"Mount up," he ordered her, holding two guns on the three assailants.

"They have my derringer," she whispered.

"Unbuckle the gunbelts carefully," he commanded the men. "Throw them down. Her derringer with them."

The men did as he ordered, and he kicked the weapons out of their reach. Noah swung into the saddle behind her. Sliding an arm around her waist, he wheeled the horse around and galloped between two buildings. He raced across the Plaza and slowed at the next block. Drained and shaken, she slumped against him. "Thank you. I should have let you see me home."

"Damned right," Noah said, shifting her curtain of golden hair over her shoulder. It was silky to touch, smelling sweet, like fresh apple blossoms, and he inhaled deeply. He wanted to go on holding her, her closeness reminding him of how long it had been since he had had his arms around a woman. So damned long. For just a moment he remembered all the lonely nights he had spent drinking in the saloon, trying to drown his memories of Fanchette.

His thoughts were suddenly pulled to the present by the woman in his arms. The realization that she was wearing nothing except her nightgown and cape, and the clear recollection of a glorious glimpse of long, shapely legs, stirred his desire. He headed toward the sporting houses, because he assumed that was where she belonged despite her protests. She was probably paid well by the wealthy man whose house she had just left. She was lovely, and Noah's senses were assailed. He leaned forward to brush her nape with his lips. She gasped and twisted around.

"Sir!"

"You smell sweet, Miss—"

"Thank you! Just keep your distance," she said,

drawing herself up, making him grin as she turned her
back to him again. She was a feisty one! And when
he delivered her to the house, he intended to come in
and partake of little Miss Goldie's talents. He was
acutely aware of her luscious body pressed against him,
her rounded bottom, her slender waist encircled so
easily by his arm, her straight back and slender wrists
and long coltish legs. He had been in town only hours,
but it seemed as if he should have heard of such a gem
as Goldie.

"Which house is yours?" he asked as they headed
down the street past bordellos. The broad street
stretched before them, cactus and rocks in the bare
yards, light spilling from open doors, and music carrying in the night.

All of April's fright and exhaustion evaporated as
she realized he had assumed she was a lady of pleasure. She twisted in the saddle to glare at him. Light
spilled from a saloon that still held customers, washing over his face, and she was startled to see the deep
blue of his eyes. Then she remembered his question
and drew herself up.

"I don't live in one of these houses!"

He grinned with a flash of white teeth that dazzled
her as if she had looked into bright sunlight. "Not
many ladies slip out and cross town at night all alone,
climb trees to gain access to an upstairs bedroom—
and then go home to regular family life. You live with
your parents? Or is some poor husband being—"

"If you hadn't rescued me, I would—" She bristled
and snapped her mouth shut. "I live alone! And I
wasn't going to a tryst with a lover!"

He chuckled. "Where do you live, Goldie?"

"Turn around and go back to the corner."

"Since when does a beautiful young woman live
alone in a rough frontier town like this?" he asked in
mocking tones as they changed directions.

"Since I came to live here! The schoolmarm lives
alone."

"And how old is the schoolmarm?" he persisted
with an undercurrent of amusement. Goldie was angry

and defensive, but he felt sure that if he shook her, money she had been paid for the tryst would tumble out from her pocket. And he had seen the schoolmarm today. She was in her middle years, as big as a man, and as safe living alone as he would be.

"I don't know!" April snapped, looking up at him again. A mistake. His white teeth gave him a rakish look, his smile was as warm as sunshine, and she had to laugh.

"All right! She's over forty!"

With her laughter, Noah experienced a ripple of pleasure that surprised him. Her white teeth were small and even, her laughter throaty, infectious. Catching her chin, he turned her to face him. "As I live and breathe! What a smile!"

April thought the same about him, but she wasn't about to tell him.

"Turn west at the next corner. You're the most infuriating man I've ever met! But I—"

"More infuriating than that scum you just encountered?"

"No. You—"

"Ah, thank heaven for a small gift! I'm better than those three. That puts me slightly above a snake! More in the lizard category, eh?"

"Will you let me finish a sentence?"

"Of course. I'll listen attentively," he said, leaning closer, his breath warm on her nape.

"Now, don't do that!" she snapped, twisting around, her anger resurging.

"Do what?" he asked in innocence, his mouth only inches away, his voice dropping to a level that was a rumble, almost a caress. She was having a strong reaction to him, one she wasn't accustomed to experiencing. Only one man held her heart, and he had died long ago, when they both were little more than children. This man was a stranger, annoying and infuriating.

"Don't do what?" he persisted, repeating his question.

"Sit so close to me," she said, barely able to get

out the words as embarrassment flushed her face. She
lived in a town overrun with men. She sang to them
and entertained them, but she kept a wall around herself that always separated her from them. Until now.
No invisible barrier existed with this man, and the
more time she spent with him, the more nervous and
uncomfortable she became. And for all her experience
in dealing with masses of men, she had virtually no
experience in a one-to-one relationship, certainly not
with a man like Noah McCloud.

"I certainly can't help the fact that I'm sitting close
to you. This saddle isn't made for two," he explained
in the most reasonable tone possible. "Why does it
disturb you so?"

"You know why!" she exclaimed, her cheeks burning as she stared straight ahead and wound her fingers
in the horse's coarse mane.

"I disturb you."

"Yes, you do," she admitted, unaccustomed to being coy or flirtatious. "Turn north here."

"You have a good sense of direction," he compli-
mented her cheerfully. "Most women don't know east
from west."

"There's my house at the end of the block."

"And you live all alone?" he drawled, making a
shiver run down her back. His fingers moved back and
forth lightly on her wrist. His thumb was rough and
callused, and each feathery stroke stirred a tingle, but
she wouldn't acknowledge it. He had a way of turning
her admonishments around and teasing her with them.

"Yes, I do. And I'm sorry, but I can't invite you in.
It would be scandalous, and contrary to what you think
about me, I lead a very proper life!"

"Do you now?" he asked in a joshing voice that
tickled like feathers.

"I play the piano at church on Sunday. I was not
climbing in that upstairs window to meet a man."

"There was no man involved in what you did?"

"Well, there was a man, but Patrick—"

"Aha, Patrick! I knew it! But all victory from hav-

ing guessed correctly is squashed by the fact that there
is a Patrick in your life.''

April didn't know whether he was teasing or not,
but she decided the wisest course to follow was to let
the infuriating man think there was a Patrick in her
life. She slipped down off the horse. ''Thank you.''

With another fancy dismount, swinging his leg over
the horse's withers, he dropped to the ground. ''I'll
go to the door with you, and if you want me to check
and make sure your house is safe, I'll be glad to.''

''I'm safe, and I can get to my door. Adios, and
thanks.'' She hurried to the door to unlock it, but in
her haste she fumbled the key and dropped it. A strong
hand picked it up. The corner of his mouth lifted in a
mocking grin as he inserted the key and opened the
door. He stepped inside and held the door. ''Come
in.''

Now she had to worry about getting him out! Taking
a lucifer from his pocket, he reached out to light a
lantern.

The match flared, and Noah McCloud glanced at
her. Her face glowed in the light, golden hair streaming over her shoulders, her cheeks pink from the night
or from his teasing. Her eyes were so pale they were
silver, unforgettable and unique, their beauty captur-
ing his interest.

His curiosity was rampant. No decent woman lived
alone, so she had to be kept in this house by the man
whom she had just slipped away from. And if she were
available to pleasure men, Noah wanted to be one of
the partakers. He knew part of his fascination was
simply the length of time since he had held and loved
a woman, and part of it was the pain over losing Fanchette. But another part was the loveliness of the young
woman staring up at him. In spite of what he knew
she had to be, she looked beguilingly innocent.

The light from the flickering match danced on his
features as April looked at him. His skin stretched
tautly over his cheekbones, a stubble of beard barely
showing on his firm jaw. His blue eyes dominated his

features and fascinated her. Clear and dazzling, his
gaze heated as his attention shifted to her mouth.

April's breath stopped. The way he stared at her
mouth, the hungry look on his features, made her lips
part and tingle until she realized how she was responding. As she stepped back, the flame reached his fingers. He swore, the match went out, and they were
plunged into darkness. There wasn't a movement or a
sound, yet she was totally aware of his presence. Finally he struck another match to light the lantern.
Feeling as if she were standing too close to a blazing
fire, she moved away from him.

Curious about her, Noah glanced around her small
house. There was a cast-iron wood-burning stove in
the kitchen, a round oak table, and a brass lantern
which hung from the ceiling. Braided rugs lay on the
polished pine floor, books on pine shelves. Whatever
else she was, she was neat and tidy. There was an
appealing warmth to the room. His attention shifted
back to her, her wide eyes staring at him intently. Remembering how she had felt pressed against him, he
wanted to reach for her.

"Good night," April said firmly, her heart thud-
ding.

" 'Night, Miss Piano Player," he said, doffing his
broad-brimmed hat and leaving.

When she heard the hoofbeats of his horse, she went
to the window. He was tall and straight in the saddle,
his broad shoulders powerful, and she remembered
every word he had said to her, every touch, the brush
of his lips across her neck. Memories swirled, heating
her blood. Her pulse quickened while she busied herself locking up, trying to shut out the disturbing
thoughts. She was amazed that the slight encounter
had stirred such strong reactions.

Noah's thoughts churned as badly as April's. When
he had ridden into town this morning, he had felt a
sense of expectancy. His trip down the Santa Fe Trail
had been hard. Crossing the mountains was always
tough, and the dry, cactus-covered land seemed to go
on forever. Albuquerque loomed like an oasis. In the

distance, beyond the western edge of town, cotton-woods lined the banks of the Rio Grande. He had ridden west along the Mountain Road to the Plaza and its surrounding shops. The spires of the San Felipe de Neri church on the northwest corner of the Plaza were beacons against the blue sky, and within hours a friendly blacksmith had given him a brief history, including the fact that the church was over one hundred and fifty years old.

Noah took a room in an adobe hotel, Los Alisios. It was only one story, but it stretched back to surround a courtyard that had a splashing fountain and native plants. He liked the West. The people there always seemed willing to accept a man without questions about his past, and the adobe structures held no dark memories of his Alabama home. His brief stint in a Union prison also made the long stretches of open land welcome.

Noah thought about the past hour and laughed, remembering Goldie toppling out of a tree into his arms. When he had heard a window close and looked up to see her inching her way down the tree, he had been captivated. She must have been concentrating so much on her descent that she hadn't even heard his approach. What a lovely bundle to drop into his arms! Whoever the lucky man was that lived in that monstrosity of a house, Noah envied him. He laughed again, shaking his head, determined to learn more about the woman with silvery-blue eyes and golden hair.

The following night, as usual, April stood at the edge of the stage, singing her ribald song and twisting her hips provocatively. When she glanced down, she saw Noah McCloud, one long leg folded with his booted ankle on his other knee, his black hat pushed to the back of his head. Locks of curly black hair showed above his lean face, his blue eyes danced with devilment, and a lopsided smile was on his face. As he raised his glass of whiskey in a mocking toast to her, she remembered telling him emphatically what a proper life she led.

For just an instant her voice faltered, and she almost
forgot her words. She began again, singing heartily
until she changed to a ballad. All the time she sang,
she tried without success to avoid glancing continually
at Noah McCloud, who lolled with graceful ease at the
table in the front row.

She swayed slightly as she closed her eyes and tried
to forget McCloud. Her thoughts shifted to Emilio, his
dark eyes pervading her memory as she tried to steady
herself. The saloon soon became silent except for the
sound of her voice and the occasional jingle of spurs.

A haze of smoke clouded the narrow room. In the
dusky gloom were the pale ovals of men's faces, longing revealed in each one's eyes. As her voice filled the
room, Noah felt a prickle across the back of his neck.
He had been shocked, his jaw actually dropping when
he had looked across the candles and realized it was
Goldie, the beautiful young woman he had rescued.
Then he grinned, remembering her insistence on how
proper she was. Proper! Her dress was split above her
knees and it fit her gorgeous figure like skin, dipping
down daringly over luscious breasts. He wasn't wrong.
It was Goldie, all right, and she looked as marvelous
as she had felt last night in his arms. Proper—only one
kind of woman could be found in any saloon in the
West! He recognized her voice, and as she launched
into the slow, lyrical ballad, he became mesmerized.
Her eyes were closed, and she sang from her heart as
if to a lover.

He hadn't heard a woman sing the way this one did.
Some dance halls and saloons had women with nice
voices, but most couldn't sing at all. They usually just
revealed enough leg and derriere to make up for talent.
This one's sultry voice transformed the saloon. Every
man there responded as if he were alone and she were
singing only to him. The temperature seemed to climb,
and Noah remembered how soft she had felt, how she
had smelled like apple blossoms in springtime. Her
voice floated in the air, wrapping around him like a
warm velvet cloak, making his heart thud, making him
want to hold her close.

She opened her eyes to look directly into his. Her silvery eyes darkened to the color of slate. They were as captivating as her voice, binding his attention, drawing his senses. A compelling urge seized him to get up and pull her off the stage into his arms. He felt caught, staring into her wide eyes, and then he realized she was caught too. *She was singing to him.* Her voice came like soft fingers, playing over his nerves, coaxing, and seductive, while she stared at him wide-eyed. Tension sparked between them as fiery as the flickering candlelight. His heart beat slowly in his chest as April continued to beguile him with a haunting love song.

She finished and there was a moment of silence before her audience was galvanized into cheering and applauding. The piano player burst into a honky-tonk rhythm, and she belted out another bawdy song that made the men laugh and cheer. The spell between them was broken, and Noah sipped his whiskey, watching her with bemused appreciation as she strutted across the stage with an exaggerated twist of her hips.

He made a vow he would get her in his bed before the next snow fell. She spun around, feet planted widely apart while she looked down at him. He raised his glass in another salute, repeating his promise to himself. She sashayed to the front of the stage and knelt gracefully as she reached up and slowly pulled her lace handkerchief out of her dress.

Again he was caught, but this time his gaze had dropped from her eyes to that tantalizing scrap of lace that was appearing from between her breasts. Noah felt as if he had fallen into a fire. The creamy flesh of full curves was revealed, and then the bit of lace came sailing over the candles. He stood up and caught it, barely cognizant of the shouts from the audience. He rubbed it slowly across his cheek while he watched her, and beneath the powder and rouge, he could swear her neck and cheeks flushed with embarrassment.

Was she one of the girls who earned her way with her body as well as by song and dance? If she was, he wanted her tonight. Then it dawned on him that she probably had lied to him last night because she belonged to another man. Whatever that man paid her, Noah would pay more.

As she took her bows and disappeared, he was up and moving, striding through the side doors to hunt for her dressing room.

"Hey, mister! You can't come back here!" A brawny giant of a man blocked his path.

Noah reached into his pocket and withdrew a handful of silver cartwheels, Mexican dollars. He held them out to the man, who took them eagerly.

"Turn your back while you count your money!" Noah snapped.

"Okay, mister, but don't cause trouble."

"Wouldn't think of it," Noah drawled, already forgetting the man. A flock of chorus girls passed him like a bevy of brightly colored birds, each in feathers and a silken dress. The odor of powder and perfume overpowered the crowded area. Some gave him curious glances, others smiled and gave him lingering appraisals.

"Where's the singer?" he asked one, and she jerked her head in the direction of a door. He hurried to it and knocked.

"Yes?"

She stood in the center of the tiny room, her arms raised as she unfastened the back of her dress. Her back was to the mirror and he glimpsed the reflection of her bare back that curved down to her tiny waist, her skin flawless and golden.

"You can't come in here!" she snapped.

"I'm already in here," he remarked, closing the door behind him. "Thanks for the handkerchief, Miss Proper Church Piano Player."

"You don't belong in my room! And I do happen to play the piano at church!" she exclaimed, blushing, her voice becoming breathless.

"And it merely slipped your mind that you sing in a saloon at night?"

"No, it didn't. I didn't care to mention it. I'm changing my dress."

"Go right ahead. I'll help with your buttons—"

"Get out!"

He laughed. "I'll turn my back. Change and let me take you to the hotel for dinner."

"Sorry, but no thanks," she answered without pause, out of years of habit of declining men's invitations.

"Thanks again for the handkerchief. Considering where it's been, I'll treasure it," he said in a husky voice, his gaze lowering to her bosom. "I forgot what you told me—what's his name?" he asked, curious about her, moving closer to her.

"Whose name?"

"The man. Where you climbed out of the window. I don't really give a damn, I'd just like to make you a better offer, a better arrangement."

"Will you get out of here?"

"Sure. In a few minutes," he said, moving closer. She held the back of her dress together and stepped back so that her legs were pressed against the dressing table. Her reflection caught in the mirror, a tantalizing glimpse of bare flesh still showing above her hand tightly gripping her dress. He moved closer, his pulse pounding, watching the changes come over her as he approached. Anger darkened her eyes; suddenly she yelled:

"Vladimir!"

Stepping away from her, Noah faced the door. It swung open and the same brawny man filled the doorway. His fists were knotted as he entered the room. "I warned you not to cause trouble."

"Stop right there," Noah said softly.

The revolver seemed to jump into his hand. April didn't see him move, but now he held the biggest, longest revolver she had seen, yet he handled it as if it were a toy. She was accustomed to men carrying six-shooters, but she had never seen a man draw as quickly or with such ease.

"I don't mean the lady any harm," Noah said qui-

etly, reaching into a pocket. His hand came away with
a clink of money. "I just want to talk. I've already
saved her once from some ruffians." He swung his
arm, and two gold sovereigns arced through the air.
Vladimir caught them easily, his brown eyes going to
April with question.

Frowning, she nodded. "I'll be all right. Thanks,
Vladimir."

He nodded and left, closing the door behind him.
She faced Noah as he put away the revolver, sliding it
into the holster on his thigh, giving her a mocking
smile. She raised her chin.

"I don't want him hurt, but I don't care to spend
my evening with you."

"How had you planned to spend your evening?"

"I'll go home now."

"Alone?"

"Very much alone," she said stiffly, trying to avoid
looking him in the eye. Something irresistible and disturbing was happening.

As he moved closer, she glanced up, and was en-
snared. He had the bluest eyes she had ever seen, the
deep blue of sapphires. His gaze lowered to her mouth,
and her lips tingled. The distance between them narrowed. Caught in a silent contest, and knowing she
couldn't call Vladimir back, she backed up until she
touched the dressing table. Noah McCloud had a faint
smile, curiosity and desire showing in the depths of
his eyes.

"Don't," she whispered.

"Don't what? I'm not doing one thing to you," he
answered easily, moving a step closer, the mocking
light in his eyes taunting her. He was only inches away.

"Don't, please!" she whispered as she looked away.

He placed his finger under her chin and slowly
turned her to face him. "Look at me," he commanded.

"Please, I love someone else," she said softly.

Noah ignored her whispered plea, leaning down to
lightly brush his lips across hers. Hers were incredibly
soft, tantalizing, her body enticing. He narrowed the

remaining distance between them with a quick step, his arm circling her waist to pull her close. He bent over and kissed her, his mouth moving across hers slowly, feather-light and ticklish, a coaxing torment.

Shock buffeted April. For a moment she resisted while sensations rocked her, his arm crushing her to his lean, powerful body. His fingers splayed on her bare back and his tongue touched her lips. Her mind reeled, thoughts stopping, her pulse racing as she yielded. Her desire unfolded like petals of a rose beneath the kiss of the sun. His tongue thrust between her lips into her mouth.

Shock hit Noah with equal force as he felt the instant stiffening of her body in a brief resistance. Her kiss seemed so innocent. If he didn't know about her saloon performance, her tryst, he would swear it was her first real kiss. And a real kiss he intended to give her. His deep voice was a rasp in her ear.

"Put your arms around me," he commanded. His mouth pressed hers, his tongue thrusting deeply now, and she wrapped her slender arms around his neck, aware of the touch of warm flesh and hard muscle. Her fingers tangled in his soft, thick curls and she thought she was going to faint in his arms.

Noah's blood thundered. She was sweet and fiery beyond anything he had ever experienced. Her smooth back beneath his hand was bare, and he trembled with desire. Her kisses were more than he had hoped, making his heart thud violently. He wanted to possess her, her body, which seemed so frail, yet was soft, supple, and a flame against his. A sob rose in her throat, muffled by his mouth. He let his hand drift down the open back of her dress, feeling the sweet curve of her spine.

She pushed suddenly and twisted away from him. His gaze flicked to the mirror to catch a glimpse of her bare back. After her kiss, the room was tropical, his senses stormed, his breathing ragged.

She seemed to be feeling those same sensations, except her eyes sparkled with anger.

"Get out!"

"Come have dinner with me."

"No!" April gasped. Resolutely she shut her eyes, but not before he had seen them fill with tears. Concern surged in him that he might have caused her pain. "Are you all right?" he asked, seeing how young and vulnerable she was.

"I love someone else. Leave me alone, please," she whispered.

He clamped his teeth together, watching her tears about to brim over. "Don't cry. I'll leave," he said, grinding out the words. He ran his fingers lightly along her cheek, then strode angrily from the room. He stopped outside her door, breathing heavily, questions swirling along with his stormy emotions.

It had to be the man whose window she had climbed out of. But why the tears? Perhaps he was married and that was why she had to sneak out of the window, yet if her heart was given to another, why had she been so disturbed by Noah's kisses? Noah had no answers. He didn't even know her name, except he had heard men call her Songbird.

He glanced at her closed door. He wanted to know who she was, and who the man was who loved her. And in the meantime, he had to find a woman named Danby.

When April opened the door, her heart pounded fiercely. She felt a strange mixture of relief and another emotion—she wouldn't admit to disappointment—which made the tenseness go out of her shoulders. She hurried outside to her carriage and drove home along the darkened streets, her emotions seething.

She had loved Emilio Piedra with all her heart, and remembered vividly his beautiful dark eyes and curling black hair. Visions of the terrible gunfight in which he had been killed flooded her mind. She had been so young, only a child in some ways, yet with her past, growing up an orphan in a pleasure house, she was old beyond her years when her half-brother Luke Danby had found her and taken her back to live with him in San Antonio. He had married Catalina Piedra, and

Catalina's younger brother, Emilio, had won April's heart. She had expected to love him always, and it had been a shock tonight when Noah McCloud had kissed her and she had responded.

Men had tried before, as forcefully as Noah Mc-Cloud, but their kisses had been nothing, meaningless, and repulsive. Soon her reputation had spread so that they left her alone. Even new soldiers coming to town learned quickly that she wasn't interested in being courted. Except Noah McCloud. His kiss had awakened confusing responses that shocked her. Twelve years old, she had been a child with Emilio; at eighteen, he had been little more than a child himself.

Noah McCloud was a man. Powerful, confident, teasing—his kisses were fiery. Remembering made her loins tighten in a startling manner. His riveting blue eyes had seemed to bore through her to her soul; his lean, strong body made her want to melt against him. She felt as if she had crossed some invisible line tonight between innocent childhood and womanhood, some awakening that had been infinitely subtle, yet had changed her deeply.

Noah McCloud. She ran the name over in her mind. She could have gone to dinner with him tonight. She felt disappointed that she had so emphatically rejected his offer. She was so accustomed to rejecting any and all offers, and she had been so shocked by his kisses and her violent reaction to them, however, that she hadn't been thinking clearly.

She had promised Emilio to love him always, yet she knew he would want her to go on with life, just as she would have wanted him to if the situation had been reversed. She wondered about Noah McCloud. Had he been a soldier? His soft drawl wasn't local, more like the southern boys she had met during the war.

As she turned from the road in front of her house, she glanced at the Dodworths' to see a white lace curtain move. April waved, knowing one of the Dodworth sisters was still peering through the window. Her thoughts churning, April unhitched the horse, fed and watered him, fixed herself a solitary dinner, and finally lay awake in bed that night, disturbed by memories of Noah McCloud.

Early the next morning she glanced out to see a man sitting tall in the saddle as he approached her house. Her heart seemed to stop and then start again erratically.

It was *him.* Noah McCloud swung out of the saddle easily, dropped to the ground, and strode toward the door. She rushed to a mirror to glance at herself, then looked down, smoothing her blue calico dress. Her golden hair was in a braid wrapped around her head. She pinched her cheeks so they would be pink, and rushed to the door while he knocked loudly.

When she swung it open, her heart beat with an unaccustomed eagerness. "Good morning! I saw you—" Her words ceased and her smile faded. His eyes blazed with anger, his shoulders were stiff, his jaw firm.

"May I come in, April Danby?" he asked, the raspy words ground out in fury.

3

She stepped back and ushered him into the room, closing the door behind him. "Please sit down," she said. "And tell me what's wrong."

"I'm Noah McCloud from Alabama."

"I know that," she said, mystified by his tone. She assumed he was waiting for her to be seated, so she made her way to the sofa. Instead, he strode to the fireplace as if he couldn't sit still because of his agitation. He seemed to fill the room, to overpower it as if the walls had closed in on them. She tried to maintain her cool composure. She hadn't done anything to stir his anger, and she didn't know what had brought about such a change in him.

In spite of his frighteningly abrupt manner, she was aware of the hammering of her pulse, and equally aware of the fine appearance he made, standing so tall. He was wearing soft faded denim that molded to the muscles in his legs. His brown boots were dusty; his black hat sat squarely on his head. He stood with his fingers splayed on his hips.

"Perhaps, Mr. McCloud, you should tell me why you're so angry."

"I came to Albuquerque to find you, April Danby."

"Me?" She stared at him in amazement. "I don't know you."

"Doesn't the name McCloud conjure up any memories?"

"No," she said, becoming mildly annoyed. "I don't know a McCloud."

Suddenly he crossed the room in long angry strides, reaching down to pull her to her feet, his hands gripping her upper arms tightly. His eyes blazed, and April's heart lurched. She wanted to scream or run, but instead she lifted her chin in defiance.

"Unhand me!"

"I ought to shake you until your teeth fall out of your head!" Noah snapped, fury boiling in him as he gazed down into her wide eyes that were filled with fear.

"I don't know you—or I didn't until two days ago. I don't know any McClouds—"

"What a pretty little liar you are!" His gaze swept past her, going over the room. "This nice house you live in all alone, your horse and fancy carriage—how many single young women can afford such luxuries?"

"Sir, it's none of your business, but I earn a good living."

"Not this good! I've known singers before. Dammit!"

Her temper flared. With a twist she tried to break free, but he held her fast. "I don't know what you want with me," she said, realizing that she was at his mercy. She was pinned in his grasp and couldn't get loose. No one would hear her scream.

"You couldn't have spent it all. If you'd done that you wouldn't be here and working. Where's my gold?"

Stunned, she looked up at him. "Have you lost your mind? I don't have your gold, Mr. McCloud."

"If you don't have it, what have you done with it?"

He was beginning to frighten her badly, and she knew it wouldn't be long before he became violent. Her mind raced for some temporary measure to placate him until she could get to safety. "I'll go get it," she said suddenly. "I didn't know I'd have to."

Noah's eyes narrowed. He studied her intensely as he tried to control rage that had been burning in him since the moment he entered her house. She was an inveterate liar, an actress, as cool as the most convincing cozener. She looked fearful and confused, but she had to be lying through her pretty white teeth.

While he watched her, April's heart beat wildly. If she could just run outside, she could get help. The neighbors would see her and one of the Dodworths would probably send for Sheriff Pacheco. For once in her life, April was thankful for the Dodworth sisters.

"If you'll unhand me, sir, I'll get your gold."

With a wary expression he released her. She rubbed her arms and smiled at him. "You sit down right there. It'll take me a minute." She walked toward the bedroom and Noah followed her with his eyes. Her voice was breathless, her face pale, and for the first time since he had met her, she wouldn't look him in the eye. His suspicions grew. He had to fight the urge to grab her and shake her, to force the truth out of her.

"It's in my bedroom. My goodness, you shouldn't have stirred up such a storm," April said brightly, barely knowing what she was saying. She dashed to the door abruptly and yanked it open.

Before she could move any farther, however, the door was slammed shut with a bang. April saw his strong hand holding it closed, and felt his arm band her waist. She struggled, kicking and yelling with all her strength. He pushed her forward against the door and held her.

Her body twisted against his, and Noah drew a sharp breath when her bottom pressed his groin. She was so slender, he had to use all his self-control to avoid hurting her. He spun her around and pushed her back against the door, spreading his legs so she couldn't kick him as easily. He held her arms pinned at her sides. Her breast heaved as she gasped for breath, and damned if she didn't look innocent! If he hadn't had the letter in Ralph's own handwriting . . .

"Where's my gold!" he snapped.

"I don't know what you're talking about," she said, terrified now. She found herself unable to cope with his strength, his absurd accusations.

"Look at me!" His eyes burned with rage. "I'm going to get my gold," he said in a deadly quiet voice.

"You have the wrong April Danby."

"There can't be two in Albuquerque. No, I have the right one." He caught her chin and held her face as her eyes flew open wide to stare at him.

"You don't remember Ralph McCloud?"

"Ralph McCloud? No."

"You lying little witch," he said. "My younger brother wrote to me just before he died. You took him in—he referred to you as an angel."

Noah watched the change in her. She blinked and her lips parted. "Ralph . . ."

He paused and stared at her. She was a singer, probably on occasion an actress, and she was doing a damn good job now. She sounded as innocent and confused as a baby, light dawning in her eyes. Damn her. Every time he was with her, he became as gullible as a schoolboy. He almost believed her emphatic declarations of innocence, and every time he looked at her mouth, he could feel his anger and purpose ebbing. She had the softest lips he had ever kissed. Soft, sweet, fiery . . . He pulled his thoughts away from that course abruptly.

"Your memory stirs," he said cynically, still having to control a violent urge to shake her.

"I remember Ralph. He didn't tell me his last name. I never knew."

"Sure enough," he said in the same scathing tones.

Even though she was trembling, she drew herself up. "I didn't. And I have no idea what you're talking about. He didn't have any gold when he was here."

"Like hell he didn't," Noah said quietly. Her eyes quickly flashed with an anger that matched his own, and her trembling ceased.

"He didn't."

"He had *half* our family gold. He wrote to me he had hidden it with you."

"That's not true!" she cried. April's emotions had undergone another storm. Noah McCloud's unreasonable fury had goaded her into anger. Yet beneath her anger ran an undercurrent of awareness. She was keenly conscious of his hands on her arms, of his strength, and of the nearness of his body.

"He didn't hide anything here! He was barely alive! He couldn't have carried gold with him. If he had any, I don't know what he did with it."

"You're lying," he said flatly, leaning down so his eyes were level with hers. For just one moment his heart skipped a beat as he gazed at her. She had the largest, most compelling eyes he had ever seen. Flecks near the pupils gave her ash-gray eyes a tint of blue. He swore under his breath. She was a lying little witch who could cast a spell effortlessly. "You listen to me, April Danby. I won't give up. I lost everything I had in that damned war." There was a fierceness to his expression that made her cringe. She didn't understand how he could change so rapidly. Last night he had stirred warm and tender emotions in her, but now she was frightened.

"That gold is all I have left and I intend to have it. I won't give up. Sooner or later you're going to give it to me."

"Can't you understand, I don't have your gold. I don't know anything about it!" she cried, angry and fearful at the same time. "Most folks here don't know I took your brother in, either."

"I'm not leaving Albuquerque until I get my gold. You'll have me for your shadow from now on."

"I don't have it!" she exclaimed, wondering how she could convince him.

"I'm going to get it back," he repeated. He wasn't getting anywhere with her and his rage was growing. "I promise you I'll get it!" He strode out the door to mount up, his hands shaking. But in spite of logic, in spite of Ralph's condemning letter, Noah wanted to haul her into his arms and kiss her. Anger and longing tormented him. She's just another pretty woman, he told himself. A cheating, lying little temptress who has the McCloud gold!

Shaken, April watched him ride away, furious over his arrogant assumption that she had his family's gold. And beneath her anger was disappointment. She shook her head and closed the door with more force than necessary. Damn that man! The reactions he stirred in her were unsettling. She didn't want to be attracted to him, to have her heart jump at the sight of his tall figure. Memories of his lighthearted teasing that first night haunted her. And worse than his gentle banter and mocking laughter were the memories of his touch, his arms around her. She squeezed her eyes closed until they hurt. She didn't want to think about Noah McCloud's kisses or his strong arms. She wouldn't! He was unreasonable, infuriating, frightening . . . Uselessly she tried to cling to her anger, but it kept slipping away. It was replaced by a void, a sense of loneliness that she hadn't known in years.

That night as she sang, she looked over the edge of the stage into the smoke-filled room. Noah McCloud sat at the front again. His jaw was set, and he watched her with a hungry, burning gaze. She tried to keep her attention elsewhere, gazing into the haze of smoke and closing her eyes when she launched into her ballad. The moment when memories of Emilio always came was replaced by a startlingly clear recollection of a recent kiss, of Noah McCloud's face bending over hers.

Her eyes flew open, meeting his gaze, and one of his dark brows quirked upward. His long body was relaxed, and he sat with an easy grace while he watched her. She was caught in his fiery look, and her voice throbbed with an emotion she wouldn't identify.

Noah felt a shiver run across his nape, and a hush came over the room. April sang, looking down at him, and as his anger fell away, longing rushed in to replace it. Her haunting song reminded him of dreams gone past, of Fanchette's softness—only it wasn't Fanchette's dark eyes that danced in his thoughts, it was the silvery eyes that were both seductive and innocent.

Her voice throbbed and her sultry breathlessness made him recall the softness of her body pressed against his. Time and place ceased. Only April existed, looking down at him with her wide eyes, singing to him in a voice that beguiled his senses.

His groin tightened as his body responded to her. He shifted, frowning, thinking about their last encounter and his gold. Suppose she had been telling the truth? Yet Ralph would never lie to him. He should know by now better than to trust a woman, he thought bitterly, remembering Fanchette. He watched April strut back to center stage. Tonight she hadn't thrown a handkerchief into the audience, and when she left, he sat quietly finishing his drink before he strode out of the Brown Owl. He mounted quickly and rode around to the back into the shadows to wait.

In a few minutes he heard a horse approach, and Noah backed his bay gelding up so he would be out of sight. When April emerged, a Union officer stepped out of the shadows.

Lieutenant Mott Ferguson blocked April's path. She stood with a deep blue cape thrown around her shoulders, a bonnet hiding her hair. " 'Evening, Miss Danby. That was mighty fine singing,'' he said cheerfully, doffing his hat.

"Thank you."

"I thought maybe you'd let me take you to dinner tonight," Lieutenant Ferguson said, and Noah immediately and irrationally hoped she would refuse.

"Thank you, Lieutenant Ferguson. I should go home."

"Come one, you don't have to go home. There's no one waiting. You'll be all alone. It's just dinner."

"You know I don't go out much. It might start talk."

"Eating dinner at the hotel after work won't start talk. I'll see you home afterward."

In the quiet of the night Noah heard every word of their polite argument and he was tempted to step forward and get rid of the lieutenant.

"I'm sorry, not tonight."

"Come on, Miss Danby, you'll grow into an old lady like old Miss Lenora." Stepping close, he slipped his arm around her waist.

"You're the prettiest woman in this whole town."

"Lieutenant!" She pushed against him.

Yielding to his emotions, Noah acted impulsively, urging his horse forward and dismounting swiftly. "I believe the lady just said no."

"Who the hell are you?" Ferguson asked, moving away from April.

"I'm taking Miss Danby to dinner." He turned to her. "Sorry I'm late."

With more calm than she felt, April stepped closer to Noah McCloud. "Lieutenant, this is Mr. McCloud. Mr. McCloud, Lieutenant Ferguson."

"Noah McCloud," Noah said, extending his hand. He faced a man the same height as his own. Ferguson was as thick in the shoulders, and his body moved with the ease of a soldier fit from training. In spite of the friendly handshake, his hazel eyes flashed anger.

"McCloud? The name sounds familiar." He frowned and studied Noah. "Are you from these parts?"

"No. I'm a long way from home."

"And judging from the way you talk, you were on the losing side," Ferguson remarked. "McCloud. Any relation to a Rebel who died in Albuquerque last year?"

"My younger brother, Ralph," Noah answered stonily.

"Fortunes of war. What brings you to Albuquerque?"

"I wanted to visit my brother's grave, see where he died. I'm just passing through," he replied, feeling an instant flare of antagonism at the note of satisfaction in the other man's voice.

"Oh? Going where?"

"Out west," Noah answered, aware that Ferguson was asking more questions than was considered polite in western society.

For a moment an uneasy silence descended, and then Lieutenant Ferguson picked up his reins. "Well, I'll leave you two. Good night, Miss Danby."

"Good night," she said quietly, knowing she had made him angry. As he rode away, she looked up into Noah McCloud's scowling countenance.

"Thank you for intervening. I can get home by myself now."

"No, you don't! I've just made an enemy as it is. He'll see us ride away from here, and you're not going to add to his anger. We'll go to the hotel and I'll buy you dinner, just like I told him.''

She started to protest, but then looked into his blazing eyes and nodded. "I wouldn't want to cause you trouble with Lieutenant Ferguson. He carries a lot of influence in this town.''

"You've already caused me enough trouble for a lifetime,'' he said quietly. "C'mon.'' He tethered his horse to the back of her buggy and climbed in beside her to take the reins. April glanced at him sharply, wondering if he tried to take control everywhere he went. He stared back at her, his brows arching quizzically, anger still burning in his gaze.

She looked away hastily, perturbed by his curious glances. She almost wished she had accepted Lieutenant Ferguson's invitation to dinner. He couldn't possibly be as difficult to deal with, or as disturbing to face, as McCloud.

In front of the hotel, Noah came around the buggy to help her. His hands went around her waist to lift her down, and she rested her hands on his forearms, feeling the coil of tight muscles. The instant her feet settled on the ground, she stepped away from him. As if he didn't notice her reaction, he took her arm lightly and led her into the Los Alisios Hotel.

She walked in silence, gazing at the parlor with its bare plank floor and dark mahogany furniture. It was the town's newest hotel, but she really didn't see it. All she was aware of was the height of Noah McCloud's shoulder beside her, the length of his stride, his fingers resting so lightly on her arm. When she glanced up at him, a muscle worked in his jaw, and a fierce expression was on his face.

They entered the dining room and were seated by the window at a table covered in white linen. She seldom went out with men, and an uncustomary nervousness plagued her as she gazed across the narrow table at McCloud. He had hung his hat on a hook at the door, and dark locks curled on his forehead. His hands were scarred, his fingers long as he held a menu.

The prices were exorbitant. Dinner would cost seventy-

five cents. He must have some of his gold right now
if he could afford to take her to dinner! Oxtail soup,
chicken soup, loin of mutton, steak, and cream-
fricasseed chicken were on the menu, and as she de-
liberated, he asked, "How about the steak, Miss
Danby?"

"It's too expensive!" she blurted, then realized how
inexperienced it made her sound.

For an instant his features softened, a brief flicker
of a smile showing. "Do you like steak?"

"Yes, but the chicken soup sounds fine. You don't
need to do this," she said, unable to calm her nerves.
She knew she sounded nervous, but he had put her on
edge with his smoldering rage. His gaze seemed to
peel away every vestige of clothing she wore.

He motioned to the waiter and ordered steaks while
April stared out the darkened window at the saloon
across the street.

"Calm down, Miss Danby."

Her head snapped around. "I *am* calm!"

"You look ready to fly into a million tiny pieces. Of
course, I can understand why you're nervous. If I had
taken someone else's fortune—"

"When will you get it through your thick head that
I don't have your gold!"

"Then why are you so nervous?" he shot at her,
leaning forward and speaking in a rasp that was just
above a whisper.

She blinked and straightened up, leaning back in the
chair as if trying to put as much distance as possible
between the two of them. His brows arched, his eyes
narrowed—damnable sapphire eyes that seemed to
pierce right to her feelings—and he studied her. "Answer my question."

She tried to look away from his gaze, but it was like
trying to smile while eating a green persimmon. With
an almighty effort she succeeded, and looked down at
her fingers locked in her lap, her knuckles white as
snow. "You would make the devil nervous!"

"That wasn't what I asked," he said, pronouncing
his words slowly and clearly, as if she were a child.

She could tell without looking up that he was leaning close over the table. *"Why are you nervous?"*

Her patience snapped and embarrassment flooded her. "You make me nervous because you're unpredictable, you stand too close, you touch me too often, you're too disturbing, you breathe on me . . ." The words seemed to come like an unleashed torrent, pouring out of her without any means to make them stop. And to her horror, all his anger vanished; amusement made his eyes dance.

Noah bit back laughter. She was so damned nervous and young and lovely, it was hard at moments to remember his gold or his dreams and the terrible aching loss of his family and home. She made him forget everything except her.

"I breathe on you?" He couldn't resist teasing her, watching her cheeks go from pink to glorious rose. Her wide eyes developed a spark that made him want to reach for her and silence what was coming.

"Will you stop compounding the difficulties!"

"What difficulties? I breathe on you?"

Anger made her forget everything else, and she leaned forward only inches from him. Noah wanted to pull her into his arms so badly that he ached.

"Why does my breathing on you disturb you so?" he asked softly.

They had both strayed far from the subject of gold, and his eyes held a twinkle. In spite of his unpredictability and her nervousness, she saw the ridiculousness of the moment and she laughed. "You know exactly why!"

He thought his heart would slam through his ribs with her laugh. She had the damnedest sense of fun, which surfaced in unexpected moments, and he like her for it. He ought to be twisting her arm to get the truth from her, and instead he was laughing with her and loving every second of it. *Fool and idiot. Double, double fool. She's pretending and lying. She's gorgeous. She's fun.* It was something he hadn't experienced often with a woman. *She's an actress. An actress who can fool, and mesmerize, and mislead.*

Breaking into the moment, the waiter appeared with steaming plates of thick, buttered steaks, the brown juice running onto the plate with fluffy white potatoes and dark gravy. As hungry as he had been half an hour earlier, Noah silently cursed the arrival of his dinner. For the next few minutes Noah was engaged in conversation with the waiter, and then they ate in silence.

She chewed the tender steak, relishing each bite, a treat she seldom allowed herself.

He watched her rosy mouth, observed her closing her eyes, and all his appetite momentarily fled. If she enjoyed something as simple as a steak so much it sent her into a rapture—what would she be like in bed? He poked at his dinner, glancing continually at her, watching her eat, aware that she had given herself over totally to the pleasure of eating, for a moment losing her fear of him.

She focused on him. "This is delicious!"

"I'm glad."

"You're not eating."

"Yes, I am."

She paused to drink her water, studying him, and her straight pale brows came closer together in a frown.

"What's wrong?" he asked.

"I don't understand you."

He leaned forward. "Well, that's something we have in common, because I find you an enigma, Miss Danby."

"I can't be much of a puzzle to anyone."

"And why am I a puzzle to you?"

"You're furious with me because you think I have your gold, yet you take me out and spend a small fortune to feed me when it's unnecessary."

His emotions were at war. He knew too well the treachery and deceit pretty women were capable of. This one was either blatantly lying to him or she was as innocent as she protested to be. And he couldn't accept the latter when he remembered Ralph's letter.

"Two steaks aren't a fortune. This dinner became necessary when I interfered with you and the officer, and I don't care to see you starve."

"I wouldn't have starved! And I'm greatly relieved to hear it isn't a fortune."

"Do you always order chicken soup when a man takes you to eat?" he asked, unable to resist teasing her.

"I don't go out with men," she said bluntly, studying the dining room.

Again, he was surprised. "Damned if you don't sound like you're telling me the truth!" This time his voice filled with disgust, anger back in his expression.

"I am telling you the truth."

"You're young, beautiful, single. You sing in a saloon. I caught you climbing out a man's window. Don't tell me you go straight home and stay alone night after night."

"I have friends."

"Ah, I'm sure!"

"Lady friends. I play the piano at church on Sunday mornings and at prayer meetings on weeknights. I'm in a ladies' sewing group. I'm good friends with Melissa Hatfield as well as Octavia Littleton. I eat dinner with both families often and help Octavia's sister, Drusilla, with her new baby."

"And what men do you go out with?"

"Not that it's any of your business, but I don't. You can ask around town if you don't believe me."

He fully intended to do just that. She was becoming more of a puzzle to him than ever, and he couldn't cope with his emotions when he was around her. "Why don't you go out with men?" Noah asked. He was curious to see what convoluted answer she would give him, because he didn't believe her for one second. She was beautiful, seductive, enticing, and fun. She sang in a saloon. *Not go out with men!* About as much as he never went hunting!

While he scowled and his stormy thoughts seethed, she gazed out the darkened window where they could see lights from the saloon down the block across the street. When she didn't answer, he persisted. "Why don't you go out?"

"I was in love with a man and he was killed," she said softly.

"In the war?" Noah asked.

"No, before the war."

Foolish answer. She was too young—eighteen, he would guess. The war had started five years ago. "You were a child before the war," he reminded her.

"I was," she answered, realizing he didn't believe a word she said, but she didn't care. She had never discussed Emilio with another man and she didn't want to talk about him now.

Noah could see the stubborn lift of her chin, the frank stare that suddenly made him suspect she was telling the truth. "How old were you?"

"Twelve."

"That's too young to fall in love."

"No, it isn't."

"Under twenty is too young to know what your heart really feels," he argued.

"I wasn't too young. I was in love forever," she stated forcefully with a toss of her head. "I'll never forget him."

Noah imagined how she would look with her hair down over her shoulders. "No one else has made you forget him even for just a second?"

Her eyes widened, a look of consternation crossed her features, and her cheeks turned pink. Instantly she looked down at her hands in her lap, but he had seen the silent answer in that brief moment of revelation.

"Miss Danby," he said in a lowered voice, drawing out her name, wanting to make her respond to him.

"His name was Emilio and I loved him," she said, struggling to gain control of her emotions. She faced him defiantly. "I'll always love him."

She seemed so damned young. One minute she was seductive, the next he thought she was sly and a thief, and the next she made him laugh and forget everything else. "That's why you were upset when I kissed you," he said gently.

"Where are you from?" she asked, and he knew she wanted to change the subject. He couldn't figure her out, couldn't decide what was truth and what wasn't. All he knew was what was in his brother's letter, and there was no doubt about it.

"Alabama. Didn't Ralph tell you?"

"No," she answered, and a harshness returned to his features. "I don't have your gold, and for heaven's sake, don't spoil this wonderful dinner!"

He bit back a laugh, keeping his features solemn and wondering what kind of spell she had worked on him. He cut his steak and took a bite.

April continued to eat, ignoring Noah McCloud's constant, curious watchfulness. The steak was heavenly and it had been a long time since she had eaten one cooked to perfection. When the Hatfields invited her to eat, their cook inevitably burned every shred to darkened chars that barely resembled food. This, however, was thick, juicy, and tender beyond description.

Noah McCloud remained silent throughout the rest of the meal, and back in her buggy, she faced him. "Thank you for the wonderful dinner. I can get home by myself."

"No. I fed you, so you can put up with my company for a little while," he said, taking the reins from her hands.

She stared at him as her usual annoyance with him returned. As if unaware of her feelings, he said, "Tell me about Albuquerque. How long have you lived here?"

"I came when I was fourteen."

"Fourteen! Where's your family?"

"A long time ago I left my half-brother in San Antonio. He had just been married, and his wife was with child so they couldn't leave San Antonio."

"What about your parents?"

"I don't have any," she said stonily, flatness coming to her voice, and he found another puzzle to her.

"You had some parents once upon a time. What happened to them?"

"I never knew them. Someone took me away from my mother when I was only a few years old."

"So where did you grow up?"

"With a lady in Santa Fe."

"So she's like a mother to you?"

"Sort of. Yes, she is."

"What's her name?"

"Lottie."

"And where is she now?" he asked, turning on the lane to April's door. She glanced to her right and saw one of the Dodworths pop back out of sight away from the window.

"There's one of the Dodworths."

"Who are they?"

"My neighbors. They're elderly twin sisters who married brothers. The brothers were killed gold mining in Colorado Territory, and now the sisters live together. They always look to see what I'm doing, and now they'll gossip about your escorting me home."

He glanced over his shoulder. "Do you mind?"

She shrugged. "Not if you leave quickly and don't give them fuel for the fire."

He pulled on the reins to halt at her back door. "Give me your key."

He lifted her down, and then his hands dropped from her waist immediately. He opened her door, and in minutes he had the lamps glowing. She faced him. "Good night, and thank you again for the marvelous dinner."

"Let's talk a minute."

"The Dodworths—remember?" He made her nervous now, because he overwhelmed her, and she could feel the deep-running current of anger that had briefly abated during dinner. He stood by the fireplace while she faced him. Tension increased between them, and she lifted her chin, gazing back into his stormy eyes.

"The Dodworths be hanged," he said quietly, and any hope of getting him out of her parlor swiftly vanished. "Sit down, Miss Danby, and tell me about meeting Ralph."

April knew it would be a waste of time to argue with him, so she sat in the rocker. "I found him in my dressing room. He was bleeding badly and begged me to hide him. Within minutes Lieutenant Ferguson and another Union soldier were at the door wanting to know if I had seen him. I told them I hadn't. Ralph asked me to take him home with me and he refused to let me get him a doctor. I let him sleep in my bed, and when I woke the next morning, he was gone. I got Doc to go search for him, and he came back to tell me that Ralph was dead.''

"The doctor found my brother?"

"Yes. Excuse me a minute," she said, rising to leave the room. She remembered the gold ring that Doc had given her. She got it out of a tin box in her bottom drawer and took it back to Noah to hand it to him.

Gold glinted dully in his palm while he drew a quick intake of breath. "It's my mother's ring," he said, sounding vulnerable and hurt for the first time since she had known him. "Her name was Mirabelle. Mirabelle Windham McCloud. The Windhams were from Baldwin County too."

"I didn't know. I'm sorry." She stood close to him and he gazed down into her eyes. As before, when he looked at her so intensely, she felt a pull that was like the tide. She had to fight the urge to lean closer.

His eyes darkened and he caught her arms tightly, the anger rising in him. "Dammit, where's the gold!"

"I don't have it!" she exclaimed. Her gaze dropped to his mouth for an instant, and her emotions came violently and swiftly, as if she were tumbling over a cliff. He swore, and desire flared in his eyes. She saw a hungry longing in him that was impossible to misread. While he fought his emotions, her anger grew.

"I don't have your gold and I've never had anything more than that ring!"

"My brother didn't lie, and he wrote that you had his gold.''

"Well, I don't lie either!"

"No?" he asked in cynical tones, his dark brows arching. "Miss Pious Piano Player who sings and dances in a saloon. Who keeps trysts after midnight! Have you ever lived in a bordello?"

His question caught her by surprise. She waited an instant too long to answer him, and saw the contempt come into her expression.

"Get out!" she ordered, furious with him and with her reaction to him.

"How long ago did you leave it? You're very convincing, Miss Danby. And I'd pay a lot more for your services than I paid for those two steak dinners," he drawled.

The rage within her flashed like a flame bursting to life. Without knowing what she was doing, she raised her hand to slap him. Before she could, he caught her wrist, holding her tightly. "All those nights alone you talked about," he said softly, taunting her. Beneath his mockery anger flowed. He leaned closer. "I want my gold."

"I don't have it! Get out of my house!" she cried, afraid of him, unable to cope with the storm of emotions he caused.

"I'm going, but I won't give up. Sooner or later you're going to give it to me," he threatened in a voice that sent an icy chill rushing over her.

He left, striding across her floor, his boots scraping the boards, spurs jingling. He slammed the door behind him, and if the Dodworths had missed his entrance, they couldn't miss his exit.

Feeling slightly sick, April squeezed her fist against her middle. He didn't believe her. He thought the most contemptible things about her—and at the same time, she wanted him to stay!

"Emilio," she whispered, feeling as if part of her past were slipping away, being pushed aside by a stranger who spun her life around. Why, of all men, was she attracted to Noah McCloud? She squeezed her eyes shut, trying to shut out the clear impressions of him, the all-too-clear recollection of his kisses, his laughter and teasing, the strangely gentle note that came to his voice at moments when he believed her.

She picked up a pillow and threw it across the room with all her strength before going to her room to climb into bed.

The next day Noah was ushered into Aaron Yishay's office, a long, narrow room in his adobe house. Beneath a ceiling lined with *rajas,* ax-split cedar poles, he had an examining table, glass-fronted bookcases, shelves that held apothecary bottles and equipment, a broad oak desk, and two armchairs. Motioning to his visitor to have a seat, Aaron sat down behind his desk, gazing at Noah with curiosity. "Now, what can I do for you, Mr. McCloud?"

"I wanted some information from you. According to Miss Danby, you found my brother on the trail when he died. He was the Rebel she befriended over a year ago."

"She told you this?"

Noah nodded, having a feeling there was something significant in the question, although not a flicker of change had come to Dr. Yishay's expression. "Is that correct?"

"Yes. He was already dead when I found him. I notified Lieutenant Ferguson. The army was after him. He was wounded badly." He squinted at Noah. "How on earth did you find out Miss April took him in? I didn't think anyone knew about that except Mama, Miss April, and me."

"My brother wrote a letter to me and posted it from here."

"Lord, I don't know how he had the strength to manage it! Judging from his wounds and from what Miss April told me, I don't know how he lasted as long as he did."

"Sir, did you find anything on him—any bundles, something like that?"

"He had a ring in his hand. I gave it to Miss April."

"She returned it to me. Was his horse there?"

"Yes."

"No sign he had been attacked?"

"Mr. McCloud, your brother died from those wounds. It was unbelievable that he made it as far as he did, but there was no sign that he was attacked. It looked like he finally fell off his horse and was probably dead when he hit the ground. His trail was bloody as hell."

"I see. Do you know Miss Danby very well?"

Aaron Yishay stroked his beard, his dark eyes as bright as a sparrow's as he studied Noah. "Yes, I do. I've known that young lady since she came to town."

"And do you trust her?"

"I assume you have a decent reason to ask a question

like that," he said with a surprising note of steel coming to his soft voice. "Yes, I trust her. I'd trust her with my life."

Noah stared back in turn, wondering how well Aaron Yishay knew April. "Since you're a doctor, I assume you can keep things confidential, and I'd appreciate it if our conversation is kept quiet."

Aaron nodded. "It will be."

"My brother was carrying something valuable. He posted a letter saying he was leaving it with April Danby. She says she never received anything from him."

Noah stared into implacable brown eyes. "Mr. Mc-Cloud, if Miss April says she didn't receive whatever it was, she didn't. She is as honest as grass is green, and that is a fact."

"So was my brother," Noah said quietly.

"You can ask Mama, Mrs. Yishay, about Miss April if you want a woman's opinion, but I promise you, you can take the lady's word. She won't lie to you. She wouldn't hurt anyone or take something that doesn't belong to her. She risked a lot to befriend your brother, and when she came to get me to go after him, I wanted to tell the army men. I thought that would be the right thing to do, but she wouldn't let me. Your brother didn't die in prison because of Miss April."

"I'm aware of that," Noah said stiffly.

"Don't let the fact that she sings in a saloon fool you. She's as proper as Vesta and Lesta Dodworth. Probably more, because she doesn't spy on her neighbors." He came to his feet, leaning forward over his desk so fast it startled Noah.

"And let me warn you, don't you harm one hair on Miss April's head or you'll answer to me!"

The thought of the five-foot-five doctor threatening Noah made him bite back a smile. "I won't harm her," he answered solemnly. "I just wanted to find out a little about her."

Aaron Yishay hurried to his door, opening it to call, "Mama!"

"I'm coming," came a feminine voice, and in seconds

Noah rose to his feet as a woman the same height as Aaron Yishay bustled into the room, her brown eyes filled with curiosity.

"Mama, meet Mr. McCloud. Mr. McCloud, this is my wife, Mrs. Yishay."

"I'm happy to meet you, ma'am."

"Mama, tell Mr. McCloud how much you trust April Danby."

"My goodness," she said, studying him more intently, "I trust that sweet child completely. April couldn't harm anyone."

"Well, thank you, ma'am," Noah said, flushing with embarrassment as he faced both of them. "I just needed some questions answered about the lady."

"He's that Rebel's brother," Aaron said softly. "Thank you, Mama."

She nodded, still studying Noah. "It was nice to meet you, Mr. McCloud," she said, and left, her husband closing the door behind her.

"Where are you from, Mr. McCloud?" he asked, returning to his seat behind the desk.

"Alabama."

"Where were you during the war?"

"I fought with the Alabama Twentieth Regiment. We were at Vicksburg. I went through the siege and fall, and then later was taken to a Union prison in Rock Island, Illinois. I was in prison for eleven months."

"Where's your family now?"

"I don't have any family left. They all died during the war."

"Sorry," he said, and the anger seemed to leave his dark eyes. "Your mother too?"

"I think she died from grief. They said she got pneumonia."

Doc Yishay gazed at Noah with speculation. "Where are you staying?"

"I'm at Los Alisios." Noah stood and offered his hand. "Thank you for your time," he said.

Aaron shook his hand, walking beside him. "Are you just passing through?"

"More or less."

"Well, our talk was confidential. You asked me what you wanted to know. Now I'll ask you what I want to know."

"Yes, sir?"

"Did you come to Albuquerque to get whatever your brother left behind?"

"Yes, I did," Noah answered truthfully.

Aaron stroked his curly black beard and nodded. "If Miss April says she doesn't know a thing about it, she doesn't."

Noah nodded. "I'll keep that in mind. Thanks for your time."

"No trouble at all," Aaron Yishay said, smiling suddenly, revealing two widely spaced front teeth and crooked eyeteeth. "Maybe you need to get to know Miss April better."

"I intend to, sir."

Noah went striding down the path to the gate. He mounted and rode away without looking back until he reached the corner. When he glanced back over his shoulder, he saw Aaron Yishay on horseback, a bowler hat jammed on his head as he rode in the direction of April Danby's house.

On Saturday April went outside to wash her laundry in the big galvanized tin tub. In a land that was warm all year long, there were signs of spring everywhere. New leaves were on the trees, grass was all around, and flowers burst into bloom in tended gardens. There was a cool freshness in the morning air, promising a warm day. As April bent over the washboard, she sang while she worked.

"For all the gold you have, you could hire someone to do that," drawled a deep voice.

4

"How long have you been there?"

"Long enough to see you can use some help wringing out those wet things." Sauntering toward her, Noah rolled up his sleeves.

"There isn't a man in this town who does laundry, except Mr. Dolan, and he charges for his services."

"I won't charge you, and now there's one other man in this town who does laundry."

"I don't need your help, thank you!" she snapped, trying to push a stray lock of hair out of her eyes with her arm. She was conscious of his fresh white shirt, his faded denims. She wore a patched green gingham, her hair was in disarray, and she had soapsuds up to her elbows. He reached over and caught the wayward strands of hair, tucking them behind her ear. His warm fingers brushed her flesh, and the touch stirred her awareness of him.

He finished rolling up his sleeves, revealing muscular arms sprinkled with curly dark hairs. His hat was pushed to the back of his head, and curls tangled beneath the broad tilted brim. Exasperated, and embarrassed by her appearance, she glared at him.

"It doesn't bother you one bit that you're not wanted!"

"I don't think you really mind having a little help."

"I mind a great deal!" she snapped, unable to imagine him actually doing laundry. "And you'll resort to your usual brute force eventually, wanting to know where your gold is."

"I haven't hurt you," he said quietly, and her cheeks flamed.

"You've *frightened* me."

His lips firmed as if he were biting back a smile. "You haven't acted frightened." He picked up a dress and dipped it in the tub and began to scrub.

"I don't want you to wash my clothes."

"Why not?" he asked, squinting up at her.

"Well, it doesn't seem proper."

His eyes sparkled with laughter that was unmistakable this time. "Afraid I might see your drawers?"

She laughed. "Maybe so!"

"I'll leave those for you to wash, I promise," Noah said. He was, as usual, surprised and pleased when her humor surfaced. He thought she looked just as pretty leaning over a tub of sudsy water with her hair tangled as she did prancing around on a stage in a silk dress. Her disarray made her more approachable, and he was amused by her bristly reception. "Is this how you usually spend your Saturdays?"

"Yes."

"How about another steak dinner tonight?"

"And more questions and accusations afterward? No, thanks."

He paused and flung his hat at a branch on a tree, where it caught and hung, swaying slightly. "I'd like to talk to you."

"If you keep calling on me, there'll be a scandal."

"Miss Danby, I can't believe you'd stir a breath of scandal in old Albuquerque!"

She laughed and gazed across the washtub at him, into blue eyes that were level with hers. His face was only inches away, his lips wide and firm and inviting. She drew a sharp breath and straightened up.

"My wash isn't getting done," she said in a shaky breath, bending over the washboard quickly. They were both using the same tub and her hands collided with his.

"Sorry! There isn't room for both of us."

"Sure there is," he said good-naturedly. "If you want, go sit in the shade and rest a spell."

"If I do, you might wash my drawers," she drawled, and he grinned. They worked in silence, and she soon forgot the laundry she was washing, because all her attention was taken by continual brushes of her hands against his. She was intensely aware of his proximity until she said in exasperation, "This is too crowded. I'll wash, you rinse, wring them out, and hang them up for me."

"Sure enough."

They scrubbed her wash, April slanting curious glances at him as he worked. "Where did you fight in the war?" she asked, trying to steer the conversation away from herself and onto a harmless topic.

"In Mississippi, Louisiana, and Alabama. I was in the Battle of Vicksburg."

She paused to look at him. "I heard that was bad. That they cut off all supplies." She had heard Luke talk about Vicksburg, the casualties, the people reduced to eating rats to survive. "My brother said that was one of the turning points of the war."

"That's right," Noah replied, his voice flat. "It gave the Union control of the Mississippi. Thirty thousand people surrendered. The civilians were paroled."

"What happened to the soldiers?"

"I don't know what happened to all of them. I was sent to a Union prison in Illinois."

"My brother fought for a time. Thank heaven he came home from the war! So many didn't."

"I don't understand how your brother could let a thirteen- or fourteen-year-old sister go off all alone," he said grimly, taking a sheet from her hands to plunge it into the rinse tub. He remembered she had as much as admitted she lived in a bordello. She looked as innocent and young as a spring flower, yet he had guessed correctly when he had asked her about living in a pleasure house. As he squeezed water from the sheet, he studied her, because he couldn't figure her out. She always pushed him away, and her kisses weren't those of an experienced, worldly woman.

She canted her head to one side to frown at him. "You're thinking about your gold," she accused.

"No. Actually, I'm thinking what a contradiction you are, Miss Danby. You look like a young miss still in the schoolroom, as if you've never been in love with a man, yet you live alone, sing in a saloon, and at one time used your body to earn your keep."

To his surprise, she grinned. "I did no such thing. And if this goes on through all my washing, Mr. McCloud, I can do without your help!"

Rinse water dripped on his boots while he felt as if he were sinking into quicksand. Here we go again, he thought. She's going to lie to me, another bald-faced lie, and I'm going to believe her. "You've already admitted to living in a house of pleasure," he said, and her eyes twinkled.

"Yes, I did, so you just naturally assumed the worst."

Startled by her answer, he realized her past might explain the incongruities in her life now. "Why were you there?"

"A man left me there when I was a baby, and the ladies cared for me until my half-brother Luke Danby found me and took me home with him."

"I'll be damned!" he exclaimed, astounded and chagrined. "Why didn't you explain? You knew what I would think."

"Your boots are getting wet," she observed, and he began to wring out the dress he was holding. "And I didn't particularly care what you thought," she added in haughty tones. He leaned across the tub of suds so swiftly he startled her.

"You should've cared." He bit off his words and straightened up while she tossed her head.

"Because you would have treated me differently? Those women are human, and they deserve to be treated fairly."

His mouth curved up in a sardonic smile. "Fairly is just fine," he drawled in a husky voice, "but they don't usually object to certain advances." His amusement seemed to heighten when she blushed. Her hair was blowing in her face and perspiration dotted her brow. Her hands were too soapy to brush the hair out of her eyes, so he reached out to tuck some silky strands behind her ear. Her skin was soft, petal smooth, and he was aware of touching her. He saw the flicker in her eyes and guessed she was experiencing the same sparks as he. She had been raised in a sporting house. Maybe she was as innocent as she proclaimed. Innocent where men were concerned—not where the McCloud gold was concerned. He had damning proof of that.

"Anyway, that was long ago."

"I still don't see how your brother could let you go off by yourself when you were only thirteen or so."

"I was old enough," she said. "And he couldn't really leave town with me. You see, while I was in San Antonio, I heard that our mother, Hattie Danby, was still alive, remarried to a man named Castillo. I didn't tell Luke, because he needed to stay home with his new wife, and when Emilio died, it was difficult for me to be around them. They were so happy, but Catalina, with her black hair and black eyes, resembled her brother, and it hurt to be with them. Also, I hoped I might find Hattie. She was told that I had drowned, and she thinks Luke was killed violently in the wagontrain ambush when she was taken captive. She should learn she has two healthy children. I wanted to find her. I've been singing onstage since I was five years old, so I knew I could earn my keep, and I know how to keep out of the way of men."

Her words had the solid ring of truth, and Noah suddenly realized that she led one of the most solitary lives of anyone he had ever known. He thought of his own childhood. He had been pampered, protected by two doting parents. He had a brother he loved, friends, and parties and a beautiful home, while April Danby had grown up in a sporting house.

"What a hell of a life you must have had," he said quietly, voicing his thoughts. She raised her head, her hands pausing on the washboard while she shrugged her slender shoulders.

"Children accept what life hands them. It didn't always seem that bad," she answered, and he knew by the tone of her voice that there had been times when it was bad.

Warm wind blew across the bare ground as the sun beat down on them. She scrubbed as if oblivious of his presence, but he didn't seem to notice. He was lost in his thoughts about her. How innocent was she? Her kiss had been almost like a first kiss. The memory of it made his desire kindle, yet he had to keep his head around her if he wanted to get back his gold. No wonder she wanted the gold and would go to such great lengths to keep it.

"Under the circumstances," he remarked dryly, "I don't know how you've survived on your own. Out here men respect proper women and six-shooters, little else, especially not a beautiful young woman on her own who was raised in a sporting house. I think you've been damned lucky."

"Thank you for the nice compliment. And I'm careful."

"Not careful enough," he grumbled.

"Besides," she added lightly, "I'm not alone all the time." She handed him dripping laundry. "Luke's best friend is a Kiowa, Ta-ne-haddle, who married the woman who took care of me as a baby. Lottie was like a mother to me. Ta-ne-haddle won't settle down and Lottie is part Apache, so she doesn't mind his nomadic way of life. They're never far away for long, and Ta-ne-haddle has made it clear in Albuquerque that anyone who bothers me will have to answer to him."

"There's always the drifter that doesn't know a damn thing about Ta-ne-haddle! I didn't until right now, and I've been in your house. If I didn't have any scruples, there wouldn't have been any way for you to stop me from doing whatever I wanted."

"You're beginning to sound like my brother," she said with a mischievous note that grated on his nerves. "And there are townspeople who've stood by me when I've needed someone, the Yishays, the Hatfields. I have friends."

Noah shook out a dress, held it up, and looked at her quizzically because it was tiny, far shorter than April's other dresses. She laughed and tried to shake the wayward locks of hair away from her face. "That isn't my dress. I do the Dodworths' laundry for them, because they both have stiff bones."

"You do their laundry and they gossip about you?"

"Well, until you came to town there was nothing to gossip about! They bake cakes for me sometimes. They haven't really done me any harm, and they're eighty years old. When I'm eighty, I hope someone will help with my laundry."

"Have children and you'll have help."

"I'm not marrying," she said lightly, pushing two dresses into the tub.

She thought he was standing beside the clothesline. Instead, his fingers lifted her chin, and she gazed up into unfathomable blue eyes. "If you don't marry, it'll be the most colossal waste of womanhood," he drawled softly, sounding sincere and looking concerned. Her heart missed beats, feeling as if it were skittering around in her rib cage. She tried to smile and keep her voice calm.

"You can't understand what I'm telling you. I love a man who is no longer alive." She wondered how convincing she sounded. How could Noah McCloud have such a devastating effect on her so effortlessly? Most of the time he seemed unaware of it, but occasionally she thought he felt something too.

"Well, you're very much alive. If he was any kind of man at all, he'd want you to pick up and go on with your life."

"I'm going on. And so is this laundry if you'll get back to work," she said, but there was nothing firm in her voice. In fact, she was breathless. There was an unpredictable quality about him that disturbed her, an attraction she couldn't resist.

"Yeah, sure," he said, moving away from her, a scowl on his features. He stood with his feet braced apart, his back to her as he hung up wet clothing. He wore his six-shooter low on his hip. Her gaze drifted down his long legs and she made an effort to look elsewhere.

"What kind of childhood did you have?" she asked,

washing furiously, as if she had to be done in the next five minutes. She tried to ignore the rapid beat of her pulse. His slight touch and his words indicated there were moments when he saw her as a woman, and not just as someone who had taken his gold.

"I grew up on a plantation and we lost it during the war. My family's all dead."

He said it so quickly and in such flat tones that April paused to stare at him. He continued to pin her clothes to the wire she had strung from a post to the house. His body was lean, hard, yet she saw the defiance in his stance and knew full well he was fighting hurt over his losses.

"I'm sorry."

He glanced over his shoulder at her. "The same thing happened to hundreds of others."

"That never makes it easier."

They stared at each other, and she wanted to reach out and touch him, to console him in some way. "I don't have your gold," she said quietly, and saw the clamping of his jaws, the hard look that came to his eyes. He turned around to finish pinning up clothes that sagged only inches above the ground.

"Who the hell put up this line?" he asked, stepping back with fists on his hips to study it.

"I did, and it does the job."

"Barely. You hang one heavy thing on here and you'll have to do your wash all over again. If you strung this, you must have a hammer."

"In the toolshed."

He followed the wave of her hand, disappearing in the shed, only to reappear with the hammer. In a few minutes the clothesline was restrung. It was low enough for her to reach, but also high enough off the ground that her dresses weren't in danger of dragging in the dirt.

"Thank you," she said, tossing out the sudsy gray wash water. He emptied the other tub.

"Let's pack a dinner basket and ride down to the river."

"I have a list of tasks to do before I go to work

tonight. Besides, I'm surprised you'd want to picnic with me when you think I've stolen what's rightfully yours. Or else you're beginning to believe me.''

Staring at her, he stood with his fists on his hips. He didn't believe her, and he intended to get what was his. So far he simply hadn't come upon any reasonable method to do so. Where a woman was concerned, he couldn't resort to violence. In spite of his certainty that she was lying about the gold, he was beginning to understand her better. He knew why she had such an air of both worldliness and innocence. The worldliness came from her independence, her background, her saloon singing. The innocence came from being shut away, not going out with or allowing men to call. Noah had asked around town enough now to know she had a reputation for absolute coldness where men were concerned. That reputation caused the few people who knew he called on her to stare at him with open curiosity, or to frankly ask him if he had known her before she moved to Albuquerque. And he couldn't explain why he wanted to go on a picnic with her. Not even to himself.

''Show me your list.''

While she aired two rugs and packed a basket of food, Noah curried the horse and quickly repaired a broken slat in her shed. Not a mention had been made about gold, but she knew it was on his mind the whole time. Once while he was searching in the shed for tools, she caught him rummaging through things and knew he was looking for his gold.

While he still worked outside, she finished her tasks and then sponged off. She brushed her hair vigorously before trying it behind her head, then changed into a pale yellow dress of printed lawn, the long full sleeves finished with ruffles. She carried a fringed China silk shawl, the only extravagant item she owned. When she paused to study herself in the mirror, she laughed at her reflection and leaned forward to whisper, ''Idiot!'' She was happy. Noah McCloud had been pleasant and helpful all day. He always seemed to generate an undercurrent of excitement, and she had to admit she looked forward to going to the river with him.

Self-consciousness grew as she went through the house, her cheer replaced by a nervousness she seldom experienced over her appearance. She began to worry that perhaps she shouldn't have changed. She paused with her hand on the knob, and he knocked.

She opened the door, standing only inches away from him. "Miss Danby—" he began, and then his gaze dropped down and he stopped speaking. He looked at her in a consuming glance that went from head to toe and back again.

"You look pretty," he said simply, warmth in his voice and appreciation clearly showing in his gaze. She was glad she had changed her dress.

"Thank you." She blushed, pleased by his compliment. "You were going to ask me something?"

"Oh?" He stared at her blankly and raked his hand through his hair, black curls springing back beneath his fingers. "Oh! Do you want your horse turned out to pasture? We can hitch mine to the buggy."

"Yours is saddled. We'll use Raven."

He nodded. "We'll be ready to go in just a few minutes."

She picked up the basket of food and a blanket. Noah took them from her and held the door as they left.

He hitched her black horse to her buggy and they rode to the wide Rio Grande. The town was in the distance behind them, the river cool and inviting.

"This is an old town," April explained, "established by the Spanish after their conquest of Nuevo Méjico in the sixteenth century. The town was founded by Don Francisco Cuervo y Valdés, who brought some families here. He named it after his patron saint, Francisco Xavier, and the viceroy of New Spain, the Duke of Alburquerque. Then it was changed to San Felipe de Alburquerque, and finally Albuquerque, dropping the first R. Albuquerque has grown because it's on the Chihuahua Trail, the old Camino Real, or Royal Road, that led from Chihuahua to Santa Fe."

Noah watched her as she talked, thinking he could listen to her forever. Her soft mellow voice was feminine and soothing. Her throat was slender; she was willowy and tall for a woman. Her lashes fluttered and she cut a glance at him, catching him staring at her.

"I heard the town was occupied by Confederates during the war."

"It was occupied by the Union under a Captain Enos. Luke and Catalina didn't want me to stay, so I went to San Antonio during 1862, but later I came back here. When Captain Enos heard General Sibley was coming, he loaded wagons to go to Santa Fe. He set fire to the storage house to destroy the remaining supplies, but sympathizers put out the blaze. It wasn't long before the Union returned under a Colonel Canby. I was told Sibley buried eight Napoleon cannon outside town rather than let them fall into the hands of the Union Army. I came back in the summer of 1864. Ta-ne-haddle and Lottie came with me."

"You must not have been back long when Ralph was here."

"That's right. It was winter, cold and snow, with many soldiers in town."

Noah slowed the buggy and stopped in a spot beneath the shade of tall cottonwoods. It was spring, and new green leaves were on the trees. Along the riverbank was a shady spot, and April sang softly as she helped unload the buggy and spread a blanket.

Noah listened to her, enjoying the song, watching her constantly, always torn between curiosity and anger. He got two of Ta-ne-haddle's fishing poles from the wagon, and in minutes he had them baited and in the water. He propped them on the bank and sat down while she spread cold biscuits, berry preserves, and two red apples on the blanket.

It wasn't long before he caught a bass large enough for their lunch. She watched while he cleaned it and cooked it over a blazing fire.

The first bite of flaky white fish was delicious and she told Noah, "What a marvelous cook you are!"

"Anyone can fry a fish," he answered with amusement.

"Not so!" she said, relishing each bite.

"You must like fish as much as steak. I don't think I've ever seen anyone enjoy eating as much as you do."

Her eyes twinkled and she wiped her mouth daintily. "At Miss Kate's we had the worst cook. Radtke Quackenbosch—we called him Quack—he was nice, but he couldn't cook. I eat often at the Hatfields' and their cook is equally bad. I really think Mr. Hatfield likes things on the well-done to burned side."

"The Hatfields?"

"Melissa Hatfield is my best friend. The only time I've had really good food is when Lottie and Ta-ne-haddle come to stay or when I was with Luke. And the steak dinner you bought me. This is wonderful."

"Thank you. I'm limited to fish and a few things like that," he said, trying to imagine what kind of life she must have had as a small child. "Miss Danby, when you were a child, didn't you see a bad side of life?"

"Very," she answered matter-of-factly. "I didn't think I would ever like a man in my whole life, but of course Emilio changed that."

"You said a man took you to Miss Kate's. Do you mind my asking what man?" he asked. He was curious about her and was trying to sort out her past.

"My stepfather. According to Miss Kate, he didn't know who my father was, and he didn't want me. He told my mother I drowned."

"Damn. I'd think you'd want to kill him if you found him."

"I did for many years, but now I'm older and I know it would just hurt my mother. Nothing can change the past." She shrugged. "Now I would let it go if she's happy with him."

"Maybe women don't hang on to the past as much as men," he said. "If you found her, you'd just let it go—all these years you've been separated from her,

the life you've led? You wouldn't make him pay for it
in the slightest?''

"Not if it meant hurting my mother," she said.
"What would we gain?''

She didn't sound like a scheming little vixen who
would take a man's gold. She tilted her head to one
side. "What's wrong?''

"Just trying to figure you out," he said.

"What do you plan to do when you leave here?''

"Go on west. I'll get some kind of business. I've
helped run Bel Arbre," he said, the last word pronounced *awba*.

"Bel Arbre?''

"My home," he answered gruffly.

"You don't want to go back and start again?''

"No!''

"You must know how to raise cotton.''

Blue eyes leveled like twin cannon on her. "I don't
ever want to go back. It's all gone now." He dug in
his pocket and pulled out a rock. As she stared at it
in his strong hand, she saw it was a piece of stone or
brick.

"See this?" He jiggled the stone in his hand, running his finger over it. "That's all I have left of Bel
Arbre—a broken piece of one of the bricks from a
fireplace," he said gruffly, and she hurt for him and
his losses.

"I lost all my family, our home, most of my friends,
and the woman I loved. I don't want to go back.''

"I can understand," she said, thinking how difficult
it must be to lose everything when you had so much.
"That's somewhat like my reasons for leaving San Antonio. It hurt to be reminded constantly of Emilio.''

He poured two glasses of cider and leaned back
against the trunk of a tree to watch her while they
talked. Her golden, silky hair fell softly on her back,
tied with a ribbon that he wanted to reach over and
pull loose. Dappled sunlight spilled through the leaves
and played over her, and he wondered if she had any
idea how pretty she looked. When she relaxed, she
seemed guileless, but if he gave her a heated look,

flirted, or teased, she blushed and became slightly un-
sure of herself.

"When did you start fighting during the war?" she
asked.

"Shortly after the outset of the conflict," he said,
stretching out his long legs. "I was young when I went.
I'm twenty-six now."

"I'll be twenty soon."

"My father was still young and he let them talk him
into serving."

"Your poor mother!"

"I know," he said grimly, "but he couldn't stay out
of it."

"What was your house like?"

"It had twenty-eight Doric columns, galleries running all around the house, and a big central hall down-
stairs. Twin rows of twelve big oaks grew on either
side of the drive up to the front entrance, and fan tran-
soms were over the doors. You could sit on the galleries and watch company come up the drive beneath
the oaks. The house was made of cypress and bricks
that we fired on our own place. Papa built Bel Arbre
when he married Mama."

Noah tossed his hat down beside him. A breeze ruf-
fled his curls as he leaned back against the tree and
stared at the river while he talked. April could envi-
sion the house that he described, and Noah McCloud
a young man in it. His voice softened, and his features
lost their harshness as a faraway look crept into his
eyes.

"I was the oldest, so Papa took me with him when
he rode out to oversee work on the plantation. He
bought more and more land. Always wanted land. He
bought land across the road from his place and then
later behind his place. He said when I married, he
would give me the land across the road, and Ralph
was to have the land behind Bel Arbre."

His voice held a wistfulness that she had never heard
before, and she knew he was lost in thoughts about
his home. She ached to reach out and touch his hand,
wishing he hadn't lost so much. She knew that was the

reason he had become so hardened that he found it difficult to trust others.

"When Papa and I both left, Papa decided before he went that Ralph was to see to it that half of our gold was kept safe. One half he buried on the place." His voice became harsh as he gazed at clumps of grass blowing in the breeze. "I went back and got that after the war, before I started out west."

"You're carrying all that gold with you now?" she asked, aghast. Many men in the West would shoot for little more than twenty dollars' gain.

"No, Miss Danby," he answered in cynical tones. "It's very safely tucked in a bank in Kansas City."

"Go on, you were telling me about your family and Ralph taking the gold," she reminded him, hating the harshness that had returned to his voice and his features.

"Anyway, Papa thought Ralph would be home with Mama and might need the other half, so he left it in Ralph's charge. Papa couldn't resist getting in the war—Lord, how he hated Yankees for interfering in his way of life."

"I'm sorry you lost your home, but I can't favor slavery," she said quietly, thinking of her own past, and how terrible it would have been to belong to strangers.

Noah had been caught in memories of home; he heard the conviction in her voice and guessed she was thinking of her own upbringing, which had been left so to chance and the care of strangers. "No, I don't favor slavery either, but I hate what we lost. Yankees burned our house. Mama went to Dothan to stay with a sister, and that's when Ralph joined the army. He was so young, only fifteen, but the South needed every man who could fight. I don't blame him, I would have done the same."

"How on earth did he carry a lot of gold with him?"

"He didn't. He buried it or left it with people he could trust, but as his unit moved west, he took it with him. I don't know how he managed to keep it through the two years he was with the army. When he went off

to fight, I think Mama just gave up. I couldn't get
letters home often and she didn't know where I was or
if I was alive or not. Then Papa was killed at Resaca
in Georgia when 'Cump' Sherman attacked on his
drive to Atlanta.'' Noah spread his hands on his thighs,
rubbing his palms against them. ''It's good to be out
west and away from the memories. There are good
memories, but right now the bad still overshadow
them.''

"I'm sorry," she said gently. He raised his head to
gaze into her eyes.

He smiled, creases bracketing his mouth. ''I
shouldn't dwell on the losses. There were good times.
We had balls and parties that would last for days. We'd
barbecue meat in a pit, and that was good food! We
had a bed of pink and white peonies that ran along
one side of the house, and when those flowers would
bloom in the springtime, Mama would say it was time
for a ball. The house would be turned on end getting
ready for it.'' Noah pulled out his ''Arkansas tooth-
pick,'' the long double-edged blade glistening in the
sunlight. He began to peel one of the apples, letting
the long peel unroll as he worked carefully. ''Ralph
and I could hunt possum and coon and quail and deer,
all kinds of game. We had miles of cotton. We had a
slave—Doby was his name—he taught Ralph and me
how to fight.'' Noah cut slices of apple and handed
her one. It was crisp and juicy, and she ate it while he
talked.

"Papa probably would have thrashed us if he had
caught us, but we'd go down to the river where there
was a clearing back in the bushes and Doby taught us
how to throw a punch.''

"I'm surprised he'd hit his owner's sons!"

Noah grinned, his teeth white and even. ''That's because one time I got in a fight on the place with a boy
from a neighboring plantation, Buford Tatum. He was
two years older and twice as big as I was at the time.
I came out a poor second. Doby saw the fight, and he
didn't like his family getting whipped. Besides, I
taught Doby to read.''

"I didn't know slaves could read."

Noah shrugged, laying aside the apple and putting his knife away. "Some could. Mama taught two of the house slaves. I used to take a book down to the river, and Doby started asking me about it one time. He was a field hand, but he was interested in my books, so I'd sneak off and teach him, and when he could read, I used to slip the books out to him. Doby didn't think I ought to take a beating like I did from Buford, so he told me to meet him down by the river. I don't think Papa would really have objected, because he believed in winning a fight, but Mama would have stirred up a fuss if they had caught us at it." He grinned again. "Every fight I've won, I feel I owe to Doby."

"Do you know what happened to your slaves?"

"I know what happened to Doby. He was killed defending Bel Arbre when the Yankees burned it. Powerful muscles aren't much match for a rifle." He tilted his head back against the tree.

"There were many good times, though. The balls were fun, all the neighbors and friends would come, the house would be full of people. Papa would get out the best liquor he owned." For a time Noah stared at the river, and she knew he was remembering home and boyhood. She wondered whom he had loved—she was sure there was at least one who had danced in his arms, shared his kisses. Longing besieged her as she stole glances at him. His attention shifted to her. "I guess you didn't have many dances, did you, Miss Danby?"

She shook her head. "The only one was a fandango I went to with Emilio."

"The only one?"

She laughed. "Don't look as if I suddenly turned green! I dance on a stage every night, you know."

"That's a hell of a lot different," he said gruffly.

"You don't miss what you don't have," she said. "Besides, I've never wanted to go with anyone else."

"What was Emilio like? Was he twelve too?"

"No. He was eighteen and the most handsome man I've known," she said, looking beyond Noah at the river. A dreamy, wistful expression came to her features and brought an inner glow to her. Noah drew a deep breath. Again he had to fight an urge to reach the short distance and touch her. Her voice changed, and Noah heard a tender note of longing. He thought it would be wonderful to stir such feelings in a woman like April Danby. He forgot his gold, forgot her occupation, and focused all his attention on her. His gaze shifted from her luminous, wide silvery eyes to her rosy mouth. He had thought Emilio was a young boy, as young as April. He was amazed to learn an eighteen-year-old had fallen in love with her, yet he was beginning to understand why.

"I met him when Luke took me back to San Antonio. Luke was engaged to Catalina at the time. The men were so rough and rowdy at Miss Kate's, I usually tried to avoid them. I thought I'd never, ever fall in love!" She cut a glance at Noah and laughed, and he smiled in return, knowing she was lost in her thoughts. He pictured a little golden-haired girl drifting in the background of a sporting house.

"I'd never really known a boy, and Emilio was gentle, and he loved to read like I do. He played the guitar and liked to dance and was so handsome. He gave me this necklace," she said, pulling the golden heart from beneath her collar. Noah reached out to take it in his hand, letting his knuckles rest on her thin collarbone.

"He said the necklace was his heart; I would have it always. And I promised to wear this heart always."

"That was a long time ago, Miss Danby."

"There are some things time doesn't change."

"Life *is* change," he said softly. He leaned closer, caressing her throat with his hand that held the necklace, tilting her chin upward with the other. He almost kissed her, and he saw she would let him. Her lashes fluttered, her cheeks flushed, and he wanted to lean down, but he thought about his gold and resisted.

April held her breath as his indigo eyes filled with longing. His fingers were warm beneath her chin. Her heart hammered violently, as her gaze dropped to his mouth, and she wanted to be kissed.

She saw in his eyes the moment he thought about the gold. His expression changed; his features became harsh as he inhaled deeply. He shifted and frowned, staring at her, but this time the look was cold.

"I want my gold, Miss Danby. It's rightfully mine." He reached beneath his shirt and withdrew a yellowed, torn scrap of paper. He carefully unfolded it as he moved close beside her, their shoulders touching.

At first she thought the paper was smeared with dirt, but when she took it in her hands and saw the shaky signature that read "Ralph," she realized it was blood. Swiftly she scanned the letter, which was barely legible:

> Noah:
>   I made it this far. The gold hidden . . . with April Danby in Albuquerque. If I don't get home, tell Laura Lee I love her. Give part . . . my share to Miss Danby.
>
> R.

She frowned and read it again, looking up into blue eyes that were as hard as steel. "I swear to you, I don't know a thing about your gold."

"That's my brother's handwriting," he said harshly.

"He asked me to get pen and paper for him and some men's clothes to travel in."

"Why in the sweet hell didn't you get him a doctor?"

Her head snapped up and she glared at him. "Because your brother was also a strong man who was very determined! If I hadn't done what he asked, he would have ridden away that night. I told you before, I wanted to get a doctor, but he refused. He was afraid the doctor would turn him over to the Union soldiers. He had killed a Union officer," she said, hating to see the grimness in Noah's features. "They were after him when he hid in my dressing room. I told you that too. I brought him home and he demanded I get the clothing and paper and pen and not go to the doctor. He threatened to leave, and he would have!"

Looking away from her, Noah ran his fingers through his hair in a distraught manner. Her anger at him evaporated as she saw the pain in his expression.

"I'm sorry. Your brother was brave and strong. I don't know how he lasted as long as he did," she said in sympathy, reaching out to touch his wrist.

The contact made him turn to gaze into her eyes. As his hurt vanished, so did her sorrow, because she was caught up again in the disturbing attraction that flared so easily between them. He was only inches away, and for a second she couldn't speak or breathe.

With an effort she withdrew her hand. She felt heat rise in her cheeks as she stood up and walked to the river's edge. Green water splashed against a boulder in the center of the river, spray sparkling in the sunlight.

In seconds he joined her. "April, my brother was as honest with me as sunshine is hot," Noah said solemnly.

"I don't have your gold," she said, looking him directly in the eye. "I swear to you, I don't! I don't know anything about it."

Anger surged in him. He couldn't believe her because Ralph's letter was damning. Clenching his fists, he grabbed her by the shoulders, his fingers biting deep. "Dammit. You saw his letter, with his blood spattered all over it!" He closed his eyes and spun away from her as if he had to move away before he did something violent.

"I can't help what the letter says. I'm telling you the truth."

"I have to believe my brother. I knew him longer and better. I can't beat it out of you. My fine southern upbringing makes it impossible for me to strike a woman," he said bitterly. "I was taught to treat ladies respectfully, no matter what kind of liars they were!"

As her anger surged, she brushed past him. "I'm going home."

His hand snaked out and caught her, spinning her around. She gasped and flung her hands against his chest, her silvery eyes going wide.

"I can't hurt you, but I won't leave here without it," he said tightly, fighting anger, fighting attraction. He didn't want to think her eyes were spellbinding. He didn't want to look at her mouth and yearn to place his lips on hers, "I'll be your shadow if I have to stay until I have a long white beard."

They glared at each other, but in spite of his harsh words and his anger, she saw desire flame in his eyes, and she wanted to feel his arms around her.

She couldn't pull free and he didn't release her. They continued to stare at each other, both gasping for breath while minutes passed.

"You little witch," he whispered, but all the force had gone out of his words, and he pulled her to him. He groaned, closing his eyes, hauling her against him to hold her tightly. With deliberation he lowered his head, and his mouth covered hers. His tongue thrust against her closed lips. April trembled in his arms, her resolve melting with the swiftness of butter beneath a flame. Her arms slipped around his neck while her mind argued with her heart. Arguments stopped. Thought stopped. She was lost as his tongue forced her lips apart and then played in her mouth, stirring feelings that were as intoxicating as wine, taking her sweetness, giving her strength, demanding more.

Noah shook with desire. She was slender and sweet, her breasts soft against him, her mouth setting him aflame. She had been loved by a gentle eighteen-year-old boy when she had been only twelve—she was as innocent as a spring rose and as sensuous as the most seductive woman. He wanted her. He bent over her, molding her to his length, feeling his blood thunder in his veins while he kissed her passionately, wanting to make her moan, wanting her to cling to him wildly, wanting to feel her hips press against him.

She twisted away from him, both of them breathing hard, both staring at each other, warring emotions easily visible. She didn't want to respond to him. He was a hard man, after his gold, going on west. There was nothing about Noah McCloud that was quiet or gentle like Emilio.

Noah began picking up their things, working
quickly, trying to curb the urge to reach for her again.
He was torn between believing her and believing his
brother's letter. He didn't need to get involved with
her—he needed to keep a clear head. In minutes the
buggy was loaded and they headed back to April's,
where he helped her down. He paused with his hands
on her waist.

"I won't leave here until I have what's rightfully
mine."

She nodded solemnly. "Thank you for your help
today."

Wondering how many kinds of fool a man could be,
he mounted his horse. He had helped her do her laundry, mended her shed, curried her horse, eaten a picnic dinner with her, and kissed her. And he expected
her to hand over his gold!

Before he rode away, she reached up to grasp his
reins. "I really don't know anything about it."

"Miss Danby, I swear to you, my brother wouldn't
have lied about this."

He turned his horse, the bay gelding flicking its tail
as he rode away.

He spent two weeks dogging her, trailing after her,
watching her house at night, eating with her, spending
lazy afternoons with her, and his nerves and patience
stretched thin. As much as he wanted to reach for her,
he curbed the impulse, but it took more effort each
time. She attracted him and infuriated him. In sleepless hours he decided on a course of action that should
convince her he intended to get what was rightfully
his.

5

On a warm Friday night during the last days of spring, while April sang at the Brown Owl, Noah rode toward the Cantina Encantada. He had heard the owner liked to gamble with patrons on occasion. If he bought the Brown Owl, which would be difficult, April Danby would go to work at the Encantada or at El Paraíso. El Paraíso was a dobie, a small adobe building, with cracked windows and cottonwood stump chairs, a doggery he would buy later. Noah wanted to start with the Encantada, then he'd get El Paraíso, and last, the Brown Owl. The Encantada was a hewn log building, long and narrow, with a shake shingle roof and glass windows. In addition to being a sound structure, it was in a choice location next to the stage depot. It would be a good business investment.

And when he owned the three saloons, there wouldn't be any place left in Albuquerque where April could get a job because the other saloons and cantinas were men-only, no singers, no women. By then she would have to admit she had his gold, or use it to survive.

It was almost dawn when Noah returned to his hotel. Now he was the new owner of the Cantina Encantada. It had been a wild game of faro and he had won more than he had hoped for—the saloon and an old adobe hacienda built back before there was much town. The man who had wagered the house was living in one room of it, and Noah thought he had lost it without regrets. Noah would worry about the house later, move into it or sell it, whatever seemed best. Right now he wanted to concentrate on the saloon. His jaw was set.

Eventually April would have to admit she had the gold. Enough pressure and she might capitulate. In spite of people's stories that seemed to prove April to be what she said, he had to believe Ralph, who had had no reason to lie.

During the next week he spent all his waking hours taking care of his new saloon, changing the name to McCloud's Place. As long as he was the owner, it was going to earn a dollar. He had familiarized himself with the way the games in the saloon were played before he tried to win it. The game favored the house, but they played with old square-cornered cards, and after nights of observation and playing, he could beat their system, winning on the cathop that counted double. When he set up his own faro game, Noah intended to hire an experienced dealer.

Noah implemented his changes immediately, working in the early hours before dawn and during the mornings. He kept the saloon open afternoons and nights. As soon as he could, he started looking for a new bartender.

Early one morning as he sat in the shade of a scrubby juniper in front of a piñon-log cabin, he talked to a man who had been recommended for the job. Duero Corinto was a short, stocky man. He had been chopping wood when Noah rode up, and together they sat down to talk.

"Estoy enteramente a su disposición," Duero said cordially. He offered Noah a tin cup and held out a bottle.

"Gracias," Noah answered politely, knowing how courteous some of the local people could be when visited in their homes. He watched the amber liquid pour into the cup, drank, and choked, coughing and blinking his eyes as the fiery liquid went down. "Whoo! They said you know liquor!"

Duero Corinto laughed, his teeth stained brown from tobacco. "You develop a taste for tis-win, Indian whiskey. I lived with the Apache for a while."

"I thought I'd tasted every kind of whiskey, but this

is new." Cautiously he took another sip. "I just became the new owner of the Encantada."

"*Sí*. I heard."

"I want to make it a better place. I think it can earn good money."

Duero nodded his head, waiting quietly, and Noah began to develop a liking for him. "I heard you used to tend bar."

"*Sí*. I can do the job."

"Why did you quit?"

"I was at the New Mexico House. I worked for five different owners. It was a nothing job."

"Doc Yishay said you're an honest man."

Duero grinned and shook his head. "That Doc! He's a good man."

"Well, are you?"

"Honest? *Sí.*" He waved his hand toward the cabin behind him. "Does this look like the home of a dishonest man?"

Noah smiled. "Do you remember how to tend bar?"

"Who forgets?"

"Want a new job as barkeep?"

"I have a good job at the lumberyard. I don't have to stop fights, dodge bullets, clean up after drunks."

"I'll pay you a monthly wage of seventy-five dollars and five percent of the profits. In six months we should have an idea how much we can earn and we'll renegotiate then."

Duero lowered his tin cup and stared at Noah. "You give me part of the saloon plus seventy-five dollars a month?" he asked, amazement making his voice a whisper.

"I want someone I can trust, someone I can leave the business with. I can't be there every minute—far from it. I don't know much about saloons right now."

Grinning, Duero thrust out his hand. "You got a new barkeep."

"Good. You start as soon as you can give notice and leave the lumberyard."

"I start today. I can work double if Mr. Adderson wants me to stay until he hires someone."

"Good," Noah said, pleased with Duero's replies. "The first thing I want to do is get rid of the Taos Lightning. I don't give a damn what you do with the stuff, but it's the worst damned whiskey—"

"It's distilled at Rio Hondo. It's supposed to have a wheat base, pepper, tobacco, and sometimes, rumor has it, gunpowder." Duero refilled Noah's tin cup. "They sell it all over the West."

"Not in my saloon." Noah shook the cup slightly. "And no tis-win!"

"You're a strong man, Mr. McCloud. White men can't stomach tis-win," he said with a grin.

"I've already wired the Rocky Mountain Brewery. We're serving good liquor, no red eye. If they want cheap whiskey, they can go down the street. We'll sell five-cent-a-drink beer. Know where I can hire someone good with a six-shooter?"

Duero's brown eyes were full of curiosity, but he kept questions to himself. He stared into space a moment while he thought. "I don't know. Perhaps Tobias Lente."

"I want a peaceful saloon. I'm going to pay a fighter to keep it that way. If I'm going in the saloon business, it's going to be as good as I can make it. The best in the territory, I hope."

"Ahh," Duero said, nodding. "Perhaps Tobias or Uvaldo Zucal."

"Tell them to contact me if they're interested. Can you help with some remodeling?"

"*Sí.*"

"I know Lean Henry handles money on occasion for his patrons. We can do that too. I'll charge two percent interest per day to lend money."

"Some places charge twenty percent each day," Duero said impassively.

"That's akin to highway robbery. I'll put in safe-deposit boxes; we can hold gold dust for the miners, have a foreign-currency exchange. No shin plasters or greenbacks accepted for the gambling or drinks. We can discuss business more when you come by the saloon. And the new name is McCloud's Place."

"Sure, boss."

Both men stood up and shook hands again. Then Noah rode off to town. Eight hours later, he continued the same conversation as they stood behind the bar of the saloon. "Duero, I want honest people working for me. I'll pay good wages for people I can trust. I want you to talk to them first, I'll go with your recommendations."

Duero laughed. "Doc must have done one dandy good selling job. I'll have to thank him."

"He said he would trust you with anything. I'm riding to Santa Fe. Hire two men to go along to help bring back supplies."

"*Sí*. It's through Apache territory. My wife was Apache. She was killed," he said flatly. Noah decided not to pry, and Duero quickly continued, "I can get you through safely."

"I need someone here while we're gone."

"You have a good man. Hosea Shorne. You can trust him, and he's worked in saloons for years."

"Good. Can you leave tomorrow?"

"Day after. Then I'm through at the lumberyard. And I'm finished there for today. How can I help here?"

Noah looked at the crowd in the saloon. "You can get behind the bar right now. Two bits or a pinch of gold dust a pony. And we'll use good whiskey."

"*Sí*, Mr. McCloud."

"Duero. You can call me by my given name, Noah."

"Sure, boss."

By three in the morning the crowd had gone and only one man lay sprawled in the corner, snoring as his chest rose and fell evenly.

"You got a broom?" Duero asked.

"There's an old straw one back there."

"I saw it. You need a new broom, boss. Get a turkey-feather one. We'll sweep each night. There should be five to fifteen dollars in gold dust on this floor."

Noah laughed and rubbed his jaw. "Damn, I never thought about what gets spilled."

"There's no one waiting for me at home," Duero said. "Anything we can do now?"

"Sure, if you're willing to work. Get a hammer."

Noah had learned long ago how to use a hammer and saw, and with Duero's help he began rebuilding parts that needed it.

The next day he ordered new furnishings. Duero and Hosea helped him hang new signs painted by Will Brinks, a local artist. Over the door was the largest one: McCLOUD'S PLACE. And beneath it, flanking the door, were two long signs: "Billiard Hall . . . Cold Beer," and "Beautiful Women . . . Music." Noah knew all his employees—the six dancing girls, the dealers, the mixologist who would work when Duero wasn't on duty, and the piano player.

Many days he caught a glimpse of April riding past his place on her way to the Brown Owl, in the next block. Once, as he was standing in the doorway looking at the summer batwing doors woven of stiff rattan, April rode past and he waved to her. She nodded coolly, and his emotions were plagued with a mixture of feelings. He wanted to stride into the street and talk to her; he wanted to show her his saloon, which he was growing more pleased with each day; and he experienced a twinge of guilt over his motives in obtaining the saloon.

He had interviewed all the dancers, and decided to keep them, but the more he talked to them and heard their sad stories, the more he felt nagging uneasiness about April. She shouldn't sing in a saloon. He stood with his fists on his hips and stared out the window of his tiny office. She was sweet and innocent and not the same type as others who performed in saloons. He swore, sitting down behind his desk to go over a list of figures. He shouldn't care! An hour later, after refiguring repeatedly, he strode through the door to talk to customers and get his mind off April Danby.

Two weeks later McCloud's Place was almost completely renovated. New round-wick Rochester brass lamps hung from the freshly painted ceiling, brass spittoons gleamed as well as the brass rail at the bar, and the small platform was ready to serve as a stage for dancers. With Duero's help, Noah rode to Santa Fe, where he bought a wagon and hauled two billiard tables and a roulette wheel to Albuquerque.

In the middle of July, at three in the morning, Noah had his sleeves rolled high and was hammering a new shelf in place behind the bar. By nine o'clock in the morning he was aching with weariness. He hadn't slept for the fourth night in a row, but the place looked better every day. Profits were already coming in, and the faro, keno, and roulette were raking in good returns.

He wanted to bring April over to see the new interior, the new fixtures, the polished old ones. He rubbed the nape of his neck and silently cursed himself. He wanted to show it to her. He was doing it all to put her out of business, *to hurt her*, yet at the same time he wanted her to see it. He knew if there was no issue of missing gold between them, her eyes would sparkle. She would praise his work and make him feel as if he had done something twice as good as he actually had. He could imagine her standing in the empty room, looking around.

"Jesus," he exclaimed, and tossed down his hammer to stomp out the back door, almost colliding with Aaron Yishay.

"Whoa there!"

"Sorry, Doc," Noah said, going to the pump to splash cold water on his face. "What are you doing out here?"

Doc was seated on a stump in the shade of the building, whittling a small block of wood. "Mostly hiding. Mama's washing curtains today, and at our house, that's trouble. If I'm not there, I won't have to get involved in it. She thinks I'm delivering Mrs. Clackenwill's baby."

"Won't she ask Mrs. Clackenwill about the baby?" Noah asked, leaning against a wagon and grinning, relieved to find something to take his mind off his own troubles.

"I'll tell her it was false labor. Mrs. Clackenwill

will have that baby any day now. Besides''—he squinted at Noah and grinned, his dark eyes twinkling—''Mama's used to my tricks. She knows I'm hiding and she's probably relieved to have me out of the way when she does the curtains in my office.''

Noah laughed and scuffed the dirt with the toe of his boot. ''You can come inside to wait if you want.''

''And have you give me a hammer and put me to work—no, thanks. Just as soon wash curtains. I didn't know you were interested in saloons.''

''I am now.''

''That's why you said you were looking for an honest man you could hire.''

''Right. Thanks for recommending Duero. I think he'll be fine.''

''He's dependable. I hear you won a house too. The Old Morelos place.''

''You know about it?''

''Everyone who's been here very long knows about it. Old place, but solid as this ground.''

''I've been too busy to look at it. I'll probably sell it.''

''That right? That sounds like a good idea. Ever owned a saloon before?'' he asked, whittling, sending little chips of pale wood falling over his feet and knees.

''No. I'll learn.''

''Figuring on hiring a singer?''

''I might.''

Aaron Yishay grinned. ''You decided I told you the truth about Miss April. She's going to sing here.''

''No and no.''

''You still think she took your gold?''

''So you know it was gold.''

''Still aim to get it back from her?''

''Yes.''

''McCloud, I'm glad you got into business here, because you're going to grow old waiting for that gold.''

''No, I'm damn well not!'' Noah paced restlessly, turning his back on Aaron. He now wished he was alone.

"How you figure that? She can't give you what she doesn't have."

"You don't know that!"

"That why you bought the saloon?"

"Yes."

"To go into competition?"

"Not exactly. I intend to put her out of work."

Aaron Yishay lowered his knife and block of wood to stare at Noah. "I heard you go help her with all her chores on Saturday and Sunday, and that you've taken her down to the river for a picnic."

"I used to help her, but lately I've been busy with my saloon. How'd you know that?"

"Vesta Dodworth talks to Mama. Vesta is the real gossip, not Lesta. Isn't your behavior contradictory?"

"I have to do something." He ground out the words.

"She's telling you the truth."

"She could have fooled everyone in town, and you know it. She could have fooled you."

"Son, you look as miserable as a coyote with his toe caught in a trap."

Noah almost snapped off a harsh answer, but then he took a second look at Yishay's bright eyes, and he sighed. "Damn, one minute I want to bring her over here and show her all I've accomplished, and the next minute I'm planning how to ruin her and force her into giving me what's rightfully mine. If you laugh, so help me—"

"Son, I'd never laugh at a man in deep trouble, and I'd say you're in about as deep as a man can get. Why don't you settle down and forget that gold? Life might be a heap better."

"If you had a brother you could trust as much as you trust yourself, and he said April Danby had the family gold, would you believe it or not?"

"I see your point. But remember, things happen. Sometimes things we don't plan happen. I know April. If she had your gold, she would give it to you. I'd trust her with everything I own, and Mama would too."

Noah ran his hands through his hair. "I just can't give up. It's a hell of a lot of money. A hell of a lot."

"Son, I hear a lot of things. People talk to doctors, they seem to trust us. You're not the only one who's been talking about gold lately. I heard a rumor that your brother, the Rebel, had some Union gold. That's why he killed a Union officer."

"I don't know anything about that. All I know is, we sent Ralph off with our family gold. Do others in town know about Ralph and the gold?"

"Surely you didn't think this was a big secret between just you and April?"

"Well, yes, as a matter of fact."

"You don't look like a naive man. News about gold always travels."

"Damn." Noah picked up a rock and tossed it as far as he could throw. It bounced across bare ground, finally coming to rest yards away. "I'm going back to work."

Aaron Yishay folded his knife and stood up.

"What are you doing?" Noah asked. "You can stay here."

"I think you can use some help," Yishay said quietly, and Noah wasn't about to argue.

When April sang Saturday night, she wore a new dress. It had taken her months to make, and with Melissa's help she had spent most of her evenings the last few weeks sewing the spangles on it. It was emerald-green faille, cut low in front, and the neckline was trimmed with white point-duchesse lace and green feathers. The bodice fit tightly, and the skirt split to her knees on both sides and was edged with a dark green ruche. When she looked down at Noah McCloud, he nodded imperceptibly and lifted his drink in a salute.

His smoldering anger had been disturbing. Now he gazed at her intently, but the anger was gone. There was no mistaking the mocking approval as his eyes slowly drifted down over her and just as deliberately crawled up inch by inch. His gaze set her aflame, as if he had brushed her legs and body with his hands instead of merely a look.

Noah sipped his whiskey and watched her, his body responding as she leaned over the stage and looked into his eyes. Her voice was as tantalizing as a caress. Mentally he stripped her; the tight, low-cut dress left little to the imagination, and the images in his mind were a scalding torment.

She pulled a lace handkerchief from her deeply cut neckline, and as always, it brought the house to their feet. Cowmen yelled and stomped, the ones near the stage clamoring to catch the scrap of linen and lace. Except Noah McCloud, who sat quietly watching, a taunting smile on his face.

April walked to the edge of the stage to kneel down and sing. When she was so close, singing legato, her voice throbbed with feeling, and her gaze locked with Noah's. A tremble ran through her as she watched him. She drew the handkerchief across her lips and breasts, and then she flung out her arm to toss the lace over his head.

He stood up suddenly, his arm snaking out to catch the handkerchief. He sat down as men cheered, and then the saloon grew quiet. As she sang, Noah held the handkerchief in his open palm and slowly closed his fingers over it until the handkerchief vanished from sight in his fist.

The anger was back in his eyes, and she understood his threat. She knew his new saloon was open and reportedly doing well. Tonight was actually the first time in over a month he had been in to the Brown Owl. With a toss of her head she crossed to the other side of the stage and stayed as far from him during the rest of her performance as possible.

When she entered her dressing room, he was already there, leaning against the wall. He straightened and came forward when she stopped in the open doorway.

"You don't belong in here."

His gaze lowered insolently, inching downward in a slow appraisal.

"Stop studying me like I'm a horse you're about to purchase!"

The corner of his mouth curved in a taunting smile. "I came to ask you to dinner." While he talked, he came closer, and with each step her pulse skipped faster.

"No. I'm sorry. Melissa Hatfield is visiting me tonight. She's waiting at home."

"Hatfield? That's the name of the man who owns the house where I caught you."

"My best friend is his daughter. Will you stop staring at me!"

He reached over her head to close the door behind her. His voice lowered. "Every man out there has looked at you as much as I have, and some of them with worse intentions."

"I don't want to hear about your intentions!" she tried to snap, but the words came out breathlessly. "And they didn't look at me the way you do!"

"The hell you say!" he remarked lightly, a teasing note back in his voice. "How do I look at you that's different?" he drawled, and she felt on fire. He stood too close, his questions were too intimate, and his bold gaze seared like a flame.

"Please leave so I can get dressed."

His expression was sardonic as he watched her. He tilted her chin upward.

"You weren't meant to live like a hermit. You were meant for a man. To be loved until you faint, to use all that smoldering passion that comes through when you sing."

"I sing to Emilio's memory." She jerked away, her cheeks flaming.

"Memories make cold bedfellows," he said. His words mocked her. "I'm going to get what I came for. I can't spend the rest of my life following you around, waiting for you to make a slip."

"It would take the rest of your life, because you're after something I don't have."

"If you don't have a job, you'll have to use the gold," he said quietly, and she heard the threat, like a blade of cold steel placed against her throat.

"You can't get me fired. Lean Henry won't listen to you."

"Lean Henry will listen to money. I'm the new owner of the Cantina Encantada."

"If you could afford to buy a saloon, why do you need the gold?"

"Saloon owners are often not the most settled citizens in a town. I won the Encantada in a wager, the same way, I believe, that Lean Henry won the Brown Owl. There aren't a lot of saloons in town that need a singer," he said quietly.

She panicked for a moment, but quickly regained her composure. "I can move to another town, or go back to San Antonio."

"You may just have to do that very thing. Or you can cooperate. I'll give you a share," he said coaxingly, but his eyes were as hard as crystals.

"I don't have it! Leave me be, Noah!"

"I won't give up," he said. He leisurely assessed her from head to toe, and then he was gone, closing the door quietly.

For an instant she stood in shock. Then, trying to rid herself of her worries, she hurried to get dressed. She changed into a demure blue gingham that fastened to her chin, then braided her hair swiftly. She tried every way possible to look chaste and cool and remote, but was still unable to get his husky voice and taunting words out of her thoughts. Worries alternated between fear that he would force her out of work, and anger at his assumptions, and a burning response to his relentless gaze. She leaned forward to stare at her wide-eyed reflection, wondering why she had such a startling reaction to a man who was so vastly different from Emilio. She ran her hand across her collarbone, feeling the necklace Emilio had give her so long ago, and silently vowed that she would not let Noah McCloud unnerve her.

That night Noah sat quietly across the street beneath a tree and watched April move around her parlor. She sat in her rocker quilting and talking to her friend,

who must be Melissa Hatfield. That first night, April
must have been taking Melissa Hatfield's place in bed
while Melissa slipped out for a tryst. Noah had to admit he was relieved. He swore silently when April extinguished the lamps and went to the curtained
bedroom. The taunting images of her going to bed
made his body throb with desire.

Her windows became dark, but he still waited outside to see if he could catch her slipping out to some
hiding place for the gold. In spite of her protests that
sounded as truthful as anything he had ever heard, she
had to have it. He came again the next two nights
around five in the morning. Business at his saloon was
at its slowest then, and he dozed in his saddle, feeling
sure that sooner or later she would do something to
reveal where the gold was hidden.

One night, as he sat quietly watching her house, a
shadow moved. Instantly his soldier's instincts came
to life. His eyes narrowed, and he sat tense and still
while his gaze swept the area.

6

Black shadows shifted, and a man's form materialized, gliding into April's house. Noah dismounted and ran for the house, not bothering to keep quiet until he reached the door. Then he moved as silently as possible, stepping inside.

His eyes had already adjusted to the dark, and he strained to hear as he crept toward the parlor. The moment he stepped to the doorway, he saw a man silhouetted against the window. Noah pulled his six-shooter.

"Don't move," he ordered, cocking the hammer.

"Who the hell are you?" came a raspy voice.

"Who is it?" April called from the bedroom.

The intruder answered at the same time as Noah, both answers blurring, and Noah remembered what she had told him.

"Who is it?" she called more emphatically.

"Noah McCloud!" he snapped. "Are you Ta-ne-haddle?"

"Yes. Who're you?"

Noah put away his revolver, then struck a match to light a lamp. A dark-skinned man in a white shirt and denim trousers faced him. A thick black braid of hair hung down his back.

"Mr. McCloud!" April said, fury choking her voice.

Noah picked up a lamp to light the wick and turned to see April. She stood in the doorway in the flickering lamplight, her golden hair tangled and tumbling over her shoulders. A plain white cotton wrap covered her from her throat to her toes. His heart lurched, because she held as much sensual appeal as she did on a stage in a tight-fitting silk dress.

"Ta-ne-haddle!" she cried, as a smile lit her features. She ran and threw her arms around the Indian's neck. Noah felt a tug of envy as he watched the one-eyed man scoop her up easily and hug her in return, kissing her cheek before he set her on the floor. Never had Noah seen her so enthusiastic, and his envy deepened.

"Where's Lottie?"

"She didn't come with me, but I met a trapper who had just been through town . . ." He paused, and his gaze went over her head. One cold, black eye studied Noah. "He said some man has been taking you out, but word has it you don't like the man, that he's forced his attention on you."

"That's not altogether right," she said. Noah heard the amused note in her voice, but he didn't take his gaze from Ta-ne-haddle, who simmered with silent threats.

"This is Mr. McCloud. And this is my friend Ta-ne-haddle. Mr. McCloud is the man you heard about. He thinks I have a large cache of gold that belongs to him."

Noah could have groaned aloud, because instantly Ta-ne-haddle seemed to draw himself up, and his hand drifted to the knife in the scabbard at his waist.

Noah reached beneath his shirt and yanked out his brother's letter. He held it out to Ta-ne-haddle, who read it and then looked down at April.

"I did take his brother Ralph in. You remember, the Rebel I told you about."

"The one who died?"

She nodded, and he reread the letter before looking at Noah and handing it back. "If she told you she doesn't have your gold, she's telling the truth. She doesn't have it."

"Young single women can't afford to live in this style. My brother never lied to me. He was here and he had the gold at that time."

"You don't know he had the gold at that time. And

she lives in this style because she earns her keep by singing—''

''Singing won't pay for all this.''

''And her brother sends her money from time to time,'' Ta-ne-haddle said quietly. Noah's gaze flew to hers.

''Is that true?''

She nodded, and exasperation filled him. ''Why didn't you tell me, instead of allowing me to think you earned the money for this all by yourself?''

''Because you haven't always given me a chance, and usually people believe what I say,'' she said with a contrariness Noah thought was purely feminine, ''so I expected the same of you.''

''April, you go back to bed. Mr. McCloud and I can discuss this.''

''I don't want you to fight,'' she said, looking from one to the other.

''Go on to bed,'' Ta-ne-haddle urged softly.

''Maybe the lady wants to stay to protect me,'' Noah drawled, taunting her. She glared at him, then returned to her bedroom, slamming the door behind her. She climbed into bed, but she couldn't sleep. She sat in the dark listening for sounds, but there was nothing but silence. The minutes seemed like hours, and finally she couldn't bear not knowing what they were doing. Impatiently she threw back the covers and climbed out of bed. Holding her robe close around her waist, she went to the parlor. The house was empty.

It wasn't like Ta-ne-haddle to leave after only saying hello. And it wasn't like him to leave without telling her. She opened the back door cautiously and looked around. To her horror, a body was stretched on the ground.

With a cry she ran toward it, and recognized Ta-ne-haddle's inert form. She flung herself down beside him, terrified that Noah had killed him. The moment she touched him, however, Ta-ne-haddle stirred.

''Are you all right?''

He sat up, and blood trickled down his jaw from the

corner of his mouth. His cheek was dark, his eyes puffed, and blood ran from a cut on his arm.

"You've been fighting!" she cried. She wondered what he had done to Noah, because she had never known Ta-ne-haddle to come out the loser in a fight. "Did you kill him?" she asked in sudden fright, looking around for another body.

"No, but I'd like to!" he grumbled. He staggered to his feet to go to the pump.

"Where's Mr. McCloud?"

"I hope roasting in hell," he said, sticking his head beneath the pump. April grabbed his hand so he had to pay attention to her.

"Where is he? Did you hurt him?"

He squinted at her. "Do you care?"

Her cheeks burned and she was glad for the darkness. "Well, I don't want you to kill the man."

He gave a grunt, continuing to study her while he raked his tangled hair back from his face. "He'll be all right. Maybe we better have a talk."

"I think you hurt him!" she exclaimed, because his gaze slid away in a guilty manner.

"He's as tough as an old grizzly."

She put her hands on her hips. "What did you do to him?"

"How much do you care?"

Embarrassed, realizing how she was sounding, she walked to the house. He fell into step beside her. "I asked you a question, April."

"I don't want him hurt just because he's laboring under a false notion."

"Laboring under a false notion!" Ta-ne-haddle echoed in disgust. "Why didn't you tell me that you didn't want me to hurt him before we left you?"

"You did hurt him!"

"Not as much as he hurt me. Or maybe about the same, but I didn't know this was the way the wind was blowing."

"The wind isn't blowing any sort of way!" she snapped.

"I'm not going to argue with you about this."

"We're not arguing," she replied stiffly. "You can do whatever you want to do to Noah McCloud!"

"Slit his throat? Scalp him?"

"No!" she exclaimed. She knew how adept Ta-ne-haddle was with a knife. Then she laughed. "All right! I told you I didn't want you to fight. It isn't his fault his brother wrote that he gave me all his gold."

"Do tell. Maybe you better tell me all about that night you gave his brother shelter."

"Come inside and I'll get a bandage for your cut."

When they sat down, she asked, "Did you ever scalp anyone?"

"No. I was too young when I was taken back east by the soldiers."

"What do they do with the scalps?"

"They're booty," Ta-ne-haddle replied, stretching out his legs and leaning back against the settee. "The returning war party charges back into the village firing rifles and shooting arrows, reenacting their attack. Each warrior sets his woman on his horse, circling the camp and singing. The scalps are stretched on hoops and held high by the women to honor their braves. If there are no dances planned for that evening, the grandmothers carry the scalps in a march. The following day there is the Scalp Dance. The scalps are placed on poles, and the women take the lances of their warriors, dancing around the trophies. They make feints at the scalps to imitate the killing of the enemy."

His voice lowered as his eyes gazed into the distance. She wondered how much he missed his Indian heritage, and if he would ever make peace with his own people.

"April, what about this Noah McCloud?"

"He's all right. He thinks I have his gold, and that makes him angry, yet he can be very nice sometimes." She knew she was blushing and that Ta-ne-haddle couldn't be fooled.

"Looks as if I owe the man an apology. I started the fight."

"How badly did you hurt him?"

"Not too bad. Where's he from?"

"Alabama."

"Does he work?"

"He owns a saloon now, McClouds's Place."

"He ought to earn a living fighting," Ta-ne-haddle said, rubbing his jaw. In the quiet of her kitchen they talked for an hour before he told her he needed to get back to Lottie.

"She's not far, just south of town a few miles. We'll both be here to visit soon."

"I hope so. Don't you get tired of roaming?" she asked. She was always curious about his way of life.

"No." He shook his head. "Maybe it's my Kiowa blood. We're Tsa'-hop, movers, we follow Da-e-dal, the great star. I love to roam. And Lottie does also."

She remembered how she had traveled with them, when she was younger. Lottie and she would sit around a campfire at night, and Ta-ne-haddle would tell them Kiowa legends.

"I'll go now," he said. His eyes were still swollen from the fight. "I see I'm not needed to protect you from McCloud," he added dryly.

April blushed as she kissed Ta-ne-haddle good-bye.

The next day, during the middle of the bright, sunny morning, she saw Noah as she was walking toward the general store. He was across the street, just coming out of the hotel. She gasped and stopped to stare at him. He noticed her standing there, and he crossed the wide dusty street. He had a blackened eye and a bruise on his cheek, a cut across his jaw, and his hand was bandaged.

"Good morning," Noah drawled, tipping his hat. "I guess you're right, Miss Danby. You do have a protector."

"Well, you two are a sight! Ta-ne-haddle looked as bad as you do! And did this do anything to convince you of my innocence?"

Something flickered in his eyes and he stepped closer. The moment he did, the morning changed. She saw only him—his broad shoulders, his long slender face, and his unfathomable blue eyes that bound her to him.

"Innocence?" he said in an entirely different tone of voice, changing the connotation of the word. "I've already reached my own conclusions about your innocence. And I know what I'd like to do about it," he added.

She burned from the unmistakable implications. They stood on the edge of the street with people passing all around them, yet for a moment they were alone in the world. She focused all her attention on Noah, who held her mesmerized with his gaze. Her lips were dry and she felt as if she couldn't draw a breath. She licked her lips. Her tongue slid across her lower lip until she realized how intently he was watching her and she clamped her mouth shut. His gaze was mocking, the tension growing and pulling, making her want to tilt her head up, close her eyes, and lean closer to him.

"If we weren't in the center of town in the middle of the morning, I'd oblige," he said softly.

It took two heartbeats to realize what he had said. She stepped away, glaring at him. The spell vanished as quickly as it had been conjured up.

"He should have just finished you off!" she snapped, and spun on her heel to walk away. With a chuckle he caught up with her.

"Hey, wait. After causing me trouble and pain last night, the least you can do is be civil."

"The least you can do is leave me alone! You are beginning to bother me a great deal, Mr. McCloud!" she snapped, facing him.

"Is that right? All you have to do to get rid of me is hand over what's rightfully mine."

"Oh, how I wish I could! I don't have your gold. There's one thing I must say, though, your brother was a far nicer man than you!"

Noah looked startled as she left him. She swept into Hatfield's General Store, passing the cracker barrel and potbellied stove. She was immediately assailed by the smells of plug tobacco, fresh-ground coffee, and leather from the boots and saddles. As she moved down the aisle, a look of determination crept across her face. Usually she enjoyed lingering in the store with its myriad items, the hams hanging from the rafters, the shelves of Epsom salts and paregoric, new bolts of colorful gingham and muslin materials, but today her mind was on Noah McCloud, not supplies.

Fresh eggs were nine cents a dozen, white soap was five cents, an eight-pound bucket of lard was forty-six cents. April made her purchases in a turmoil, as if a summer whirlwind had played havoc with her emotions.

He was in the saloon Saturday night, but she didn't talk to him afterward because when she stepped outside, Lieutenant Ferguson was waiting. " 'Evening, April. I enjoyed your singing tonight.''

"Thank you," she said, allowing him to help her into her buggy.

"I'll see you home if I may," he said politely. April couldn't think of any way to refuse, but she always felt uncomfortable with him. He was polite and pleasant, yet the looks he gave her weren't. His hazel eyes seemed filled with curiosity, speculation, and burning lust. She had heard two of the dancing girls talk about him—both had been favorably impressed, but he wasn't the man for April.

Letting his mount follow, he climbed up beside her to take the reins. She pulled her shawl around her shoulders and lifted her face to the stirring breeze. A pale moon rose high in the sky. "I've never heard anyone sing as pretty as you do."

"Thank you. Where are you from, Lieutenant?"

"My home was in Pittsburgh, but I won't go back there."

"You didn't like it?"

He shrugged. 'My folks never had much. I like the army life, being an officer. There's opportunity out here, opportunity in the army.''

"Do you still have family back there?"

"Yeah, plenty of that. There were eight boys in my family. We're scattered all over, and I suppose some of them are still in Pennsylvania. Where'd you come from, Miss Danby?''

"My family is in San Antonio. I only have one brother."

"Who's that half-breed Indian and his squaw who stay with you often?''

"His name is Ta-ne-haddle," she said coolly, wondering how Lieutenant Ferguson knew about him.

"Don't get in a huff," he said. "If you had to fight the Apache and the Comanche with us, you might feel differently about Indians."

"Not about my friends. They're like family to me. Lottie's the closest I have to a mother."

"Yeah. I heard you were taken from your parents when you were a baby and raised by a woman in Santa Fe. I didn't know it was Lottie—sorry."

At her house, he jumped to the ground quickly and reached up to swing her down out of her buggy. His hands rested on her waist. "The garrison is having a picnic Saturday afternoon. I'd like to take you, Miss Danby."

"Thank you, but—"

"Miss Danby," he said softly, "give me a chance. You won't ever go out with me."

"I'm sorry. I'm having company that afternoon. I don't go out with anyone," she replied.

"You've gone out with that McCloud. You're the most beautiful woman in town!" Mott Ferguson said. He leaned close, his voice lowering as he slipped his arms around her waist.

"I should go inside," she said. "Please, Lieutenant. My neighbors—"

He pulled her to him roughly, bending over her. His arms held her tightly to shut off her protest as his mouth covered hers. She clamped her lips shut and her body stiffened.

She struggled against him, remembering Noah McCloud's kisses. His had set her on fire, yet were almost as unwanted as the lieutenant's. She loathed Ferguson's kisses; they did nothing to stir up a warm response. In seconds, she managed to push him away.

"Sir! You mustn't!"

"You women always clear your conscience with a flock of protests," he said with amusement, and April bristled.

"I wasn't clearing my conscience," she answered quietly, trying to hold her temper.

"Good night, Miss Danby. Sweet dreams to you."

While he rode away, she hurried into the house, rubbing her lips with the back of her hand. She had hated his kisses and his glances that seemed to undress her. And his assumption that her protests were a sham was an insult. Yet she couldn't understand her own reactions, because Noah McCloud often gave her the same blatantly searing appraisal, as if he were undressing her in his mind. He kissed her when she had fought him, he tormented, annoyed, and on occasion frightened her, yet her pulse drummed wildly when he touched her. She was acutely aware of his presence, and her skin didn't crawl at his touch. Far from it. Oh, Lord, how far from it!

Why the difference? At least Noah would never insult her the way Lieutenant Ferguson did. So why was Noah so attractive, while Lieutenant Ferguson was almost repulsive?

It was a question that thousands of women had probably asked themselves. Never again would she ride home with Mott Ferguson. She drew the curtains in the bedroom and sank down on a rocking chair. She sang as she remembered Noah's smoldering appraisal and how he had bent over a washtub rinsing her clothes. Mott Ferguson wouldn't do her laundry. She smiled and thought of her Saturday afternoons with Noah. They were never at a loss for something to discuss, and she could tell him all her worries.

Hidden among the trees behind her house, waiting in the shadows, Noah felt on fire. He had watched Ferguson kiss April, heard her protests, and had to fight a compulsion to step forward and punch the lieutenant. He rubbed his knuckles, sore from his encounter with Ta-ne-haddle. The Indian was a mean, scrappy fighter, and Noah didn't want to tangle with him again.

All the time he had fought, he had tried to avoid really injuring the man, because he suspected April Danby wouldn't speak to him again if he hurt her friend. Noah swore softly. She had tied his life in knots and he didn't see any hope of unraveling them easily.

Sunday morning she got to church early. It was a hot summer morning, and high white clouds filled the blue sky. Church bells rang in the still air, and it promised to be a glorious spring day. The church windows were open, and fans lay in the pews. By the time she was playing the first hymn, the air had become heated. Dressed in her best pink gingham, April played with gusto, raising her voice in song.

This was the time of the week she loved the most. Her nightly performances in the saloon were only a way to keep a roof over her head and food on the table. She didn't like the rough saloons or the ribald men. She always tried to remember there were few women in the territory, and many men were lonesome. On Sunday mornings, however, she played out of love. She liked the people who came to the little white church. The piano there had been donated by the Will Carters when they moved from St. Louis. Two keys were missing, but they were in the highest octave, and she didn't need them anyway. While she played and sang on Sundays, she could enjoy the families who surrounded her. She often pretended that she had a family sitting in the pews, dreaming that Hattie and Luke and Catalina, Ta-ne-haddle and Lottie were there. Sometimes as she played, she pretended Emilio sang in the congregation and that she would go home to cook for his family after church. When the service was over, her fantasies faded but for an hour each Sunday morning she gave vent to all her longings, protected by the kindness of the friendly people around her.

This Sunday she had ridden to church with Melissa and Mrs. Hatfield, who were taking her to their home for dinner after church. Melissa, her black curls tucked demurely beneath a blue bonnet, sat beside her mother on the front row, only a few feet from April. Melissa's voice lifted clearly in song, her cheeks pink as roses, and April knew the sparkle in Melissa's eyes and color in her cheeks weren't from the ride to church.

Across the aisle sat Patrick O'Flynn. As much as the Hatfields tried to keep Melissa from seeing Patrick, they couldn't keep the two from attending church. It was the one chance Patrick had to see Melissa regularly. He sometimes even got to talk to her, particularly on days like today, when Ned Hatfield stayed home from church. Patrick's cheeks were as pink as Melissa's, and his brown eyes sparkled brightly. His red hair was parted in the center and combed down smoothly, every strand in place. While he sang, his glance kept straying to Melissa.

Reverend Wilfred Nokes, a man bigger than almost any other in town, welcomed his flock in his booming voice. Sun streamed through the high window behind him, shining on his bald head. April played the second hymn while everyone's voice rose in unison.

In spite of the singing, the sound of galloping horses could be heard. Gunshots blasted through the calm morning. April faltered and people stopped singing, a murmur of fear running through the congregation that was as palpable as the morning breeze through the windows.

7

Hoofbeats, shouts, and more gunshots came. Reverend Nokes strode down the aisle and went outside, while the congregation stared silently after him. A small child began to cry, and the men left to follow Nokes outside. April rushed out in time to see him stride down the wooden church steps into the rising cloud of dust formed by the milling horses. Men galloped in circles outside the church, whooping and firing their six-shooters into the air.

Reverend Nokes held up his hands and shouted at them as two men from the congregation moved past April to his side. Ed Greenbaum drew his revolver, and instantly Nokes pushed his hand down.

"No! Someone might get hurt!" he shouted above the din.

He waved his arms, yelling at the riders. They whooped louder and began to circle him. April's anger changed to fear that someone would get hurt badly.

"Great saints in heaven!" Selma Hatfield exclaimed, coming to stand beside April. "Thank heaven your father isn't here, Melissa."

"Someone will start shooting."

"The preacher needs some help," Patrick said grimly, and Melissa clutched his arm.

"Patrick, please don't go out there. Please!"

April's gaze swept the riders, looking for the leader. She spotted the flamboyant man instantly, and had no doubt that he was in charge. Above bare broad shoulders, golden hair streamed behind his head. If the situation hadn't been so annoying and frightening, she would have smiled at his audacious mien. He rode like he was born to a saddle. Bear claws were tied in a necklace around his neck, and the broad-brimmed hat on the back of his head held long eagle feathers streaming back from the band. Bare-chested, he wore leather trousers and boots with shiny silver Mexican spurs. April became angry as she watched him taunt Reverend Nokes, riding back and forth past him, whooping like the wildest Apache warrior.

Determined to do something before one of the men opened fire, she stormed across the ground and stopped in the path of the golden-haired man. Grinning, he pounded toward her.

She stood with her fists on her hips, ignoring shouts of the men on the porch of the church, ignoring Reverend Nokes's pleas for her to come back. If the riders had intended to actually harm someone, they would have already done so, and while they wouldn't back down from the men, they might if confronted by a woman.

The blond's big sorrel stallion loomed closer. April felt locked into a contest of wills, but she stood her ground. Defiant, terrified, yet determined, she watched the horse throw up its head and roll its eyes.

At the last moment the rider tugged the reins, and the sorrel thundered past her, only inches away. As he passed, the golden-haired man leaned down and scooped April up with one arm, shouting and laughing.

She clung to his shoulder and saddle, glaring at him. She was jostled and shaken while they galloped along, and finally he reined up and looked into her eyes. She gazed into deep blue eyes and skin as burnished as copper, but shock momentarily made her speechless— she thought she knew him. The flicker of a frown crossed his features, and his eyes narrowed to stare at her. He threw back his head and laughed, pulling her closer. She could smell the whiskey on his breath, then quickly turned her face, so his kiss only brushed her cheek.

April slapped him as hard as she could, her palm

making a crack against his skin. "Stop interrupting the worship of good people."

. He blinked, and a hard expression changed his features. "Yes, ma'am. You're a brave one."

"And you and your bunch are a cowardly lot to come disturbing families who want to worship the Lord. Now, why don't you leave us!"

He lowered her to the ground and looked down at her, tipping his hat before turning back to his men. *"Vamos!"* he shouted. He fired his revolver rapidly three times in succession, and waved his hand. April watched him as he galloped away. Who was he? She felt sure she knew him, but she couldn't remember from where or when.

Members of the congregation as well as Reverend Nokes rushed up to shake her hand. They chatted about the past moments until talk about her actions was distorted beyond recognition. Melissa was adither as they later rode to the Hatfields'.

"I don't know how you had the courage to do that!" she said.

"Land, child, don't ever do anything like that again!" Selma Hatfield exclaimed, holding tightly to the reins as she drove the buggy home.

"I didn't stop to think about it," April said, secretly thankful that Mr. Hatfield stayed home with a foaling mare. He was too quick to draw his pistol, and she didn't think he would have hesitate to open fire on the ruffians.

As if to echo her sentiments, Melissa said, "Pa should have been there this morning. He would have run them off right fast!"

"That he would, Melissa Jane, but there might have been more people hurt," Mrs. Hatfield pronounced somberly. April silently agreed with her. Deep down she held little like for Melissa's father, and she hoped he was still busy with the mare.

When the buggy halted at the house, the Hatfields had a new colt. They went to see the wobbly infant, his long legs spread apart and short tail switching.

"Isn't he beautiful!" April breathed. She wanted to

hold him, yet knew the mare would be happier if everyone left her baby alone.

"What was this I heard about a shooting at church?" Ned Hatfield snapped. "I was just about to ride out that way."

"Rowdies, Mr. Hatfield," Selma Hatfield answered. "Come along, girls, and we'll help Mr. Ching get dinner on the table." Both girls hurried to the house after her. All three women knew they should get away from Ned Hatfield's questions.

Cook, maid, butler, and yardman, Mr. Ching lived with his striped cat in the attic of the Hatfield house. Now, beaming with delight, he served hot brown biscuits and steaming roast beef.

As soon as he had finished the prayer before dinner and had carved the overcooked roast beef, Ned Hatfield returned to the subject of the shooting.

In spite of the burned food and Ned Hatfield's grating manner, April enjoyed her dinners with them. It gave her a sense of family, and she enjoyed Melissa's company. As she glanced from father to mother to daughter, it was still difficult to imagine how Melissa belonged to them. Like a redbird with two sparrows for parents, Melissa sparkled. She had smooth ivory skin, dark brown eyes, and lovely features. Selma Hatfield, who was as nice as anyone could be, had sallow skin, mouse-colored hair, and a thin face with a long nose. Nor did Melissa inherit her beauty from her father, who was five feet, eight inches tall, barrel-shaped, with a bulbous nose, unruly brown hair, and a broad jaw that was constantly jutting out in stubborn anger.

When Melissa was only eight years old, the Hatfields had come to Albuquerque. In Missouri Ned Hatfield had farmed, earning a meager wage that he used to support his family until the Hannibal and St. Joseph Railroad had wanted part of his land. Because of hills and a river, Hatfield's land was the only way the railroad could complete its line without detouring miles out of the way.

When the deal was made, Ned sold the rest of his

farm, took the cash, and went to New Mexico Territory to open a general store. From a small one-room adobe hut it had flourished to the building now occupying half a block across from the Plaza.

As Ned Hatfield passed a plate with a thick slice of beef, he glared at her. "That fracas this morning at church—I heard something about your stepping in the path of desperadoes and ordering them to stop."

"She was very brave, Papa!" Melissa exclaimed.

"Listen, April, you don't have a pa, so I feel it's my responsibility to say to you what a father would—it ain't a woman's place to face down gun-toting waddies!"

"Yes, sir. I thought they were probably just young boys who were still celebrating Saturday night," April answered quietly. "I didn't think they would hurt me. Sometimes men will respond more quickly when approached by a woman than when confronted by a man."

"Mr. Hatfield's right, April," Selma added gently.

"I think it was the bravest thing!" Melissa cried in April's defense, her face turning red.

"Bravery can get you a bullet through the heart!" Hatfield snapped. He stabbed a hunk of roast beef and waved it at April. "You leave handling bandits to the men!"

"Yes, sir," she answered demurely, aware that Melissa was embarrassed by her father's admonition.

"And don't you ever try anything so foolish, Melissa Jane. Women just don't know the dangers in life. I should have been at church. I hope those desperadoes return next Sunday. I wouldn't have let them ride away as free as birds. Ought to hang the ringleader—that would teach them not to interfere with God-fearing people!"

"What shall we name the new colt?" Mrs. Hatfield asked. April was relieved to have the subject changed.

After dinner April and Melissa went out to sit on the fence and watch the new foal.

"Isn't he the prettiest little thing?" Melissa asked. She looked all around. "April, may I come visit you this afternoon? I want to meet Patrick. I told him I'd be at your house about the middle of the afternoon."

"It's all right with me Melissa, but if your pa catches you, there will be trouble."

"Please. I haven't seen Patrick for days now!"

April bit back a smile as she gazed into Melissa's wide eyes and nodded. "All right, but I pray none of us gets caught!"

"I don't know what makes Papa so mean and hateful! But it would have been safer at church this morning if he had been there," she repeated, returning to the subject.

"I don't know, Melissa. Someone might have gotten hurt badly if shooting had started."

"You could have been carried off by those men. I don't know what I would have done if I had been scooped up like that!" She scooted a little closer and her eyes sparkled. "Wasn't he exciting? Next to Patrick, he's the handsomest man I've ever seen! I saw him kiss your cheek."

April laughed. "I do believe, Melissa, that you had rather it had been you instead of me!"

"I'm not that brave, but I wish it had been me! I almost fainted just looking at him!"

"Maybe you're not as much in love with Patrick as you think you are," April remarked.

"Of course I am!" Melissa tossed her head. "But that man was something to see! All that gorgeous yellow hair and . . . and . . . everything about him!" she added, scarlet flooding her cheeks.

"We better go inside if you want me to invite you over in front of your folks."

Melissa hopped down off the fence. "You're right. Papa will be sound asleep before long. He always naps on Sunday afternoon."

April put the incident at church out of mind until the next time she went to work. As she approached the saloon, she realized how her bravery in facing the ruffians was going to be exaggerated enormously. A banner in front of the Brown Owl proclaimed "The

Songbird—The Beauty Who Chased Desperadoes from Albuquerque.''

Inside she faced Lean Henry, the owner. Lean Henry was a man of mystery who had appeared in Albuquerque in the middle of the night. He had won the saloon in a game of faro, and set up business. He lived above the saloon, and his first year in town, rumors had circulated about his past. People said that he had fled the law after robbing a bank in St. Joseph, Missouri, that he had hit a vein of gold in Colorado, and that he was wanted for killing a man in Mississippi. Whatever his past, April found him to be fair and reliable, and that was all that mattered to her. A man's past was his own business.

Once he had asked her to dinner, but when she politely refused, he shrugged, gazing down at her solemnly. ''Want to go another time, April, or do you want to keep business and pleasure separate?''

''I think I should keep business and pleasure separate,'' she answered, aware that he was twenty years older than she. He smiled and nodded, and had never asked her out again.

''The town's buzzing with talk about your bravery,'' he said when she entered the back door.

''I saw the banner. I didn't do as much as Reverend Nokes did, and the whole congregation was behind me.''

''That's not what I heard,'' Lean Henry drawled, rubbing his black beard.

''I don't think the riders ever intended to hurt anybody. I think they just wanted to stir up some trouble after a long Saturday night. The banner is foolishness.''

He winked. ''Good business. We have a crowd tonight. Who's the man who's always at the front table?''

She didn't have to ask whom he was referring to. ''Noah McCloud.''

''I've talked to him. He's hard and cynical, honey,'' Lean Henry said, watching her steadily.

''I'll be okay.''

Lean Henry shrugged. "You ever want him out of here, just give me the word."

"Thanks," she said, then quickly moved past him to her dressing room. Later, when she stepped onstage and began to sing, two things were different. Three cowmen, dusty from the trail, sat at the table where Noah often sat. Her eyes searched the gloomy corners of the saloon as she sang, but she couldn't spot Noah anywhere. But she did see the golden-haired man come through the swinging doors and go to the bar.

This time he wore a shirt, but he still stood out in the crowd with his feathered hat, the bear-claw necklace, and two six-shooters in holsters on his narrow hips. His shoulders were broad and bony, but he was slim-waisted. His lean hard body was revealed by his tight trousers and the shirt open to his waist.

Men moved aside for him. Leaning against the bar, one boot heel hooked over the brass rail, he watched her. He pushed his hat to the back of his head and drank deeply from a bottle of tequila. Every time April glanced his way, she met his direct and steady gaze. He grinned at her and winked, and once again she had that fleeting impression of having met him somewhere else.

Before her song was over, he threaded his way through the crowd to a table in front of the stage, where two men sat drinking. He leaned down to say something to one of them, and she saw the man scowl. Her attention shifted as she strutted across the stage.

A table crashed to the floor, and April looked over to see the three men brawling. Instantly the other men in the crowd were on their feet, fists flying as they joined in the fray. April continued to sing amidst pandemonium while the piano player pounded the ivory, trying to drown out the racket.

April dodged a chair that smashed onstage. A bottle flew over her head. Lean Henry motioned to her to get offstage as he headed toward the side with a Winchester in his hand. In a minute gun blasts added to the din, but she was already striding for her dressing room, wondering if Sheriff Pacheco would come or leave it to Lean Henry and his boys to quiet the bedlam.

She changed quickly to her red silk dress. As she fastened the hooks, someone knocked on the door and she opened it to face the golden-hair man. He stepped inside and closed the door behind him.

"I came back to apologize for stirring up a ruckus when you were singing."

"I'm surprised you're still standing."

He grinned. "The fight didn't last long. I just wanted a table close enough to see you, pretty lady."

"Thank you."

"I really am sorry. I didn't get to hear all of your song."

"You can come hear me sing in church next Sunday," she said lightly. Something about him was appealing in spite of his peccadilloes.

He glanced beyond her at the mirror. "Turn around and I'll fasten that middle hook for you."

"I can get it."

"Turn around," he ordered lightly.

She did, because it was easier to let him fasten the hook in the middle of her back than it was to struggle with it herself. He stepped toward her. His fingers were deft and warm, brushing her skin before he fastened the hard-to-reach hook.

"Now I have to comb my hair for the next song."

"Can I watch?"

"Actually—"

"Please."

She laughed and nodded, sitting down in front of her mirror and running a brush through her hair.

He strolled around the tiny cubicle, touching her green silk dress, running his hand across the feathers. "They call you Songbird."

"That's right," she answered, powdering her face lightly and brushing rouge on her cheeks. She glanced over her shoulder to find him leaning against a wall and watching her. "Where are you from?"

"The territory. The Sangre de Cristo Mountains

north of here. And you're the prettiest woman I've
seen west of the Mississippi.''

"Thank you," she answered dryly. She was sure he
told dozens of women the same thing.

"I guess the bravest, too, to stand out there in the
middle of all those horses. How come the prettiest
lady in town plays at church and sings in a saloon?''

She shrugged. "That's the way life is on the frontier. The good goes with the bad. Out here you find
lots of people doing things they shouldn't.''

His grin broadened and he sat down astride a
straight-backed wooden chair, gazing at her over the
back. "I like to hear you sing. My mother always sang
around the house.''

"Thanks," she answered perfunctorily, looping her
hair in curls and pinning them on top of her head.

"You must not have any family here.''

"How'd you guess that?'' she asked, glancing at him
in the mirror, which distorted his handsome features
and made his face appear inches longer.

"A ma and pa wouldn't want you singing here; a
husband sure as hell—pardon me, sure as gun's iron
wouldn't want you singing in a saloon. That doesn't
leave much of anyone else.''

"You're right.'' Their gazes met in the mirror, and
in spite of the trouble he had caused everywhere, she
liked him. "Are you in town often?''

He shook his head, and a shady look came over his
features. She knew he was hiding something. He
shifted restlessly and stared at her with his hands resting on his thighs. April's attention returned to her hair,
but her curiosity didn't die. Seldom had she met a man
she was curious about, but this one stirred a chord of
familiarity and she kept trying to place where and why.
Had he been a regular at Kate's when April was growing up? He looked too young, only a year or two older
than she was.

"I go back onstage now.''

His crooked grin surfaced. "I'll go back to my table
down front, where I can see and hear you, Songbird.''
He held the door open. Before she stepped through, she

glanced up at him, studying him closely, and she saw
that he was younger than she had thought—decidedly
too young to have been a customer at Miss Kate's, so
that wasn't where she had seen him before. He caught
her chin in his hand, gazing at her intently.

"Time, April," Lean Henry said, appearing in the
hall. When he glanced at the other man, his eyes narrowed.

"Good-bye," she said, hurrying away.

True to his word, the blond sat in the front row.
While he watched her steadily, a man moved through
the crowd swiftly toward him. The man said something to him and jerked his head in the direction of the
door.

Sheriff Pacheco burst through the swinging doors,
paused, then ran toward the front, charging toward the
golden-haired man.

8

With ease the blond vaulted onto the stage. He doffed his hat at April, raised both hands in the air in apology, and ran backstage with men following behind him. She continued singing as if nothing unusual was happening. Gunshots were fired, and then the commotion from the back stopped.

As soon as she could, she found Lean Henry. He was cleaning his Winchester in the small room that was his office, and the faint smell of gunpowder lingered in the air.

"What happened just now?" she asked.

He squinted at her above the spiraling stream of smoke rising from the cheroot clenched between his yellow teeth. "Sheriff's after a gang. He told me that there was a bank robbery. That's all I heard before he ran out the door after them."

"Those are the men who disrupted church last Sunday."

"I'll be damned! Sheriff Pacheco will get them."

"He might not this time." She thought of the golden-haired man and how quickly he had jumped to the stage and run out the back. "Bank robbery? He didn't seem that fierce."

"That's because you're a pretty woman. If he disrupts church next Sunday, I wouldn't step right out in front of him again. Pacheco said something about murder."

"I'll remember your advice," she said, heading for her dressing room.

The next morning, she saw Sheriff Pacheco sitting outside in front of the jail. He was leaning back against the adobe wall while he whittled. His dusty booted feet were propped on the rail, and he was talking to one of his sons, Bernardino Pacheco, who was also a deputy. She changed her course and crossed the street, to meet him.

"Good morning, Sheriff, Deputy."

"Morning, Miss Danby," they chorused in unison. Sheriff Pacheco pushed back his hat to look up at her.

"That was quite a commotion last night."

"Sorry it was during your song, but duty comes first."

"I understand. Who was the man you were after?"

"Man's name is Tigre," he said, drawing out "Tee-gray" as if to emphasize his importance.

"What's he done?"

"I heard about you confrontin' him at church. Don't tangle with them boys again, Miss Danby."

"He's wanted in the territory for murdering a man," Bernardino Pacheco added.

Disappointment flared in April. "He seemed nice," she said, voicing her thoughts without realizing she had spoken, until Sheriff Pacheco frowned.

"Desde luego! A pretty woman brings out the nice-ness in a man, Miss Danby, but he can be pure poison through and through. In addition to murder, the outlaw is wanted for bank robbery and train robbery. 'Nice' isn't what the man is!"

"I suppose you're right."

"You see him again, you tell Lean Henry to send for me."

"Sure enough, Sheriff," she said as she walked away. Murder. The golden-haired man, Tigre, was an outlaw, and a bad one. She remembered him as he leaned against the wall of her dressing room, grinning confidently while he watched her. He hadn't seemed so fierce or evil then.

She suspected he was far away from Albuquerque by now, so she put him out of her mind and finished her errands. As she started home, a tall, familiar fig-ure caught her attention. Her heart skipped a beat as Noah McCloud headed toward her.

"You've been away from Albuquerque," she said when he rode up beside her buggy. He swung his leg across his horse's withers and dropped down in the buggy beside her. In a lithe maneuver he looped his horse's reins to the back of her buggy. He settled in the seat and looked at April.

Her heart drummed as she felt his shoulder press against hers, and she gazed up into his blue eyes.

"I've been to Santa Fe to buy some things for my saloon. While I was there I went to Miss Kate's."

April's pleasure at seeing him evaporated. "You were checking on me."

"I was trying to get more information about you. I don't know you very well, Miss Danby. My brother's letter says one thing, you say another."

"And did you come to any new conclusion?" she asked, now annoyed that he was in her buggy and spoiling the morning with his suspicions.

"They corroborated your story."

"I told you the truth about my past, I'm telling the truth about your brother and the McCloud gold."

"You sound damned convincing, Miss Danby," he said quietly. "Only one thing keeps me from believing you."

"What's that?"

"My brother's letter."

"I don't know one thing about your gold!" she snapped, drawing back on the reins to stop the horse. "You can just get back on your hor—"

"Simmer down," he said in a friendly tone, taking the reins from her hands and flicking them. "It's too pretty a morning for trouble." He raised his face to the sun. "This is one of those special days. It's not too hot, not too windy or cold, it's just right." He looked down at her as she studied him, amazed at his friendliness. "Let's enjoy the ride," he said. His voice was calm, but she heard the note of steel underneath and she suspected he had something else on his mind that he intended to tell her. "Is your Kiowa friend still here?"

"No, not in town."

"Who is he? I had to fight for my life to keep him from killing me, and I'd swear he quoted Shakespeare to me."

"He probably did. He loves poetry and doesn't forget anything he reads. He went to school back east."

"Damn, and he came back here to just roam?"

"That's what he likes. His mother was a captive of the Kiowas. When he was young, soldiers came and captured her. He was sent east to live with her family. After she died, he came back to this part of the country.

"You're from the East. It was foolish for you to go to Santa Fe. It can be dangerous to travel around out here if you don't know the land."

"I got along. I heard some wild tales about you while I was gone."

"Those tales, as often happens to tales around here, have been blown out of proportion." She tilted her head, smoothing her brown gingham dress over her knees. "Have you talked to Doc yet?"

"Yes, more than once, and each time I've gotten a lecture in your behalf. If anybody in this town thinks you are a saint, the Yishays do."

"They're good to me."

"They're trusting people."

Before she could question him on his last statement, he pulled to a halt at her back door. He jumped down easily and swung her to the ground, releasing her immediately. She saw the cold harsh set to his features, the glacial blue of his eyes, and knew he had something on his mind.

She reached up to get her bundles from shopping. Long arms stretched out, and Noah lifted down a jug of horse liniment and a new shovel.

"Getting ready to dig?" he said, studying the shovel in his hands.

"My shovel broke this spring, so I ordered a new one," she replied. She wondered if he would think all her purchases were paid for with his money. She picked up a sack of flour and a jug of kerosene.

"Let me have those."

"I'll manage, thank you," she said stiffly, but he took the sack of flour from her anyway. She was aware he had shortened his stride to match hers. He opened her door and they paused, staring at each other in another clash of wills.

"Just set my packages down here, thank you," she said coldly. As he set her things down and stepped outside, she saw the anger flare in his eyes. She walked into her house and slammed the door, locking it. To her relief, he didn't protest, and she leaned against the door, her heart pounding, anger swirling and rising like a river current.

Noah swung into the saddle and urged his horse forward, his jaw set grimly. She could always stir him up. Her wide, lovely eyes looked guileless, her voice always rang with sincerity.

He had heard the stories circulating about April Danby since his absence. He'd heard she had rushed out of the church to stop a gang of desperadoes from riding into town to raise hell, that she had ordered them away from Albuquerque. He had also heard that Reverend Nokes had hidden behind her skirts while she had argued with the wild ruffians. Another version had her blasting away with two-six shooters while the congregation and the reverend had cowered in the church. Suddenly Noah laughed, wondering what had actually happened. He could easily imagine her facing a gang of rowdies and standing her ground. He hated her one minute, but admired and desired her the next! Damned if it hadn't been good to see her this morning. If only . . .

He swore, pushing his hat back on his head. Suddenly some deep instinct sent a silent warning to him. The nape of his neck prickled, and years of soldiering made him doubly cautious. He turned swiftly, his gaze sweeping the empty street behind him. The only thing he glimpsed was the briefest black shadow moving out of sight behind a house. It could have been shadows of leaves from a cottonwood, or no shadow at all, merely his imagination, but his intuition said it was someone following him.

He stared at the spot, right next to an adobe house. Tall pink hollyhocks grew in a patch of dirt in front of it, and a cottonwood only yards away provided shade. Nothing moved, nothing looked out of the ordinary, yet he suspected he was being watched.

He settled back in the saddle, riding slowly while his mind raced. He needed to find out who it was and why. For over a week now he had thought someone was following him occasionally, and whoever was doing it was good at it. He suspected it might have something to do with April.

He wanted to have another talk with Lean Henry. There were still gaps to fill, still statements April Danby had made that he wanted to verify.

After April sang that night, Noah followed her home, resisting the temptation to confront her. He scowled in the darkness, thinking of her warmth and laughter. She shouldn't lead a solitary life, working and going home alone. He stopped outside her house and with surprise watched her knock on her own back door.

When it opened, another woman was silhouetted in the doorway, and beyond her stood a red-haired man. The curtains were drawn on the parlor, something April never did, and Noah's curiosity rose. He dismounted and made a wide circle through yards and lots around her house. He found a horse tethered to a tree in a field behind the house.

Noah waited where he could see the horse and still be in shadows. Finally the man emerged, a hat jammed down on his head. He hurried to his horse in long strides, mounted up, and rode away. Noah couldn't see his face because of the shadows caused by the man's hat, so it wasn't anyone he recognized. He sat down on a log to wait and watch April's house, something he had done night after night, to no avail.

It was two hours later before the lights were extinguished, and he decided he should wend his way back to his horse and ride back to the hotel. He stood up, brushing off the seat of his pants, when a hoofbeat

sounded. It was faint and far from him. Nothing stirred
in the night except shadows of leaves that wavered
when the breeze blew, but Noah was curious. It was
too late for April's neighbors to be out.

He sank down on the log again, listening to night
sounds. It was a full ten minutes before he heard the
crack of a stick. He sat as still as stone, his hat pushed
down over his head to keep his face in shadow. Someone was passing not far from him.

Footsteps were barely discernible, and occasionally
Noah heard the jingle of spurs. He realized it was
someone accustomed to tracking. He thought of Ta-
ne-haddle. In seconds he raised his head and squinted
in the darkness. At first he was unable to pick up any
movement, but then he saw a shadow shift. In a moment he caught sight of another change in the dark,
and saw a man creep across the open ground. Noah
squinted and saw that the man was bare-chested. Two
big pistols were buckled on his hips, and he wore a
broad-brimmed hat on his head and a necklace of bear
claws above his bare chest. It wasn't the Kiowa. Noah
had heard about the rowdies who had disturbed church
and how April had stopped them. And he had heard a
description of the wild man who had led the pack, a
man wanted for murder. A man with a thousand-dollar
reward on his head—dead or alive.

A thousand dollars was a lot of money. Noah stood
up, his hand closing around the butt of his pistol. He
removed his Colt from the holster and edged forward,
keeping in shadows. He moved slowly, taking care
with each step, because he knew the man would hear
the slightest sound.

Tigre Castillo. Noah had heard Sheriff Pacheco say
his name. It was as flamboyant as his appearance. Tigre. Why was he sneaking up on April's house? Pure
coincidence? Because of April's friend? Or because of
April? Noah had heard he had been in the saloon and
had gotten away from the sheriff. He stepped with care,
inching forward, freezing with surprise when he heard
the sharp click of rocks hitting glass.

He saw the man was tossing pebbles at April's bedroom window, and some of the tenseness went out of his shoulders. That wasn't the action of a man hell-bent on evil. Noah drifted closer and heard the window rise. April appeared as a blur of white nightgown, her hair cascading down over her shoulders, and momentarily Noah forgot Tigre Castillo. His mouth went dry, and he thought of her clad only in her nightgown. A thin layer of material was all that covered her warm body. He stared at her while Tigre asked her to let him come inside and talk to her.

Noah's senses came alert and fear for her safety returned. Why did Tigre Castillo want to talk to her in the dead of night?

And then it dawned on him. April Danby might not have stepped up bravely to confront a stranger. Tigre Castillo might have the McCloud gold.

9

April closed the window. "Melissa, someone wants to talk to me."

"It's the man who caused trouble at church," Melissa said in awed tones. "Papa said he's wanted for murder, that Sheriff Pacheco is after him."

"I'm going to listen to what he has to say," April said, pulling on her wrapper.

Melissa caught her arm. "April! Suppose he wants to rob us! Suppose he wants to hurt you!"

"I don't think he will. Let go of me, Melissa."

"No! He's *wanted!*"

"He's already had the opportunity to hurt me, and he hasn't. He isn't going to hurt me now."

"You don't know that! And if Sheriff Pacheco finds out we let him inside—if Papa finds out—"

"Melissa, let me go. The man's waiting at the back door."

"No! I can go for the sheriff if I climb out the window. Or we both can. We can get away from that man! He could do all sorts of terrible things. He—"

"He could, but he won't," Tigre drawled, and both women spun around to face him. He stood in the bedroom doorway, one long arm stretched overhead propped against the jamb. "I didn't know you had company."

"This is Melissa Hatfield, my friend. I know your name is Tigre. And I'm April. We should go to the parlor to talk."

He made a sweeping bow. "After you, ladies."

"I'll leave you two alone to talk," Melissa whispered, licking her lips. His blue eyes slid over her, and Melissa yanked up her wrapper, holding it to her chin. She blushed furiously at the faint smile that hovered over his mouth.

"No, you won't, Miss Hatfield," he said. "Come along, or I'll bring you along, but you're not going out the window to get Sheriff Pacheco."

"Come on, Melissa," April said calmly, worried that Melissa's fright would set off a violent reaction in Tigre.

Holding her wrapper closed, Melissa scurried past him, moving to the parlor. She sat on the settee and locked her fingers together tightly in her lap, looking like a frightened child.

"Would you care for some cold cider?" April asked, trying to make things seem normal.

"Thank you, I would," he replied. He sat down across from Melissa and smiled at her. He was bare-chested, and he gave his hat a toss, raking his fingers through his long blond hair. He looked like a wild man in April's small parlor. He was overwhelming. His weapons and the bear claws around his neck gave him a fierce appearance that his white teeth and cocky grin couldn't offset. The shining silver spurs jingled when he moved.

When April had served golden cider and sugar cookies, she leaned back in the chair to face him. To her relief, he had been talking to Melissa about her new colt—how he had learned there was a new colt, April couldn't imagine, but Melissa had relaxed, and was responding in a polite voice to his questions.

"Miss April, you know Sheriff Pacheco is after me. I have to get out of this area before someone gets hurt, but I have something I want to ask you to do for me."

He was handsome and tough, his skin burnished, and he was armed to the teeth. He appeared formidable, but now, as April sat so close to him, she thought again how young he looked. To her amazement, there seemed to be a vulnerable note in his voice.

"How do you know you can trust me?" she asked. "I won't break the law."

"I'm not asking you to break the law," he said solemnly. ''And I think I can trust you, because you're good. You've been good to me, and you're brave.''

''What do you want me to do?'' she asked. Her curiosity seemed insatiable. She was unable to imagine any reason this strange, fiery man would need her help.

He stood up so suddenly it startled her. With long strides he left the house. Melissa and April looked at each other in uncertainty.

''What on earth can he want you to do?'' Melissa asked. Her eyes had developed a sparkle, and April saw that she had lost her fear of Tigre.

''I don't know. I can't think of anything.''

''Are you going to do it?''

''I don't know what he wants.'' She fell silent as he reentered the room. He carried bulging saddlebags. When he placed them on the floor beside her, she heard the unmistakable clink of coins.

He knelt down beside her to take her hands. ''My ma and pa are coming to Albuquerque this summer to buy more sheep. They always stay a few days at the hotel, and Pa goes to the saloons when they come to town. You'll probably hear of 'em. Would you see that they get this? I want them to have it.''

April was aware she was probably holding the gain from a bank or train robbery or worse. Her conscience mulled over the request while Melissa's face paled.

''April! Yes, she will,'' Melissa answered him. April knew Melissa's fear had resurfaced, that she was afraid of what he would do if April refused his request.

''I'm not giving this back where it came from,'' he said with a stubborn lift of his chin. He looked directly into Melissa's round eyes. ''I just want to get it to my folks.''

''It doesn't seem right,'' April said. ''I think I would be breaking a law.''

''April!'' Melissa sounded agonized.

''I won't hurt you if you refuse, but I'd be indebted to you forever if you'll do this for me. I want to do this for my folks. I can't take it back where I got it. Please.'' The word came out on a strange note in his voice, and April suspected there were few times in his life he said please.

She couldn't answer, but stared at the saddlebags and wondered what horrible crimes he might have committed to gain the money.

"I earned it breakin' broncos in Texas," he said suddenly. It was a flat lie, April knew. "That's what you can tell anyone if a question ever comes up. You can say I told you how I earned it."

"They said you murdered someone," she said, trying to decide what to do. She wondered about his past, because as terrible as his crimes sounded, he hadn't hurt her or anyone else when she had been around him.

A harshness came to his features. For an instant April's heart jumped. He looked fierce and angry as he glared at her.

"My pa's a sheep man, a nester. And cattlemen don't like sheep, or sheep ranchers, or men who live in sod huts," he said. April knew that was a fact as true in Albuquerque as it was in other places in the West.

"We settled north of here in the Sangre de Cristos near Taos when I was eight. We had three good years before they started trying to drive Pa out. They burned down our barn, then killed our sheep and our horses. First it was one thing and then another. They wanted to buy Pa out, but he wouldn't sell. He fought back. The burning and fighting went on for the next three years. My mother was terrified. Then they finally caught my father and gave him a beating that nearly killed him." He paused, his eyes cold and harsh, gazing beyond April. "He stuck it out, fought back, and rebuilt. He always said the day would come when the sheep man would have his rights protected by law."

Tigre strode to the empty hearth. The lamplight highlighted his prominent cheekbones. "I caught three men polluting our well. When we fought, they intended to kill me. See this scar."

With a clatter he lifted the necklace of bear claws. A thin white ridge of scar tissue ran across his collar-

bones. "The man who did this meant to cut higher.
He was trying to slit my throat." He let the necklace
fall in place and faced them with his hands on his hips.
There was a quiet anger in his tone. "I killed one in
self-defense and the other two fled. Their boss was a
powerful man in our part of the country, and by sundown there was a posse after me.

"When they caught me, I didn't get to stand trial. I
wasn't in a courtroom and I didn't have a judge. They
just decided to hang me. Pa and his men came to my
rescue, and I escaped. So I'm wanted for murder."
His blue eyes blazed, a muscle working in his jaw. "If
I hadn't killed that man, I would have been dead. See
these other scars." He pointed to a faint white line
across his chest, one under his arm. "They're from
that day," he said bitterly. "I've committed robberies
too," he admitted. He stared at April, and she thought
she had never seen a man look so cold and hard and
bleak. "I shouldn't have asked you to do this, but my
folks are good people."

"So may the people be that you've robbed," she
said steadily. She heard Melissa gasp and felt Melissa's foot give hers a nudge.

"I'm going."

"Wait a minute," April said quietly, and he paused.
"I'll do it."

Something flickered in his eyes, and his expression
softened. He came across the room to take her hands
in his again. "Thank you," he said hoarsely. She
gazed into eyes as blue as the sea, and she felt drawn
to him.

"You're a beautiful woman," he said softly, still
holding her hands. Smiling, he sat down in the chair.
His white teeth were perfect and even, creases brack-
eted his mouth, and a dimple showed in his cheek. "I
think my folks will come to town sometime this summer. You can tell them I'm heading toward California."

He glanced at Melissa. "But I'll come back here
when things cool down."

Melissa blushed and smiled at him. "I wish I could

show you my colt,'' she said shyly. April turned to stare at her, astounded at the change in her attitude toward Tigre.

"Maybe I'll stick around long enough to see him,'' he said, and the tone of his voice slipped a little lower. When he glanced back at April, his voice resumed its normal timbre. "My father is Javier Castillo. Ma's name is Hattie.''

April was still staring at Melissa when he said the names that struck her as forcefully as if he had slapped her face. *Ma's name is Hattie.*

April didn't move a muscle, but suddenly her head buzzed. She stared at Tigre Castillo. His eyes narrowed and he cocked his head to one side. "What is it, Miss April?''

"When I first saw you at the church, you looked familiar,'' she said as if to herself. She studied him carefully, guessing now why she thought she had met him before.

"Is something wrong?'' he asked.

"April, are you all right?'' Melissa asked, and her voice seemed to come from far away.

April's ears roared and her heart pounded as she stared at him, unable to answer.

"What the hell is wrong?'' he asked. The harsh look returned to his features and she could see a faint resemblance to Luke in the set of his jaw. There was also some resemblance to her own appearance in his large eyes and golden hair.

"Do you have brothers or sisters?'' she asked, the words coming in a whisper.

He frowned. His eyes narrowed and then widened, sweeping over her features. She realized he had come to the same conclusion. And without another word, she knew she was facing her half-brother.

10

"April, what's wrong?" Melissa asked again, but April barely heard her question. She felt devoured by Tigre's gaze.

"I didn't think about it when you said your name was April. I had an older sister who died," he said, and wonder filled his voice. "I never knew her, but her name was April Danby."

April closed her eyes. After all the searching she and Luke had both done to find their mother, here was their half-brother and the answer to Hattie's whereabouts.

Strong hands gripped her upper arms and pulled her to her feet. She gazed into Tigre's probing blue eyes.

"Who're your parents?"

"I never knew my mother, Hattie," she said, her voice quivering. She stared at him and then they embraced each other tightly. She clung to him with her eyes closed, thinking: I have a family. Another brother. Hattie lives north of here in the mountains near Taos.

He leaned away, holding her arms again. A sardonic smile lifted one corner of his mouth in a crooked grin. "Damn, it's grand and at the same time—what a shame to find out the beautiful lady is my sister!"

"April!" Melissa cried, standing up to stare at both of them, her eyes round with shock. "You're his *sister?*"

"Yes! Oh, *yes!*" April and Tigre laughed, looking into each other's eyes.

To April's surprise, tears stung as she gazed up at him. "I've hunted for Hattie. Luke—*our* half-brother— has hunted for her."

"Luke? I thought people called him Lucius. I thought he was dead. Ma said he was killed in an ambush."

"How wonderful for both of you. !" Melissa cried, moving closer to them. Tigre reached out to slip his arm around her shoulder and pull her into their circle. All three hugged, laughing and crying at the same time.

When Tigre's grip relaxed, Melissa smiled up at him. "You have a wonderful sister!"

He gazed down at her, his face only inches away. His eyes studied her features while his arm held her close against his side. "I know that already. This is one of the best days of my life!" His voice grew husky while his gaze flicked to April, and then back to Melissa to gaze into her eyes.

His hand drifted across her shoulders, lightly brushing the nape of her neck. She pulled her wrapper high beneath her chin and blushed hotly as she sat back down.

"I really haven't thought about a sister I never knew. I thought you were dead. Ma thinks so! Pa said you drowned," he said, puzzlement filling his voice. "Pa was there when you drowned. He said you were washed downriver and they never found your body."

She sobered then, remembering when Luke had told her what had really happened. She knew it would forever change Tigre's view of his father if he learned the truth. His features became solemn as some of his joy faded, and she realized he was as sensitive as he was handsome. He seemed to know what her thoughts were without her voicing a word.

"What happened to you, April?" he asked. "I can see in your eyes that it wasn't good."

"Then you can see more than most men on this earth," she answered. "Sit back down." She debated telling him a lie, but she suspected he would see through her deceit. How did a man who was a murderer and thief develop such sensitivity to people? Yet she knew Luke was shrewd and intelligent; why wouldn't his brother be also?

"Melissa knows about my past, but few people in town do. When I was barely more than a baby, someone took me to a house of pleasure, where the ladies raised me until our brother, Luke Danby, learned my identity. Luke took me back to San Antonio with him. He's an attorney now, but he has been a U.S. marshal."

Tigre grinned and stretched his long legs in front of him. "Balderdash! My brother a former U.S. marshal, sworn to uphold the law!" He sobered. "Ma thinks both of you died violently. She thought Lucius—Luke—was killed in a wagon-train ambush when they came west. She's always called him Lucius."

"He goes by 'Luke' and he's hunted for her—that's how he found me. He was looking for Hattie."

"All three of you have different fathers?" Melissa said, looking back and forth at them in amazement.

"I didn't know mine," April stated.

"She never talked about him," Tigre answered solemnly. "All she would ever say when I asked questions was, 'I don't want to remember because it's too painful.' So I stopped asking her about him or about you long ago. And we thought Luke was dead. She told me once he was hauled behind the horse of a man named Domingo Piedra."

"Yes, but he survived. He's badly scarred from it. Domingo Piedra is dead, and Luke is married to his daughter."

Tigre's brows arched. He opened his mouth to speak, but the sound of horse's hooves stopped him. All three listened as someone rode up to April's door. Tigre stood up and his hand went to his six-shooter.

"It's the middle of the night," Melissa whispered. "Who can that be?"

"Tigre!" Pounding sounded on the back door and Tigre ran past them to the door.

A slender young man in a red shirt stood there, his chest heaving. "Get out. The sheriff's coming. Some old lady said there were men here. Sheriff's only a few blocks behind me."

"Dammit."

April and Melissa had followed him to the back door. April caught his arm. "Tigre, tell me where to write to Hattie."

"Address it to Javier Castillo at Taos." He gazed at April. "I want to talk to you longer, but not now. I'll be back." He swept his arm around her to kiss her cheek. " 'Bye, sister," he whispered, and she laughed, letting her hand trail over his cheek. He looked down at Melissa, and suddenly his arm went around her waist and his head lowered. He kissed her full on the mouth.

Melissa's hands flew up to his arms as if to push, but they rested there lightly. When he released her, her eyes opened slowly to look up at him. He winked at her.

"C'mon, Tigre. For Lord's sake. Kiss 'em later!" The man held a tight rein on his horse. Tigre vaulted into the saddle.

" 'Bye, loves," he said, and was gone, moving away at a gallop.

April closed the door. "Extinguish the lamps. Quickly!"

Melissa rushed to do as April said, and in minutes the house was in darkness. "The cups of cider!"

April gathered the dishes and carried them to the kitchen. As she started back to the parlor, she heard horses.

"Get to the bedroom, Melissa. Get back into bed." April grabbed the heavy saddlebags and carried them to the bedroom. "If they come in to look for him, where can I hide these?" she asked, more of herself than of Melissa.

"My portmanteau!"

"No. If they find them, I don't want you involved."

Pounding sounded on the front door, and April's mind raced. "Put them under the pillows. Quick!"

April handed over the heavy saddlebags, hearing the coins clink. She pulled her wrapper tight and went to the front door, taking her time, trying to give Tigre every second possible to get away. She closed her eyes and prayed for his safety while another burst of pounding came from the door.

"Just a minute," she called loudly, and waited.

There was a minute's quiet, and then pounding came again. "Open the door, Miss Danby!"

She still waited, trying to ignore her wildly beating heart. Beneath her fear for Tigre's safety, a current of joy was running. Another brother. And she would find her mother now.

Fists beat against the door.

"Who is it?"

"Sheriff Pacheco, Miss Danby. We have the house surrounded. Open the door."

She slipped the bolt and opened the door. "I need to light a lamp. Land sakes!" she exclaimed. "Sheriff Pacheco!"

He stood with rifle drawn, looking past her while two of his deputies, Bernardino and Reubel, milled around on horseback behind him. There were other men beyond them in the darkness.

"Where is he?" he asked, stepping into the parlor.

She went to the lamp and lit it quickly while men entered the parlor. Ned Hatfield pushed into the room. "Where's my daughter?"

"She was asleep in bed," April said calmly. "What's this all about?"

"We heard you let a man in this house. A man with long yellow hair."

April hoped her expression was one of tolerant exasperation. "Sheriff Pacheco, Melissa has been here with me all evening since I returned from work. We've been quilting, and we were asleep before you came here. We haven't had any man in this house."

"Melissa!" Ned roared outside the bedroom door.

In a moment Melissa opened the door. "Papa! What are you doing here?"

"Would you like to search the house, Sheriff?" April asked dryly. "That way you might be satisfied, and we can get back to sleep."

"We'll do that."

"Get dressed," Ned commanded his daughter. "I'm taking you home with me."

"Papa, it's the middle of the night! April and I were asleep."

"No one has been here?" Ned asked, looking at April.

"No one," she answered emphatically. She realized she was learning to lie. There was no way on earth she would turn her brother over to the authorities.

Sheriff Pacheco looked all around the parlor. "That old busybody. It's probably the Dodworths' damned imagination again!"

"Melissa Jane, has a man been in this house to-night?" Ned asked sternly, his face crinkled in a scowl.

"No, Papa," Melissa answered, her eyes wide and round. "No."

Sheriff Pacheco sighed. "Damn. Sorry, Miss April, if we disturbed you. Are you coming, Hatfield?"

"Papa, let me stay. I'm not dressed, and we were asleep!"

"Go back to bed, Melissa," her father said gruffly, and stomped out. "Next time, Pacheco, ask that biddy some questions!"

"She sent Doc to get me. It's Doc who should ask questions."

The door closed on their conversation, and April looked at Melissa, whose eyes sparkled with mischief. She clasped her hands together and danced to her toes. "Oh, April, this has been the most exciting night of my life! Tigre Castillo! He shouldn't be wanted for murder for defending himself."

A little bell of alarm went off inside April, and her eyes narrowed as she gazed at her friend. "Melissa, he's my half-brother. I like him and I trust him, but that doesn't change that he's a wanted man," she said gently. "Don't forget Patrick."

Melissa's cheeks became pink. "Don't be absurd! I haven't forgotten Patrick! But Tigre Castillo is excit-ing, and to find you have a brother! I'd be delirious to

discover he was my brother. And now you know where
your mother lives, and she's coming to Albuquerque!''

"I know. After all this time—it's hard to believe it's
true. Hattie Castillo.'' She thought of Luke. "I have
to write to Luke and tell him. He'll want to be here
to see her. Go on to bed, Melissa. I have to write to
Hattie, my mother,'' she said, lingering over the
words. She remembered the times when she had been
a little girl and had wanted her mother so badly, had
wanted to talk about her mother to other children, to
say, "My mother did this'' or "My mother did that.''
"My mother, I can't believe it, Melissa.''

Melissa spun around and hugged her. "I'm so happy
for you. To find your mother and to find out that Tigre
Castillo is your brother!''

"I have to write to Hattie and Luke right now. I'm
too excited to sleep.''

"So am I! When do you think he'll be back, April?''

Again April looked closely at Melissa's sparkling
eyes, and she felt a premonition of dread. Tigre was
an exciting, handsome man, unlike any other man in
Albuquerque. He was far different from the polite,
somber, twenty-six-year-old Patrick O'Flynn. Patrick
was hardworking and quiet, living a long distance from
the family he had left behind in Ireland. April had
heard all about his family of eleven children and the
poverty they lived in. Patrick was the eldest, and he
had left home so there would be one fewer mouth to
feed. He had come to America when he was fifteen
and worked at first one job and then another until he
reached Albuquerque with a wagon train that had come
over the Santa Fe Trail. He was tired of traveling, of
odd jobs, and he decided to settle. Land was abundant
and cheap, and he took his savings to purchase enough
to get a start. He fought for the Union, returning home
to Albuquerque to try to get some sheep and start
again. He had met Melissa at church.

For Melissa to fall in love with a man like Tigre
Castillo could be a terrible thing. Yet the sparkle in
her eyes was brighter than ever before, her cheeks more
flushed, and excitement bubbled in her.

"Melissa, be careful. Tigre isn't a man to love."

"April, I don't love him! How could I love him? I just met him. I can't be in love with him!"

"I hope not. It's bad enough for you to love Patrick, who's a good man, and one your father should like. Tigre would never be acceptable to your father, and Tigre can't ever give a woman a decent life. He's on the run, Melissa, and he has been all of his adult life."

"You don't even know how old he is."

"From what Luke told me, Tigre must be two years younger than I am."

"Almost my age," Melissa said breathlessly, and April shook her head.

"Melissa, he's an *outlaw*. He's wanted for murder, and it doesn't matter how justified it was, he's still a wanted man."

"It matters all the world whether it was justified or not. If he'd had a real trial, he wouldn't be wanted!"

"You don't know that," April said, her thoughts shifting to her discoveries. "Melissa, my mother thinks two of us died violently and the other one is wanted for murder."

Melissa's joy vanished, to be replaced by a look of compassion, and she put her arms around April. "Oh, April! When she gets your letter, think how happy she'll be."

April clung to Melissa, thinking about Luke, about Tigre. She straightened up and wiped tears away. "Sorry. I'll write the letters so I can post them both as soon as possible."

"Tigre Castillo, " Melissa said aloud, her voice dreamy. "April, what will you tell people about your parents—how you found your mother?"

"I'll just tell them a man passing through the saloon told me about Hattie and Javier Castillo. Castillo isn't an uncommon name in these parts. No one has to know their son is a wanted man."

Melissa nodded solemnly. "I'll tell Mama soon, because she'll be so happy for you. Mama and Papa both have always worried about your not having any family."

April couldn't imagine Ned Hatfield worrying about her. He always seemed to gaze at her with cold disapproval and treat her with an aloof politeness. But she knew Selma Hatfield did worry about her and had tried to be a substitute mother on many occasions, a fact April had always appreciated. She would be happy for Selma to know that she had at last found her mother.

April got paper and pen and sat down at her narrow oak desk to write to Luke. She knew what this letter would mean to him. He had searched for his mother for so many years, and April knew that underneath his toughness, he was a tender, loving man. It had hurt him terribly to be unable to find his mother after the ambush when he had been so young.

She wrote quickly, spilling all her thoughts onto the page.

> Dearest Luke:
>   You will be shocked to read my news. Our long search is about over. And I've discovered we have a brother—Tigre Castillo.

As soon as she had completed the letter, she started one to Hattie. She composed the letter carefully, pausing often, lost in memories. She remembered how she had tried for several years to find Hattie and then had given up the search.

She smoothed the paper out, thinking about Luke, imagining his green eyes when he read her letter. Suddenly her throat burned and tears swam in her eyes. All these years—Hattie didn't know all of her children were alive.

When she finally stretched out in bed, she talked with Melissa in the darkness until almost dawn. Melissa fell asleep first. April lay quietly, her thoughts spinning over Tigre, wondering if he had gotten safely away from town, and when she would see him again. She also wondered if she could ever convince Noah McCloud she was telling the truth.

* * *

When she stepped outside Tuesday night after finishing her last song, Noah was waiting on his horse.

"Evening," he drawled, dismounting.

"Good evening, Mr. McCloud. I'm surprised you're
not at your place."

"I've hired me a good man, Duero Corinto, and
I've given him a small cut of the business. That gives
a man an incentive and an interest in the place."

"I know Duero Corinto. He hasn't worked in a saloon lately."

"No. He worked at the lumber mill last. Now he's
a barkeep. He's a hardworking man, honest, and am-
bitious, and I think he'll be a good man. I don't want
to be tied there day and night."

She gazed up at him as he sat beside her in her
buggy, lifting the reins. He had his good points, there
was no denying that. If only he believed her! She gazed
at his profile, aware she was staring. She felt a longing
sweep over her that made her want Noah McCloud to
scoot closer, to touch her arm lightly as he did often,
to make her laugh. And she knew it was foolishness.
He intended to force her out of work. She clamped her
lips together and stared straight ahead.

"You had company last Saturday night. You're getting social, Miss Danby, for someone who used to be
alone most of the time."

"How do you know I had company?"

"I know what goes on in town and in your life."

"Are you spying on me?"

"I might be. All you have to do to get me to leave
you alone is—"

"I'll tell you again. I don't have your gold. Not a
penny of it!"

"Such protests of innocence, yet a man slipped away
from your house late Saturday night, and I'm sure he
didn't want anyone to see him. Who was the man?"

"I shouldn't tell you one thing about him!"

"A lover! Why, Miss Danby, you have a secret life
after all."

"There's no such thing! Melissa Hatfield was over

and she's in love with Patrick O'Flynn. Her father
doesn't like Patrick, so she begged me to let them
meet at my house.''

"As I recall, Ned Hatfield has a rather foul temper.
Aren't you taking a big chance?'' he asked.

"Melissa deserves to get to see a nice young man
like Patrick O'Flynn,'' April continued. ''It isn't right
for her father to keep them apart simply because Patrick is Irish.''

"I agree with you,'' Noah said solemnly.

"That's why you found me climbing out of the tree
that first night,'' she said, remembering clearly.

"How's that?''

"I was in Melissa's bed so she could meet Patrick
and warn him. Her father had heard they were going
to meet, so he went after Patrick. You simply assumed
the worst.''

He chuckled. "Now, what would you assume if you
saw a beautiful young woman climb out of an upstairs
bedroom window in the dead of night?''

She laughed, tilting her head back, and Noah suddenly wanted to slip his arm around her. There was
something infectious about her laugh.

"You're right, I suppose!''

"That was the first man at your house last Saturday.
There was a second.''

"Do you stay all night long?'' she asked, her cheeks
turning pink.

"Sometimes,'' he answered. Even though he didn't
stay all night, it wouldn't hurt for her to think he did.
He watched her closely. "Why did he come to call?''

Her lashes fluttered, and he saw a brief second of
panic before her features became impassive. "He came
to visit. He was the man who interrupted the church
service.''

Noah caught her arm, making her face him. "Why
did he come, Miss Danby?''

"That's none of your business.'' He saw fear in her
expression. They reached her house and he helped her
down, his pulse beginning to hammer. How easily she
could work hand in hand with a man who was a thief

and murderer! At last Noah thought he might be getting closer to forcing her to admit the truth.

He opened her door, went inside and lit the lamp, and then turned to face her. "Tigre Castillo has the McCloud gold, doesn't he?" Noah asked, his gaze roaming over her kitchen.

"No! Get out!"

"So he does have it," Noah said grimly. She was in a panic over something, unable to hide her fear. "And he must have brought some back to you," Noah said, moving past her to the parlor.

"No!" she cried. She remembered the saddlebags filled with Tigre's money, and icy fear gripped her.

"At last we get to the truth," Noah said, standing in the middle of the parlor. She glanced toward her bedroom, and then looked at him. He had seen the look, and he turned to stride for the bedroom while her heart plummeted.

Noah wondered if April had ever lied before, because she wasn't any good at it. She followed him, stepping around in front of him.

"You have no right to be in here!" she exclaimed, and then clamped her lips shut. In the middle of her bed where she had left them lay the saddlebags bulging with Tigre Castillo's stolen money. Noah crossed the room to them and picked them up.

Coins clinked, and he turned around to give April a look that was both angry and satisfied.

"So you had a thief in it with you," he said quietly.

11

Tigre leaned over his horse, galloping west away from Albuquerque. There was no sign of lawmen behind them, and his thoughts had drifted back to the night's revelations. He had a brother and sister! The idea shocked him each time he thought about it. April would write to Hattie, Tigre knew, and also he knew how happy this would make her.

Melissa Hatfield. Something tightened in Tigre's chest when he thought of her. Both women had been sweet, and he longed for the company of a female who was sweet and innocent and not as hard as the sun-baked ground.

They slowed, and Barrigona rode up beside him, the two men a contrast: Tigre tall in the saddle, Barrigona short, paunchy, constantly eating. He chewed a hunk of dried beef, wiping his hand across his mouth. "We go to California now, Tigre?"

As they rode northwest toward the Cebolleta Mountains and long-extinct volcanic cones, Tigre reined and turned to look behind him. There was only the moonlit landscape, the alluvial plain of the 1,885-mile-long Rio Grande, land covered with scrubby creosote bushes and sagebrush. They were in Bernalillo County, one of the five counties in the territory that stretched from Texas to California.

"If they don't come after us, I want to go back." Another of the five men who rode with Tigre caught up with them.

"We're headed for California now, boss?" Coco Moore asked.

Barrigona shifted in the saddle, his short legs relaxed over the horse's girth, his broad shoulders splashed with moonlight.

"Not yet," Tigre answered quietly.

"How's that? I thought you said—"

"I'm going back. You boys ride on. I'll catch up with you eventually."

"Go back! Man, you're loco!" Barrigona exclaimed. He pushed his hat to the back of this head, the broad brim framing his round face and black eyes.

"I'm going back," Tigre said with a stubborn determination.

"It's that damned Songbird. Tigre, there's women in every town. Pretty women," Barrigona said.

"I'll meet you fellows in Tucson. Okay?"

"Don't go back. You want to hang?" Coco asked in his rasping voice. "I ain't going back."

"I didn't ask you to. I won't get caught. I'll see you in Tucson or Monterey," Tigre argued stubbornly.

"Hell, there are women better-looking than that dancing gal!" Barrigona continued. "I'll show you two when we get to Tucson."

"No," Tigre said, and reined his horse. "I'll be there in another two months, or don't wait for me. You two tell the others." Tigre turned his horse and flicked the reins, urging the stallion to a canter. He rode toward Albuquerque without looking back. Finally the sound of hoofbeats faded, and he slowed and turned in the saddle. A cloud of dust spiraled into the air in the distance. He headed southeast. He wanted to talk to April again. And he wanted to see Melissa Hatfield again. Just once he wanted to hold Melissa Hatfield in his arms and kiss her.

That night as he lay stretched on the ground asleep, he moaned and moved restlessly. Suddenly he yelled and sat up. He was wringing with sweat. He ran his fingers through his hair, shaking his head to get his hair away from his face. He had dreamed that he had a ranch and a house, and Melissa was in a big bed with her arms outstretched, pulling him down to fit closely against her. In the next instant she disappeared into blackness. It had been a long time now since he

had dreamed about a house and a woman in it. He
swore softly under his breath. The dream had seemed
so damned real.

He stood up, yanking off his blanket. In minutes he
was mounted and headed back toward Albuquerque,
passing the Isleta Pueblo in the distance. He'd camp
close to town and ride in at night to try to see both
women. He thought about his dream. A ranch house
was something as forbidden to him as the moon. A
wanted man couldn't put down roots. All his boyhood
years he had expected to grow up and have a ranch
just like his father. Now that dream could never come
true. Every time he thought of California, common
sense would finally set in. He was constantly reminded
that he would never get far enough away that he could
lead a normal life and not be afraid that someone
would discover he was wanted for murder and theft.
He swore bitterly, thinking of April earning her living
in a saloon. Hattie would want April to go home with
her, and yet April was not only a grown woman, she
was one as accustomed to independence as Tigre. He
wondered about his older brother—a former U.S. marshal! The thought conjured up a grin that faded as
curiosity arose over Luke Danby and what kind of man
he was. For a moment Tigre felt cheated. He had never
known his brother or sister—he was condemned to
roam on the wrong side of the law.

That morning he cut his long hair, shaved, and removed the bear-claw necklace. He removed one holster and pistol, pulled on a white shirt, and pulled the
feathers out of his hatband. He then mounted up again
to ride into town. In ten minutes he had a bag of supplies and food. And, more important, he knew exactly
where Melissa Hatfield lived and which room was hers.

During the night he watched the house, and as if his
dreams had conjured her up, she suddenly appeared
out in the yard. He had almost stepped forward when
her father came out behind her.

"Papa, isn't this night grand?"

"Damned hot in the house!"

"It isn't hot out here. And look at the stars. Did

you ever see anything so beautiful? Look how they shine."

Tigre listened to the enthusiasm in her voice and he longed to be the one with her, to have her all to himself. He could imagine the sparkle in her eyes.

"Selma, come out here!" Ned Hatfield called.

The door opened and a slender woman stepped outside and moved to a chair. "My, this is twenty degrees cooler than in the house," she said. Her voice was soft with a faint drawl. Her speech was hesitant, as if she weren't certain of her words.

"Let's sleep out here tonight," Melissa said, and Tigre held his breath, and closed his eyes and prayed for the first time that year.

"Too damned much trouble to haul everything out here, and that fool cat of yours will get right in the middle of us!"

Melissa tried to hide her soft laughter, but Tigre heard her.

"Can I sleep outside?"

"Yep. No harm in that, except you'll have Old Tom with you, and then the early-morning birds."

"I don't mind."

A back door opened at the neighboring house and a man's voice called, "Is that you, Ned?"

"Sure, Paul, come join us."

Tigre settled back, knowing he was in for a long wait. He had asked around and knew the names of the three families who lived on the block—the Hatfields and the Kleins on this side of the street, the Volkels across from them. Paul and Etta Klein joined the Hatfields in the yard, sitting on wooden chairs, enjoying the night air while Melissa and Selma Hatfield served glasses of lemonade.

Ned Hatfield stretched and said, "I spoke to Bob Worth today. He's been to Santa Fe and they think they'll have a railroad. A Major Gunn was there; he surveyed a route from Atchison. They're looking for investors."

"Won't that cost too much? The stage is practical," Paul said.

"Worth quoted them as saying ten thousand dollars a mile."

"My word!" Selma exclaimed. "Papa, you're not—"

"No. Not a cent," he answered.

"That's too much money," Paul added. "They'll never raise it. If they build it, they'll have to fight Apache and Comanche and Kiowa all the way."

"Edgar Griggs's cousin was in the bank today. He said they had another Apache raid in Pinos Altos. Rumors are the Apache and Navaho have joined. General Carleton has been there to look over the situation."

"The trouble can't get any worse than that."

"They're opening Fort Bayard east of Silver City, but that will give protection to Pinos Altos."

"Griggs said there are about four hundred people living in Pinos Altos now. The miners are working six hundred placer lodes within six miles."

"You'd like to be with them, wouldn't you, Ned?"

He chuckled, the sound carrying in the quiet night. "Sometimes I would, Selma."

"Yeah. It's tempting, all right," Paul Klein said. "I heard there's some action in the upper Moreno Valley. Placers were discovered near Elizabethtown on the western side of Baldy."

"There are still a lot of fights over land titles. The Treaty of 1848 recognizing Spanish holdings complicates ownership."

"Yeah. The Office of Surveyor-General they created before the war to settle things has just added more to the problem."

"Hear you have a new foal."

They talked about the new colt, the latest wagons to arrive in town up the Chihuahua Trail, the weather, and the Fiesta at summer's end.

Tigre sat on the ground in the shadows of a clump of cottonwoods where he could see Melissa. Moonlight splashed over her. He sat without moving, watching her slender arms as she lifted them to scoop curls off the back of her neck as she fanned herself. She gazed up at the moon, and conversation waned. Finally the Kleins went home, and within a quarter of an hour the Hatfields said they were going inside. Melissa said she still intended to sleep outside, cat or no cat. She went inside with her parents to get her bedding, and Tigre's heart pounded.

Upstairs lamps flickered to life behind gingham curtains. Melissa didn't pull hers, and his pulse thudded violently as she walked around the room, flinging off her gingham dress. Tigre felt as if desert winds were singeing him. He had moved to the west side of the house when she came near the open window. Her white camisole fitted snugly, dipping low where it was tied with a pink ribbon over flesh as smooth and rosy as peaches. He ran his hand across his sweating brow.

Turning her back to the window, she wriggled, and all her clothes were gone. The window hid her below her tiny waist, but above her waist, the sight of her bare back made his blood roar in his ears. He drew a sharp breath, the image of her indelibly carved in his memory. A white cotton gown dropped over her head, and her beauty was hidden again. He stood as still as stone, watching her comb her hair, imagining her without the nightgown. The lamp went out.

He moved back into the darkest shadow. He waited silently while she came out, a white blur gliding through the darkness to a wooden bench. She stretched out bedding and finally lay down, propping her head on her hands.

He waited until all the lights in the house had been extinguished long enough for her parents to fall asleep, and then he moved closer.

"Melissa!" he whispered. She sat up instantly. "Melissa, it's me, Tigre Castillo," he added quickly.

She yanked the sheet to her chin. "What are you doing here?"

He sat down on the bench beside her. "I came back to Albuquerque because I wanted to see you."

"Me?" she asked breathlessly. She glanced over her shoulder at the house. "If Papa saw us . . ."

"Do you think they're asleep?" he asked, but all he could think about was her. Her hair fell over her shoulders, black ringlets tumbling in a curly profusion. The top button at the neck of her gown was unfastened, revealing a triangle of pale skin.

"Papa sleeps like a bear in winter, Mama always says. I guess they are."

He reached out to take a silky black curl and let it slide through his fingers. "You're beautiful."

Suddenly she drew a swift breath. "How long have you been out here?"

"I just rode up a few minutes ago," he lied. "I left my horse back a ways and walked."

"I'll have to remember to pull my curtains," she said shyly.

"And I'll pray you forget to pull them." He let his fingers rest on her shoulder. She didn't protest, so he moved his hand closer to her throat. "How old are you?"

"I'm sixteen. And don't tell me that's young!"

"I wasn't going to. I'm not much older. Anyone in particular courting you?"

"Patrick O'Flynn. Papa doesn't approve of Patrick."

"Your papa sure as hell wouldn't approve of me," Tigre said softly. He let his fingers drift across her nape, hearing her quick intake of breath. "But if he did, I'd come courting, I swear to you, I would." He moved closer and his voice was husky and soft. "I don't have time, Melissa. I can't come courting and take you to dances and bring you flowers. I have to ride away from here, maybe forever. And if they catch me before I get to Mexico, they'll hang me."

"Oh, no!"

"Yes, they will."

"Seems like something could be done. Mr. Castillo—"

"Tigre. It's Tigre Castillo. Call me Tigre."

"Your half-brother used to be a marshal. Maybe he can do something."

"No one can do a damned thing," he said, stroking her throat, watching the flutter of her lashes and the parting of her rosy lips. He leaned closer. "Melissa?"

he asked, savoring her name and drawing it out. "Melissa," he repeated in a whisper, treasuring the moment.

"Yes?"

"Can I kiss you just once so I can carry the memory of your kiss with me?"

Again her lashes fluttered, and she looked down, smoothing the sheet over her drawn-up knees. "I bet you say that to all the women."

"I might have said it before," he stated solemnly, "but I've never meant it before." He placed his finger under her chin in order to look directly into her eyes. "I mean it with all my heart." His voice sounded gruff while his blood pounded in his veins.

"You can kiss me," she whispered, closing her eyes and lifting her face.

He slipped his arms around her waist, pulling her tightly against his chest. He lowered his head to place his mouth over hers and kiss her, trying to use control. His tongue thrust into her mouth. Her arms wound around his neck, and her tongue touched his, thrusting against his, setting him on fire.

They kissed wildly and Tigre knew he would love her all his life. She was sweet, passionate in her innocence. He wanted her desperately, and he had to shut his thoughts to tomorrow and enjoy the moment. He bent over her, kissing her. She was sweet—oh, Lord, so sweet. He was on fire with desire, throbbing until he felt as if he would burst.

Finally she pushed him away. "We must stop."

He ached with need for her that he knew he would be unable to fulfill. As he stood up and walked away from her, he burned with longing, trying to gain control over himself.

"You better go," she whispered.

"Melissa!" came the call of a deep male voice from the house, and a door banged.

Instantly Tigre dropped down, crouching low as he ran. Hugging shadows and trying to get out of sight, he ran to the few cottonwoods that offered any protection.

"Melissa, is someone with you?"

"No, Papa. I was singing softly."

"Young lady, are you telling me the truth?" Ned hollered, doubt and anger in his voice as he came striding out. "I heard someone." Tigre stood flattened against the trunk of a tree, then hoisted himself up on a lower limb and waited. He watched Ned Hatfield stop beside Melissa and look all around.

"Dammit, miss, don't you lie to me. I heard someone talking to you. That damned Patrick is here, isn't he?"

"No, Papa! I promise he isn't."

"If you lie to me, young lady, over that damnable Irishman, I'll lock you in that house for a month! Patrick O'Flynn!" he shouted. "Stay away from my daughter! I know you're there! You come back and you'll get a bullet through your heart for trespassing, do you hear me! Dammit, Melissa Jane, get inside!"

"Papa, Patrick isn't here! All the neighbors will hear your shouts!" she exclaimed. She was crying now. Tigre clenched his fists, shaking with anger. He wanted to confront her father, to tell him to stop being a tyrant to her.

He also wanted to court her like other men in the town could. He leaned back against the trunk of the tree, his eyes closed as pain engulfed him. He hated running and thieving! He loved ranching and reading, and had always thought he would have a home and family like his folks—

His thoughts were interrupted abruptly by a shrill cry from Melissa. "Papa!"

"You told me he wasn't out there! If Patrick O'Flynn isn't hiding out there in the dark, then why are you so scared for me to go look!"

"You don't need to search the yard for someone who isn't there! I'm going inside."

"Damned right!" Ned said, striding directly toward Tigre with a six-shooter held high.

"Papa, you might shoot someone innocent."

"Shut up, Melissa! No one belongs near my property or my daughter in the middle of the night."

Melissa began to sob, covering her face with her hands. Tigre wanted to drop down and confront Hatfield, and give him a punch in the jaw for the way he treated his daughter.

"Get in the house!" Ned thundered at her.

Melissa whirled around, scooping up her bedding and racing over the ground. Her white nightgown billowed out as she ran, her curls bouncing. Tigre hurt for her, but his attention was on Ned Hatfield, who was moving closer. Tigre held his breath as Ned stopped right beneath the branch. All he had to do was look up. Tigre wouldn't draw on Melissa's father. He wouldn't risk shooting her parent.

Finally Hatfield moved on, walking slowly and carefully, making very little noise. Tigre sat completely still. His muscles began to ache, but he wouldn't move. He heard a twig snap, and in a few more minutes Hatfield passed a few yards away, heading to the house. He paused and turned to face the trees.

"Damn you, Irish! Stay away from my daughter. I'll never let her marry you, and I'll shoot you dead if I get a chance. Don't think I don't know you're out there! I saw you with her."

He turned and stomped back to the house, no longer taking care to be quiet. Tigre waited. He relaxed, but he stayed on the branch for another five minutes before dropping lightly to the ground. He moved with sure-footedness back to his horse, thankful he had dismounted over half a mile from the Hatfield house.

He turned south, riding away from town to hunt a campsite far enough from Albuquerque to be safe. The next night he was back watching the Hatfield house.

Once Ned Hatfield came outside and walked all around the house, standing on the back steps a long time, but finally he went inside. It was a hot night, and the Hatfields left the doors and windows open. Melissa came to sit beside her bedroom window and gaze outside. Tigre cursed the bright moonlight that kept him from crossing the yard to talk to her, but couldn't take the risk. Black curls framed her face as she leaned on the sill.

"Melissa," he whispered, knowing he was too far away for her to hear, but wanting to be with her more than ever.

Two nights later the bright moon was gone. Wearing gloves and a black shirt, Tigre left his horse two miles from the house and began walking. He moved silently across the yard, climbing the cottonwood that grew beside her window. He settled against the trunk to wait for Melissa to come to her room. When she appeared, she closed the door.

"Melissa!"

She paused and frowned; then her head jerked around and she dashed across the room to the window. "Tigre!" she gasped. "You mustn't! If Papa finds out—"

"He won't. I had to see you. When they go to sleep, I'll come inside where I can talk to you."

"It's too dangerous!" she said as her eyes widened.

"It's worth the risk. I have to see you before I go."

She bit her lip and nodded, a frown furrowing her smooth brow. She moved away from the window and turned out the lamp. He waited while her door opened and light spilled inside. He could hear voices as her mother talked to her and finally told her good night.

Tigre waited while the town and the Hatfield house both grew dark and quiet. Finally Melissa appeared at the window.

Without her saying a word, he moved. He had removed his spurs, and he made only the slightest rustle as he climbed across the open space through the window into her room. He turned to reach for her, and she came into his arms at once, her arms winding around his neck while he bent his head.

"You're all I've thought about," he whispered gruffly. "I should be with my men riding to California, but I can't leave Albuquerque because of you."

"Tigre . . ." The word was a sigh of yearning, and then his mouth covered hers and all words ended. He shook with desire for her, relishing the sweetness of her kisses as her soft body pressed against his. While they kissed, he moved toward the bed, but she pulled away.

"Tigre, if Mama got up and came in—she doesn't knock first. You'd never get away."

"Shh, Melissa," he said, guiding her closer to the bed.

"I mustn't," she said, yet her protest was weak.

His knees touched the feather mattress, and he sat down. He pulled her down on his lap, and he thought his blood would boil from the pleasure of holding her against him. "Melissa—Lord, you're sweet!" he breathed, pausing to look at her. He gazed into her eyes, memorizing each feature, trying to store up images to last him a lifetime. He ran his fingers lightly over her face, her lips, her cheek, and down over her slender throat.

He watched her as his hand slid slowly down to her breast. She gasped and closed her eyes, but she didn't stop him. He moved his hand lightly, relishing the feel of her high, soft breast. Her eyes grew round while he opened the gown and freed her breasts, cupping them in his callused hands, burying his face between their enticing softness.

She wound her fingers in his hair and held him close while he kissed her. He felt her response, until finally she pushed him away. "Tigre, it's too dangerous!"

"Shh," he said, bending his head to kiss her.

The creak of boards in the hallway was the first warning to reach him.

Tigre heard a step outside the door. He dropped down, sliding under her bed as Melissa flung herself under the blanket and lay still.

He heard the footsteps come into the room, then saw bare feet and the hem of Selma Hatfield's gown. He waited while Selma went to the window. She turned around and left the room, leaving the door open behind her. He lay still, waiting for Melissa to act. She lay still as minutes ticked past. Finally Melissa swung her feet out of bed and closed the door quietly. She waited, leaning against the door for several minutes. He scooted out.

"Tigre, I'm so scared for you. You should go. I think they watch me more closely since that night I slept outside. And I'm not allowed to sleep outside anymore unless the whole family does."

He slipped his arm around her waist, drawing her to him.

"Mama's awake now. I want you to go. I'm afraid—"

He bent his head and kissed her long and deep before he paused. "I'll be back tomorrow night before midnight."

She nodded and he kissed her again before he stepped over the sill. His gaze swept the dark, quiet yard and street; then he climbed into the tree and in seconds was on the ground.

He waved at her, and hurried away, keeping in dark shadows as best he could. He reached the open ground, where there wasn't any cover, and he had to pray that Ned Hatfield wasn't watching out a window. He mounted his horse. His body ached with need for Melissa. He loved her and wanted her. He wanted to court her, to come calling and take her out and dance with her. He swore softly. He should get out of Albuquerque. Every night that he came to town increased the risks he was taking, but he couldn't leave yet. She was the sweetest, most desirable woman he had ever known. He hated the life he was caught in, wanting to change it, wanting to make Melissa Hatfield his wife.

Wife. The word was like magic, and conjured up silken nights with Melissa in his arms, children, a home. He groaned aloud and tried to change his thoughts, angling around town in a circle and heading south.

12

Noah McCloud shook his arm free from April's grasp and picked up the saddlebags that bulged and clinked.

"It's not what you think!" she exclaimed, trying to take them out of his hands.

He unfastened the straps of leather and turned one upside down. April gasped, stunned at the shower of gold that cascaded down on her counterpane. For an instant both of them were transfixed at the sight. Then he swore and turned to grip her tightly by the shoulders, giving her a shake. Anger burned in him.

"You lying little vixen!" he snapped in a quiet voice. "I knew if I waited long enough—"

"That's not your brother's gold!" she cried, grasping his wrists and trying to pull his hands away. "Let me go! That isn't your money or mine!"

"Half of that statement is correct! This is just part of what I want."

"That isn't yours! It wasn't your brother's! It isn't mine! I'm telling you the truth!" she cried. She struggled in vain to free herself from his grip that held her fast.

"Dammit. Who does it belong to, then? Don't tell me your brother from San Antonio sent it!"

"No!"

"It's the McCloud gold, and you're in this with that damned outlaw, Tigre Castillo. I know he's been here, and he gave you this, didn't he?"

The question hung between them, and his eyes narrowed. A look of disgust made his lip curl contemptuously. "You're a beautiful little thief who probably took advantage of Ralph."

"I didn't, and it's not what you think!"

"What wild story are you trying to invent? I can see your mind racing over lies now, trying to select the right one."

"No! I haven't told you, because I shouldn't."

He made a deprecatory sound, and his disgust became even more obvious.

"It belongs to my half-brother, Tigre Castillo."

Noah's eyes narrowed. "You have a half-brother in San Antonio."

"I have another one. Tigre Castillo came to see me Friday night. He asked me to keep this money to give to his parents. He told me the circumstances that caused him to kill a man."

"You lying witch, spinning yarns that my gullible, innocent brother probably believed," he said in a tight voice. "I know enough about people to know how damned deceitful they can be. Particularly women!"

"You're so cynical and hard. I pity you! Have you ever trusted anyone?"

"Yes, I have, and it brought me a hell of a heartbreak."

"Well, more's the pity, because the world does hold honest people. And I'm being honest now. Tigre left this with me. He wants me to get it to his parents. He said they will come to Albuquerque soon—Hattie and Javier Castillo. When he told me their names, I knew he was my half-brother. Hattie Castillo is my mother." She saw a flicker of surprise in McCloud's expression. She met his searching gaze without wavering.

Noah held her shoulders, watching her, and all he could do was to silently call himself a fool. She sounded damned truthful. It fitted. And he believed her.

"That's why you wrote a letter to Mrs. Javier Castillo," he said, studying her.

"You know I sent a letter?" She was astounded that he would pry into her life. "You are the lowest sneak—trailing around after me—"

"You have my brother's gold hidden somewhere, and the only way I can find it is to keep after you."

"I don't have it! This is Tigre Castillo's gold!"

Noah studied her. He knew about the letter posted to Mr. and Mrs. Javier Castillo in Taos County. Dammit, why did April Danby always sound so truthful? Her eyes were wide, facing him defiantly and openly. Fires of anger flashed in them, and he was sure the gold on the bed must belong to Castillo.

"You're the sister of a murderer," he said quietly. "That may change your standing in the town."

"Not as much as your midnight visits will!"

While he held her, he became aware of the small bones under his hands. A silky lock of her hair fell over the back of his hand and a faint smell of lilacs drifted up from her skin. Her skin was beautiful, smooth and flawless, and he could imagine stroking his fingers over her slender throat.

He tried to push aside such thoughts and concentrate on the matter of gold. His gaze lowered to her mouth, though, and desire for her flared in spite of their differences. His gaze met hers again, and he saw the same knowledge in her eyes. A calm look had come over her features. Her lips parted and her pulse beneath his fingers was skipping wildly. She wanted to be kissed, and that made him want her more.

He could have groaned aloud with agony. He was drawn to her, he believed her. With an effort he ignored the tension that was growing between them, the pull that made him want to slip his arms around her tiny waist and crush her softness against him. "The sheriff will watch you now as much as I do."

"I don't intend to announce the news. As a matter of fact, I didn't intend anyone to know my relationship with Tigre except Melissa, and she won't tell. I don't want Tigre hurt."

"You know the gold is tainted," Noah said in sardonic amusement. April never ceased to amaze him.

She moved away and he let her go, his hands dropping to his sides, but he had seen the worry in her expression. "I know it's tainted, but as he pointed out, he can't give it back, and if I don't do this for him, he'll find another way."

"Better to do as he asked, since he's a murderer," Noah said dryly.

"I promised to give it to Hattie and Javier. I wrote to them, but I didn't mention the gold in the letter."

"And did you write to your mother that her present husband gave you away to a bunch of soiled doves in a rough frontier town?"

"No," April said, biting her lip. "And I don't intend to tell her. It will hurt her terribly, and it may cause trouble between them."

Her answer made Noah's respect for her increase, and he scowled as he listened to her talk.

"I have to see her and talk to her. It seems impossible to think I really have my mother. And another brother."

Noah heard the wonder and joy in her voice, and he understood how she felt. He had lost his family, and there were moments when it tore at him. She glowed with happiness in spite of his accusations, and he couldn't doubt what she was telling him.

"I wrote to Luke too, so he—" She stopped and frowned. "I suppose you already know that."

Noah flushed, suddenly wishing he didn't have to pursue her so relentlessly. Whenever he forgot the gold, he was drawn to April. If circumstances were different . . . He closed his thoughts to that. "Yes, I know you sent both letters."

"Then you know I'm telling you the truth."

He had made his decision. As he gazed into her wide clear eyes, he knew one thing. He was a fool where women were concerned. He believed her. *He wanted her.*

He shrugged and bent down to scoop the gold back into the saddlebags. April leaned down to help him, taking the bag from his hands to hold it wide open. Their shoulders brushed and he turned to look at her. She was only inches away, and the urge to touch her heated his blood. As if she could plainly read his thought, she moved away.

When he finished refastening the bag, he tossed it

down and followed her into the parlor. "It's late," she said.

He sat down, a crooked smile appearing. "You can wait a few more minutes. Tell me more about your newly found family."

"Would you like some cider?" she asked. She knew she shouldn't be so hospitable at this late hour, certainly not to a man hell-bent on causing her trouble, but she couldn't resist. She wanted him to stay.

"I don't suppose you have anything stronger in the house?"

"No, I don't."

"Then cider is fine," he said, following her to the kitchen. He sat down at the oak table, dropping his hat on an empty chair.

"I made apricot kolaches today," she said, placing a bowl with golden-brown balls in front of him.

"What are kolaches?" he asked, picking one up to bite into it.

"They're Czech. There was a girl at Miss Kate's that taught me how to make them."

The pastry crumbled in his mouth, the apricot adding a tart tang. "Ah, these are good. Do you like to cook?"

She bobbed her head, smiling at him. She was aware of his nearness, his long legs stretched out beside her chair. She lost all her appetite, and wished she didn't have such an intense reaction to him.

Noah resisted the urge to lean forward so he would be closer to her. "You know it will complicate your life when people learn about your relationship to Tigre Castillo. He's wanted for a lot of crimes. I've seen the list in the sheriff's office."

"I told you, no one knows except you, Tigre, and Melissa."

"None of us will talk, but if Hattie and Javier Castillo come to town and people learn they're your parents—April, someone will make the connection. The sheriff will remember coming to this house to search for him."

She looked away from his steady gaze. "I suppose

you're right, but they can't do anything to me simply
because I'm his sister. I have a lot of friends here.''

"For his own sake, he ought to stay away.''

"He's gone to California. He explained to me why
he was wanted for murder,'' she said. She wanted
Noah McCloud to know the truth. She told him,
watching the slight shake of his head.

"Too many times good men get on the wrong side
of the law. Look at my brother—he was wanted for
murder. I know whatever Ralph did was justified, because he was good through and through. Hell of a lot
better man than I am,'' he added softly. "I'm sure
you'll agree,'' he said, his voice becoming lighter.

She smiled at him, and thought again that she liked
having him here to talk to. She could tell him things
and know they wouldn't be spread around town.

"Think your brother will come to Albuquerque?
And your folks?''

"I hope so. I know it will be upsetting for my
mother to discover I didn't drown. You're right about
that, but I had to let her know I was alive.''

"Yes, you did, but it'll still be a shock,'' he said
solemnly, watching her. Sitting so close to her, gazing
into her eyes, he thought how beautiful she was. Self-
sufficient, loyal, beautiful. Her eyes sparkled when she
was happy, her lips looked as soft as they felt. If he
could just forget the gold, forget what she had done . . .

The sound of hoofbeats was clear in the night, and
then a knock came at the front door. April glanced in
uncertainty at Noah before she rose to go to the door.
He followed behind her, his hand resting on his six-
shooter.

She opened the door to face Aaron Yishay. "Doc?
Come in.''

Taking off his hat, he stepped inside and faced Noah.
"Ah, McCloud. How are you?''

"Fine.'' Noah shook hands in greeting while April
closed the door.

"Would you join us in cider and kolaches?''

"I can't turn down an offer like that,'' he said, smiling at both of them. He acted as if it were the middle

of the afternoon instead of the dark hours of early morning. "You were sitting in the kitchen. Let's go back in there."

As soon as he settled at the table and April handed him a cup of cider, she asked, "Did you want to see me?"

He chuckled. "You're scandalizing the Dodworths. They came to my house and said some man was over here. They were afraid you might not be safe. Mc-Cloud here wasn't threatening you, was he?"

She laughed along with Noah. "Not this time," she said lightly. "I'd think the Dodworths would be afraid to get out at night to go to your place. Why didn't they just come over here and ask me?"

"Well, suppose it had been a bandit? He would have just turned his gun on them too, and that wouldn't have been any help. I'm going to have to have Mama give them a little talking-to. This is the second time recently they've stirred up a fuss over nothing. Of course, the last time, there wasn't anyone here at all when Sheriff Pacheco and his boys arrived."

"Will Gerta be worried about you?" April asked, trying to avoid talking about the sheriff's visit.

"No. She thought it was all foolishness—as I did— but we had to be sure. Now I'm glad I did," he said, taking another kolache. "We're getting a new bunch of soldiers in here tomorrow. They're on their way to Fort Bayard. Apache are on the warpath. Ever fought Apache?"

Noah nodded. "I encountered some north of here."

"You ever need a man to deal with Apache, you got the best there is working for you right now."

"Duero?" Noah asked, trying to pull his glance from April and pay attention to Aaron Yishay.

"Lots of stories about Duero and the Apache," Aaron answered. "He can fight them, track them, and get along with them. One story is that he had an Apache squaw for a time."

They sat and talked, and Noah finally relaxed. He enjoyed Aaron Yishay's stories about people in town, enjoyed watching April laugh. He relished her soft,

rich voice that could touch him like a caress. As they
both listened to a story about the occupation of Albuquerque by Mexican forces, he reached out to move
a lock of her hair away from her cheek. She didn't
look at him, appearing to be aware only of Doc's story,
but her cheeks became pinker and her lashes fluttered
in a manner that made his pulse jump.

Finally Doc stood up and stretched. "As much as I
like the company, the roosters will be crowing soon."

'I'll ride back that way with you, Doc," Noah said
as he stood up. He wanted to linger, to stay with April,
but the hour was late, and he didn't trust himself. He
wanted badly to touch her, to hold her.

They thanked her for the cider and kolaches and told
her good night. Noah mounted. Doc glanced up at
him. "Just a minute, McCloud. Forgot something."

He hurried back to April's door and knocked. She
had just turned away, and she went back to open the
door. Doc's eyes sparkled and he looked at her with
curiosity.

"Miss April, is this the one?" he whispered.

She laughed, her cheeks flushing with heat as she
glanced past him at Noah, who sat waiting on horseback. "No, Doc, he definitely isn't the one!" she
whispered in return. "I think he'd like to wring my
neck over his brother's gold."

"Is that so?" Aaron turned to study Noah.

"Doc!" April chided in a harsh whisper, afraid
Noah would inquire about their conversation.

He grinned and nodded. "Good night, Miss April.
He's not a bad sort."

She smiled and closed the door, leaning against it
and laughing softly. . . . *not a bad sort*. There were
times he was absolutely marvelous. Like tonight after
the first awful moments when he had thought the gold
in the saddlebags was his. But after that, he had been
fun. She hummed softly as she put out the lamps.

The next two days and nights, Noah was busy with
the saloon and didn't see April. Business was good,
and he had to increase some of his supplies of whiskey. He was learning what sold best, what he didn't

need to stock. On Tuesday it was almost dawn when he returned to his hotel. With his thoughts on business he crossed the lobby in long strides, his spurs jingling with each step. He unlocked the door to his room and entered the darkened room. The window was open wide, the curtains billowing inward with the breeze. As Noah picked up the kerosene lamp and reached for his matches, he felt a prickle across the nape of his neck. He knew he wasn't alone.

"I was beginning to think you weren't coming back here at all tonight," drawled a soft voice from the shadows. Noah spun around, shock making his heart slam against his ribs.

"Noah, darlin', I've been waiting and waiting to see you for the longest time."

13

Hattie sat in the wagon waiting for Javier, watching him stride down the dusty Taos street. Leaves drifted through the air on the warm summer afternoon. Javier's arms were loaded with packages. His long legs and springy strides were the same as Tigre's, and for a moment she thought of her son. It had been two years since she had last seen Tigre! She tried to hold on to happy memories and not let sadness invade her mind. There were too many regrets in the past to dwell on them, too many losses.

Javier was tall and broad-shouldered, one of the strongest men in the area. She always felt as if the Lord had given her Javier and Tigre as compensation for her other losses. From the first, Javier had seemed to adore her, and he had given her a good home and a son. She smiled at him as he plunked packages down behind her in the wagon, then climbed to the seat beside her, pulling out a tattered envelope.

"You have a letter from Albuquerque."

"Tigre?" she asked, her heart leaping as she reached for the letter.

"No, sorry, Hattie," Javier said gently, handing her the letter.

She turned it in her hands, looking at the address in one corner with the initials A.D. "I don't know anyone in Albuquerque. It must be someone who knows Tigre."

"You might open it up and read it," Javier said dryly, smiling at her as he flicked the reins. The wagon moved down the street, circling the plaza to head east out of town toward their ranch. Beyond the adobe buildings and houses of Taos rose the shaded purple slopes of the Sangre de Cristos. The slopes shimmered with dark spruce and aspen leaves that dangled and danced in the wind like jewels. The sky beyond was a brilliant blue backdrop, white clouds moving over the peaks.

Hattie turned the letter in her hands a few more times. She rarely received letters. Tigre could read and write as well as she could, but she knew that under the circumstances she shouldn't expect him to write letters home.

"I'll swear women love to conjure up a mystery! You're turning that thing, wondering who sent it. Any man would have torn it open and read it by now," Javier said with a chuckle. He draped his arm around her shoulder to give her a hug. She smiled up at him, momentarily forgetting the letter. In spite of all these years of marriage and their age, Javier could still make her heart skip. He made her feel young and desirable.

He gazed down at her, his velvety dark eyes changing, passion flaring. "I'll be glad when the drive home is over," he said.

She nodded as he brushed her forehead lightly with a kiss. She straightened up. "Javier, we're in town! People will talk."

"Balderdash! Let 'em talk. I still have the prettiest woman in these parts and I like to look at her and kiss her!"

Hattie smiled perfunctorily, sliding her finger under the flap to open the envelope.

"It's a woman's handwriting." Javier didn't answer and she smoothed out the sheet of paper.

Dear Hattie Castillo:
  I must warn you before you read further—my letter will give you and Javier Castillo a shock.

Hattie frowned and started to speak, then clamped her mouth shut and read: "I met Tigre."

She looked up. "This is from a woman who's met Tigre."

"Oh?" Javier frowned. "What's she say? He isn't married, is he?"

"I don't know. I haven't read that far." She went back and read aloud: " 'Tigre has been in Albuquerque. He left something for me to give you.' "

"The boy has probably left us money again," Javier said, his voice becoming gruff. Hattie knew how deeply Javier loved his son, and how bitter he was over the justice he had been dealt. "I don't need his money and I wish to heaven the boy would keep it, put it in a bank, and take a new name and a new life! Damn, if I could just see him and talk to him!"

Hattie patted his knee. "He loves you or he wouldn't want to give you anything," she said. "Just think about that part of it." She smoothed the letter on her knee. "Anyway, he must be in love to trust her with money!"

"Go ahead and read."

" 'He said he thought you would come to Albuquerque this year.' If only he would have stayed until we got there!" Hattie exclaimed.

"He might not have been able to stay. Go ahead."

" 'Tigre told me your names, Hattie and Javier Castillo. My mother's name was Hattie, so I had to ask him about you.' " Hattie's voice became quiet as she read swiftly, holding the paper up in shaking hands." 'My name is April Danby.' Javier!" Hattie exclaimed, looking up. To her amazement, all color had drained from Javier's face as he turned to take the letter from her hands.

"It can't be," he whispered.

She frowned, looking at him a moment longer. She held his hand as she read, leaning close against him, " 'I have been searching for you for a long time. I have a half-brother, Luke Danby, an attorney, who lives in San Antonio Texas. I hope this doesn't come as too great a shock.' April and Lucius are both alive!" Her head swam and she clenched her fists, squeezing her eyes shut momentarily. "All these years I thought they were dead." She didn't look at Javier, who sat grimly silent beside her. Her thoughts tried to absorb the news he had just read. She gripped Javier's arm tightly. "Javier, they're both alive," she repeated, and tears filled her eyes. "Both April and Lucius! Luke. He must go by 'Luke.' They're alive. We have to go to Albuquerque. Oh, Javier!"

For the first time she noticed him. His face was gray and drawn, his eyes as cold as ice. He looked years older in just the few minutes that had passed. "Javier, what's wrong?"

His chest heaved and he looked down at her. "Wrong? Nothing's wrong. That's just a shock to think that you don't have two children and suddenly find out you do." He hugged her, pulling her against his chest, but she frowned. She didn't find the usual comfort from his embrace, because she knew that for one of the very few times in his life, Javier had just lied to her.

She was unable to fathom why he wasn't rejoicing—she couldn't believe it was because he wasn't their father. Javier was loving and good, and these weren't small children who might become a responsibility to him. They were grown. She pulled away and looked up at him. He turned to stare ahead at the path.

"Did you finish reading?"

"No, not quite," she said, reading the last in a rush: " 'I hope you can come to Albuquerque soon. I have posted a letter to Luke and hope he will also be here. Ta-ne-haddle, a Kiowa brave, found him and nursed him back to health after the wagon-train attack. He searched for you for many years. I hope this hasn't been too great a shock, but I had to write. I want so desperately to see you. My love, Your daughter, April Danby.' "

"She doesn't say anything about where she lives or who cares for her. Can we go next week?"

"Next week?" He laughed, but it was a mirthless, harsh sound. "That's impossible. You know I have someone coming to buy those ewes. I can't up and leave without taking care of business first. Albuquerque is several hundred miles away. We'll go, but I can't leave the place without notice, and I'll need time to get ready.''

"Javier, something's wrong," she said solemnly, running her hand over his hard knee. "What is it?"

"Wrong? Not a thing. It's just a shock to discover we now have three children instead of one.''

A wall had come up between them, and it lasted all the way home. It lasted until they were in bed, but then Javier loved her as if it were the last time in his life. Afterward he buried his face against her throat, and to her amazement, she felt tears.

"Javier! What's wrong?"

He raised his head, his wide black eyes devouring her as if they had been married for days instead of years. "I love you, Hattie. I always have and I always will.''

"I love you too.''

"I hope you continue to love me.''

"Of course, I will," she said, sobering. Her joy faded as she realized something was bothering him. He rolled away from her and soon was asleep, but Hattie lay awake in the darkness. She was much too excited to sleep. She offered another prayer to the Lord for bringing her children back to her, praying that Javier's problem would disappear.

In the night she stirred, and realized he was gone from the bed. She saw him outside, moving restlessly back and forth on the long porch. His cheroot tip glowed bright red in the black night, and she wondered what was worrying him. She hadn't noticed a thing until the letter, but she couldn't see how he could be unhappy to learn that her children were alive. It couldn't be that, yet every time she asked him about going to Albuquerque, he changed the topic of conversation without giving her an answer. She frowned, wondering about him, worrying about it.

A week later, she waited for him on the back porch of their log house. They lived in the valley between two mountains, and the air was cool and crisp. In the distance she could see a flock of sheep and the two dogs that helped guard the flock. Their house, made from ponderosa pines, was comfortable and was big enough for a large family. Tigre's room was empty, and she wanted to bring April back to live with them if possible. She shifted impatiently, her gaze sweeping over the land. Their stream rushed over rocks as it tumbled along the valley. And then she spotted Javier's hat bobbing as he strode along the far side of the corral.

She confronted him as he was coming in from the barn. "Javier, I want to talk to you now."

He paused and she realized how solemn he had become in the past week. "Yes?"

"I'm going to Albuquerque—with or without you, I'm going."

His shoulders seem to sag, and for the first time since she had met him, Javier looked defeated. "Hattie, these are grown children. It might not be like you think to meet them."

"I have to! I can't ignore them now that I've found them." She was aghast that he hoped she wouldn't want to see them.

"I'll take you," he said wearily.

"We should leave two days from now."

He nodded and started past her. She caught his arm. "Javier, what's wrong?"

"Nothing. Except that I'm busy all the time."

"Are you afraid I'll want to bring April back here to live?"

"If that's what you want, I don't mind. We have room for her. We had Tigre before."

"You won't mind if I ask her to come stay with us?"

"No, Hattie. Whatever you want. But she's a grown woman and she has already made a life of her own. She may not be interested in coming here."

"I know that, but I want to ask her. She may need help."

"Whatever you'd like to do."

"That isn't what's been worrying you?"

"No."

She took his hands in hers. "Don't shut me out of

your life. Is there some problem with the land, or the horses, or the water?''

He hugged her, crushing her to him. "I love you, Hattie. Please always remember I need you too.''

Amazed, she leaned back. "Javier, for God's sake, what is it? What's wrong?''

He moved away. "No more than usual, and less than sometimes.''

She watched him go and felt an ache in her heart. She had lived with him long enough to know when something was disturbing him badly. She had butter to churn and material to dye, so she returned to her chores, but her mind was on Javier all through the day.

Three times, emergencies arose that caused Javier to postpone their departure for Albuquerque. The first one Hattie accepted without a qualm; the second, she was quiet and tried to reassure herself that it had been important—one of the men came to get Javier to see about sheep that had been stolen. But the third time she waited grimly for him to return home.

The aspen would turn golden before another two months. After that there would be the threat of snow, and he would postpone their trip until springtime. She couldn't allow that. When he hung up his gunbelt, he turned to look at her solemnly.

"I'm going to Albuquerque—with or without you,'' she said, her voice clear and firm.

"We'll go. In the morning.''

Javier kept his word, and they began the trek southward. They rode in the wagon with two of the hired hands who went along to help carry supplies back to the ranch. Hattie's excitement mounted with each mile that passed, but Javier was as quiet and solemn as he had been the past weeks. She realized he might be blaming himself for her being separated from April for all these years. The next day, as they rolled along flat ground, she laid her hand on his knee.

"Javier, if you're tormenting yourself about giving up the search for April when you thought she had drowned, then I want you to stop worrying.''

He turned to stare at her, his black eyes unfathomable.

"I realized that might be what's been worrying you," Hattie continued gently. She ran her fingers across the back of his neck. "You've been the best husband I could hope for. I don't blame you for thinking that she had drowned and couldn't be found. I didn't see the need to keep searching for her either."

"Hattie," he said, his voice sounding agonized, "I shouldn't have done what I did."

"Don't fret over it! You've been so good to me. You were a good man to marry me when you knew all I'd been through," she said, burying her face against his arm. "I love you, Javier. There's no need to blame yourself for anything concerning April."

"Hattie . . ."

She looked up. Furrows creased his brow, and he looked grim. "What is it?" she asked.

"I . . . I should have done things differently."

"Don't blame yourself!" she exclaimed. She hated to see him in torment. "I love you. And nothing can undo the past. We just have to take the present and be happy! Stop fretting. I love you so!" she exclaimed, and slipped her arm around his waist to hug him. His arm dropped over her shoulders and he held her close. Her face lay pressed against his clean cotton shirt, and she felt his warm body beneath the thin layer of fabric, his heartbeat strong and steady.

14

Noah stood still in shock. He recognized the voice. As long as he lived, he knew he would never forget that soft, enticing voice that had a husky note, that made his heart beat quicker.

"Fanchette!"

She laughed, a deep throaty sound. "Go ahead and light a lamp, darlin'. I've been waitin' and waitin'."

Blankly, still in a state of shock, he struck a match. In seconds the lamp flared to life and he looked around. Fanchette sat in the straight-backed rocker. Her midnight tresses, crimped and parted in the center, were caught up high behind her head. Dark ringlets fell over her shoulders and down the back of her neck. Her eyes were deep brown, and as beautiful as he had remembered. Her skin was smooth, her mouth red.

She looked like a vision, unreal in the small frontier town where women usually dressed in gingham, calico, and muslin. Her blue faille dress was edged with lace, its skirt trimmed with a gathered flounce. The sleeves were underlain with puffs of white silk, and the dress looked like the latest Paris fashion, as if there had been no war, no hardships and deprivations. The low, square neckline pressed lightly against the creamy rise of her full breasts. His breath caught as his gaze drifted down, and for a moment he remembered how he had held her in his arms, how her soft body felt beneath his.

"What are you doing here?" he said, dazed. He was unable to fathom why she would be in New Mexico Territory, why she would be in his hotel room. Where was her husband? Questions swirled in his mind as she smiled and stood up.

"It's late and I should have done the proper thing and waited until tomorrow. I told them I was your sister and got them to let me in your room," she drawled seductively. She slowly crossed the room toward him. His heart jumped while memories stormed his senses. This was his first love. She had been the first woman in his life, and for a long time she had been the only woman. He remembered the pain when she had broken the engagement.

"I'm a widow, Noah," she whispered, his name sounding like No-*ah,* the accent on the last syllable. There was still a tinge of French in her southern drawl.

"I wanted to step in front of a Yankee bullet when I got your letter," he said gruffly, his pulse pounding.

She closed her eyes and then opened them. "I can't ever tell you how sorry I am, what a dreadful mistake I made."

"Go back to Alabama, Fanchette," he said bitterly.

"Oh, Noah!" She began to weep softly, standing only inches away. Her perfume assailed him, the same sweet fragrance she used to wear years ago. She turned her head, her eyes closed as tears spilled over her cheeks. His gaze raked over her. The low-cut dress hugged her full curves, her breasts larger now. For a moment he looked at the cleft between her milky mounds, and his body responded to his need to hold her.

"Don't cry!" he said.

"I hurt you so badly. I don't deserve anything, but I made a terrible mistake. Noah, I was just a young girl, bewildered by the war!" She raised her face and brushed away a tear. Her eyes were bright and she looked gorgeous with tears sparkling on her dark lashes. "I was lonely and young and frightened. Families were dissolving and homes were being destroyed, and you were so far away fighting battles that few of our brave boys returned from. But I was wrong! I was so wrong! I've loved only you."

He stared at her, torn between wanting to pull her

into his arms and forgive her, and the memory of how he had been hurt beyond any pain he had ever experienced.

"You should strike me for what I did to you!" she exclaimed, lifting her face, looking him in the eyes. She licked her lips, watching him, and he felt as if he were drowning in her black eyes. She was his first love . . .

"I couldn't possibly hit you," he whispered in a hoarse voice.

"Noah, *mon chèr*," she drawled, and raised her arms. "I want to marry you. I want you to come home with me . . ."

Without conscious thought, he slipped his arms around her. She pressed herself against him and his head tilted, coming down to kiss her, his arms tightening. Fanchette. Boyhood. Before the war, when there had been a future and peace and family. She was bound up in so many memories of his past, and he held her tightly, as if he could recapture some of that through her kisses.

"I was so foolish, darlin'," she whispered. "I made the worst mistake and I had to see you, had to find you and tell you."

Noah cupped her head with his hand and kissed her deeply. Words weren't important now. Her body fit against his and her kisses were sweet and hot. Fanchette. How many hours in battlefields so far from home he had dreamed about her, and now she was in his arms, clinging to him and telling him how sorry she was, that she was free again.

By dawn she lay in his arms in bed, gazing at him intently. "I owed you this night for a long, long time," she whispered, kissing his jaw. His hands stroked her body and he held her close to him.

He gazed at her, wanting her again. How good it was to have a beautiful woman in his arms, to feel her soft body against his in the night. He thought about marriage, and the image of April Danby floated into his thoughts. Noah frowned, shifting away from Fanchette. She propped herself up on her elbow and gazed down at him. Her dark hair fell over her shoulders, spilling across his chest. Her skin was pale and smooth, and his desire for her became all-important as he pulled her down in his arms.

It was midafternoon when April saw them leaving the hotel together. Fanchette was laughing as Noah helped her into a buggy. Something hurt as she watched them, and April told herself it was foolishness. She and Noah McCloud were enemies—or almost enemies. Nevertheless, she wondered who the beautiful dark-haired woman was. Her hand rested on Noah's arm possessively. He looked down at her as if he would devour her with his eyes.

As the days passed, April saw him more and more with the same woman. He rarely came to the saloon anymore, and finally she began to wonder if he had given up the notion that she had his gold. Then one night two weeks later, he was back again. The moment she looked down through the haze of smoke and gazed into his eyes, her heart lurched, and then pounded violently.

When she sang her ballad, she sang to him, watching him. A frown came to his face, yet he gazed back steadily at her until the world seemed to disappear. The saloon filled with men seemed to vanish, and only Noah McCloud was there. For two beats after the song had finished, she still watched him, turning abruptly to move across the stage. Later, when she tossed her handkerchief, a man moved across the space between tables and snatched it out of the air before it fell near Noah's chair. Noah had made no attempt to catch it.

That night when she stepped out the back door to go home, Noah was waiting.

"I thought maybe you had decided I was telling you the truth about the gold."

"Not at all." He rode beside her buggy. "Time's passing and I need to get the gold and get home," he said, gazing into the darkness. His voice held a distant note. She glanced at him, knowing the beautiful woman she had seen him with lately had caused the change in him. April had heard the woman was from Alabama, Noah's home state.

"Who's your friend?" she asked, and felt a strange premonition that they were on a touchy subject.

"Fanchette Viguerie Craddock. She was engaged to me during the war. She's the first woman I ever loved, the only one," he said. He looked at April. "I'm going to marry her."

His voice was solemn, and his words caused a strange sense of loss in April. She raised her chin and studied him as he rode beside her, his back as straight as a fencepost. "How nice," she said, but her voice was flat and without enthusiasm.

"I want to get my gold, go home, and marry Fanchette. I'm going to rebuild the house I lost. Fanchette will go home, wait for me, and we'll be married when I return."

"So you decided to go back to the South and raise cotton."

"It's all I really know except running a saloon."

"Lean Henry said you're doing well with your business."

Noah shrugged. "I've been lucky with it. It's a nice business as long as I keep order."

They turned on the path to her house, and she stopped in the backyard. Noah dismounted and waited, no longer swinging her down out of the buggy as he had always done before. As they moved toward her door, they both reached for the knob at the same moment, and his hand folded over hers. While he withdrew it at once, his eyes narrowed and their gazes locked for a moment. Tension flared between them.

"Give me your key."

She handed it to him, and their fingers brushed. April was inordinately aware of the faintest contact. While he unlocked the door, she stared at his broad shoulders. She knew she would miss him. If only the gold hadn't been an issue between them! He was the first man whose kisses had stirred her since Emilio. She tried to brush aside the thoughts, telling herself

Noah McCloud was marrying another woman and moving to Alabama. She mustn't think of his kisses.

He shoved open the door on the empty kitchen and stepped back to let her enter first.

"I'll light a lamp," he began as April's knees hit a hard object. She yelped, starting to fall, but Noah caught her. He swore, and a chair scraped on the floor.

"Something's happened," she said, feeling for familiar furniture and finding only space.

A match flared to life, the tiny flame providing sufficient illumination. April gasped, her hand flying to her mouth while Noah swore. Drawers were spilled, the walls had gaping holes hacked in them, the tables and chairs were overturned, and dishes had been broken.

"Oh, no! Why would anyone do this?" she asked, dazed by the wreckage.

Noah lit a lamp and picked up a fallen chair, bits of dishes crunching underfoot as he led the way into the parlor, which was just as wrecked.

"Why would anyone do this?" she repeated in a daze. "I haven't got any enemies. I don't have any money."

Noah turned to look at her, watching her kneel in the rubble of her possessions. She picked up a tintype of Luke and Catalina. April looked stunned, her face pale as snow, her hands trembling. He wanted to pull her into his arms and comfort her. She clasped the tintype and picked up a book Luke had given her. It had been tossed down and walked on, wrinkled pages fluttering out.

"It's only *things,* and things aren't really that important," she said in a forlorn voice. "But for so many years I didn't own anything . . ." Her voice trailed away and she looked up at Noah and drew a deep breath. "What could they want?" She gazed at the ruined parlor.

"The same thing I do," Noah answered quietly, watching her closely. He would bet every dollar he owned that she wasn't acting, that it hadn't occurred to her why someone had almost destroyed her house.

And for the first time, doubts assailed him about his accusations against her. "They wanted the gold," he stated quietly.

April's eyes flew wide. "I don't have any gold!" she cried. Noah believed her, and he had to reassess a lot of things. He knew she wasn't acting. She might be good on the stage, but she wasn't this good. Her eyes narrowed and she stared at him. "Did you do this?"

Surprised, he realized that would be a natural assumption, and he thanked fortune that he had been in the front row at the saloon all evening long. "No, I didn't," he answered. He saw the doubt in her eyes and he couldn't blame her. "You saw me. I was right there in front of you all evening."

"You could have had someone do it for you while you stayed at the saloon."

"I could have, but I didn't."

As April stared at him, he met her gaze. His eyes were wide and guileless, but she knew how men could lie and steal and cheat. Yet it wasn't like Noah to hire someone to do this work. He was a loner, and he took care of his own errands. She knew that from the past few months since he had arrived in town.

She ran her hand over her forehead, her eyes widening as she gazed up at him. "Someone thinks I have gold? I can't believe that!"

"What other explanation can you give for this? Whoever did this was searching for something," he said solemnly, bending down to stand a table upright again. He righted the overturned settee.

"What are you doing?"

"I'll help you straighten things out. You should tell the sheriff. Do you want me to go get him?"

"In a moment," she said, running her hands along her skirt. "Right now I'd rather have your company."

Noah stared at her, frowning as she picked up a slashed pillow and began to gather up clumps of strewn goose feathers. She kept turning the pillow in her hand, white feathers drifting about her feet. "I didn't have anything that was mine for so long. This shouldn't be so important to me . . . ." Her voice faded and he crossed the room to catch her in his arms, holding her against him.

"Go ahead and cry over it. It's no sin to shed a few tears."

She clung to him tightly, burying her head against his chest. She was glad for his quiet strength and his understanding. "I made most of these things. Luke made the rocking chair for me . . ."

"Sorry, April," he said softly. It was the first time he had called her by her first name, and in spite of her shock over her house, she noticed the change in him. She tightened her arms around him, giving vent to tears for a moment. In spite of her sorrow and shock, she was aware of his strength, his long, lean frame pressed against her. Gaining control of her emotions, she moved away.

"I'm glad you're here," she said, speaking so softly that he barely heard her.

"I'm glad too," he answered, studying her. Her dresses, except those she wore onstage, weren't stylish and fancy like Fanchette's. Her hair was natural, not crimped or braided with pearls winding in it, but she was as beautiful as Fanchette. He studied her profile, her full lips that were rosy and soft, her straight nose and broad forehead. He hated what had happened to her, and promised himself he would find whoever had done this. He was also thankful he had decided to go talk to her about the gold tonight. His gaze went over the furniture. "They sure as hell were looking for something sizable."

"What do you mean?"

"Look at the room. The rocker is fine. Most of your books are okay unless they were in the way of something behind them. It's the big things, where someone could hide bags of gold, that have been chopped up or smashed."

"You're right. I guess this just makes you all the more certain I've lied to you," she said in a level voice. Noah studied her, wondering if her control was growing thin again.

"On the contrary," he said quietly. "For the first time, I'm beginning to think you've told me the truth."

Startled, April stopped stuffing the goose feathers back into the torn pillow. "Why?"

"Your reaction to all this."

"I can't follow your line of reasoning, Noah Mc-Cloud, but if it took this to make you see the truth, then maybe this isn't that big of a disaster after all!" She picked some books off the floor and righted a chair, working quietly.

As he watched her, he wanted to hug her. In spite of the disaster and her shock, she was picking up the pieces. And now he believed her—she didn't have the gold and never had known anything about it. If she didn't have the gold, though, where was it and why had Ralph written that she did?

She looked up at him, her eyes flying wide. "Tigre's gold!"

Noah moved ahead of her to the bedroom to light a lamp while she went to the armoire. "Lord, it's gone!"

"What's worse, it'll be proof to whoever broke in here that you have the gold and you know where the rest of it is," he said grimly. "April," he said, catching her wrist, "come with me to get the sheriff. I don't want you to stay here alone."

She gave him a faint smile. "You can't stay with me all the time. I'll be safe. You get Sheriff Pacheco and I'll pick up while you're gone."

"No," he said forcefully. "Please come with me."

She stared at him a moment, shrugged, then nodded. As they rode along the street in the quiet night, she voiced her worries.

"Who could have done that? No one knows about the gold except the Yishays and Ta-ne-haddle and Melissa. No one else knows."

"More people probably know than you realize," he said solemnly. "Aaron Yishay told me as much. And people probably know I'm here after it." Worries plagued him and he studied her in the dark. "April, could you stay with friends for a while? Go stay at the Hatfields' or the Yishays'?"

She stared at him, and he couldn't tell what she was thinking. She drew herself up in the saddle, sitting straight as a ramrod. "I can take care of myself, and it's not your place to worry about me."

And then he realized that for the past half-hour he had completely forgotten Fanchette. He frowned and stopped watching April, suddenly aware that his gaze had been lingering on her. Feeling a rush of guilt for forgetting Fanchette, he looked away quickly. His mind shifted back to the problem at hand, reassessing the evening. "April, it's a quarter of a million in gold bullion and ingots. There are people who would gladly murder for a fortune like that."

"I can't go live with someone else."

"Do you know how to use a pistol?"

"Yes. I have a derringer."

"I'll get you a six-shooter. Will you carry it all the time?"

"If you'd like," she answered in a peculiar voice, and he wondered whether she really would.

Sheriff Pacheco returned with them, swearing about all the calamity. He frowned, running his hand across his forehead. "You don't know why this happened?"

April stared at him and then looked at Noah.

"Sheriff," Noah said, "I'll tell you something, but I'd like it kept as quiet as possible."

"What's that?"

"April doesn't know anything about it, but one night, almost a year ago, my brother, a Rebel soldier, stopped in her dressing room and then followed her home. He wrote to me that he hid our family gold with her. She's innocent in this and didn't know one thing about it."

April stared at him, amazed at his statements about her innocence. She had hidden his brother, and after all this time, she didn't see how trouble could come from admitting it. "Sheriff, he's trying—"

"I'm trying to tell you the situation," Noah interrupted. He moved to slip his arm around her waist, and squeezed her tightly, as if hoping to signal her to keep quiet about Ralph. "She's innocent, but someone thinks she has our gold."

"Mr. McCloud, I've heard rumors about the gold for two months now. Some say it's a hoard of a million dollars in gold you're searching for. Speculation was that you're hanging around town looking for it. At least until you bought the saloon. That sorta killed some of the rumors.

"Do you have any idea about who could have done this?" Pacheco asked.

Noah's arm was still around April. She was intensely aware of being pressed to his side, aware of the deep rumble of his voice. She couldn't understand why he was still holding her. "No, I don't. I wish I did."

"Miss April, you shouldn't stay here alone," Pacheco warned.

"I'll be all right."

"Ma'am, begging your pardon, whoever did this is a mean, ornery cuss. You're a beautiful woman. There are a lot of drifters and outlaws who pass through these parts who wouldn't think twice about taking a pretty lady with them. Especially if they thought she could tell them where she has gold hidden. And, Miss April, you shouldn't say much about that Rebel. The army takes a sour view of people who help wanted men. And that goes double for that Castillo outlaw. Don't confront him again. Let the men handle it. Mr. McCloud, can't you see to it that she stays with someone?"

"I'll try," Noah said, "but as you know, Miss Danby has a wide streak of independence."

"Well, that can get a woman in a hell—sorry, in a lot of trouble in these parts."

There was a knock on the door, and all three turned to stare at it. Sheriff Pacheco withdrew his six-shooter. "I'll answer it," he said. He moved toward the door, and April glanced up at Noah. He still had his arm around her, and she had no inclination to move away.

"Get back out of the way, April," Noah said, moving her toward the door to the bedroom. He leaned down to whisper, "And don't admit one word about harboring Ralph."

"Yes, sir, Mr. McCloud," she said primly.

His hand dropped to his holster and he stood in front of her. She peered around him to see Sheriff Pacheco throw open the door and raise his pistol.

Vesta Dodworth's jaw dropped; then she screamed and reeled, her knees buckling.

"Damn and tarnation!" he swore. "Miz Dodworth! What are you doing out at this hour?" He caught her, helping her inside to a chair as she fanned herself with a lace handkerchief. She gasped and moaned.

"I never expected to have a pistol waved in my face!" she said faintly.

"This is Mr. McCloud. McCloud, meet Miz Vesta Dodworth. This is the man you always talk about," he said under his breath to her.

"How do you do, Mr. McCloud. I saw the three of you come in and I thought there might be some trouble. I thought I should come see . . ." Her voice trailed off because she had noticed the condition of April's parlor. April knew the news would be spread over Albuquerque before the next sundown. "What happened?"

"Some thieving varmint broke into Miss April's while she was away. Now, maybe you better get back home and lock yourself inside."

"Oh, my gracious! My gracious! April, dear, you poor thing! What can Lesta and I do?"

"It's late, and there's nothing much any of us can do tonight," April said. "Thank you. You didn't see anyone coming or going from my house earlier, did you?"

"Good heavens, no! Wilma Hawkins came to call, and we chatted for hours."

"Let me see you home," Sheriff Pacheco said, taking her arm.

"Thank you, Sheriff. My word, a body isn't safe. April, you can come stay with us."

"Thank you, Mrs. Dodworth, I'll be fine."

"Miss Danby, want me to send my boys to help put things back together?" Sheriff Pacheco asked.

"No, thanks. I'll manage."

"You take care of yourself," he said sternly, and looked at Noah. "You should see that she does."

Sheriff Pacheco left with Vesta Dodworth, and as soon as they were gone, Noah faced April. "I mean it. Don't tell anyone that you sheltered Ralph. There's a lot of gold missing. Someone is after it, and the less said, the better. I was going to give you a good hard squeeze if you started to say something more about it."

So that was why he had kept his arm so tightly around her. She nodded. "Thanks for all you've done."

"You're not going to sleep anyway, so I'll help you pick up the pieces."

"You don't need to."

"I know I don't. I may have brought all this trouble on you. No one bothered you after Ralph was here. The trouble didn't start until after I came to town."

"Don't blame yourself. But at least now you don't have to try to buy out Lean Henry and put me out of work," she added lightly.

His scowl deepened. "Sorry about that too."

"I was teasing," she said gently.

"I was going to do exactly that. I'm sorry."

"It's all right. I understand," she said, wishing now he would stop condemning himself. She began putting her house back in order.

Noah moved a heavy chest back in place in the bedroom. Her bed had been slashed, and April smoothed it over. He watched her while he worked, pausing to openly study her when she climbed on a footstool to put a folded blanket back on a high shelf. Her dress pulled tautly over her breasts, and her narrow waist was outlined. He suffered a compelling urge to go lift her off the footstool and into his arms. The blanket fell, because she wasn't quite tall enough to get it on the shelf. He couldn't resist and moved to her side, lifting her down.

He caught her by surprise. There was nowhere to put her hands except on his shoulders, and for just a moment he let his hands linger on her waist. He didn't want to release her. His chest felt tight, and he gazed down into her ash-colored eyes, questions flooding him. Why was he still reacting to her? He was in love with Fanchette, engaged to Fanchette. Now he couldn't blame his deep reactions to April on the fact that he had been so long without a woman. He had a beautiful, exciting woman waiting at the hotel, and he shouldn't be drawn to April, or feel his blood heat as he watched her.

She stepped away abruptly as the blanket toppled out again, and Noah caught it. He pushed it back on the shelf easily, and when he turned, April had gone back to the parlor to work. Frowning, he stared after her, and then made an effort to put her out of his thoughts while he worked twice as fast.

Within the hour they were both working in the same room again. He straightened up to watch her. "You shouldn't stay alone."

"Whoever did this will also realize that I don't have anything hidden. I can't run forever, and I can't move in with someone else."

"Damn," he said quietly. "Just be careful. Is it general knowledge around town that you receive money from Luke?"

"I don't know."

"If it isn't, someone might think just as I did, that all this was McCloud gold. I think you're in danger." They gazed into each other's eyes, and all she could think was that he was engaged to a beautiful woman now.

"Don't worry about me," she said sharply. "It's not your place to worry."

He turned away and they both worked in silence until she stopped and found him surveying the room.

"What's wrong?" she asked him.

"I was thinking about Ralph's letter."

She picked up a patterned red-and-blue quilt and

folded it. "I've been thinking about his letter too. There are several possibilities."

"What have you thought of?" he asked.

"First, whoever was searching for something may have found it and gone."

"I rule that out," he said. "There's too much destruction. It looks as if someone searched long and hard."

She placed the quilt on the foot of the bed. "Someone else may have found the gold long ago and taken it, and I never knew a thing about it."

"Or Ralph might not have been clear enough to know what he was writing."

She shook her head. "I was with him. He was clear in his thoughts. There's another possibility. Ralph may have hidden a note here that will tell us where he left the gold, because he wasn't carrying gold with him when he was with me. Not any that I saw."

Noah nodded. "I agree. That seems most likely." His gaze swept the room.

"I'll search for a note. This is enough work for tonight. I'm finally getting sleepy."

"Let me stay in the parlor. I don't think you should be here alone," he said. He feared for her safety, as he felt drawn to her more than ever.

"I have to stay by myself," she said firmly. She wanted him there, but was unable to forget his engagement. "You can't be here tomorrow night and the next and the next."

"I intend to find out who did this as soon as I can."

"You may never find out, and you know it. No, go home, Mr. McCloud."

"Say my name, April," he said. His voice was husky, making her forget their argument as she became aware of his nearness.

There were several heartbeats of silence. "Noah." It sounded different from any other name she had ever said. Why did it take such an effort? "Now, you go home," she said, feeling the tension pull between them. There was an attraction that held invisible fire, and it was impossible to avoid. His eyes narrowed before he turned away from her, jamming his hands into his pockets.

"I'll go now. If you need help—"

"Thank you," she answered quietly, wanting him to stay, and knowing her feelings had nothing to do with her need for safety. She followed him to the door, where he paused, studying her. She couldn't get her breath as she gazed into his stormy expression.

"You don't look as if you've gone all night without sleep and had your house torn to pieces."

Or learned that you're getting married, she thought. "I'll be all right."

"Whoever did this is capable of violence," he said grimly, looking beyond her. "How do you get word to that Kiowa that you need him?"

She shrugged. "I don't know. I've never had a real emergency before. Word just gets to him. He's always close, but I don't know how to find him."

"Well, I'll put out word in town tomorrow that he's needed. Good night, April," he said, jamming his hat on his head. He left, and she stood in the silent house, his words echoing in her mind repeatedly: ". . . *Fanchette will go home and wait for me . . . we'll be married . . .*"

It hurt, the cold fact that he would go back to Alabama and marry his first love. She tried to stop thinking about him, but it was impossible. She finished picking up her broken things, her mind going over the conversations they had had, the times they had spent at the river. She had always thought there would never be another man who could stir her feelings as Emilio had, but she had to admit there was one now.

She tried to shift her thoughts from Noah to the missing gold, but she couldn't.

Meanwhile Noah rode into the field behind her house and dismounted. He tethered his horse away from her place and walked back to sit on the hard ground, listening to an owl hoot and to the distant yip of a coyote. Fanchette would just have to wait. He was afraid for April's safety. He saw that a light still burned in

her parlor, and he wondered if sleep was as lost to her
as it was to him.

As April walked down the street toward the general
store, she saw Noah and Fanchette waiting for the
stage. They were directly in her path. Noah looked up
and smiled, and Fanchette turned her head to stare at
April, so there was nothing to do but go meet Fanchette. April's sweeping glance took in Fanchette's
stunning traveling dress of russet glacé silk trimmed
in black lace. Her parasol matched her dress, as well
as the pert little russet bonnet perched on her head
and tied beneath her chin. She looked impervious to
dust and heat. Her skin was creamy, far paler than
April's, which had been exposed to the New Mexico
sunshine. Lace gloves covered her tiny hands. Like her
dress, her hair was the latest fashion. Crimped, parted
in the center, braided, and looped on the sides of her
head, it was pulled back to reveal onyx earrings in her
dainty ears.

As beautiful as she looked, it was Noah standing
beside her who was breathtaking. He wore a leather
vest, white shirt, and blue denims, his hat pushed back
casually on his head. April was once again struck with
how handsome he was.

And she became acutely conscious of her own hand-
made blue gingham, which was plain, and the simple
blue bow in her hair.

"April, I want you to meet my fiancée, Fanchette
Craddock. Fanchette, I've told you about April
Danby," Noah said, his arm around Fanchette's waist.

"*Enchantée.* I'm so happy we could meet before I
catch the stage!" Fanchette exclaimed with far more
enthusiasm than April could muster. "You're the one
who helped our darlin' Ralph." She stepped forward
and gave April a little hug. A heady perfume assailed
April's senses. "And Noah owes you a hundred apol-
ogies for thinking you've been living on Ralph's gold."

"It was an understandable mistake," April said,
amazed Fanchette had come out with such a state-

ment. She felt thrown off-balance by Fanchette's self-assurance and happiness.

"I keep telling him there's enough left at home, home being Alabama, that he doesn't need the Mc-Cloud gold. After all, the late Mr. Craddock left me everything, and his sympathies were such during the war that our home was not destroyed. *Sacrebleu!* Noah doesn't need so much as another pinch of gold dust. But you probably know by now that my fiancé has a stubborn streak." She laughed, and April smiled and couldn't help liking her. She was sunny, sophisticated, and the most beautiful woman April had ever seen. She looked like a china doll, not a hair out of place.

"Yes, I do know a little about that," April admitted, glancing up to find Noah watching her. "If you'd trust me, I'd promise to send word to you in Alabama if the gold ever does turn up."

"I trust you," he answered in a somber tone. "But I'm staying to look around a little more. I'll sell my saloon before I leave."

"It is impossible to imagine Noah running a saloon!" Fanchette exclaimed.

"You're brave to come all this way alone," April said, studying her. The sun was rising high in the sky, beating down and promising a scorching day, yet beneath her parasol, Fanchette looked cool and fresh.

"Oh, I'd be terrified to do such a thing. Papa came with me as far as Santa Fe, where Cousin Raoul lives! I insisted that I be allowed to come to Albuquerque to see Noah without all my protectors. One of our house servants and my mammy came with us, and they can't wait to see Captain McCloud again," she said, smiling up at Noah and revealing dimples in each cheek. She bestowed her smile on April next.

"I hope you have a good trip back to Alabama," April said. She tried to sound polite, yet knew her voice had a stiffness to it. She wanted to get away from them and their happiness. Away from Fanchette, who was radiant over Noah.

"Thank you. It's been interesting to see so much of the world. I'd never been out of Baldwin County before,'' she said in her soft southern drawl, her hand still resting lightly on Noah's arm. "If you ever come to Alabama, we'd be so happy to have you visit us.''

"Thank you, Mrs. Craddock,'' April said.

"You must call me Fanchette.''

Noah listened to the exchange between the two, and his emotions were stormy. Fanchette was breathtakingly beautiful, the embodiment of a boyhood dream. He had wanted her for so long, dreamed of her so many times, possessed her, and now he didn't want to put her on the stage for Alabama. Yet, at the same time, it was April whose arrival had quickened his pulse, April who held his attention. He knew part of Fanchette's breathtaking beauty was created by her expensive, fashionable wardrobe, and part of her attraction was bound up in his dreams of the past.

Both women dazzled him. It had seemed so right to take Fanchette in his arms, to renew his pledge of marriage that she had broken long ago, but as he gazed down at April, he felt as if he had lost something precious. She cut a glance at him, then instantly returned her gaze to Fanchette. He noticed her cheeks becoming pink, and he wondered what was going through her mind. And the thought of her pining away for a lost childhood love was beginning to grate on his nerves more and more. It was a waste of a woman who was warm and loving, who should have her own family.

"Noah told me you sing, and I just think that's marvelous! How wonderful to have a talent and be able to use it. I'd be terrified to get up on a stage. It makes my heart palpitate to think about it!''

April laughed politely and realized there was a world of difference between her life and Fanchette Craddock's existence.

"I'll be on my way,'' April said quietly, hurting in a manner that surprised her. "It was nice to meet you.''

"Oh, Miss Danby, *chérie*, it was so nice to meet you! I hope you can keep my Noah out of trouble until he decides to stop this silly hunting for gold. It was probably stolen from poor Ralph anyway. Do come to Alabama to visit us,'' she said, flashing another spectacular smile.

''Thank you.''

''Right now, I can't wait to get home and announce our coming marriage to everyone in the county!'' she exclaimed, smiling again at Noah, who stood solemnly staring at April.

She nodded to him and left, walking away from them and feeling as if the hot morning sun was suffocating her. Wisps of hair had slipped from the ribbon and curled around her cheeks in spite of her bonnet. She felt damp with perspiration from the heat, her feet were dusty from crossing the road, and she was acutely conscious of her gingham dress. It hurt to watch Noah with Fanchette. She had to keep reminding herself that it was absurd for her to hurt so much over Noah. Absolutely absurd. Where was her deep eternal love for Emilio? She and Noah McCloud had been more enemies than friends. As swiftly as that argument rose to mind, however, she realized that they had become friends. She found him easy to talk to at times, exciting to be with. Clamping her jaw down, she went into the cool interior of the general store. As she shopped, she heard the stage rumble past, sending a cloud of dust dancing in its wake.

She moved closer to the front window and watched as it stopped. A group of men unloaded boxes and trunks. A passenger alighted, and then it was time for Fanchette to board. She turned to Noah, lifting her arms and standing on tiptoe as he pulled her to him and kissed her. A suffocating pain engulfed April. She turned away, moving down the long aisle, unaware of her surroundings, finally acknowledging that she had fallen in love with Noah McCloud.

15

Dazed, April ran her errands and hurried home, thankful she hadn't encountered Noah on the way. She was afraid he would take one look at her and guess excatly how she felt about him. She needed to get her emotions composed before she saw him again.

As she first came in sight of her house and the buggy by the front door, her heart lurched. She thought Noah might be waiting, but then she recognized the Hatfields' buggy.

As soon as she halted, Melissa climbed down to help April carry her packages inside. "I guess word's already all over town," April said. "It'll take me a long time to get my house back like it was. Thanks for coming to visit."

"I wish I deserved the thanks, but I don't know what you're talk—" Melissa had followed April inside, and now she stood with her mouth open in surprise while she stared at the shambles of a room that was usually neat and tidy. "What happened?"

Surprised, April stopped to look at her friend, and for the first time realized that Melissa had her own problems. Her skin was pale as snow, and a frown creased her brow. "Someone broke in last night and did this. Noah, Mr. McCloud, thinks they were searching for his gold."

"How dreadful! Oh, April, you can't stay here! I'd be terrified to come back home."

"I'll be fine," she said, wondering how many people she had reassured that morning. "What's wrong?"

"Why would anyone think you have the McCloud gold? I thought that was a secret."

"Probably because Noah McCloud is searching for it. You know how rumors and gossip go through a town."

"I'm so sorry!" Melissa said. "I can't believe someone would do this. Mama will want you to come stay with us."

"I'm all right. Enough about my problems. What about yours?"

Instantly Melissa's eyes clouded with worry. "Patrick wants to see me. He says he has to."

"You want to meet here again?" April asked quietly.

"Yes. I think he knows about Tigre!" Melissa said as if her heart were breaking in two. She gripped April's arm. "I don't know what to do! I love Tigre, but I hate to have to tell Patrick."

"Tigre! You only saw him that one—" April bit off her words as she saw Melissa's cheeks turn bright pink. "You've been seeing him! I thought he went to California. When?"

"He's slipped back at night."

"Where do you meet?" April asked, aghast as she mulled over the implications.

"In my room," Melissa admitted, her face turning crimson.

"Your room! Melissa, if your father catches him, he'll shoot him! And he will catch him if he's going to your room at night."

"I know it, but I have to see him." She grasped April's hand. "I love him! April, he's wonderful, and so gentle."

"He's wanted for murder!" April said softly. She stared at her friend, astounded and worried. "You can't love him!"

"I know I shouldn't, but I can't help it."

April became silent, thinking she couldn't even take her own advice. She loved Noah McCloud as surely as there was a sun in the sky, and it was as unwise and foolish as Melissa's love for Tigre.

"Melissa, Tigre hasn't asked you to run off with him, has he?"

"No. But I love him." Suddenly she burst into tears. "I love him! I adore him."

April hugged her, feeling infinitely older, when little more than three years separated them in age. "Melissa, you can't find happiness with him. He can't settle, he can't have a family. The sooner you break it off, the better off you'll be," she said, knowing the advice would go unheeded.

"Tigre's wonderful. Oh, April, he's wonderful." She frowned and moved away. "And Patrick is wonderful too in his own way. He isn't exciting like Tigre, or as dashing and brave, but he's a good man and he really loves me. And he has humor and patience—something that my father has never had. I don't want to hurt him."

"Then don't, Melissa. Patrick is good," she said, thinking of the tall redhead. "He adores you and he would give you everything in his power. It's so hopeless to love Tigre."

"But I do. Yet I can't bear to tell Patrick."

"You had better weigh the choices long and hard before you make a final decision." She started to add that Tigre would bring only heartbreak, but then April thought better of it. How was she to know what life with Tigre might bring? There were places where he could go and assume a new life and live as peacefully as an average citizen. She suspected that more than one man in Albuquerque had a new identity and new family, having left behind a tragic past.

"Both are good men," she said finally.

"That's what makes it so difficult. I thought I loved Patrick."

"Maybe you don't love Tigre as much as you think, if you don't want to tell Patrick about him. If both could court you in a normal manner, you might feel differently about them. Tigre causes a stir wherever he goes, but don't mistake that for love."

"I know. Part of me loves Patrick," she said in a whisper. "I don't want to run from the law, to love a man who may hang."

"Then there's your answer," April said gently.

Melissa wrung her hands together. "No, because I love Tigre too! He's marvelous and his kisses almost make me faint."

"Maybe you shouldn't make a choice yet. Take more time."

"I don't know what to do. But Patrick insists on seeing me."

"You can meet here again. What night would you like?"

"Tuesday," Melissa suggested.

"Fine," April agreed, concerned for her friend.

"Thanks, April. Let me help you with your things." They worked together, Melissa talking about the two men in her life while April tried to keep her thoughts off Noah, an impossible task.

That afternoon she rode to the Brown Owl to go to work. She had to pass McCloud's Place on her way to Lean Henry's saloon. She sat stiffly in the buggy, trying to stare straight ahead. She knew that Noah was inside, and she longed to see him. Each day she had watched the progress he was making on his saloon. He had enlarged the building and hauled in new furnishings. At first it had been a threat, because he seemed to be able to acquire saloons too easily and force her out of work, but now the threat had vanished. Although he finally believed her, he still watched her as intently as ever, and she supposed that was his manner with everyone. This morning as he had stood beside Fanchette, every time April had glanced into his blue eyes they seemed to be trying to probe to the depths of her soul.

She tried to avoid looking at the saloon. She was tempted to glance over just to see if she could catch sight of him. Compulsion was too strong, and she turned her head to gaze inside the dark interior. Although she was unable to see anything, she was acutely aware that he was only yards away. She turned away quickly, knowing that if he were watching, he could easily see her staring. Piano music floated in the air through the open door, and she wondered what he was doing. She turned behind the Brown Owl, glancing back to her right at Noah's saloon. He was only a block away. Separated by a block and an engagement.

April drew herself up and shivered in the sunlight, feeling a chill. Fanchette Craddock was a lady, a silken, beautiful southern lady who had grown up with servants, who was accustomed to the life Noah had known. She didn't sing in a saloon to support herself, nor did she work and talk with coarse frontiersmen. April clamped her jaws together and tried to stop making futile comparisons. All they had had were a few kisses, something casual to him, something forgotten. His Saturday visits had stopped with Fanchette's arrival, and April missed his companionship.

Noah watched her drive past. He had been standing at the bar talking to Aaron Yishay, who stopped in about four times a week. Aaron had seen her first. "There goes Miss April."

Noah turned to see her sitting in her buggy, her back straight, her blue gingham dress buttoned primly to her chin. Her profile was to him, and he wanted to go out and speak to her. He watched her gaze coolly toward his saloon.

His eyes followed her through the window as she turned to go behind the Brown Owl. She glanced back in his direction once more, and he was still tempted to hurry out and speak to her. It dawned on him that Aaron Yishay was looking at him expectantly and had been talking.

"Sorry. What did you say?"

"I asked how long you're going to stay in town."

"I don't know. I want to find out who broke into April's place, and I want my gold."

"I heard you got engaged to the lady from Alabama."

"Fanchette," Noah answered, wondering if anything happened in Albuquerque that Aaron Yishay didn't know about.

"That's a long distance for the lady to travel. Guess she knew you from before."

"We were engaged once before, and she married

Samuel Craddock while I was fighting. She's widowed now, so we'll marry and I'll go home to Alabama," he said, knowing Yishay would worm it out of him sooner or later. "I'm going to the back to work. Bring your drink and look at what I've done."

Aaron followed him the length of the long barroom to the back door. "Hear you're going to sell beer on the Plaza during Fiesta."

"That's right. I'm building a booth right now."

"Miss April's going to sing."

Noah gave him a surprised look. "I'm amazed the town ladies would permit it."

Aaron chuckled. "She'll sing the sweet stuff that she does on Sunday mornings in church. All the ladies in town approve of Miss April."

They stepped through the back door onto dusty ground. Piles of freshly cut lumber filled the air with the smell of sawdust and pine. Two men were hammering on joists for the roof. Noah was enlarging the saloon, adding fifteen feet to its length. He had the area framed in with lumber, and soon would lift the walls in place. Aaron Yishay stood in the sunlight and gazed around. "Seems like a hell of a lot of work for a man who's going to quit business and leave the territory."

Noah felt a flicker of annoyance, not getting the response he had expected. "It'll be a better saloon."

"It'll be damned expensive to sell. You're changing this into the fanciest saloon in the territory."

"It's turning a dollar right well. When the addition is finished, I'm getting a new back bar," Noah said, picking up a board to mark it off to saw. "Sit down on that barrel." He motioned with his hand. "I saw a back bar in Santa Fe that I can buy. It's five feet longer than the one I have now, and that'll make it thirty feet long. It has a beveled mirror with a carved hardwood frame."

"I hear you moved into your house."

"I decided I might as well save money and live there. Actually, if I were staying, that house would be promising. I like it."

208   *Sara Orwig*

"Mighty big."

"I grew up in a big house. Bel Arbre was three stories high. This one just spreads out like a watermelon vine." He bent over the board, measuring carefully.

"How much danger do you think April's in?"

Noah raised his head to gaze into the doctor's curious black eyes. "A lot," he answered solemnly. "It doesn't help for her to live alone or to travel back and forth to the saloon and sing."

"What's her singing have to do with anything?"

Noah shifted impatiently. The thought of April prancing around onstage in front of cowmen and drifters had bothered him lately more than he cared to admit. He shouldn't care, but every time he saw her ride past in her buggy, visions of her performing floated into his mind. He wanted to go pull her down off the stage and tell her to go home. "April's a fine person. She ought to marry some nice man and have a family," he said, and the words had a hollow ring to them.

"I think Miss April is in love," Aaron said quietly.

Noah's head snapped up, and he felt as if he had been hit by a lightning bolt. And then common sense set in. "She can't be! She never sees anyone," he snapped, staring at Aaron. "Who's the man?" he demanded brusquely.

"Son, for an engaged man, you're mighty touchy about the subject of Miss April's love."

Noah's patience was gone. "Who's the man?"

"She loved him a long time ago."

"Oh, hell. Emilio Piedra," Noah said as the stiffness went out of his shoulders. He bent over his work again, but in seconds he glanced back at Aaron who sat blandly sipping his drink and smiling at Noah.

"You did that on purpose, didn't you?"

"What?"

"Told me April's in love. You think I'm in love with her."

"Are you?"

"No, I'm not," he declared forcefully. "I love Fanchette. I'm going to marry Fanchette."

"Son, you don't have to convince me."

Noah glared at him. Yishay's meddlesome nature annoyed him, yet he liked him and enjoyed his company. "If I didn't love Fanchette . . ." he said, and his voice faded. His gaze drifted off and he forgot Aaron Yishay while he thought about the possibilities. If Fanchette were still married to Samuel . . . Now that Noah knew, April wasn't lying about the gold, now that he had a thriving business in a town he liked, with friends in the town . . . April . . . He thought about her wide ash-colored eyes, her laughter, her sensuous kisses that always made his blood heat.

He swore and bent over the board to go back to work.

"Someday April will fall in love again," Aaron Yishay said airily, and Noah wished he would go back to the bar.

"I hope so. Waste of a wonderful woman as it is."

"You really think April's wonderful, huh?"

Noah straightened up. "Doc, gét off my back about April."

"Oh, I didn't mean anything. You're engaged and you're going back to Alabama. It's just nice to hear a good man sing her praises. She'll fall in love and marry. April's not the kind to wither on the vine. I'll tell you what, McCloud. I'd bet a half-acre of land that Miss April is married before her twenty-second birthday."

"I hope you're right, and I'm not taking that bet."

Aaron chuckled and stood up, waving his empty glass at Noah. "I'll be back, McCloud. Damned good whiskey. Fine saloon. A truly fine saloon," he said as he left.

Noah stared after him in consternation. The thought of April falling in love bothered him, he had to admit. As much as he hated to think about her living alone and singing onstage, he found it more disconcerting to think about her falling in love. By twenty-two. He bent over the board, sawing vigorously. Then he lifted it up to carry to Hosea and Juan, who were working.

"Here's the board you needed for the back door," he said. "I'll cut the other two now."

He went back to measure the next one, his thoughts drifting again to April.

"Boss," Hosea said, holding the board upright in place. "This is a foot short."

Noah stared at it and swore. He marched over to look. "I'll redo it." He carried it back grimly, tossed it on a pile, and picked up another long board in its place. He bent over it to measure, and wondered if April would wear her green silk dress tonight or the red. He swore again, throwing down a piece of chalk. If he didn't get his mind off April, he wouldn't get anything built! He gazed around at the new structure. It might be difficult to sell soon, because it was going to be a sizable investment. And there were moments when Alabama seemed damned far away. He raked his fingers through his hair.

"Hosea, can you cut this lumber?"

"Sure, boss."

Noah marched through the framework and around to the side of the building, pulling out a cheroot to light it. It was still an hour before dark, too early for customers to flock to the saloons. Another hour, and music would come from Lean Henry's place as well as Noah's. And April would be singing. He wanted to go watch her. He swore softly, torn between his loyalty to Fanchette and what he wanted to do. Aaron Yishay hadn't helped matters. Why couldn't he get April out of his mind?

He threw down the cheroot and ground it out. As he headed back to work, his jaw clamped shut and a steely glint flickered in his eye.

16

When Tuesday night came, as April sang, she couldn't help but keep thinking about Melissa and Patrick. She prayed that Melissa had made the right choice. Life with either man could be risky and dangerous because of her father. Ned Hatfield was the only man who disapproved of Patrick, however, whereas every lawman in the West was after Tigre, including the bounty hunters and his enemies.

April couldn't keep from glancing at the table where Noah used to sit night after night. When she finished singing a song, before the next performance, she went to her dressing room to change. She tried to force her thoughts to Melissa's problems, to try to avoid facing the ones that plagued her own mind.

Melissa Hatfield paced April's parlor, waiting for Patrick. For the tenth time she peered at her face in the mirror, straightening the braids that were looped and pinned over her ears, frowning at the wayward curls that had already escaped from the plaits. She smoothed her pink lawn dress, adjusting the full sleeves and smoothing the lace that fell over her wrists. If Papa saw her in her good dress, his suspicions would stir! She was thankful he had been at the store when she came to April's, and she hoped he would work late and go to bed early. She stared at her image, her eyes wide, her lips rosy. Which one did she really love, Patrick or Tigre?

Where was Patrick? Impatiently she went into April's darkened bedroom to peer out the south window. The field behind the house was empty and dark. A bright harvest moon hung low on the horizon, a big

yellow ball that looked almost like the sun. Stars glittered and an owl hooted, a forlorn cry in the night that
made Melissa shiver and move away from the window.

A quarter of an hour later she heard a faint rap on
the back door. When she went to the door, her heart
pounded. For an instant she thought of the break-in.
Praying it was Patrick, she opened the door.

"Melissa," he said, slipping inside quickly and
closing the door after him. With the deliberation that
characterized all his actions, he removed his hat and
hung it on a hook by the door. His white cotton shirt
and tight denims were spotlessly clean, his red hair
parted in the center and combed down. She thought
he looked so handsome.

"I had to see you."

Torn with indecision, she gazed up at him, wishing
he had stepped through the door and swept her into
his arms the way Tigre would have. "Come into the
parlor, Patrick."

"Why couldn't you see me last week or the week
before? Or talk to me at church?"

"I'm sorry," she said in a strained voice. He turned
her to face him, frowning, his brown eyes clouded
with worry. A stray lock of red hair fell over his forehead and he brushed it away.

"I can't keep sneaking around to see you. I want
you to be my wife."

"Oh, Patrick!"

He slipped his arms around her, pulling her to him
as he lowered his head to kiss her. Melissa's arms
wrapped around him and she raised her mouth to his,
kissing him in return, though she was torn with indecision that only grew instead of diminishing.

"Melissa," he said, raising his head, "I love you."
He took her hands and led her to the sofa to pull her
down on his lap. He gazed at her solemnly, and all
she could think of was how much more exciting Tigre
was. He would always slip into her room in the dead
of night, and the moment he entered, he would shower
her wildly with kisses, never giving her a chance to
talk.

"I've got a good flock of sheep," Patrick said earnestly. "I want to ask your father for your hand. If he won't agree to our marriage—"

"He won't. Papa doesn't change his mind," she said bitterly. She knew that only a few men in town would suit her father. A very select few. "He always talks about Hiram Holloway, the rancher's son who collects bugs and doesn't even like to talk to girls."

"If your papa won't consent," Patrick continued doggedly, "I want to go north, to Colorado Territory. We can build a house there and have a fresh start." All the time he talked, he stroked her hair, her shoulders, her throat. "I love you. You're the most wonderful woman I've ever known," he said awkwardly. The same words came to Tigre so glibly, yet she knew Patrick said them from the depth of his heart, and she was deeply touched.

"Patrick." She buried her face against his neck and clung to him. She couldn't marry and leave Tigre, but she didn't want to let go of Patrick either. He was solid, and good, and dear to her.

"Melissa, you're crying!" he said, aghast. "Don't, oh, please don't cry. I'll do anything . . . there's no need to cry."

"Patrick, I can't say yes," she said, sitting up and facing him.

"I love you. I need you." He looked as if she had just plunged a knife into his chest.

"I . . . love you too!" she gasped, trying to hold back her tears, "but I'm not ready to marry."

"Why not? We talked about it before. You sounded ready."

"Patrick, I have to think. There's someone else."

"Someone else?" he asked, frowning at her. His hands grew still. "You've been seeing someone else?"

She nodded. "And I like him a lot, but I like you too!"

"Who is he?"

She caught her lower lip with her teeth, gazing at him with indecision. His scowl deepened. "Who is he, Melissa?"

"He's wanted for murder."

"An outlaw?"

Miserably she nodded and started to cry. "I'm sorry, but I can't say yes, Patrick."

"And you can't say no," he added bitterly. He gazed down at her and pulled her against his chest, stroking her hair. "Don't cry. I won't rush you. I love you, Melissa. I want you to be my wife and the mother of my children. I'll do everything I can to make you happy."

She knew he had left the rest unsaid—that an outlaw couldn't do much to make her happy, couldn't give her what Patrick would. She slipped her arms around him to hold him. "I shouldn't ask you to wait, but—"

"Shh. You don't have to ask. I'll wait. You'll make the right decision. You want the same things in life that I want. We've talked about it before. I even know what kind of house I want to build for you."

He turned her in his arms, gazing down at her. Suddenly his arms tightened, hauling her hard against him as he leaned forward to kiss her passionately. His kiss lengthened while he caressed her, until Melissa's body softened against him. Her arms tightened around his neck, and she responded fully to his lovemaking. For the first time his hands roamed down over her curves, making her moan, making her hips thrust against him. He was more passionate than ever before, and she responded wildly to him. She wished she could shut out all memories of Tigre, all desire for him. When Patrick's hand slipped beneath her skirts and played over her thighs, Melissa groaned and caught his hand. She sat up, gasping for breath.

"Patrick, stop."

"I'll stop," he whispered, "but I want you and I love you." His hands still caressed her, drifting up over her breasts that strained against her soft dress. He kissed her, silencing her words. In seconds his hands had tugged the buttons free and opened her bodice, leaving only her chemise over her pale skin. He bent his head and kissed her breast through the material and she wound her hands in his hair.

"Patrick, stop!" she cried out. She slipped off his lap and moved away from him, trying to straighten her clothing. She crossed the room to cool her desire and get her emotions composed. Her pounding heart slowed to a regular beat and her breathing became normal while she wrestled with what to say to him.

"Melissa." He turned her to face him, holding her with his hands on her shoulders. Suddenly, hoofbeats sounded, and both of them paused to listen. "Patrick, it might be Papa!"

Frantically she tried to smooth her dress and hair. "You have to go!"

"I can hide in Miss Danby's bedroom. My horse is hitched blocks from here."

She bit her lip and watched as he hurried to the bedroom. She ran to a mirror. Her mouth was red from Patrick's kisses, her cheeks pink, and her hair mussed. She smoothed her hair quickly, because the horse was right outside now. She glanced around, snatched up April's pot of rouge, and smudged some on both cheeks as the pounding on the door started.

She raced to the door to throw it open. "Papa!"

"I just got home, Melissa Jane, and your mama told me she allowed you—what happened to your face?"

"I was trying April's rouge, Papa. She's at the saloon."

"Dammit! You get that washed off your face! You look like a painted hussy. It's damned dangerous for you to sit here alone while she's down at that den of iniquity. Get your things and come home."

"Oh, Papa, please. I told April I'd be here when she came home. We're making a quilt together. You know I'm trying to get that done as a surprise for Mama's birthday."

"Dammit, this isn't safe."

"Papa, please," she said, her voice growing soft while she smiled at him. "I'll be safe, and the Dodworths always watch the house until after April gets home. Please let me stay."

"Oh, dammit!" He pushed past her and came into the house. For a moment her heart stopped beating.

She was terrified he would find some evidence of Patrick. He stood in the middle of the room.

"See here—April has all these bits of material she's saved and dyed for me," Melissa said, knowing her father would be bored in seconds if she talked about quilting.

"This house is just so damned isolated."

"Papa, I'll be all right. It's only another hour until April comes home, and I'll bet if you go look, both the Dodworths are peeking out the window now."

He glared at the door, turned on his heel, and went to a window to lean around cautiously and look outside. "They are watching, as a matter of fact."

"Oh, Papa, please. I want to get my quilt done."

"Oh, hell. All right, you can stay until midnight. I'll come back and take you home."

"Papa, please!"

"Midnight or now," he said, and Melissa knew he wasn't going to yield further, so she nodded.

"And this is the last time you're to stay here alone while she's gone. Do you understand that, Melissa Jane?"

"Yes, sir."

"Lock this house up good when I go."

"Yes, sir."

He stomped out and she locked the door, leaning against it to listen as he rode away. She went to the darkened bedroom. "Patrick?" she whispered.

"I'm here," he said softly, at her elbow. "Shh, Melissa. I know your pa. He could ride a block, dismount, and sneak back to look in the windows."

"I know it. I think you should go while you can."

"I don't want to go until we get things settled," he said stubbornly.

"I can't settle anything, because I don't know what I want."

Silence stretched between them and then he pulled her to him. He kissed her passionately again, drawing out the kiss until once again she yielded, softening, clinging to him. Finally he released her. "Work out a time to come when April's home. She'll give us privacy.''

''All right. Patrick, I'm sor—''

He stopped her words with a quick kiss. ''Don't ever say that. I think you'll make the right decision. You're an intelligent woman, Melissa. Now, go walk around in her parlor so he can see you moving around. I'll slip out a window.''

''Oh, Patrick, please be careful,'' she said, suddenly terrified for his safety. She knew her father wouldn't hesitate to shoot to kill.

''Don't worry. I understand men like your pa. That's why I left Ireland. Good bye, sweet love.''

He gave her a little shove, his words echoing in her mind. *Sweet love.* For Patrick those were flowery words, yet she didn't need flowery words. Other things were more important. Her emotions seething, she did as Patrick had instructed, moving around the parlor, picking up her quilt to study it. Not a sound came from the bedroom; she kept straining to hear him leave, but after ten minutes had passed she knew he was gone. She had never even heard the slightest scrape. She was tense, listening for any disturbance outside, half-expecting gunshots or hoofbeats or shouts.

Nothing happened, and finally she moved around, pulling shut April's gingham curtains and going to the darkened bedroom to give vent to tears that had threatened for an hour.

When April returned home, Melissa was still sobbing. As soon as April sat down, Melissa poured out her worries. ''Patrick asked me to marry him and I told him no. He wants me to think about it.'' She sobbed violently while April sat close by in the rocker, waiting for the paroxysms of crying to subside.

''Melissa, you must love Patrick too, or you wouldn't be crying over your decision.''

''Patrick is good and he would be good to me, but when Tigre kisses me—'' She broke off and blushed. ''April, you loved Emilio. When you kissed him, did he make you feel like you would faint? When Patrick kisses me, it's not the same. It's fun, but it's not like

Tigre. And Tigre . . ." She blushed again, looking down at her hands. "He's exciting," she said.

"You have to think of your future. Have you talked to Tigre about it?"

"No. We never have a chance."

"Maybe you should try to find somewhere to meet him besides in your bedroom, someplace where you can talk and be more rational."

"I'm terrified he's going to get caught, yet I can't send him away."

"I'm sorry. Melissa, you must tell him the gold was stolen when my house was broken into. I'm sorry, but it's gone."

"I hadn't thought about that!"

"And his folks are coming to visit. He'll want to see them." Hoofbeats sounded, and April rushed to the window. "It's your father."

"He won't let me stay and he won't let me ride home alone since your house was broken into. Mama said to try to get you to come home with us."

"I'll be all right. Nothing's happened since that night. You better dry your eyes."

"Oh, my! Papa will want to know why I've been crying." She pinched her cheeks to make them pink, then dried her eyes. "Thank you, April, for letting me come over here tonight."

April nodded and opened the door to greet Ned Hatfield. In a few minutes the Hatfields departed and she stood in the doorway waving to Melissa. The moon was high now, crickets chirping, the air pleasantly cool. April stood watching the Hatfields ride away. She hoped Melissa made a sensible decision soon, or there would be a tragedy.

A shadow moved, and April's eyes narrowed, studying the darkness while she could still call out to Ned Hatfield for help. Someone was seated on horseback across the street in the shadows of the houses. It was a man with a hat pulled low, and he was watching April. She closed the door behind her, going down the step. The light that had poured out the door was gone, and her eyes adjusted to the night. She squinted, trying to see, moving forward as chills ran down her spine.

She opened her mouth to call to the Hatfields, but the man on horseback moved. It was Noah. Her heart seemed to stop and restart at a faster pace.

He came forward across the street and dismounted, spurs jingling as he stepped down.

"You gave me a start!" she said. "I saw someone watching my house."

"I didn't mean to frighten you, but I'm concerned about your staying alone since that damned Kiowa hasn't shown up yet!"

"Don't refer to Ta-ne-haddle that way!" she admonished him, but there wasn't any real bite in her voice. She hadn't talked to Noah since that morning when she had met Fanchette Craddock, and she was happy to see him, pleased that he was concerned about her.

"Yes, ma'am!" he answered in a lighter tone. "How long do you think Miss Hatfield can go without her folks finding out about Patrick O'Flynn meeting her here?"

April gazed up at him in the darkness and debated whether to trust him with her concerns. "It's worse than that. Tigre didn't go away. He camps near here and slips in at night to see her."

Noah swore quietly. "He'll hang if her father catches him and doesn't shoot him first."

"I know. I'm worried about him, and there's nothing I can do to help either one of them."

"She's in love with him?"

"She doesn't know, but Patrick has asked her to marry him."

There was a long silence. She couldn't see his eyes beneath the shadow of his hat brim. "Lives get so damned complicated," he said with surprising bitterness, and she wondered what was troubling him. He couldn't be that worried over Melissa and Tigre.

"I better go inside," she said reluctantly. "You don't need to stay and watch my place. I'll lock up."

"I'll watch for a while. I don't have to be back yet."

They heard hoofbeats that grew louder, and instantly realized that someone was approaching. Noah rested his hand on his pistol. "Maybe you should go inside until I see who it is."

"It's probably someone passing through town," she whispered. She was conscious of his presence as her gaze wandered over his broad shoulders and long, lean frame. In minutes three pinto ponies came into view, with riders on two mounts, a child in front of one.

"Ta-ne-haddle!" she exclaimed, and hurried forward to meet them.

Noah relaxed and watched them. He was thankful the Kiowa had come to town, because he worried constantly about April's safety. She greeted them and walked back in front of their horses. The Kiowa slipped off his easily and walked beside her, talking quietly.

"Noah, you know Ta-ne-haddle. This is Lottie and their daughter Dawn. Lottie, meet Noah McCloud."

While she said hello, the sleeping child stirred, looked around, and saw April. "Cissy," she said, holding out her arms.

Laughing, April took the child and hugged her, and Noah felt something tighten around his heart. April looked so natural holding the sleepy child, talking to her softly, smoothing her long silky black hair. Instead of holding to a lost love, she should have her own children, a man to love her.

"Let's go inside. Noah, come with us."

"No. I should get back to the saloon."

Laughing, she caught his arm. "Come inside. You told me a few minutes ago you didn't have to go back."

She gazed up at him, smiling. The dark-skinned child looked at him with curious round black eyes and he nodded. "I'll get the horses unsaddled in a few minutes," Ta-ne-haddle said. Noah held the door open and they all went inside. He blinked as he stepped into the light, and then he looked at the family he had just met. Dawn was a beautiful child with a button nose and thickly lashed, luminous black eyes. She clung to

April, calling her Cissy, and April glowed with happiness as she talked to Dawn.

"I'm glad you got here," Noah said to Ta-ne-haddle, extending his hand for a handshake. It was the first time he had seen the Indian since that introductory encounter, and he gazed into an impassive one-eyed stare. He turned and caught Lottie studying him. She flashed him a smile, and he decided Ta-ne-haddle was a fortunate man, because she was a beautiful woman.

"I've heard abut you, Mr. McCloud," she said. "I'm glad you and Ta-ne-haddle didn't kill each other."

"Yes, ma'am. I don't intend to tangle with him again."

"I have so much to tell you," April said while Dawn tugged on her arm.

"You see my book," Dawn urged, and April laughed, shrugging her shoulders. "There's juice and cakes," she said as she sat down.

"I'll help you with the horses," Noah offered. Ta-ne-haddle was on the verge of refusing, but as he glanced into Noah's eyes he nodded and went outside. As they led the animals to the back to the shed, Noah told him about the break-in.

"I'm worried about her safety."

"So now you know she doesn't have your gold."

"Yes."

"We can stay for a while, but after a time, I don't think April will let us stay. She knows how much we like to roam."

"Maybe by that time I can find out who did it, or find my gold. I've offered a reward for any information."

Ta-ne-haddle nodded. "Sorry I slugged you. I understood you were giving her trouble. She gave me plenty for what I did to you."

Surprised, Noah smiled. "I'm damned glad you're here. I don't think she realizes the danger she's in."

"It might be better if I move my family away from here and watch the place at night."

"That's what I've been doing, but I've got a saloon to run and there are nights that I can't get over here."

"Does she know you're watching her place?"

"No. She saw me tonight, and we were talking when you rode up."

"I think we'll stay a few days and then I'll move the family. I won't leave April unprotected."

"No one can watch her all the time. That's what worries me. She's written to Luke and he's coming."

"Luke?" Ta-ne-haddle repeated, pleasure evident in his voice.

"She found her mother." Quickly he related to Ta-ne-haddle all that had happened.

"I have prayed that they would be reunited. And she has a brother. I have heard of the outlaw, his silver spurs and golden hair. April will be safe while they're here. Do you know when they arrive?"

"Any day now. By the time they leave, I hope I have a lead on who did it."

"I'll watch every night until they come. You can count on that."

Noah clapped him on the shoulder. "Thanks."

"I don't think you need to thank me."

They had walked back to the front of the house, and stood quietly talking in the darkness. Noah's horse whinnied softly, lifting its head. "I'll leave you. I know she wants to talk to you."

Ta-ne-haddle watched Noah mount. "McCloud. Don't hurt her."

"I won't. April still loves Emilio Piedra. I'm engaged to a childhood sweetheart and I'm going home to Alabama before long. I just want my gold." If his news came as a surprise to Ta-ne-haddle, it didn't show in his impassive features. He turned and went inside, his long black braid hanging down the center of his back.

17

When Hattie and Javier began the last leg of their journey to Albuquerque, Hattie was trembling with excitement. They had joined a wagon train, and in Española, a cavalry patrol going south to Fort Craig agreed to ride with the group to protect them from Indian uprisings. There was talk among the families in the wagon train of a raid on Camp Mimbres made by the Mimbreño bank of Chiricahua Apache, led by Mangas Coloradas. Also there were rumors of Comanche raids on the Navajo at the Bosque Redondo reservation. The Mesilla Indians had even attacked the cavalry several times in recent months, so the days spent away from each town were tense, and the men kept constant watch.

In Santa Fe they saw the construction of the Palace of the Governors on the Plaza. They were delayed because the river had risen, but finally they wound their way southward. Each day as they drew closer, Hattie's eagerness increased. April—would she still have golden hair? Had Lucius changed? She should remember to call him Luke. So many women had lost babies and children in the trek westward that Hattie felt blessed to have discovered hers alive after all this time. The lost years were useless to weep over now, she reminded herself, but questions about them still ran through her mind. How did April support herself? Had a family taken her in as their daughter. Why wasn't she living in San Antonio with Lucius. April had written that Lucius was an attorney like his father. Hattie remembered all the lawbooks that had burned up during the attack on their wagon train when she and Lucius had first headed west. He must have acquired others, but she wished he could have had his father's. She thought of his handsome features, his wide green eyes and thick dark lashes, how tall and slender he had been at seventeen. Lucius—Luke and April. All her children were alive. If only Tigre could be there. Tigre. She had lost another one only to get two returned to her. She smiled and hummed a tune, but as they approached Albuquerque, anticipation made her quiet and tense.

They could see long, flat adobe buildings and houses in the distance. Cottonwoods and willows lined the riverbank, and the purple-shaded, snow-capped Sandia peaks towered in the distance. Heat rose from the plains in shimmering waves, and occasionally a snake slithered across the trail, or a lizard sat poised as still as the stones around them. Overhead, hawks circled lazily on warm currents of air, gliding and soaring. Hattie felt as weightless and airborne as the birds. Excitement made her wiggle constantly with anticipation, and a smile played around her mouth.

On Wednesday, the end of August, they rode into Albuquerque and Javier made arrangements to meet with his men the following morning at the livery stable. He intended to buy sheep and horses as well as replenish needed supplies while he was in town. Hattie gazed at all the sights, the chandler's shop, a cantina, a blacksmith's shop, a general store. This was a thriving town of about two thousand, and Hattie relished the sights and sounds. She stopped as her gaze fell on the signboard beside the doors of a fancy saloon.

"Javier, look!" she exclaimed, gripping his arm tightly. "That sign says, 'Hear the Songbird, Miss April, Whose Songs Will Melt Your Heart!' "

"A dance hall girl!" Javier said under his breath, his scowl fierce.

"You can't condemn her for that!" Hattie exclaimed. "She may have had to earn her way alone. You can't blame her for singing in a saloon or anything else she might have done or might be." Hattie was

subdued now, realizing for the first time that there was
a strong chance that April was a soiled dove. Hattie
closed her eyes as an ache gripped her. Her child had
survived and that was what mattered now. Nothing
else. If she had become a woman of pleasure, Hattie
could accept that as well.

They stopped to ask a cutler directions to the house.
On the way they passed the jail. Hattie averted her
eyes instantly, a shiver coursing through her. She
thought of Tigre, and prayed he was far from the territory and safe. As they began to pass houses, she
relaxed, her thoughts returning to April.

It had been over seventeen years since she had seen
April. Her heart pounded as they slowed and stopped
the wagon in front of a small house with flowers
blooming by the front porch. Javier jumped down and
turned to lift Hattie down. He took her arm and together they walked to the front door, where he rapped
loudly.

. The door opened and Hattie faced a lovely young
woman whom she would have recognized anywhere.
Her gaze swept over April's hair, parted in the center,
braided, and looped on both sides of her head. Her
wide eyes were silvery-blue, almost the color of ashes
on a burned-down fire, and for a brief moment Hattie
remembered April's father. April was slender and tall,
with beautiful features and skin. Hattie's heart beat
with joy.

"We're Javier and Hattie," Javier said, and Hattie
opened her arms. She couldn't wait to get acquainted.
She pulled April into her embrace.

April clung to Hattie, tears stinging her eyes. How
many, many times she had dreamed of this moment.
She had imagined it in so many ways, and it was
sweeter than she had ever expected. Oblivious of her
tears, she clung to Hattie and whispered, "Mother."
Her gaze went over Hattie's shoulders and she looked
into Javier's black eyes. His solemn countenance didn't
hold a hint of rejoicing.

Sobering, she pulled away. Hattie held her hand, her

eyes sweeping over April's features as if she were
memorizing them. "This is Javier, your stepfather."

He nodded and April nodded in return, feeling instinctively that he didn't want to touch her. She returned her attention to Hattie and caught a brief frown
before Hattie turned away from Javier.

"Come inside," April urged, holding open the door.
"Luke and Catalina and their children should be here
any day now."

"I can't believe it yet!" Hattie said, wiping away
tears and smiling broadly at the same time. "And I'll
see my grandchildren!"

"Sit down, please. I have a ham cooked and—"

"First, let's talk," Hattie urged. "I'm not that hungry," she said, looking at the parlor that was as neat
as a church altar. The cheerful gingham curtains and
fresh flowers added to the warmth of the room. The
floor gleamed with polish and a crystal vase on the
mantel sparkled in the light that streamed in from
the window. Her daughter had done well, Hattie
thought with pride. She knew it hadn't been easy for
April, even though she had been fortunate enough to
find Lucius. Life for a woman alone on the frontier
could never be easy.

"I'm so glad you're here," April said. She gazed
with joy at her mother. *Mother.* She could never say
the word enough times. Since her arrival, Javier had
barely spoken, and he kept staring at April with his
cold black eyes that looked as bleak as a winter prairie. April guessed that he was afraid Hattie would learn
the truth about what he had done so many years earlier.

"Now, start back at the beginning and tell me where
you've been and what you've done," Hattie said eagerly while Javier sat as still as if he had turned to
stone.

"I don't know what happened at first," April said
softly, almost unable to believe her words. For several
years after she had learned the truth, she had dreamed
of getting back at the man who had given her away,
who had hurt Hattie almost as badly as he had hurt

April. But she couldn't say the words now and do
something else to hurt her mother. Nothing would
change the years gone by. "I was taken in by some
ladies in a pleasure house and they were good to me.
It was in Santa Fe at Miss Kate's, and they had dancing
girls."

She could see the look of relief that flooded Javier
Castillo's features, and though she wanted to cry out
and tell him what a terrible thing he had done, she
continued with her story.

"I could sing, so I started performing with the
dancers when I was five. That's how Luke found me.
He was in Santa Fe—"

"Oh!" Hattie exclaimed, interrupting April. "Just
think, Luke in Santa Fe. So close to us. Go on, April."

"When we met, he had been searching for you. He
realized we were related, and he took me back to San
Antonio with him. By that time I was twelve."

"October the twenty-first," Hattie said.

"The next spring Luke was planning on marrying
Catalina Piedra, and his good friend Ta-ne-haddle was
going to marry Lottie."

"Lottie?" Hattie interjected.

"Lottie was at Miss Kate's. She took a special interest in me, and when Luke left with me, she followed because she didn't trust him. Of course, he
found her and took us both to his home in San Antonio. Lottie fell in love with Ta-ne-haddle and married
him. I was in love with Catalina's brother, Emilio
Piedra," April said softly, looking down at her hands.
"He was eighteen and he said he would wait for me
to grow up. Their father, Domingo, turned outlaw, and
Luke was marshal." She faced Hattie. "There was a
gunfight and Domingo killed Emilio."

"He killed his own son?" Hattie said aloud. Her
thoughts raced as she realized what April was telling
her. "He was truly a terrible man."

"Luke killed him."

"Ah, just as he deserved."

"I think Catalina would have shot him if Luke
hadn't. Anyway, Catalina and Luke married and Ta-

ne-haddle and Lottie were already married. I couldn't bear to stay with the four of them. They were all so happy, but all I could think about was Emilio. I had heard that someone had seen you around Santa Fe, so I ran away.''

"Luke let you go?" Hattie asked in disbelief. Javier hadn't said a word, and sat quietly listening, watching April closely.

"I found out later that he came after me, but then he decided he needed to be home with Catalina. I wasn't really alone. Ta-ne-haddle and Lottie followed me. You'll meet them, because they know you're coming. I knew I could earn my way by singing, and I wanted to find you.''

Her voice softened as she studied the lovely woman who was the mother she had never known. Hattie was beautiful, with large blue eyes and smooth skin that didn't reveal her age. She looked younger than April knew she must be, and joy shone in her expression. Hattie's eyes filled with tears and they hugged each other tightly, April clinging to her. "I'm so thankful!''

As April straightened up and wiped away her tears, Javier said, "Tell us about Tigre.''

"He was here again night before last. He's camped not far from here, and he said that on the last night of Fiesta he will come to town, because everyone will be at the celebration.''

"*Gracias a Dios! Me alegro. Tigre es muy valiante,*" Javier said softly, and Hattie squeezed his hand. It was the only time since his arrival that his features had softened, and it was obvious he loved his son deeply.

"He was well when he was here?''

"He's fine. He can tell you his plans,'' April said gently, knowing they both ached over their son. "Now, how about something to eat?'' she asked, trying to cheer them again.

"I'll help,'' Hattie offered.

"Do you want to unhitch your horse? There's a shed in back,'' April said, and Javier left through the front door.

All the time the women worked, they talked. They

placed slices of pink ham on the table, along with
golden biscuits April had baked that morning.

"I sing at the Brown Owl, and I can stay home
tonight, but tomorrow night I'll have to go to work,"
April said as she set a small bowl of chow-chow on
the table.

"We'd like you to come home with us," Hattie said
simply. April turned, her brows arching in surprise.
Her face flushed and she smiled. Pleasure warmed her
that they would ask her.

"You think about it," Hattie said gently. "I know
you have a life here, and we're isolated on a sheep
ranch in the mountains, but we'd like to have you.
You've had to make your own way far too long."

"Thank you," April said quietly, gazing into blue
eyes that were filled with understanding and sympathy.
She knew that the offer to come live with them was
extended warmly by Hattie only. April set a dish of
pale yellow butter on the table. "I hope Ta-ne-haddle
and his family come to town while you're here."

"I hope so too. I'd like very much to meet the man
who saved Lucius. I can't seem to remember to call
him Luke," she said, laughing.

"We'll have a fiesta in town this week, so you'll be
here for it. I'll sing Thursday and Friday evening and
on Saturday afternoon. It lasts three days."

"I hope Luc . . . Luke arrives tomorrow."

They talked, filling in the gaps made by all the years
they had spent apart. Finally they went to bed, April
on the sofa and Hattie and Javier in her bed.

Hattie was too excited to sleep, and she lay awake
in the dark. The only unhappiness to mar the day was
Javier. Whatever the problem was, it continued to
plague him. He was solemn and quiet, and seldom
joined in their conversation. She turned her head,
wanting to reach over and stroke his broad chest that
was covered in a thick mat of tangled curly hair. His
shoulders were hard, his muscles solid, and Hattie felt
a swell of love for him. She wished he would confide
in her, knowing this was the first time in their marriage that Javier had kept a secret from her.

* * *

On Thursday, Noah shaved and bathed, getting ready for the festivities. His thoughts were on April. He knew he should leave her alone. He was engaged, making plans to go home to Alabama, yet he still wanted to see her. When he entered McCloud's Place, Aaron Yishay was at the bar, his foot on the brass rail, deep in discussion with Duero. Aaron's bowler hat sat squarely on his head, and he wore his usual black suit. A stiff paper collar was around his neck. Noah joined them, and in a few minutes Duero moved away to wait on a customer.

"Aren't you taking Mrs. Yishay to the Fiesta?"

"Oh, *de cierto,*" he answered in his slightly eastern accent. Noah smiled.

"You sound as if you came from the East."

Aaron nodded. "New Jersey originally, and then we moved to St. Louis, where I grew up. I suppose the accent stuck, because that was the way my parents spoke."

"And that's were you met Mrs. Yishay?"

He nodded, looking down at his drink. "My parents were poor. Papa was a cooper, but he wanted better for me. They saw to it that I had an education, and when I was twenty-six I met Mama. Her parents didn't approve. Her father was a storekeeper, a very successful St. Louis merchant, and he had a bad temper."

"Sounds like Ned Hatfield."

Aaron chuckled and swirled his drink. "They tried to discourage us. She was eighteen years old then," he said, and his voice softened. Noah studied him, wondering if Yishay had been assailed by doubts. He rubbed his finger along the polished mahogany bar that had been varnished in layers to protect it from drinks and burns.

"Did you ever have doubts?" he asked quietly.

Dark brown eyes met his. "No. I knew she was the one woman for me."

"How'd you know?" Noah asked, knowing it was a foolish question.

"I couldn't live without her," Aaron answered simply. "Her papa offered me five thousand dollars if I would forget her and move away from St. Louis."

"Damn! That's a lot of money."

"It was more than a lot to a struggling medical student who knew how hard his parents were working to keep him in school. I refused the money. The old man couldn't believe I would. I finished school. The next offer, the stakes were higher. My life."

"He threatened you?"

"Yes. That's why we live out west."

Noah continued to wonder about Aaron's past as he studied the shorter man. "She must have loved you a great deal to come out here and leave everything behind," he said, knowing if he asked Fanchette to move to Albuquerque, she probably would refuse.

Aaron smiled and shrugged. "I've been a lucky man. You'll see, McCloud," he said, leaning his elbow on the bar and smiling at Noah, "when you marry your Mrs. Craddock, there's nothing in the world as fine as the love of a good woman. That Kiowa friend of April's, he doesn't own a thing in this world except his ponies, a few trinkets, and that big knife he wears, but he's one of the happiest men I know, because he's got a good woman who loves him more than anything else on earth." Aaron turned back to the bar to rest both elbows on the mahogany and sip his drink.

"How many children do you have?"

"Two sons. They went back east to college. Nathan lives in Chicago now; Michael lives in Philadelphia. We have two grandchildren."

"That's a long way from Albuquerque."

"Except during the war, Mama and I go to see them every two years."

Noah gazed at the doctor, wondering if his own life would someday be as settled. Whenever he thought about returning to Alabama, instead of the buoyancy he expected, he had a mixture of expectation and regret and sorrow. "*. . . there's nothing in the world as fine as the love of a good woman . . .*" April's image danced into his thoughts. "Were you ever reconciled with your in-laws?"

"No. That's a regret, but Mr. Goldring was not the kind to soften. They never saw their grandsons. Both of Gerta's parents are dead now." He took a drink and after a silence said, "Miss April's singing tonight. Have you met her parents?"

"No."

"Real pretty woman, her mother. Real pretty. Like Miss April. I better go home now and get Mama. She likes the evening. It's too hot after siesta to stir around."

"I'll go over to the Plaza, check on the booth. It's about time to collect the cash and bring it back here for safekeeping. I should see if Hosea needs more beer." The two men strolled outside.

"You coming tonight?"

"Probably," Noah answered, thinking of April. He could hear the music clearly, and images of her danced in his thoughts.

"Isn't that right?" Aaron asked, smiling at him.

Noah had no idea what had been the topic of conversation or what Aaron Yishay was asking about. He hadn't heard the past few sentences.

"Sure is," he said grimly, jamming his hands in his pockets, judging from Aaron's sly smile that the doctor knew Noah didn't have even a vague idea what he was talking about.

"She sings about seven," Aaron said softly.

"Yeah, Doc. See you later."

Aaron smiled. Noah watched him walk away, his shoulders bobbing as he took tiny steps, heading toward his house. Noah thought about the doctor and his life, coming out west so he could marry the woman he loved, leaving everything behind to move to a struggling frontier. Noah knew that Aaron Yishay thought he was in love with April. Was he? He shut the question out as swiftly as it popped into his mind. He was engaged to Fanchette. He tried to think of Fanchette, and succeeded for about ten steps until he reached the Plaza and saw the platform where April would sing. Struggling to keep his mind off April, he strolled to his booth to talk to Hosea and drink a beer.

Parades were held each day, and pageants took place on the Plaza, but at the moment the town was quiet. People thronged the Plaza, vendors sold their wares, horses and wagons lined the streets, leading away from the center of the festivities. April wasn't present, and Hosea had a hefty amount of cash, so Noah tucked it under his arm to carry it back to his place. As he started across the Plaza, he said hello to Melissa Hatfield, who was with her mother beside a tamale vendor's stand.

Melissa watched Noah walk past, her gaze sweeping the crowd, searching for Patrick. She secretly wished Tigre could be present. There had been a hanging of an outlaw earlier in the week, a man who had robbed a bank in Santa Fe and Socorro and was caught trying to steal two horses from the livery stable. Ever since the furor over the outlaw, her worries for Tigre's safety had increased. To make matters worse, her father was one of the worst and most vocal in favor of hanging the man.

"Melissa," Selma Hatfield said, breaking into her thoughts, "it's terribly hot. I'm going to the candy store and sit down on one of their benches, where it's shadier and cooler."

"Fine, Mama. I'll be all right," Melissa replied. She was happy to be left alone. She milled through the crowd as musicians climbed to the platform to play. Siesta was over and people were filling the Plaza again.

"Miss Hatfield!"

She turned to see Mott Ferguson. He smiled and removed his hat. "How pretty you look!"

"Thank you. Right now I feel wilted though. It's hot."

"You look far from wilted. Come sit down in the shade with me."

She nodded and crossed the Plaza with him to a bench beneath the overhanging roof of the barber shop.

"As soon as you're cool enough, I'd like a dance."

"Fine, but let's wait a little while."

"I'm glad Miss Danby found McCloud's gold."

Melissa's head snapped around. "She hasn't found the gold!"

His brows arched and he gazed at her with curiosity. "Oh? Are you certain?"

"Yes. She's still looking; sometimes I help her. How did you know about the gold?"

"I think everyone in Albuquerque knows about it now."

"That's what Mr. McCloud told her."

"When McCloud bought the saloon and started adding to it and fixing it up, I just assumed she had found his gold and returned it to him."

"No, not at all. As a matter of fact, her house—" Melissa clamped her mouth shut, and he smiled.

"I know about that too. Sheriff Pacheco told me. Someone broke into her house and tore everything apart—searching for the gold, no doubt."

"Yes. Mama's afraid for her, and we haven't even told Papa what happened. April shouldn't stay alone, but she doesn't scare easily."

"Sometimes bravery isn't the wisest course. Of course, others may assume the same that I did—that McCloud has his gold. She may be safe from another break-in."

"Provided it's someone who lives here and knows about Mr. McCloud's saloon." A fiddler began to play, and the music drowned out the sounds of the crowd.

"How about one dance now, and then I'll treat you to some lemonade."

She laughed as he took her hand to help her to her feet. He was handsome in his blue uniform. He left his hat on the bench, and his golden hair gleamed in the sunlight as he led her out to join the other dancers in a circle.

After one more dance and a drink of lemonade in the shade of a cottonwood, she glanced up to see Patrick standing by a hitching rail. He was watching her, and her cheeks turned pink to be caught laughing at something Mott Ferguson was saying.

"Lieutenant, I should go now. My mother will come searching for me soon if I don't."

He smiled as if he knew she had another purpose in bidding him farewell. "May I have a dance tonight?"

"Yes, of course," she said, pleased that he wanted to dance with her again, knowing that with her father present tonight, she would have little chance to dance with Patrick.

"Two dances?" he persisted playfully.

"Yes, two or more!"

"Ah, good. I look forward to the evening."

"Thank you for the lemonade. I'll see you to-night," she said, and turned to stroll back in the direction where she had seen Patrick. He leaned against the wall of a shoe shop, and her pulse began to skip as she approached him.

"Hello, Patrick," she said shyly. "Mama is sitting over by the candy shop."

"And you're out dancing with the lieutenant."

"You sound jealous!" she said, laughing. "I told him I had to find Mama."

Patrick took her hand and led her around the corner of the shop, moving between buildings where there were few people. "Dammit, you see that outlaw, you flirt with the lieutenant—"

"Oh, Patrick," she said, suddenly sober, "Mott Ferguson doesn't mean a thing to me!"

"But the outlaw does. I wish he was hanging over by—"

"Don't say that!" she cried, her voice hoarse. She was suddenly cold all over, as if an icy blue norther had swept across the Plaza. "I'll never forgive you for saying such a thing if something happens to him."

"I'm sorry, Melissa," he said gruffly, his forehead furrowed in a scowl. "It's just that I love you so damned much!"

Suddenly she softened and placed her hand on his cheek. When she was with Patrick, she loved him the most. When she was with Tigre, he was the man for her. "I love you too," she whispered, wanting to feel his arms around her.

He groaned and looked around. "Come here."

"Patrick, Mama—"

"She won't hunt you in this heat. We'll have a few minutes." He pulled her toward a shed, stepping into its stuffy interior. It was filled with rusty tools and old wagon pieces, wheels in against one wall. Patrick pulled her into his arms and kissed her. Melissa slipped her arms around his neck, yielding to him, knowing she had to come to a decision soon.

* * *

Early in the evening as she walked toward the Plaza, Hattie and Javier beside her, April was eager with anticipation. The happiness she felt over finally meeting Hattie overwhelmed her, and with the Fiesta, April would get to see Noah. He had a booth on the Plaza where he was selling beer, and while he might not work the booth, she felt he would be around. Expectation of Luke's arrival also added to her joy. She dressed in a bright red shirt and a Mexican-style low-cut red cotton blouse, her hair tied behind her head with a ribbon and a red blossom in it.

While she chatted with Hattie, Javier was as solemn as the first hour he had arrived. During their visit April never had been alone with him. He never brought up the past, and she wondered if he had any idea that she knew what had actually happened. The only time he relaxed and had a warm note in his voice was when talk turned to Tigre.

The Plaza was filled with people. Booths surrounded it and in the center was a platform on planks for the musicians. She found a chair that was brought out for her and placed near the musicians. As she waited in the chair, her toe tapped in time to the rhythm while she watched the dancers and the crowd, searching for one head of curly black hair and a pair of broad shoulders.

Disappointment flared when she couldn't see him. If he were present, she would be able to spot him, because he would be taller than almost everyone. Javier and Hattie danced, and then they moved through the crowd while April sang "Listen to the Mockingbird."

After sundown, when Noah returned to the Plaza, he stopped besides a building and watched April from the shadows. He listened to her sing an old southern song while the dancers moved slowly around the Plaza. April's voice was so clear and haunting that it had made a tight knot form in his chest.

I miss Alabama, he told himself, watching the slender girl on the platform. Her hair was tied behind her head with a red ribbon as she often wore it, and he stared at her with longing.

The sound of her voice invaded his mind. Noah pushed his hat to the back of his head and began to thread his way through the crowd. As he walked, friends spoke to him, and while they talked, April's audience clapped in time to the music.

While April sang, she couldn't see Noah in the crowd and she reminded herself over and over that she shouldn't be searching. He was engaged. He loved Fanchette, Alabama, plantations, raising cotton, balls, and hunts, and none of those were in the territory. Gold held him here, and nothing else. As the applause for her song died down and a dance started, she stepped down off the platform to look around. Lanterns blazed and a gentle breeze blew across the Plaza while the musicians strummed *"La Raspa,"* a lively Mexican folk dance. A hand closed on her arm and she turned around.

She looked up into Noah's laughing blue eyes. All evening long she had waited for this moment, and the force of it took her breath. It had been days since she had seen him, and memory was enhanced by reality. Never had he looked more marvelous than tonight, with his hat pushed casually to the back of his head. Tangled black curls fell above his forehead, and he wore a white linen shirt with a bandanna around his neck.

"I heard you sing, April. I liked it," he said, feeling breathless.

"Thank you."

"Aaron Yishay said your mother is in town."

"I want you to meet her."

His hand stayed on her arm. Awareness of everything around them vanished for her, because all she could see was Noah. She wasn't sure what she felt. She tried to think of something to say to keep him at her side, but she was at a loss for words.

"Do you sing again tonight?"

"Not until later. How's your saloon?"

"We're about finished with the roof and walls for the addition. We're putting in a floor tomorrow."

"Lean Henry says you're his big competition."

"And vice versa," he said, tugging gently on her

arm to move her out of the path of people milling past them. "Like to dance?"

"I don't know how," she blurted. "I haven't danced—"

"Since a fandango with Emilio," he finished. "Well, it's time we changed that."

"Noah, they're doing intricate steps!" She watched dancers stomp their feet and clap hands, skirts billowing as women turned. "I can't go out there."

"Come here." Music and lights diminished when he led her between two adobe buildings on the edge of the Plaza away from the crowd. The air felt cooler, and they were beyond the fringe of the crowd. Listening as the musicians started another tune, he slipped his arm around her waist. "All they're doing is this," he said. "Put your right foot forward. Now left, and step, step left again."

He led her and she tried to concentrate, but his casual brushing against her, his arm around her waist, their privacy in the darkness, made her want to turn into his arms. In minutes they were dancing, and she laughed, following his lead.

"Good!" he exclaimed, his blue eyes sparkling. "How can a dancer not know how to dance?" he teased.

Exhilaration bubbled in her like pale champagne. She laughed again, feeling as if she could always be happy with him.

Noah gazed down at her. She followed his lead effortlessly, and already danced as if she had been doing this for years. She was graceful, her slender body swaying with the music, the red dress billowing like flower petals when he turned her. The music was fast, and on the next turn Noah gave her a forceful spin. She danced away from him, twirling, laughing at him, her skirt swirling high enough to give him a glimpse of her shapely calves. She moved easily, a dancing flame that enticed him, young, beautiful, innocent, and seductive, banishing all his loneliness. She was intoxicating, drawing him with her pale eyes that looked like mist on the mountain peaks. Alabama had never seemed more long ago or far away.

He laughed, moving around her, touching her when he could, wishing the musicians would never quit, that April would never stop dancing. A nagging inner voice kept reminding him of Fanchette, but for tonight, at a harmless Fiesta, he didn't want to listen. It was only a dance. A breathtaking dance. April spun around, her willowy body swaying, and the music ended. He caught her, his arm slipping around her waist.

His heart slammed against his ribs at the feeling of her against him for only the briefest seconds before she stepped away. From the first night when she had fallen into his arms, she had intrigued him. When he was with her, she made him feel as if things were right with the world. She was so aptly named for springtime, April. She was spring to him, fresh, lovely, carrying a promise of warmth and life.

I am engaged. Fanchette is far away or I wouldn't feel this way.

The music changed to a waltz and they looked into each other's eyes with uncertainty, as if the chance to hold the other might put too big a strain on temptation. She gazed up solemnly, her hands at her sides while the guitar players sang. With a slow lift of his arms, he reached out to take her hands.

"Watch," he said, holding her at arm's length. "One, two, three, one, two, three. Count with me."

Watching him all the while, she followed his step. They moved in unison, gazing into each other's eyes.

"One, two, three. One, two, three," he counted in his deep voice while she followed perfectly. He danced to the corner of the building, where more yellow light shone from lanterns hung high on posts. She could see his eyes gazing into hers solemnly, and she wished she could go on dancing in his arms forever. Flickering shadows cast by the swaying lanterns played over Noah's handsome features, highlighting his prominent cheekbones, shadowing his hollow cheeks. Their only contact was her right hand in his left, his other hand a faint pressure at the small of her back, and her left hand resting lightly on his waist. Yet like the summer lightning she had once seen streaking out of a black sky, so with Noah, she felt invisible charges burning between them, sparking the air as they danced.

Firecrackers popped somewhere near the Plaza, their explosions less volatile than Noah's intense, unwavering study. He made her feel beautiful, special, happy. *I love him and I can't bear to think about his leaving.*

He reached out to grasp the end of the narrow red ribbon that held her hair behind her head. He tugged gently, pulling steadily until it untied and her hair swung free over her shoulders. He caught the red flower she had worn in her hair and tucked it into her neckline, his fingers brushing her warm flesh lightly. He held the ribbon as he put his hand back on her waist.

"Are you thinking of Emilio?" he asked in a somber, husky voice.

She didn't want to answer him, suddenly afraid what he would see in her eyes. She looked away.

"April."

His voice was husky, demanding. She couldn't look at him, because he would *know.* She watched the other dancers, skirts flying around trim ankles, colors whirling past.

Noah's heart seemed to beat only half as often as he watched her turn away from him, her eyes anywhere except meeting his. His gaze ran over her slender throat, her full mouth, her cheeks that were deeper pink now, and he knew the answer to his question. She wasn't thinking of Emilio. He wanted to turn and waltz back between the buildings to the solitary darkness and take her in his arms and kiss her. He wanted that more than he had wanted anything in a long time except his gold. He burned with longing. *He was engaged.* It hadn't been any time since Fanchette had been in his arms and he had put her on the stage for home, making promises to her. He was a man to keep his word, but how hard it was becoming to do so.

Fighting to control the urge to take April into the darkness, he stared at her. It was lust. She was beautiful, desirable, *present.* Fanchette was hundreds of miles away in Alabama.

The music ended and they applauded.

"It's time for me to go back to sing," she said

quickly, her gaze running over his features intently.
Handing her hair ribbon back to her, he nodded and
watched her go. She held her skirt close around her to
move through the crowd that was growing steadily now
that the darkness had fallen. Noah realized he was
clenching his fists, and he tried to relax, moving to
the side to watch her as she climbed up on the platform
and talked to the guitar players. His gaze roamed over
her, mentally peeling away the red skirt and blouse. He
wanted her in his bed, remembering his old vow the
first night in town when he had caught April. He had
planned to get her into his bed before the first snow fell.

The thought made him burn with desire. He should
go back to his saloon and forget her. Go back and
write to Fanchette, think about Fanchette. He began
to move, circling around the edge of the Plaza toward
his place, trying to keep out of the way of people.

April talked to Julio and Rogelio. "May I sing right
now instead of later?" she asked.

They glanced at each other and shrugged. "Sí, que
bueno."

They began to play, and April stepped to the front
edge of the platform to sing, her voice sweet and clear.
Her gaze swept over the heads of the dancers. Noah's
dark hat was easy to spot beneath a lantern as he
passed through the crowd across the Plaza from her.
Watching him go, wishing he cared, wishing he would
stay all evening, she sang to him alone. And then he
turned, and paused to lean against a post. It was too
dusky and he was too far away for her to see if he
watched her or not, but he had stopped to face her and
she hoped he was watching. She hoped he was thinking about her, but she knew that in reality her song,
which had been a favorite during the war, probably
made him think of Alabama and Fanchette.

She closed her eyes, seeing his sapphire eyes in her
mind, remembering the waltz, singing only to him.
She wanted him as much as she had ever wanted Emilio. When she opened her eyes, he was gone.

* * *

The next afternoon as April worked preparing dinner, she heard horses coming up the road. She dried
her hands and stepped outside to see a wagon approaching, a tall man with a hat squarely on his head
driving the team. Luke. Catalina and the children must
be inside the wagon, out of the sun. With joy April
waved and ran back to the house.

"Luke's here!" she shouted. She raced toward the
wagon, which had turned on her land.

"Luke! Luke!" she cried, rushing to greet him and
climbing up on the wagon as it halted. He caught her
arm and lifted her in easily, laughing at her, his green
eyes sparkling with delight.

Hattie heard April's cry and followed her, hurrying
out of the bedroom. Lucius was here! "Javier, hurry!
They're here!"

She felt as if her heart would burst with happiness.
If only they had Tigre, the family would be complete!
Luke's image came to mind, and as she stepped through
the door she had to pause. All these years she had
remembered the handsome, slender young sixteen-
year-old. A broad-shouldered, dark-skinned man stood
before her, and his face was lined with scars. For just
an instant Hattie was taken aback. As he gazed over
April's head, his green eyes met Hattie's, and her heart
seemed to turn over with joy. She ran down the steps
and he caught her, sweeping her up in arms as strong
as Javier's, burying his face against her neck.

"Mother," he whispered, crushing the breath from her
lungs. She thought her ribs might break, but she didn't
care. She held him, crying and clinging to him until he
set her on her feet and held her away to look at her.

"You're as pretty as I remembered," he said hoarsely,
rubbing his eyes with the back of his hand. They stared at
each other intently. So many years of searching and longing and hope were bound up in this reunion; he pulled her
to him again to crush her in his arms.

This time when he released her, his voice still raw
with emotion, he said, "I want you to meet my wife
and your grandchildren." He drew a beautiful dark-

skinned, black-eyed woman to his side. "This is Catalina. Catalina, this is my mother."

Catalina stepped forward to hug her. "I'm so happy for Luke and April and you that you have found each other. And I'm happy for my children to finally have a grandmother."

She stepped back, and three small boys moved to her side to cling to her skirt. "This is Knox," she said, ruffling the hair on the tallest boy, who was dark-skinned and black-haired like his mother. "And this is Jeff," she said, dropping her hand to the shoulder of a sandy-haired boy with big brown eyes. "And this is Emilio," she said, pointing to a small boy who had knelt down to study ants trailing across the sand. "Emilio." He looked up, locks of black hair curling over his wide forehead above his big green eyes. He stared at Hattie and she smiled at all three.

Remembering Javier, Hattie looked around and saw him watching from the porch. "Javier, come here and meet Luke and his family."

When she turned back around, Luke's jaw had set grimly in a manner she had never seen in his years as a boy. Luke had been a gentle child, intelligent, cooperative, but in that moment she realized that gentleness might not be a part of his nature now. He looked as if he were controlling rage, and with a shock she realized that it was directed at Javier.

She turned to give Javier a curious glance, and her shock deepened. He was watching Luke, and she saw he had unfastened the leather flap to his holster. He looked ready to go for his six-shooter, and her heart seemed to stop beating. Luke and Javier. They had never met before. Why would they share a burning hatred before they had spoken their first word?

Fear that she hadn't experienced in a long time hit her. Suddenly she felt as if two of the most important people in her life were in terrible danger.

18

Tigre splashed out of the river, drying himself off. He pulled on a fresh white shirt that he had prevailed on one of the ladies at the Golden Pleasure Palace to wash for him. He grinned when he thought of Tabby. Overweight, over thirty, and usually over dressed, she was fun and he always had a good time with her. Once when she was drunk, she had gazed at him with tears in her big brown eyes and told him she had married a no-good man who beat her and finally had traded her to another man for two mules. She had sobbed over that, asking him over and over all night if he didn't think she was worth more than two mules. She was good to him and she made no bones about wanting him in her bed. But at the moment, every time he went near a woman he thought about Melissa Hatfield, and his desire for anyone else cooled.

Melissa. He ached for her, longed for her. He wanted her more than he had ever wanted anything or anyone. He yanked on his pants and strode over to the box he had for her. Tabby had run that errand too, which hadn't been as easy as getting a shirt, but she finally found it, and now he had a gold ring. Tabby had told the merchant that she was buying the ring for one of her customers, a married man who didn't want it known that he was giving his lady of the evening a ring. Tigre grinned and picked up the box, taking out the small gold ring that wouldn't fit on any of his fingers. Lord, he hoped Melissa would run away with him.

As he moved around dressing and destroying evidence of his camp, he rehearsed what he would say to her. He had stayed far too long in the territory, and he had a wary feeling he had pushed his luck beyond its limits. He knew he would have to leave soon, or risk being caught. He fastened his silver spurs and buckled his gunbelt around his hips. They could go to Texas, or back east, or out west to California. Anywhere out of New Mexico Territory would be safe.

He should remain protected in the darkness, but he knew he had to quit sneaking to her house. Her father was no fool, and there were neighbors, too many chances of being seen. As Tigre folded his bedroll, visions of Melissa came to him and he paused, gazing out toward the distant mountains, seeing only her thick black curls and rosy lips, hurting, he wanted her so badly—only it wasn't a physical hurt. It was heart and soul. She was all he thought he could never have— sweet, lovely, so innocent and good, with a family that wasn't so different from his own in many ways. He swore softly, clamping his jaw tightly shut. He prayed she would go with him, knowing he shouldn't ask her, because it would cut her off from her family forever.

He paused again, guilt assailing him over what he was about to do. She loved her mother deeply, and Selma Hatfield seemed to be a truly good woman. Ti-gre swore over his dilemma, striding to his horse. This was a chance for a decent life, to go away and start again with someone at his side. He didn't think he could ever love anyone more than he did Melissa. She was perfection, fulfillment. His money could provide a fair start—ill-gotten booty, but he intended to use it. He saddled his horse and mounted, then rode north at a leisurely pace. He had plenty of time to wait until midnight.

At the thought of town and the Hatfields' house, a chill ran down his spine, and he gave a little shake, trying to rid himself of a nagging unease that plagued him. A small inner voice warned him not to go see her, but he had to. He fingered the box tucked beneath his shirt. Lord, how he hoped she would accept! It would mean going back one more time to get her. Only one more time in town. He had it all planned. If she consented, he would return for her Saturday night. They would ride north, the quickest way out of the territory. He could be across the border in no time.

His folks were at April's now, and Luke, the brother he had never met, would be there soon. Saturday night—tomorrow, the last night of Fiesta—he was going to April's to see them. Saturday night everyone in town would be at the Fiesta. April had said even the two old widowed sisters who lived across from her would be there with their friends. He would see his family and then in the darkness of early morning—if she would go with him—he would get Melissa.

Thinking of a brother—an ex-marshal—made Tigre's lip curl with a cynical laugh. The ex-marshal and his brother the outlaw. Tigre had heard about the recent hanging. Melissa had wept telling him about it, fearful for his safety. He groaned, wanting to hold her, wanting her in his arms with no barriers between them. They should be married, able to love each other without fear or worry.

A wedding night with Melissa. The thought ran through him like a flame, and he tried to force his mind elsewhere. He had miles to ride, and if he continued tormenting himself with visions and worries, he would be a nervous fool by the time he saw her tonight. He tried to think about his parents, the long journey they had had to make to reach Albuquerque, and what they would do during their stay. They would probably want April to go home to live with them.

While Tigre's thoughts wandered, a snake slithered out in front of his horse. The horse whinnied and shied, rearing on its hind legs. The snake coiled as Tigre drew his six-shooter and fired, killing the snake instantly. He fought to get his horse under control, replacing his pistol in his holster, swearing because the incident stretched his already raw nerves. It wasn't an omen, he told himself. "It was just a damned snake!" he said aloud to no one. Lifting his jaw, Tigre rode slowly north.

* * *

He shifted in the darkness, waiting patiently. His eyes were fully adjusted as he watched lights go out in first one house and then another, until finally all the houses on the block were dark. He watched Melissa's window and saw her wave a white handkerchief at him. Wearing her pink wrapper, she stood in the darkened window, a pale blur in the night, and he knew she thought it was now safe for him. His gaze swept his surroundings again. Another chill came like fog creeping in, making the hairs crawl along the nape of his neck. He shifted uneasily, suddenly wanting to postpone seeing her. Since he had escaped hanging, he had always followed his instincts. Once he even canceled a bank robbery as he and his gang rode into town to the bank. And it had been a good thing. He discovered the sheriff had a posse of men watching the bank all that week because they expected a shipment of gold on the Overland Express.

He had the same uneasy feeling tonight. He'd had it all day. He glanced up to see Melissa still standing at the window. Torn by this unusual indecision, he tossed his fears aside as foolishness. It was dark, quiet, and he was alone.

He moved stealthily to the tree by the Hatfield house and climbed, his spurs jingling in the night. Then he was inside with Melissa in his arms, and the world suddenly seemed right.

She was soft and smelled sweet as he kissed her hungrily. His hands slipped over her body, feeling her curves and warmth through the thin layers of only her wrapper and gown. He reached down, fumbling with his gunbelt to get it off as his body throbbed with desire. He lowered the gunbelt to the floor quietly, scooping Melissa into his arms to move to the bed, where he sat down and pulled her onto his lap. His hand tangled in her thick curls, soft and smelling of rosewater, and he felt as if his heart would pound through his chest as he kissed her.

He remembered the ring and shifted her away slightly, fumbling under his shirt. The box had slipped around, resting on his side above his belt, and he fished

it out, pulling her away from him to gaze into her wide
eyes. "I love you, Melissa," he said.

"Oh, Tigre, I love you too!" She started to lean
forward to kiss him, her lashes fluttering down as she
closed her eyes, but when his hand tightened to hold
her away, she looked at him curiously.

"I want to marry you," he said solemnly, feeling
as if his heart and breath and time itself had stopped
while he watched her. "I want you to come away with
me where we'll be safe." He placed the box in her
hand.

"Tigre!" she whispered, her voice filled with wonder. She opened the box and stared at the gold band,
lifting it out carefully. He took it from her, taking her
hand in his, and watched her steadily as he slipped the
ring on her finger.

"Will you marry me, Melissa?"

Her heart beat wildly. Patrick. She would never see
him again. She would hurt him terribly. It would mean
giving up her family—she would never see her mother
again. And yet—Tigre's kisses made her shake with
desire. He was a good man, and he would treat her
well. *An outlaw.* She bit her lip and gazed at him. "I
love you," she repeated solemnly, "but there are
things to think about."

"Melissa, I can't keep coming to see you. They'll
catch me if I keep it up." He held up his hand. "I
swear to you, Melissa, from this night I'll never again
rob anyone or take anything that isn't mine."

"I'm glad!"

"I shouldn't have these past years, but I was so angry over what happened to me and the unfairness of it
all. I think I wanted to strike out at the world." He
stroked her cheek. "When I was a kid, all I ever
wanted was a sheep ranch so I could live like Pa. He's
the happiest man on this earth. He and Ma are both
happy, and the ranch is beautiful. Someday I'll take
you there. It's high in the mountains where the streams
are clear and the air is cool and fresh. The trees go
straight up to the sky, blue spruce and tall aspen with

thin white trunks and leaves that dance. I'll keep my
promise and never take another thing.''

She touched his cheek, her fingertips running across
his bristly jaw. He was breathtakingly handsome,
dashing, fun, exciting. ''Tigre, it's a difficult decision.''

''I'll do everything I can for you. I love you.''

''Yes,'' she said in a quick breath.

Tigre's breath went out as his arms tightened around
her. Happiness beyond any he had ever experienced
burst in him, and he crushed her in his arms, kissing
her wildly, leaning over her as they tumbled on the
bed. His leg moved over her hip, and he pressed her
closer against him while his blood heated with desire.
Later, he decided if he hadn't been kissing Melissa so
passionately, he would have heard the creak of floor-
boards in the hall.

Selma Hatfield screamed from the doorway.

Tigre lunged off the bed, scooping up his gunbelt as
he went, scrambling for the window.

''Mother!''

''Melissa!'' came the horrified, shocked reply.

Tigre jumped through the window, almost missing
the limb of the tree in his haste. He grabbed it, dan-
gling over the ground. He swung his feet up and
scrambled along the limb to a secure spot, where he
tried to descend as quickly as possible. He yanked his
pistol from the holster, tossing the gunbelt aside. His
horse was more than a mile from the house.

He dropped to the ground and was running fast when
the back door of the Hatfield house burst open and
Ned Hatfield aimed a rifle at him.

The blast shattered the night. Tigre felt the slam of
the shot as it struck him, and he pitched face-forward.

He had taken it high in the shoulder, and he knew
it wasn't going to be fatal, but he also knew Ned Hatfield's reputation for firing first and asking questions
later. He lay still as death, knowing now was not the
time to try to run for it. He was bleeding, and on foot,
and Ned Hatfield would kill him with the next shot.

Tigre still held his pistol in his hand, his finger on the trigger.

Melissa's screams and Selma's cries mingled with Ned's bellows. Tigre heard the stomp of boots and knew Hatfield was approaching him.

"Melissa is in her room," Selma Hatfield said. "See if he's still alive. If he is, I'm going for Dr. Yishay."

"The hell you are. If he's alive, I'll finish the job."

Tigre's fingers tightened on the pistol. He could roll over, kill Ned Hatfield, and escape. But if he did, Melissa would never go with him.

Hatfield grunted with each breath from hurrying across the yard. He knelt, his fingers pressing Tigre's throat. "He's damned alive." He stood up, and Tigre heard the click of Hatfield's rifle.

"No!" Selma Hatfield cried. "If you kill that boy now, I'll tell Sheriff Pacheco you killed him when he was defenseless."

"It won't matter, he's wanted."

"I'll kill you, Papa, if you don't go for Dr. Yishay," Melissa said in a quavering voice, and Tigre could hear the scuff of feet as her parents turned around. He wanted to yell at her to stay out of it, but he was afraid he might frighten her into doing something rash.

"Melissa!" Selma Hatfield said.

"You put that damned pistol down," her father ordered. "You've disgraced us!"

Melissa was crying.

Tigre ground his jaws together, feeling helpless, knowing he couldn't kill her father, but knowing just as well that if he moved without killing Ned Hatfield, he would be dead.

"I mean it, Papa. You ride for Dr. Yishay. Tigre gets a fair trial. Move away from him, Mama."

Tigre could hear her mother's footsteps.

"You little slut," Ned Hatfield snapped. "I'll get the damned doctor, and then I'll take care of you. And when I come back, your mother is to have my pistol. Is that understood?

"As soon as Dr. Yishay gets here, I'll give the pistol to Mama."

"He's not dead. He'd better be right here when I get back."

"He will be, Ned," Selma said. "Give me your rifle."

Tigre heard Ned Hatfield leave, and then Melissa ran to fling herself down beside him. She was sobbing wildly as he rolled over.

"Tigre!"

"Don't cry," he said, hurting far worse over Melissa than from his wound. "I'm hit in the shoulder and I'll be all right."

"Melissa, get up to the house and get some clean rags so we can stop the bleeding. Can you move to the house?"

"Yes, ma'am."

"Then we'll go inside to wait. Melissa can tend your wound," she said stiffly. "Do not try to escape, because I won't hesitate to shoot. You have brought on my daughter's ruin. It won't help to see you dead, but I wouldn't have any regrets."

"Mama!"

"Get the rags, Melissa."

"I'll help Tigre inside." He stood up, slipping his good arm around Melissa. Selma Hatfield moved back out of reach behind him, and he realized she was familiar with rifles. Once again his mind raced. He knew he could use Melissa as a shield and escape, but he wouldn't do it.

Melissa cried quietly while she worked on him, and her mother stood at the door with the rifle aimed at his heart. He leaned back in the chair, feeling weak, his shoulder throbbing with pain.

"I'm sorry for the trouble I've caused," he said to Melissa.

"Don't say that," she whispered. She brought a damp cloth and wiped his face.

"Now, Melissa, go to your room."

"Mama, please."

"Do what she says, Melissa. I don't want you here

when your father returns,'' Tigre said. He looked at
her intently wondering if it was the last time he would
ever see her. In spite of her tears, her tangled locks,
and the smudges of his blood on her wrapper, she still
looked beautiful to him. ''Good-bye, Melissa,'' he
said, knowing she would never go away with him. He
could feel the hangman's noose dropping over his head,
and he leaned back with his head against the wall and
his eyes closed.

Sobbing, Melissa ran from the room. The steady
clicking of the clock was the only sound when she was
gone. Tigre sat up. ''I'm sorry, ma'am. I truly love
her, and I didn't mean to bring trouble to her.''

''I don't know how you could have expected anything else but trouble. If you had an ounce of goodness
in you, you wouldn't have hurt her this way. She's ruined.''

He looked into Selma Hatfield's eyes. ''She isn't ruined. I did little more than kiss her.''

''It won't matter. Gossip will make it worse.''

''Ma'am, don't sell your daughter short. This is the
frontier, and a good woman is like a diamond. Melissa
is good through and through.''

Selma blinked and frowned at him. Tigre closed his
eyes again and waited. In minutes Dr. Yishay as well
as Ned Hatfield and Sheriff Pacheco arrived.

''You're under arrest for murder,'' Sheriff Pacheco
said. ''Fix him up, Doc, so I can get him to jail.''

''Why bother the doc, I say,'' Ned Hatfield stated
forcefully. ''Let's get him down to the jail and string
him up. Why wait? He's going to hang.''

''He gets a trial,'' Sheriff Pacheco replied.

''Damn foolish, if you ask me. You know he's
guilty.''

Aaron Yishay straightened up from looking at
Tigre's wound. ''He can travel to the jail. I'll treat him
there. Let's get out of Hatfield's house.''

''Ned, I'll write off to the authorities for your reward money,'' Sheriff Pacheco promised.

''Want me to come with you to help guard him?''

''It won't be necessary,'' the sheriff answered.

"Doc's with me," he added with a grin. Everyone in town knew Aaron Yishay didn't carry a pistol.

"Come on, son."

Tigre went with them, his spirits sinking further when he entered the adobe jail and sat down for the doctor to treat his shoulder. When the sheriff left them momentarily, Tigre looked up.

"Doc, I have family in town. I don't want them hurt. Do you think people will find out they're my folks?"

"I don't see how you can keep it from them. Who's your family?"

"April Danby."

"Miss April?"

"Yes, sir. I wouldn't want her or my ma and pa hurt for anything."

"You should have thought of that sooner."

Tigre closed his eyes as if he had been slapped. Aaron bandaged his shoulder swiftly, mulling over the events of the night and realizing they were far more complicated than had first appeared. He glanced at Tigre and saw that his lashes were wet. Aaron's brow furrowed in a frown and he thought about his own boys, who were only a little older than this one.

"I didn't know April had another brother."

"No, sir. My parents thought April drowned right before I was born. I'm the one that stirred up the whoop-de-doo at the church, and April faced me down for it. I went to see her again, and when I was talking to her, she realized who I was. That's how she found her family."

"Do tell. Son, you got yourself and some fine people in a real pickle."

"I know that, sir. I love Melissa Hatfield more than anything on this earth."

"It won't do you any good now."

"I realize that," Tigre said. It seemed strange that they were discussing the matter so calmly when he just wanted to yell and fight and escape. He wanted Melissa, and he didn't want to hang.

Aaron finished as Sheriff Pacheco returned to the

room. "I'm through here. He wasn't hurt badly, considering." He reached down to pat Tigre on his good shoulder. "I'll send you the bill," he told the sheriff. "Good night, Pacheco. Keep a guard on him. Don't let that hothead get a posse and come down here trying to lynch the boy, or you'll have me to answer to." He stared up into the sheriff's dark eyes.

"I won't, Doc. That's a promise."

"Good night." He left, pausing beside his horse to gaze at Noah's saloon. The Plaza was quiet now, all the saloons dark except the Two Bits, where yellow light spilled from the open door of the squat adobe.

He mounted and turned his horse in the opposite direction from his house. Five minutes later, he was facing Noah McCloud in his bedroom.

"Son, you seem to have an inordinate interest in Miss April."

Coming fully awake, Noah pulled on his pants. "I hope you didn't get me up just to make that observation."

"As surely as grass is green, I didn't, for a fact. Did you know that she has a brother in addition to the brother in San Antonio?"

Noah studied Dr. Yishay. April had confided in Noah, and he didn't care to relate her private matters to others, but something had to be terribly wrong for Aaron to wake him up in the dead of night. "Yes, I do. He's wanted for murder."

"Sit down, McCloud. We need to have a talk."

19

April saw Hattie tense, and with one glance at Luke
and Javier, she knew exactly what was happening. She
grasped Luke's arm. "Luke, no."

"Get away, April. This is long overdue." He un-
buckled his gunbelt and handed it to April.

"Luke, please!" April begged, and Catalina whispered to him. "Listen to her, Luke. Boys, let's go
inside. Come right now."

Hattie watched them all in confusion. She seemed
to be the only adult who didn't know what was happening. "Luke? Javier? What is it?"

"Hattie, go inside," Javier said harshly.

"Do as he says," Luke added, while Javier unbuck-
led his holster and dropped it in the dust.

"No!" April cried, and flung herself in front of
Luke, gripping his upper arms. "You mustn't," she
urged. "It can only hurt. It won't help anything now.
It's over, Luke. *Over!*"

"April, take Mother inside and leave us alone," he
said grimly, watching Javier.

"I have to know what's happening," Hattie screamed,
going to stand beside April, turning to look at Javier.
"Javier, what is it?"

"Go ahead, Javier, tell her," Luke said with a sneer
in his voice. But Luke didn't wait for a reply. Suddenly
he brushed past the women and strode the short distance to Javier. He threw a punch with all his power,
his right connecting solidly on Javier's jaw and sending him to the ground.

"Stop it!" April cried, but Hattie caught her arm.
Javier sat up, shaking his head.

"Get up and fight," Luke snapped. "Or are you too cowardly to do that too?"

The color drained from Hattie's face, and she turned April to face her. One look at her mother's expression, and April knew she had guessed part of the truth. Hattie stormed toward Javier, who sat looking up at Luke. "I demand to know what you did."

Luke swore and picked up his gunbelt. "I'm sorry, Mother, to hurt you, but you and April and I deserved better than this man gave us." He looked down at Javier, who sat as still as a stone in front of them. Luke spat in the dirt beside him. "If you won't get up and fight like a man, I'll leave you. If it weren't for my mother, I would have drawn on you."

Javier sat with his head down. He didn't move or speak, and Luke turned, taking April's arm to lead her into the house.

Hattie gazed down at the man she had loved for twenty years. She loved him as much as a woman could love a man, yet now she saw she hadn't really known the dark side of him.

"What did you do to us?" she whispered.

He raised his head, and tears showed in his eyes. "If I could have taken back my deeds, I would have a thousand times over, but it was done and I couldn't."

"Did you try to drown April?" Hattie couldn't believe the words she was saying. Her head spun, and she felt as if the hot sun were burning through to her soul.

"Dios, no!"

"What did you do? You have to tell me, Javier."

He stood up as if an old man, unfolding slowly, brushing off his pants. "I hadn't known you long," he said stiffly, his voice agonized. "I wanted my own child; you didn't know the girl's father. She could have had . . ."

"Many men could have been the father," Hattie said bitterly. "Desperadoes, thieves, drifters. Go ahead. You have to tell me."

"I took her to a woman at a bordello and gave her to them to keep. I paid the woman to take her."

Blackness engulfed Hattie. She swayed and Javier's hands steadied her. Instantly she yanked away. "Don't touch me!" She stepped back.

"Hattie, *por Dios,* I'm sorry. I'm sorry a thousand times over."

"Javier. Do not touch me. Go home. Go away from me. You are not welcome in this house!"

"Madre de Dios, Hattie, please—"

"How could you take my little girl? How could you have been that cruel? Now you have no one. Go home."

"It's *your* home, Hattie. I've done it all for you. I know I did a terrible deed, but by the time I realized that, there was no way to undo it. I love you more than my own life. As the years have passed, I have grown to love you beyond anything I dreamed, and I have suffered a million times over for what I did. Please forgive me."

Of all the hardships she had endured, she had never dreamed she would face one like this. "Go, Javier. I do not want to see you again." She turned and strode into April's house and slammed the door. The moment it shut behind her, all her strength seemed to drain away as water tumbling out of a spilled container. Her head swam and the floor came up to meet her.

Catalina ran to her. "Look what you have done!" she accused Luke. "April is in her room crying, your mother has fainted."

"Catalina, he deserved worse." Luke picked up Hattie and carried her to the settee, where he stretched her out while Catalina went to get a damp cloth and a glass of water.

April came into the room. "I heard—" She hurried to her mother. "Is she all right?"

"She just fainted." He accepted the cloth as Hattie stirred. He wiped her forehead and held her head up. "Here, sip this." While Catalina and April watched, she drank, her gaze on her son. When he lowered the glass, she said, "I never knew."

"I know you didn't," he answered, and April saw there was a bond between Hattie and Luke that time hadn't severed.

She struggled to sit up. "I must get his things. I told him to go. He's a proud man; he will not come in to collect his belongings."

April knelt beside her, gripping her hands. "Please. All this is because of me! Don't do this. Don't send him away. I know you've been happy with him."

Hattie gazed at her solemnly and shook her head. "Luke understands. It isn't just you, April. What he did hurt many. It hurt me beyond belief to think I had lost my precious baby after losing Luke."

"That's all past!" April said. "Luke, this isn't right!" she said, glancing at him and meeting a cold green gaze that she knew was as unyielding as the ground. She turned back to Hattie. "It will hurt Tigre. Tigre is innocent in all this! Javier is his father."

For a moment something flickered in Hattie's eyes, and then the coldness returned. "No. He took my baby. Tigre never had the sister he should have had. You never had a wonderful brother you should have had. You've had a life that was hard and lonely, and perhaps dangerous. I do not know. What Javier did was a sin. I can't forgive him. Tigre was born early. I could have lost him because of my grief. No. Javier must go." She stood up and left the room to get his things, and the three adults looked at each other. Catalina was impassive, staring out the window. Unconcerned with the problems of the adults, the boys played in the kitchen, eating cookies April had placed on the table.

Luke stood up and moved restlessly across the room, glancing outside. "He's hitching up his wagon." He looked at April. "It involves more than you, and that son of a bitch had a lot worse coming for what he did. It was all I could do to keep from shooting him."

"And what will you tell your brother?"

"Tigre is his son."

"And your mother's. Tigre is your brother, Luke, just as much as I'm your sister."

He sighed. "I know that, and if he loves Hattie, he will see why I did what I did. As she said, he lost his sister because of his father's actions."

"He's coming tomorrow night while Fiesta is going."

"If he just hadn't compounded the murder with the robberies, the murder might have had another real trial and he could have been acquitted, but to add years of theft to that—there's no hope."

"He looks like her," April said. "You'll see for yourself."

Hattie returned with two bundles and a rifle under her arm. Without a word she went outside, and Luke moved to the window to watch her.

With bright sunshine beaming down on her, she crossed the yard. Javier turned to watch her. He looked older and worn, but Hattie felt no sympathy for him. She held out his things.

"Oh, *Dios*, Hattie, please," he begged.

"Good-bye." She returned to the house, wondering if she would ever feel happiness again. "I must be alone for a little while," she said, walking into the bedroom and closing the door behind her.

April went to start supper, wanting to work and move around, to busy herself some way. There was no way she could sit down and chat when her emotions were in turmoil.

Emilio tugged on her skirt. "Aunt April, more milk, please."

"Of course, Emilio," she said. He was a beautiful child with large green eyes and black hair. He looked like both of his parents, but very little like the man he was named for. It was their oldest, Knox Danby, who looked like Emilio more each time she saw him. He had grown an inch since she'd last seen him. Now he finished his cookie and slid off the chair, going out the back door and slamming it. He was seldom still, stomping and running and jumping, unlike Emilio in character, but so like him in appearance. She watched him run across the field, Jeff hurrying outside after him. Emilio set down the milk, running on short legs to try to catch his brothers.

How nice to be a child, she thought, picking up cookie crumbs.

"I'll help," Catalina said from the doorway. "Javier Castillo is leaving, and as soon as he is gone, Luke and the boys will unload our things. The boys can sleep in the wagon tonight.''

"You and Luke can have my room. Hattie can sleep on the settee, and I'll sleep on the floor. It's no trouble.''

They heard the jingle of harness and creak of wheels and April moved to the window. In moments the wagon rolled into sight, Javier holding the reins as the team headed back toward the center of town to turn north on the road home.

"Hattie can stay here.''

"She can go home with us,'' Luke said from the doorway. "I'd like for her to go with us for a while, April.''

She nodded as he crossed the room. "Where are the boys?''

"Outside.''

Luke left, whistling, a high shrill whistle that stopped all three boys. They turned around to run back toward the house and began to help Luke unload the wagon. During their early supper, April felt as if someone had died. The conversation was disjointed, sometimes light, then lapsing back into a somber mood as they were reminded of the absence of Javier. As soon as supper was over, April promised to be home as quickly as possible. She stood on tiptoe and brushed Luke's cheek with a kiss.

"Don't scowl. I sing at the Fiesta first. I have a good job.''

"Damned if you have! You shouldn't be working in a saloon. You could come home with us too.''

"Luke, we've been over that every time you've been here.''

He caught her chin to tilt her face up and look into her eyes. "You won't be torn with grief over reminders of Emilio if you come back to live with us now.''

"No, but don't you see, I'm accustomed to my independence—''

"April, you should be meeting eligible bachelors—''

She laughed and danced away from him. "Oh, Luke! Eligible bachelors! Do you know how many times I say no?''

"San Antonio is an older town with more settled

people. This is the frontier. We can introduce you into society.''

Catalina moved past them and April saw the twinkle in her eyes, and knew that she, too, was amused at Luke's efforts. Catalina shrugged. ''Your sister, my dear husband, is as stubborn as you.''

''Dammit.''

''And I have to sing.'' April dashed out the door before he could say another word, but she knew she would hear far more on the subject. Now that he had Hattie, there was far more reason for her to go to San Antonio with them. And she was tempted, yet she didn't want to leave Albuquerque. And she had to face the fact that she didn't want to leave as long as Noah was in town. When he was gone, she could go visit in San Antonio and see how she liked it, but for now she had to stay here.

Later that Friday night, after the boys were bedded down in the wagon, the adults sat in the yard where it was cooler and sipped lemonade while they talked about years past. Luke and April let Hattie know all they had done, yet carefully avoided any mention of Domingo Piedra, Catalina's father, the man who had captured and traded Hattie.

They finally went to bed, and April lay on the floor on a blanket, staring into the darkness, wondering if sleep was as difficult for Hattie as it was for her. She thought of Javier wending his lonely way back to his ranch in the mountains and what a burden he must carry. She couldn't feel the hatred Luke did. The past was done, and she hated the hurt the truth had brought to Hattie.

April finally dozed, to waken to Hattie shaking her shoulder.

''April, wake up. Someone's at the door.''

Coming alert at once, April stood up. ''It's the middle of the night. Javier?''

''No. I looked out the window. There's a horse.''

''Who the hell is at the door?'' Luke whispered, entering the room. He was bare-chested and barefoot, wearing only his pants and carrying his six-shooter. ''Everyone get back.''

He opened the door and Noah looked down the muzzle of a Colt.

"Sorry to wake you. I'm Noah Mc—"

"Noah! Luke, put the pistol down. Come inside." April bent over a lamp, and as soon as it flared to life she said, "Noah, meet my brother Luke Danby. Luke, this is Noah McCloud."

Hattie had left the room, going to the bedroom with Catalina, and Luke shook hands grimly, with barely a nod at Noah.

Noah turned to April and placed his hand on her shoulder. "Aaron Yishay woke me."

"It's Tigre!" she said, guessing something disastrous had happened.

"He's at the jail."

"Oh, Lord," she said. Noah squeezed her shoulder, aware she was wearing only her nightgown. It was as thick as a woolen blanket, yet he could feel her warm shoulder beneath it, and with her hair falling over her shoulders, it was difficult to think about Tigre's danger. He glanced at Luke, who looked friendlier now and had put away his pistol.

"What happened?" Luke asked. "Maybe I can help."

"He was caught in Melissa's room."

"Oh, no! I was afraid of that," April said, aware Noah kept his hand on her, his fingers lightly kneading her shoulder, his blue eyes studying her intently.

"Ned Hatfield shot him in the shoulder. Aaron says it's not a bad wound, the shot went clean through. He'll be all right, but they intend to hang him. And it won't go easy on Melissa."

They all seemed to hear the hoofbeats at the same time. Noah raised his head, Luke's eyes narrowed, and April glanced from one to the other in question. They heard a horse coming at a gallop. April expected it to ride past the house, but instead the hoofbeats came closer.

"What the hell?" Luke muttered, and picked up his six-shooter again.

20

A light rapping came and a woman's voice called, "April!"

"That's Melissa!"

"We'll have the whole damn town here before long," Luke grumbled as he opened the door. "Come in and join us."

Melissa's eyes were round as she stared up at Luke and looked at his six-shooter. He quickly placed it on a table and waved his hand for her to enter. The moment she saw April, she burst into tears and threw her arms around her friend's neck.

April patted her back, but Melissa cried out, stepping away from her.

"What's wrong? I didn't mean to hurt you," April said.

"Papa beat me."

"Oh, no!"

"Ladies, let's go sit down," Luke said.

Melissa shook her head. "I can't. I have to go." With tears streaming down her cheeks, she took a gold ring off her finger. "Tigre gave me this tonight. He asked me to marry him. I want you to give it back to him." She started crying, and Noah put his arm high across her shoulders, touching her lightly.

"Melissa," he said gently, "you don't have to do this tonight."

"Yes, I do." She leaned against him for a moment, wiped her eyes, and pulled away. "I told Tigre I would run away with him and marry him." Her words poured out swiftly. April studied Melissa's ashen skin, her tangled hair, and felt a twist of sympathy. Melissa

looked up at Noah. "When . . . Papa shot him . . .
when all the trouble started . . ." She paused to cry,
and all three of them silently waited. "I realized I
couldn't go through life like that. I love him, and part
of me always will, but I can't live that way, running
from the law. And I can't stay at home. It was terrible.
I won't stay there another night. I'm going to find Patrick. He's asked me to marry him and I'm going to."

"Melissa," Noah said gently, "don't do something
in haste you'll regret later. You don't have to go tonight."

"I won't regret it!" she cried. "I can't marry Tigre.
I love Patrick too and I want the quiet and the family
and the security that I know Patrick can give me. And
I won't go home."

"How far away does Patrick live?" Noah asked.

"Seven miles from here."

He looked at Luke. "Can you help with Tigre? If
you can, I'll ride with Melissa to Patrick's so she
doesn't have to go alone." He leaned back and looked
at the palm of his hand, dropping his arm from her
back. April saw the flash of anger in his eyes and wondered what he was thinking. She looked down at the
gold ring in her palm and closed her hand over it,
feeling that Melissa was probably making the best
choice she could. April knew Melissa would never be
able to face what lay ahead for Tigre.

"You two go ahead," Luke replied. "I'll get dressed
and go down to the jail now. I presume the sheriff or
a deputy is there all night."

"Oh, yeah. One of the Pachecos. There are about
eight of them that work around the jail."

"Mr. McCloud, you don't have to ride with me."

"Shh, Melissa. No more about that. We're going to
Aaron Yishay's first, and I don't want any arguments."

"Why?"

"He needs to look at your back. You're bleeding."

"Oh, please. I just want to go to Patrick's."

"We'll get there. I promise you," Noah said, wink-
ing at April, and she felt a sudden warm bond, thank-

ful he was taking care of Melissa. As Melissa turned, April saw the dark stains through her dress and knew why the anger had flashed across Noah's features. Ned Hatfield truly was a monster, and he didn't deserve Melissa.

April followed them to the door. Noah gave her shoulder another squeeze. "Cheer up, honey. Your brother's a lawyer and an ex-marhsal. Maybe he can do something."

"I hope so," she said. She felt better just knowing that Noah was present, and she was acutely aware of his casual *"honey."* She knew he had said it only because of the sad events of the night, but she wouldn't forget.

He helped Melissa mount and then swung up into his saddle, glancing back at April once more. His heart skipped beats, and for an instant all the troubles of the night diminished. April stood in the doorway with the light behind her, the strain of the evening making her forget decorum. Her form was silhouetted by the light through her gown, and his imagination could fill in the rest. Her hair tumbled over her shoulders, the top button of her gown was unfastened, and she looked gorgeous and a little forlorn. It had been a bad night, and he wished he could stay to help with Tigre and reassure her. "Melissa, wait one minute."

Abruptly he swung down out of the saddle and strode back to April. "I can't just ride away," he said softly. "I don't want you to worry. Pacheco is a reasonable man, and Aaron and I will do everything we can to help. Save your worry until all hope is gone, will you?" he asked gently.

April tried to smile, a wavering, feeble smile that didn't fool him. He touched her chin and went back to his horse.

April closed the door and turned around to face Luke, whose eyes were filled with curiosity, and suddenly she became aware of her appearance, aware of the moments with Noah, and her cheeks burned with embarrassment.

"Who is he?" Luke asked mildly.

"Noah McCloud. I better dress. I can't sleep anyway."

"April. Wait a minute. Who is he? Don't just give me a name."

"He's engaged to a woman in Alabama. He's going back there soon. He runs a saloon here, McCloud's Place. I befriended his brother a long time ago during the war—you remember. I told you about it at Christmas."

"The one who died?"

"Yes. His brother mailed a letter to Noah saying he left his gold with me. Noah came to Albuquerque to get his gold, but I don't have it. At first he didn't believe me, but now he does. He's staying until he finds his gold and then he's going home."

"Uh-huh. He must be a *good* friend, for the doctor to get him out of bed at this hour to tell him about Tigre. How'd the doctor know he should be the one to come tell you?"

"Dr. Yishay probably thought . . . well, he just probably thought Noah would like to tell me," she finished lamely. "Luke, don't be so big-brotherish!"

"And McCloud's engaged?"

"Very. I met her when she came to Albuquerque. She's beautiful and she's his childhood sweetheart."

"And now she's gone back to Alabama?"

"Instead of worrying about me, why don't we do something about Tigre?"

Suddenly Luke grinned. "Sure, Sis. You bet. Noah McCloud. Did he fight in the war?"

"Yes."

"And you just can't leave your job to come to San Antonio," he said softly. Before she could reply, Hattie and Catalina came out of the bedroom.

"What was all the commotion?"

Luke's smile vanished. "It's Tigre, Mother. I'll do everything I can to help him. He's in jail."

"Oh, no!" Hattie sat down, scooting over to make room for Catalina on the settee. "Tell me what happened."

"You tell them, April, while I get dressed. I'm going to the jail to meet my brother."

"Luke," Hattie said firmly, "we have to send someone after Javier. He must know if his son might . . ." Her voice trailed off, and everyone knew she couldn't say "hang."

"I don't see why," Luke argued.

"He's Tigre's father. That's only right. Who can go?"

"He's probably half a day's ride ahead of here. I'll go after I've been to the jail."

"He'll camp at Bernalillo, because it should be safe. He won't have traveled far."

Luke nodded and left to dress. In half an hour he stood in front of the deputy at the jail. "I'm Luke Danby, former U.S. marshal from Texas," he said, extending his hand to a sleepy deputy who looked about seventeen years old.

"Yes, sir! Deputy Secundo Pacheco," he said, shaking Luke's hand.

"Are you the sheriff's son?"

"Yes, sir. What can I do for you?"

"I'm here to see Tigre Castillo."

"Yes, sir. Right this way. Did you just get into town?" Pacheco asked, studying Luke with curiosity.

"This afternoon." He followed the five-foot-six Pacheco back to the cells, and his own curiosity rose. He peered through the bars at the handsome young man who stared back with impassive features. He was Hattie's son. The dark skin, eyes, and hair of Javier that usually would have transferred to a son had not in this case. Instead, eyes as pale as April's and Hattie's studied him, and his hair was as golden as buttercups.

"You have a visitor."

"Thanks, Deputy," Luke interrupted, stepping into the cell. "You can lock the door. I'll be safe."

"Yes, sir," he said obediently. Luke had the feeling he could tell him to open the door and let him take the prisoner and he would do so without question. And it was a temptation. Luke had thought he would see Javier Castillo in Tigre and dislike him, but all he could see was Hattie and a faint resemblance to himself. His younger brother.

Looking intently at Luke, Tigre stood up and extended his hand. He glanced beyond him at the doorway where the deputy had been, and then back to Luke. "You're Luke Danby, aren't you?"

Luke took his hand, suddenly pulling Tigre close to hug him, a warm feeling coursing through him, and he silently promised himself he would do everything in his power to keep his younger brother from the gallows.

"Sit down," Luke said in a low voice. "We need to talk."

"There isn't anything the best lawyer on earth can do for me."

"We can try for a prison sentence. That's better than hanging."

"Oh, damn. I don't see how I have any hope for anything except hanging. When did you get to town?"

"This afternoon."

"What a way to meet your brother," Tigre said dryly. "I'm not quite as evil as the wanted posters sound."

"I know. April's told me."

Tigre grinned. "And you believe her just like that?"

"As a matter of fact, I do. I trust the part of you that's my mother's son."

Tigre studied him. "I wish we'd known each other sooner."

"We can't do anything about that, but I do too. I've got some more bad news."

Tigre frowned. "I didn't know it could get much worse."

"You're in for two shocks."

"Two? You sound as if both are bad. Come on, what is it?"

"First, I love my mother, I love April—and I think I'm going to love my brother. But I can't love your father."

Tigre waited in silence, staring at Luke and wondering why he didn't continue, and also why he didn't like Javier. "You don't even know my father. Why wouldn't you like—" He bit off the words and frowned. "There's only one connection between you and him—April."

"That's right. She didn't fall in a river and drown, as you well know he told Hattie."

"God." Tigre's scowl deepened. "I don't believe you!" He jumped to his feet, his fists clenched. "You're lying. You think he did something—"

"I don't think," Luke said quietly. "I know. The woman at the sporting house told me. Your father paid her to take April."

Tigre's eyes widened and his jaw dropped. He sat down. "You think she really told the truth."

"I know she did. There was no reason not to, and I had no idea who Javier Castillo was when I found April."

"My father *abandoned* April? He abandoned a child?" Tigre asked in a hollow voice filled with shock. "Why would he do that?"

"I heard Hattie say he's a proud man. Miss Kate said he told her that Hattie didn't know who April's father was. You know she was taken captive?"

"Yes, I know."

"Your father wanted his own child. He didn't want to raise a bastard child who could have been fathered by Lord knows what kind of man."

"So he took her from Ma, and told Ma that April drowned?" Tigre sounded so agonized, Luke felt sorry for him.

"That's right, and I can't forgive him for it."

"Oh, God." Tigre moved impatiently, standing up and striding to the bars, clenching them for a moment. The white bandage was a contrast to his burnished skin. Muscles rippled when he moved. He looked too young and strong and exuberant to belong in a cell. And Luke liked him. He hadn't expected to, but he did. Tigre returned to stand facing Luke. "Something's happened between you and Pa."

"He's all right, if that's what's worrying you. I

fought with him and he had to admit what he had done. Mother told him to leave, that she never wanted to see him again.''

Tigre sat down, running his fingers through his hair. "Oh, damn, how could he have done that to her? April. All these years that sweet little thing didn't have a family. Oh, dammit!"

Luke waited. Tigre seemed quick and sharp, and Luke knew that in a moment he'd be ready for the next blow. No sooner had the thought crossed Luke's mind than Tigre glanced at him.

"Two things. What's the second? This should be a *bruja.*"

"It is." He reached into his pocket to withdraw the gold ring. "Melissa Hatfield came by tonight."

Tigre inhaled deeply, as if suddenly stabbed. A sound like a groan escaped him as he arched his back against the wall with his eyes squeezed tightly shut. Luke saw that this bit of news was going to be far worse than he had expected. And he knew how he would have felt if Catalina had turned him down.

"I'm sorry."

Tigre clenched his fists, suddenly moving away and striding to the bars to put his face in his hands, and Luke realized he was crying. Luke put his forehead on his fist, his elbow propped on his knee, trying to give Tigre silence and as much privacy as possible, because there was nothing he could do to soften the pain.

Finally Tigre composed himself and sat down. The only evidence of his inner turmoil was his ashen color and the muscle that worked in his jaw. "I'm going to hang, so I shouldn't hold her to it anyway."

"You won't hang if I can help it."

"I have a list of crimes to my name as long as your arm."

"Did you commit all of them?"

Tigre gave him a lopsided, cynical grin. "Almost all. I'm real adept at robbing stages."

"Shh. Don't ever admit it again to anyone."

Tigre looked down at the gold ring in his hand. He

rubbed his finger across it. "Did she get up in the middle of the night to bring this to you? Does she hate me?"

"No, she doesn't hate you. She was crying as if her heart were breaking, but she said she can't live through what happened tonight ever again," Luke told him frankly, knowing that he himself would want the truth if he were in Tigre's place. "She wants peace and security, and she has run away to marry Patrick O'Flynn."

"Tonight?"

Luke waited while Tigre turned red and swore and paced some more. When he had calmed, Luke continued, "Noah McCloud took her to Patrick's. She said she wouldn't spend another night at her parents' house."

Tigre rubbed the ring again. "I love her and I always will. Any more bad news?"

"Not tonight. I'll bring the family to see you tomorrow."

"Oh, no. I don't want Ma and April down here at the jail. And not my new sister-in-law. It's bad enough to have to face a new brother here—and you a lawman to boot."

"Ex-lawman, and maybe it will help. We're coming to see you. I think it's time the good people who know you stood up for you. Just remember while you're here—humble wins more friends than cocky."

Tigre grinned. "Sure, brother. Thanks."

"And get rid of the flamboyant stuff—no bear claws."

Tigre grinned and lifted them. "You like this scar better? The man I killed tried to slit my throat."

"Damn right. Get rid of the bear claws. I'll get you a suit—you can probably wear my coat. Then the world can see why you had to defend yourself."

Tigre shook his head. "Won't do a bit of good."

"Maybe. It's been a bad night, but it's almost over. See you in a few hours."

They stood and shook hands again, and Luke called

Secundo Pacheco. It took three calls before he came, and Luke suspected he had been sound asleep.

Luke kept his promise, and rode out to find Javier. It was early morning when he caught up with him on the road. Javier saw him coming and halted, drawing his rifle and waiting. Wariness gripped Luke, because Javier could easily shoot him. He untied the leather flap over his pistol but kept his hands in plain sight, holding the reins high.

"I promised Mother I'd come for you. Tigre's been arrested."

"*Maldito!*"

"I'm going back," Luke said curtly, unable to stay in the man's presence.

Javier began to turn his wagon as Luke wheeled his horse around and flicked the reins to gallop away. He put as much distance as he could between him and Javier, wanting desperately to get back to Albuquerque.

21

Mid morning Saturday, the last day of Fiesta, Luke
was back, seated at the table eating a late breakfast.
Hoofbeats thudded, and he stared at the door. "April,
you ought to live in the center of town and not on the
edge. You have more people coming to call than the
doctor and the preacher put together."

Someone pounded on the door, and Luke got up.
Frowning, he went to the door and April followed.

Luke opened it and Ned Hatfield glared at them.
"Where is she?"

"Listen, mister," Luke said, taking April's arm and
moving her behind him, "I don't know who the hell
you are, or what you want, but you can keep a civil
tongue." Luke pulled up his six-shooter and cocked
it. "Now state your name and tell me your business."

"I'm Ned Hatfield and I want my daughter. She's
friends with April Danby."

"You son of a bitch, get off this porch."

"Is she in there?"

"No, she's not, but she stopped by here last night.
I have no idea where she is now. You'll have to ask
elsewhere."

"Can I talk to April?"

April tugged on Luke's sleeve. "Yes, you can, Mr.
Hatfield, but what my brother told you is correct. She
was here, but she isn't now."

"Where is she?"

"I think she left town."

"Melissa Jane? Where'd she go?"

April shook her head. "All I can say is what my

brother said. Right now I don't have any idea where she is.''

Without a farewell Hatfield stomped away, and they closed the door. ''I hope she and Patrick are moving somewhere else,'' April said. ''It won't be long before Ned Hatfield goes hunting her.''

''Here comes the next visitor,'' Luke said, peering out the window. ''It would be easier to just sit out on the porch to greet them.''

Catalina laughed as April scooped up Emilio, who had brought her a handful of wildflowers. ''Aunt April, these are for you.''

''Thank you, Emilio. Who's coming this time, Luke?''

''McCloud.''

Aware of Luke's scrutiny, April went to the door. As Noah dismounted, she went down the porch steps to greet him. ''You didn't meet the children last night. This is Emilio Danby. Emilio, meet Mr. McCloud.''

''Hi, Emilio.''

''I brought Aunt April flowers,'' he said proudly.

''And they're beautiful.''

He wiggled. ''I want to go.'' She set him on his feet and he scampered across the yard while she looked up into Noah's eyes.

''She's delivered to Patrick.''

''Her father was just here looking for her.''

''I went with them to get Preacher Nokes. I was a witness to their marriage.''

''Oh, Noah, I hope she's happy.''

''You look pretty,'' he said softly, forgetting all about Melissa Hatfield, Tigre, and the rest of the Danbys.

''Thank you. I'm glad you went with her.''

''She's in love with two men,'' Noah said in a strange voice, ''and she tried to make a wise choice.''

''I imagine she did.''

''Here, wear these,'' he said, taking two of the lavender flowers from her hand and tucking them between the top buttons of her plain brown calico dress. His fingers brushed her throat, a touch that brought back memories of moments alone with him. He didn't look as if he had ridden most of the night or lost any sleep. As she studied him, she remembered Luke and the family.

"Noah, come inside. You haven't met my mother." He took her arm politely as they mounted the steps, and she was keenly aware of his nearness, his hand remaining on her arm when they entered the parlor.

After introductions were made and coffee had been served, Luke announced, "We're going to the jail to-day to pay a visit. I've already been there twice—once to talk to Tigre and the second time this morning to talk to Sheriff Pacheco, to tell him to double the guard. I don't want a lynching and I told him if there is one, I'd cause all the trouble I could cause for everyone involved. Of course, that wouldn't do much good for Tigre, but I think Pacheco got the message. All the Pachecos. How many of them are there?"

"Eight that work at the jail. The younger kids clean and run errands, and the older kids are deputies. He runs a tight crew," Noah said, watching April move around the kitchen, wishing he could be alone with her. He liked her family. Luke had been cool in the crisis last night, and today the women were calm. He sipped his coffee, taking one more of April's biscuits and spreading it with plum jam. Her mother was as pretty as Doc had said. Catalina and Luke were obviously in love. Whenever Catalina was within reach of him, Luke had his hand on her arm, or her shoulder, or around her waist, and Noah felt a stir of envy. Luke sat relaxed, his legs stretched to one side, his arm on Catalina's shoulders while he toyed with a lock of her raven hair. Occasionally she glanced at her husband with a look that should make him happy for a day.

Noah thought of Fanchette. He wanted the kind of marriage the Danbys had. Fanchette was like a little girl, adorable when she was happy, complacent if all went to suit her, wanting to be taken care of by the men in her life—as she always had been. Noah glanced at Hattie, Catalina, and April. They were beautiful women, as pretty as Fanchette in different ways. April

was more slender, taller, Hattie older, Catalina darker
and thinner; all were pretty, yet they were different
from Fanchette. There was an air of independence and
toughness about all three that was probably honed into
them by the land. They were frontier women, and it
showed in little ways—no flirting and coquettishness
like Fanchette, no simpering or wiles to win men to
their views. They were frank, open, warm, and loving. As long as he provided for Fanchette in the manner she wanted, she would do everything she could to
make him happy. She was a lusty wench in bed. His
gaze rested on April speculation.

She stood in front of the window washing potatoes
for dinner. She concentrated on what she was doing,
yet he knew she was listening to Luke talk, because
every once in a while she joined the conversation. His
gaze drifted down. What would April be like in bed?
Her brown calico bodice fitted tightly over breasts that
had to be less full than Fanchette's, a waist that was
tinier, particularly once Fanchette got out of her cor-
set, and legs far longer. His gaze roamed down the
yards of brown calico, but he remembered her onstage
in the saloon. She had gorgeous long legs. He drew a
deep breath, feeling warmer. He met her gaze, and
her cheeks turned pink. He stared back into her eyes
boldly, knowing he should leave her be, but unable to
resist.

She flashed him a faint smile that warmed him more
than sunshine. Then her gaze slid past him to Luke
and away, her cheeks growing even pinker. Noah
looked around to find Luke studying him with cool
speculation.

April paused as she passed the open door. "Here
comes more company."

Luke groaned, teasing her. "I used to worry about
her living here alone. She isn't alone one minute."

"Did she tell you about getting her house broken
into?" Noah asked, receiving a glare from April, but
he wanted Luke to know.

"No! And I'll have to hear about it. Who's coming
this time?"

April didn't answer, but stepped outside to hug Ta-ne-haddle and his family. The boys had spotted them coming and were gathered around, and in minutes Noah was in the middle of a family gathering. He excused himself. "You people sit right there and go on and visit. I need to get back to the saloon." As he went to the door, April went with him, stepping outside.

"At least now I can feel like you're safe," he said.

"You didn't need to tell Luke about the break-in."

"Ta-ne-haddle would have anyway."

"True. Luke wants me to go home to San Antonio with him. Hattie's going with him."

Noah touched the wildflowers, letting his fingers rest on her collarbone, wanting to slip them higher along her slender throat. He didn't want her to go to San Antonio, yet the minute he got back his gold, he would leave town. "Are you going?"

"I don't think so," she answered carefully.

He didn't want to say good-bye right now, yet he didn't have a reason to stay, and her family was waiting. "It's been a long night. Did you sleep any?"

"A little before you came."

"It's Saturday. The day to do the wash."

"That's all changed around. Now I'll do it on Monday."

"The children like you."

"I love them. Their oldest, Knox, is the one who looks like Emilio. His namesake doesn't resemble him at all."

"You might be better off in San Antonio, April. You wouldn't have to sing in a saloon."

"I know. I told Luke I'd think about it."

"The memories of Emilio Piedra have diminished enough that you could go back now?"

"Yes," she answered solemnly, her gaze going over his features with deliberation, as if trying to memorize exactly how he looked.

Noah's pulse jumped when he saw how intently she was studying him. "Wildflowers become you," he said in a husky voice, using the flowers for a flimsy excuse to touch her throat again. "Let me know how Tigre is doing," he said. He winked at her and left, mounting and riding away, and she stood watching him. In the next block he turned and waved, and she waved back. She went inside, and caught Luke watching her.

Embarrassed, she went to the bedroom to plait her hair. They were all going to the jail to call on Tigre, and she wanted to look nice. Noah. She gazed into the mirror, but she saw only his blue eyes and strong jaw, his thick curls, remembered his fingers brushing her neck. She should go to San Antonio, but oh, how hard it would be to leave Albuquerque!

Instead of taking the buggy, they walked from the house, and they were as conspicuous as a calliope. They filled the jail when they entered. All of them had come, including the children. Luke said it wouldn't hurt the children to call on Tigre in jail, and no one argued the matter. Hattie was dressed in her best blue poplin dress with a fancy straw bonnet. April, Catalina, Ta-ne-haddle, Lottie, carrying Dawn, the boys, and Luke faced Sheriff Pacheco.

"The man's had more visitors than a voting booth."

"It runs in the family," Luke remarked.

"Doc's been here, his pa, and then Tabitha—"

"Tabitha?" Luke asked.

Sheriff Pacheco glanced at Hattie, April, and Catalina and blushed. "Well, yes. This way."

April knew Tabitha was one of the sporting girls at the Golden Pleasure Palace, and she wondered if Tigre had called on her as well as Melissa. They waited while the sheriff opened his cell and all of them crowded inside. Favoring his wounded shoulder, he hugged Hattie and was introduced to the ones he didn't know. His face was flushed, but he looked pleased to see them, and April prayed he wouldn't hang. He seemed so young and vulnerable, particularly with his shoulder bandaged. He knelt down to talk a moment to each of the boys, who seemed to take to him as if they were the same age. He picked up Dawn, holding her in his good arm while she played with the bear claws that were still around his neck.

When they said their good-byes, he squeezed Hattie again. As they left, he caught April by the arm and tugged her back. "Luke said Melissa married Patrick last night."

"I'm sorry, Tigre."

"She'll be happier. I hope he's a good man."

"Patrick is good. He's reliable and good, and he loves her deeply."

He nodded, still holding firmly to her arm. "Would you send Ma back for a minute? I want a word alone with her."

April agreed to join the others in the next room, and they waited while Hattie went back to see him.

"Tigre," she said in a low voice, "I know what you want."

"Ma, Pa was here this morning. Please give him another chance."

"Don't ask me to do that, Tigre. Don't ask."

"I have to," he argued. "Ma, a man can change. That was years ago. He said he's regretted it for years."

"If he had truly regretted it, he could have gone back for her."

"Maybe he didn't know how to tell you what he'd done. By the time he could have gone back, he may have decided April was happy where she was. I don't know. All I know is that he's sorry. Ma, he can't live without you."

"Oh, Tigre, of course he can! Your father's a strong man."

"Not without you."

"Tigre, you're still a child. I can't forgive him."

"Ma, we're all together now as a family."

"It's not the same and you know it!"

"I don't think you're going to be as happy either. You're not the unforgiving, unbending kind."

"Tigre, leave me alone!" she said, pulling out a handkerchief to wipe her eyes. "I'm going. The others are waiting."

He felt desperate. He loved both parents, and the past was over, they couldn't redo it, and he felt as if his own future was gone. And when they hanged him, Tigre knew it would kill part of his father as well. If Javier didn't have Hattie—if his parents didn't have each other—the loss would be worse. "Ma. I may hang Monday morning. I have one request."

She stood half-turned away from him, refusing to look at him. "Tigre, don't do this to me," she whispered. "I hate him for what he did. I shed a million tears over April. She was so beautiful and precious."

"And now you have her. You had happy years with him, and you know it."

"Please, I must go."

"*One last request*. Please forgive Pa. And if you forgive, you have to forget."

She began to cry softly while he reached through the bars to hold her wrist.

"Is that too big a request for a son to ask? I've lost everything! Melissa Jane, my home, my family, my *life*. Can't you do this one thing for me? I know, deep down, you still have to love the good that's in Pa. And he does have good in him. Please."

Tears streamed down her cheeks as she looked at him. "I'll consider it," she answered. "That's the most I can promise."

He nodded, a muscle working in his jaw. She turned and left, drawing a deep breath before she stepped out to meet the others.

As they emerged from the jail, people turned to stare at them. Lieutenant Ferguson sat across the road on a bench in front of the Hatfield store, where April had seen him often lately, seeming to lead a far more leisurely life than most of the officers stationed around Albuquerque. Ned Hatfield came striding toward them, stopping in front of them to confront April.

"I talked to Reverend Nokes this morning. Melissa Jane's married that damned Irishman and they've run away. I've hired two men to go after them. Damned good men, but you knew what she was doing!" he snapped, stepping toward April.

"Hatfield . . ." Noah said, coming up behind him while Luke stepped forward in front of April.

Ned spun around to face Noah, who stood bareheaded in the sunshine, his sleeves rolled up. People began to gather and watch. "You! I heard you helped her get to the preacher." He advanced on Noah, who stood his ground. Ned swung a meaty fist. Noah ducked, sidestepped another wild punch, and then threw up his fists.

"This is for Melissa Jane, Mr. Hatfield." Noah's arm shot out, hitting him solidly, two quick punches that sent Hatfield sprawling. Noah stood over him. "I also took her to the doctor to get her wounds treated, wounds you inflicted from a beating. You're a sorry excuse for a father."

"You damned Rebel. You're a low-life bardog, gambler—" He came up swinging, this time moving faster, getting in a blow to Noah's jaw, then a swift left punch to his middle. Noah staggered backward and came back with two fast punches, keeping his guard up, his jaw down.

"Luke, stop them," April said.

"I wouldn't think of it," Luke drawled. "Hatfield deserves what he's going to get. Noah's the fighter."

"Amen to that," Ta-ne-haddle said dryly.

As if to prove his words, Noah suddenly moved with lightning speed, raining blows. Hatfield staggered back and went down, sprawling unconscious in the dirt.

"Damn," Luke remarked. "Next time we put money on him."

"I would have this time if you'd given me a chance," Ta-ne-haddle said. "Shall we congratulate him?"

"You ladies go on home," Luke said. "Boys, you go with your mother." They stood hand in hand, Dawn in the middle between Knox and Jeff.

Luke and Ta-ne-haddle strode forward to shake Noah's hand, and all three headed for the saloon. Noah and Luke were about the same height, taller than Ta-ne-haddle, all three broad-shouldered. April watched them go, wishing Noah were part of her family, thinking he was a wonderful man, like Luke and Ta-ne-

haddle. It looked so right for them to be together. At
the same time, a little kernel of worry plagued her,
because Ta-ne-haddle and Luke could be terribly pro-
tective of her. She studied them, hoping they didn't
get to the subject of how often he had been seeing her,
or Noah's engagement.

Tigre stood on a bunk. He had watched the fight
from his high window, and he had wanted to cheer
Noah on. He watched Luke, thinking how much he
had liked him. Javier had come earlier that morning,
and it had been a bitter, sad meeting, yet Tigre felt
his father truly regretted what he had done. One thing
he knew for sure: Javier couldn't survive without Hattie. He loved her as deeply as a man could love a
woman. Tigre wondered if he had spent all these years
trying to make things good for her just to compensate
for what he had done when he had taken April from
her.

He stared at Ned Hatfield, still lying prone in the
dirt. A cavalry officer leaned over him and motioned
to some men to come help move him. Tigre stepped
down. Melissa. How it hurt! She was married to Patrick O'Flynn.

He paced the cell and swore. He hated being caged
up, and in spite of Luke's assurances, Tigre didn't
think he could escape hanging. When he stood at the
window, the gallows were in view of the cell. A chill
passed over him and he rubbed his chest. His arm
throbbed. The doc said he was as tough as an old crocodile, and he wondered where Doc Yishay had ever
seen a crocodile, young or old, but he hadn't asked.

Melissa. He felt tears sting his eyes. He loved her.
He wanted her so badly. There would never be another
one like her. *You damn fool, there won't be another
one at all. You're going to hang.* He swore and paced
some more, lighting one of the cheroots Luke had
brought him and taking a deep puff while he thought
about all the new family members who had just been
to see him. It made him smile to think about them. He
wished he could know each one of them. And the kids.

The thought of children twisted his insides. He loved kids and wanted Melissa—

He swore and climbed back on the bed to stare at the street and the dark entrance to McCloud's Place, wishing he were inside with his brother, drinking a beer.

Noah showed them through the saloon and the new part that was still unfinished. A table was set up in a back corner where it was quiet, and the three sat down to have a drink.

"You didn't seem to need any help with Hatfield," Luke commented dryly.

"He had that coming, the bastard. Her back was raw from the beating he gave her. Do you think there's anything you can do for Tigre?"

Luke shrugged. "It depends on the kind of trial he gets. If he's got a reasonable judge, if people here don't turn on him, I told him we'd try for a prison sentence. Frankly, it doesn't look good. People have little patience with outlaws. And I hope I can persuade April to come home with me. I think once this settles down, life will be harder for her here."

Noah took a drink, refusing to think about Albuquerque without April. "What Tigre's done shouldn't reflect on April."

"Her brother is a notorious outlaw."

"Actually half-brother."

"It won't matter. He's her brother. Men won't be as respectful of her," Luke said grimly. "I know what we went through when my wife's father turned outlaw. Men gave her a bad time of it. Even men who had been family friends and should have been sympathetic. No, this is no place for her." He shifted restlessly. "She says you can't find your gold, and your brother wrote you that he left it with her."

"I believe she doesn't know anything about it. I've come to a dead end and can't pick up a rumor or any leads. But I think it's here in Albuquerque somewhere," he said, quietly discussing the gold, but thinking of April. "How long before you'll go back to San Antonio?"

"It depends on Tigre's trial, but I suspect they'll try him early Monday morning. The judge will be in town. I learned that from Pacheco."

Noah hated to think about Monday. If Tigre hanged, April would suffer another loss in her life. And every time Noah thought of Tigre, he couldn't help but think of Ralph. They would have hanged Ralph if they had caught him.

"Boss, excuse me," Duero said, and Noah glanced up.

"There's a woman at the entrance. She said to get you. It's Mrs. Yishay. She said her husband has gone to fight Ned Hatfield."

"Oh, hell. Excuse me," Noah said, and moved quickly, striding toward the door.

Luke glanced at Ta-ne-haddle. "Who's Yishay? I've heard April say the name."

"The doc. Let's go."

Noah sent Mrs. Yishay home and headed for the general store in long strides. His heart raced when he spotted Aaron Yishay standing in the middle of the wide street in front of the store, his hands on his hips, sleeves rolled up, his bowler hat squarely on his head. His black coat was neatly folded on the boardwalk behind him as if he were ready for a gunfight, but Noah knew Doc didn't carry a weapon.

"Hatfield, you whey-faced, yellow-bellied, woman-beating bully, come out here and fight!"

Noah pushed past people who had stopped to stare, then stepped off the boardwalk and began to run as Ned Hatfield stepped to the door.

"Doc!" Noah cried, pausing in the street only yards away.

"Stay out of this, McCloud."

"Doc, he's a hell of a lot bigger," Noah persisted. "Come on home."

"Stay out of this."

"Doc," Hatfield said loudly, stepping into the street, "you go on home. I ain't gonna fight a little old man like you, because like the man said, it wouldn't be fair."

"You are a jelly-spined, pink-assed fool," Aaron Yishay called out loudly enough for everyone in a three-block radius to hear.

Noah groaned. If Ned Hatfield hadn't outweighed Yishay by more than a hundred pounds, and hadn't been so mean and ornery, Noah would have relaxed, but there was no mistaking the tension growing between the two men. "Doc, please!"

"McCloud, shut up. The man's too much a lily-livered, snake-bellied coward to fight."

"That does it," Hatfield snapped. "Doc, I hope I don't hurt you bad, but you brought this on yourself." He raised his fists and approached Yishay.

"Doc!" Noah tried one more time.

He ignored Noah, moving forward with his fists raised. "You beat an innocent young girl, your own daughter. You remember this, Hatfield, the next time you start to beat an innocent, helpless woman," Aaron said, and Noah groaned again.

Luke and Ta-ne-haddle stopped beside Noah. All of them knew better than to step into another man's fight, but Noah's hand rested on the butt of his six-shooter. "If it gets too bad, I'll stop it," he said softly.

"Lord, the Doc's ten years older, besides being smaller, isn't he?" Luke asked.

Before Noah cold answer, Ned Hatfield swung. Aaron Yishay dropped down instantly, dodged away two steps, and just as quickly slashed out with his foot, landing a solid kick in Hatfield's stomach. Hatfield doubled over in pain.

The minute he bent over, Aaron Yishay's flattened hand shot out, a slashing chop to Hatfield's neck that sent him rolling in the dirt, and Noah relaxed, suddenly grinning.

"I'll be damned," Luke said. "The doc's a dirty fighter."

"He is at that," Noah remarked happily.

Aaron stomped on Hatfield's neck, stomped on his hand, and kicked him in the ribs. Hatfield lay groaning and moaning, rolling on the ground, trying to double up and protect himself.

Aaron stood over him, carefully rolling down his sleeves. "You think about that before you ever hit a defenseless woman again, Hatfield, do you understand?"

There was nothing from Ned Hatfield, and Aaron Yishay kicked him hard in the ribs again. "Do you understand?"

"Uhh . . ."

"You better get a doctor to look at your ribs." He turned to walk away, and someone let out a whoop. Somewhere else there was a burst of applause while two men rushed out of the doorway of the store to help Hatfield.

"Come meet the winner," Noah said dryly. "This hasn't been Hatfield's day. Aaron, I didn't know you had it in you! I want you to meet April's brother." Noah shook Aaron's hand. "Good fight. Why did I worry?"

Twinkling black eyes looked up at him slyly. "I think you forgot that I moved to the frontier long ago. Besides, I'm not as tall as some men. I learned a little about fighting when I was growing up in St. Louis."

"Mrs. Yishay came to get me."

"Probably scared I'd kill him. I threatened to this morning," he said pleasantly, and shook hands with Ta-ne-haddle. "Good to see you again," he said. He looked expectantly at Luke as Noah introduced them.

"Luke Danby, April's brother. Luke, meet Dr. Aaron Yishay."

"Some fight," Luke said while they shook hands.

"He deserved worse. That poor little daughter of his never hurt a fly. She'll have a few scars from last night."

"Come join us in a drink. I'll send Hosea by your house to tell Mama you're okay," Noah said, and Aaron smiled.

"That would be right refreshing, boys. Lead the way."

Tigre heard the whoops and applause. "What's all the commotion?" he asked Deputy Osmundo Pacheco as he passed the door.

"I stepped outside," Pacheco said eagerly. "Wouldn't have believed it otherwise, but I saw him do it."

"Saw who do what?"

"The doc beat Ned Hatfield to whimpering jelly."

"Why would he do that?" Tigre asked, suddenly still.

"It's all over town that he—" Osmundo looked sharply at Tigre. "Oh, sorry. I forgot. You and she, well, I didn't mean—"

"What did he do to Melissa?" Tigre asked in a tone of voice that make the deputy blink.

"He gave her a beating last night. Mr. McCloud took her to Doc Yishay." Suddenly he relaxed and his grin returned. "You should have seen ole Doc. He must be a hundred years old. He's older'n Papa! Hatfield swung," Pacheco said, throwing a wild punch and spinning half-around. "Doc just dropped down, and then, wham! A solid kick right in the gully-raker!" He kicked the air, and Tigre watched and listened to a blow-by-blow description, satisfied that Ned Hatfield was getting back a little of what he deserved. Yet he ached for Melissa, and he prayed that she wasn't badly hurt.

Deputy Pacheco danced on his toes and laughed. "Doc Yishay! Of all people. Papa always said Doc could take care of himself. I guess he's seen him fight before."

He left, and Tigre went back to staring out the window at the street, trying to avoid looking at his left, where he could see the gallows. All was quiet now, people and wagons moving up and down the street, little boys playing and a pup following them. A Mexican two-wheeled cart loaded with freight rolled past.

Tigre ate a delicious tamale lunch cooked by Mama Pacheco, and then he paced restlessly, hating the confinement of the cell. Siesta came and the town grew quiet. A small herd of cattle passed through town, stirring up dust. He'd been told Texans were driving their cattle north to market this year, and he had heard that a steer that would bring five dollars in Texas would bring as much as thirty dollars up north.

"You got more company, Castillo," Deputy Pacheco said, his eyes round, staring at Miss Tabitha as he led her to Tigre's cell.

"Unlock the door, Osmundo, dear," she coaxed, running her fingers along his jaw. He grinned.

"I'm not supposed to unlock it except for his brother, the lawman."

"Oh, come on. The man's going to hang Monday. I just want to give him a little farewell hug," she said in a throaty voice, rolling her eyes at the nineteen-year-old deputy.

"*Sí.* No problem." He let her into the cell and locked it. "Call when you're ready."

Tigre gazed at Tabby, wondering what she was doing back the second time that day. She liked him, but not that much.

"Darlin', I got your shirt all ironed for you, fresh as a daisy. You can't go before a judge in just a bandage," she said loudly enough for the deputy to hear. "Here's your shirt, love. I can't bear to see a good man hang." She handed him his shirt, then hiked up her skirts and pulled out a six-shooter, a crowbar, and a bowie knife.

Tigre stared at them, glancing at her bare legs and back to the weapons.

"You gonna take 'em, or are you going to *look* all day?" she asked with amusement.

Grinning widely, he glanced at her legs again. "I'd like to look all day, but I'll take 'em. Oh, hell, yes, I'll take 'em." He placed the weapons under the thin mattress and flung down the shirt on top of it, turning back to her, his eyes sparkling.

"Tabby, you are a *good* girl! I'll send you a reward, I swear. One more thing."

"One *more?*"

"I can't run on foot."

"I thought of that, darlin'. After sundown a horse will be hitched right behind the jail, and I paid a man to sit beside him and to give him to whoever says, 'Thanks from Tabby.' "

"Oh, Tabby, damn. Thanks." He swung her up,

spinning her around, then letting her slide down, running his hands over her.

She laughed and pulled his head down to kiss her, and he tightened his arms around her, bending over to pull up her skirt and touch her thighs. "Maybe there is *one* more thing I can think of I'd like."

That night the music of the Fiesta was loud enough to drown out small sounds coming from Tigre's cell. To his relief, one of the youngest Pacheco deputies, sixteen-year-old Miguel, was on duty. And to his joy, a female visitor came to call on the deputy. Tigre could hear her occasional giggles. He had spent the afternoon and early evening pacing and making noise so they would be accustomed to hearing noise from his cell. He worked carefully and furiously, because once the Fiesta was over and the town grew quiet, every sound would carry.

He told the deputy he didn't need a lantern, so the only light in the cell spilled through the open doorway from the front room. Tigre stood on his bed, chipping and digging away at the adobe with the knife. Then he put the crowbar between the bars and pushed with all his strength, his muscles popping, his bandaged shoulder throbbing. He felt the bar bend as he pushed. He worked steadily, praying the deputy didn't bother to look in on him. Once he heard a chair scrape, so he dropped down, stretching on the bed on top of the crowbar. To his horror, he realized he had left the bowie knife on the window ledge.

He heard the deputy pause, and Tigre looked through almost closed eyes, seeing the deputy outlined in the bright doorway. He turned and went back out of sight, and Tigre let out his breath in relief.

"He's sleeping."

"Come on, one dance."

"Papa might see me."

"Come on. We'll dance where it's dark."

Go on, go on, Tigre prayed, and heard them leave. The moment he was alone, he sprang up and worked furiously, hacking away at the adobe with the crowbar.

Exultation shook him when he yanked a bar loose. In
minutes he had two bars free, and that was all he
needed. He propped them back in place as best he
could and sat down to wait.

He guessed almost an hour passed before he heard the
clomp of boots and the soft slap of huaraches on the floor.
Tigre stretched out, his boots kicked off on the floor. He
listened as the deputy came to the door again and stood a
minute. A girl giggled. "Come on, Miguel. He's asleep.
Have another drink of tequila."

"Shh, Conchita. Don't wake him." They moved
away, crashed into a chair. Another spurt of giggles
came and Tigre heard the chair creak. He moved,
standing up and looking at the street. People thronged
from the saloon, and Tigre waited patiently until no
one was standing around on the street or passing by.
He lifted down the bars, then dropped the six-shooter,
his boots with the spurs inside them, and the knife
outside. With another look at the street, he moved as
quietly as possible, slithering through the opening and
dropping down. His wound hurt, but excitement and
the heady prospect of freedom overrode the pain.

Scooping up his things, he hurried around the building. He let out his breath when he saw a man dozing
beside the wall, a horse hitched beside him. Tigre
shook his shoulder.

"Huh?" The man peered at him.

"Thanks from Tabby and Tigre, my friend!" Tigre
bounded into the saddle.

"Vaya con Dios," the man said.

Tigre was gone, urging the horse between buildings,
his pulse racing. In seconds he had his boots on, his
belt, knife, and spurs tucked into his waistband. He
reached open country and headed west toward April's
house, veering off south.

To his satisfaction, his horse was still tethered where
he had left it the night of his capture. He led his horse
away, taking both. He would change later and leave
the horse Tabby had provided. Urging his mount to a
gallop, Tigre headed north along the river, out of New
Mexico Territory.

22

April woke staring at the ceiling, momentarily disoriented. Hattie was asleep on the settee. A rap came at the door, and at the same time, the bedroom door opened and Luke appeared with a lantern.

"April, have you ever had a whole night's sleep?" he asked in a grumbling tone. "The whole damned town comes to visit at night!"

"I don't know who it is or why," she said, sitting up. Hattie was awake now, pulling on her wrapper, and April did the same. She heard men's voices and horses, and her gaze flew to Hattie's. April knew they both thought the same thing—Tigre.

Luke opened the door and a man's voice rose. "Sheriff?" Luke asked. "What happened?"

"We've got a posse. Tigre Castillo's escaped. I want to know if he's here."

"No, he's not," Luke said flatly. "We were all asleep. We didn't even know anything about an escape."

"Danby, I let all you folks in to see him today. Someone gave him tools, because the damned bars were pried out of the window."

"We didn't give him anything, and you can search the house. My children are in the wagon. Let me tell the women."

Luke turned back to April and Hattie, his features solemn. "They want to search for Tigre."

April nodded, aware that every moment they searched would be that much more time for Tigre. She had no doubt he was riding out of the territory as fast as he could. With Melissa married, there was nothing to hold him here now.

Luke woke Catalina, and in minutes the women waited in the wagon with the children, except for April, who stood in her bedroom as Sheriff Pacheco went through the room and peered under the bed and into the armoire.

Finally the sheriff and his men were ready to leave, all of them filing out except the sheriff, who turned to Luke.

"Sheriff, we didn't give him anything. I'm a lawman who goes by the books. I intended to plead his case. We couldn't have been the only people who called on him."

"No, dammit, you weren't. That who—excuse me, Miss Danby. One of the girls from the Golden Palace came by twice. Hell, half the town came by to see him. Doc Yishay was there. 'Course, the doc wouldn't spring anybody. Four other girls from the Palace. McCloud came to see him. He wouldn't have any reason to slip something to Tigre. Barely knew him, as I understand it. I don't know why he came to call. Guess because he took Miss Hatfield to marry O'Flynn. Anyway, it's done. But we'll catch him. You'll get your chance to plead his case. Good night."

He left, calling to his men, and they rode off. The thunder of galloping hooves could be heard.

The women returned to the house and Luke closed the door. When he turned around, he grinned and Hattie laughed.

"I can't say I'm sorry. I just hope he has a hell of a head start." He hugged Catalina to his side, gazing down at her.

"I'm glad too, Luke."

"I might as well put on the coffeepot," April said. "It'll be dawn soon. I wonder how long ago he escaped, how much of a head start he has."

"If I know Tigre," Hattie said, "they won't ever catch him. He won't stop."

* * *

Several weeks later, on the third of October, as the family loaded their wagon, April told Luke she was staying in Albuquerque. Ta-ne-haddle and his family were leaving too, going to San Antonio with the others.

"It'll be a long time before we're back," Ta-ne-haddle said solemnly, taking April aside before he left. "I talked to McCloud, and he'll keep an eye on the place."

"You didn't need to do that!" she said, blushing. "He doesn't have any obligation—"

"Oh, yes, he does. He's the one who stirred up the talk of gold. If he finds his gold, you'll be safe. He didn't seem to mind," Ta-ne-haddle said solemnly. " 'If this be error, and upon me proved, I never writ, nor no man ever loved.' "

"What are you quoting?" she asked suspiciously.

"A Shakespearean sonnet," he replied with a bland air, and she made a mental note to look up the sonnet and read all of it.

"I hate to leave now," he continued, "but they want the children to be at home, and Lottie needs to be at Luke's." He smiled broadly. "We're going to have another child."

"Oh, Ta-ne-haddle! How marvelous!"

"If I didn't need to get Lottie to Luke's house before winter, I wouldn't go. I don't like leaving you in danger."

"I'm not in danger. Go, and don't worry. Please. Have you told the others the news?"

"Not Mrs. Castillo, but the others. Luke and I discussed it this morning. That's why we're leaving when they do. And it's fine to tell your mother. We just haven't had a chance."

"And what does Dawn think?"

"She wants a baby sister, of course." He laughed and held the door open for April, who went straight to Lottie to hug her.

It was another two hours before they finally left. April stood on the road waving to them, then went back to the house, which now seemed incredibly quiet and empty. For a moment she wondered if she had made a mistake in staying, but at the thought of riding away from Albuquerque and Noah, she knew she had made the only decision she could tolerate.

In minutes she glanced out to see the Dodworths coming with a cake, and they spent an hour visiting with her before they went home. She cleaned and gathered up laundry, and began to think about the gold. If they could find the gold, she would be safe. As much as she hoped Noah would stay in Albuquerque forever, she was worried about another break-in. And the gold was rightfully Noah's. While she worked, she thought about the possibility that Ralph McCloud had left a letter.

She put the laundry aside and sat down, lost in thought. If he had written a note explaining where to find the gold and had hidden it earlier, where would he have put the letter?

With a start she realized she would be late to the saloon to sing. She bathed, changed her clothing, and locked up, leaving in a hurry. When she returned home that night, she sat in the middle of her bed, still mulling over where Ralph McCloud could have hidden a letter. She got up and began to search, moving her goose-feather mattress, studying the pillows. Two hours later, she climbed back into bed, discouraged.

Three weeks from now was Aaron Yishay's birthday, and Gerta was giving him a surprise party. Noah would be there. She saw him so seldom now, partly because she had been so busy with all her family visiting and partly because she knew that was what Noah wanted. The thought of spending an evening at the same party with him sent a tingle through her, and she wriggled down in the covers, remembering his kisses and feeling more alone than she ever had before.

Hours before the party, April bathed and washed her hair, dressing in a jaconet petticoat she had made, looking at the new dress and bonnet Luke and Catalina had brought her from San Antonio. She smoothed the pink alpaca, trimmed with bias folds of deep rose satin. Rose satin covered the buttons, and the overskirt looped up on each side and fastened with rose buttons. She thought it was the prettiest dress she had ever owned. She hummed while she dressed. She intended to crimp and braid her hair in the style Catalina had shown her, but as she stared at her reflection in the mirror she remembered dancing with Noah at the Fiesta when her hair was simply tied behind her neck and how he had reached up to pull free the ribbon. If he liked her hair that way, she would wear it that way in spite of fashion, so she tied it back with a rose ribbon. She seldom wore jewelry, because she didn't own any that was really pretty except Emilio's necklace, which was the only piece she wore tonight. She studied herself before she left, wondering how Noah would see her, hoping he would think she looked pretty.

She leaned forward to glare at her image. "Simpleton!" she said aloud. "He's engaged."

She made a face and turned quickly, picking up her new duchess cap of lustrous rose satin, pulling on the cashmere *paletot* that had been a Christmas gift from Luke and Catalina two years ago. She had her buggy hitched and ready. She had asked the Dodworths to ride with her, but they were going with their neighbors the Olsons, who would bring them home early.

The night was chilly, with a yellow harvest moon, when she left home. She had a small jar of plum preserves wrapped as a gift for Dr. Yishay. She had made the preserves in late summer, with Noah helping her on a Saturday afternoon. Gerta had told her a friend would keep Aaron away from home while the guests arrived, and then they could surprise him. April was delighted, but she knew it was because of Noah more than the birthday party. A few blocks from the Yishays', Mott Ferguson rode up beside her.

"Miss Danby, how pretty you look tonight!"

"Thank you, Lieutenant," she answered perfunctorily, wondering how he could see her in the dark.

"I hear your family has all gone back to Texas. Rumors have it your brother's gone there too."

"I don't know about that."

"They say you didn't know you had a second brother until he showed up in town."

"That's right."

"That's a little hard to believe," he said lightly, smiling at her.

"You don't believe me?"

"Seems to me you'd know whether you had a brother or not. But if you say you didn't—"

"I didn't until after our confrontation at church one morning. He's gone now."

"Free like a thistle in the wind. Why didn't you go to Texas with them? Surely they asked you to."

"I have a job, Lieutenant," she answered with a bit more curtness, disliking his questions.

"Mott. Miss Danby, just call me by my first name, Mott."

"I have a job I couldn't leave."

"This party should surprise the little doctor."

"I hope so. Mrs. Yishay was so excited."

"I think half the town will be here. He's probably brought half of them into the world. He almost sent Ned Hatfield out of it. I never saw a little old man fight like the doctor."

"He's not so old," she said with a smile.

"He's old enough to be your daddy."

"That's not really *old.*"

He grinned and dismounted as they stopped in the vacant lot a block from the Yishays' house as they had been instructed to. Mott Ferguson hitched his horse to a rail and came around to help April. She wished she didn't have to arrive at his side, because Noah would think they had come together, but she couldn't see any way to get rid of him now. He took her arm, linking it through his.

"Why do you live here all alone when you have a big family elsewhere?"

"I used to have a reason—I was trying to find my mother and I heard she was sometimes in Albuquerque. Now that I've found her, I don't have a reason to stay. Maybe sometime soon I'll move to San Antonio."

"Albuquerque's loss, but I can see why you would. I just can't see why you stay now." He looked at her curiously and she blushed.

"It's hard to change. I'm accustomed to singing and living independently. If I go to San Antonio, I'll give up all of that and be dependent on my brother and his family. A man should understand not wanting to give up independence."

"A man, yes, because that's our lot in life, but it's not a woman's. Besides, if you'd relent and go out, you'd be married in no time, with your own home and family."

She laughed. "You make it sound simple."

"Look at that moon." He paused to gaze down at her. "Don't you get lonesome?"

"I keep busy," she said. She turned to walk ahead, and he fell back in step beside her, taking her arm again.

"I hope you haven't been disturbed since that break-in you had."

"No, but my family has been here most of the time."

"That half-breed go with them?"

"Yes, he did."

"He keeps close watch over you."

"I've known him since I was twelve. He's like another brother."

"I wouldn't announce that too loud around here. Half-breeds aren't popular with folks."

"There are plenty of people in Albuquerque who like Ta-ne-haddle. He's a wonderful man."

The squat adobe house with vines trailing over the flat roof and along the portal was brightly lit, with yellow light shining from all the windows. Pots of flowers hung from the protruding vigas, evidence of Gerta Yishay's gardening abilities. Lieutenant Ferguson knocked on the door and it opened immediately.

"Ah, good evening," Gerta Yishay said, her eyes sparkling, as dark as the black of her silk dress. She took April's arm and pulled her inside. "Come in, come in. How pretty you look, April, dear. Good eve-

ning, Lieutenant. And you, so handsome! Let me take
your bonnet and cape, and your hat, Lieutenant.'' She
handed the things to a servant and motioned toward
the parlor, where a fire roared in the fireplace.

They had moved the furniture in the dining room
and pushed back the chairs in the parlor so there would
be room for everyone. Guests mingled in both rooms,
and in the dining room a table was laden with food.

April drifted away from Lieutenant Ferguson, her
gaze searching the crowd for Noah, but he wasn't present. She had heard Vesta Dodworth say he was coming, though, and she hoped nothing had changed his
plans. She talked to the Dodworths, to Reverend
Nokes, and to the Pachecos, moving through the crowd
until she turned to face Mott Ferguson again. He gave
her a sardonic smile.

''Trying to avoid me?''

''Not at all. I've been talking to everyone.''

''While all I can see is you,'' he said, taking her
arm and steering her toward an alcove off the parlor.
''You look beautiful tonight, April.''

''Thank you. We should stay with the others, because Dr. Yishay may arrive at any time.'' She paused,
and as she did, she heard Gerta calling for attention.

''They're coming. Mr. McCloud's with him. Everyone gather round and we'll wish Papa happy birthday
when he comes through the door.''

April wished Mott Ferguson weren't standing so
close, with his hand on her arm, and she moved a step
away. Her pulse quickened, because Noah was coming
to the party for certain. She watched the door eagerly,
her anticipation growing. They entered, Noah swinging open the door, ushering Dr. Yishay in ahead of
him. Aaron stepped into the hall and turned to the
parlor, gazing through the wide arched opening at all
his guests.

''Happy Birthday!'' came a chorus from the crowd.

Noah appeared behind him, his gaze drifting over
the room until his blue eyes met hers.

23

Noah wore a black coat over his white linen shirt. He looked fresh, masculine, and handsome. Everyone moved forward, including Mott Ferguson, to wish Aaron well, but April felt nailed to the floor. Noah never took his gaze from her, and a faint smile tugged up the corner of his mouth as he threaded his way through the crowd toward her.

She waited, her heart beating so rapidly she could hardly get her breath while his gaze swept over her. And then he was standing only inches away.

"You have a new dress. It's pretty."

"Thank you. Luke and Catalina brought it to me from San Antonio. I didn't know you would be bringing Dr. Yishay."

"It was easy to get him to go down to my place with me."

Words. They talked, and yet all the time she just kept thinking about how marvelous he looked. She had missed him. And the times between their encounters would no doubt grow longer until he was gone, and then they would stop altogether.

While they talked about the party, Noah watched her, wanting to touch her. She was a vision with her hair parted in the center and tied behind her neck, unlike the latest styles that were fancy with braids and chignons and crimped curls. She looked young; her wide eyes were sparkling, and he was thankful she was here. Many of the guests were older, but there were people of all ages present. In fact, most of the town was there. Aaron Yishay had many friends.

"The Hatfields aren't here tonight," Noah commented.

"No. I'm sorry for Mrs. Hatfield, because she's such a nice woman."

"It's unfortunate that she'll suffer over what Ned has done."

"I want to go tell Dr. Yishay Happy Birthday," April said.

Noah took her arm and moved through the crowded room with her. She smelled sweet and he glanced down at the top of her head. He missed her. He missed talking to her, telling her little things that happened every day, telling her about his business. They paused in front of Yishay, and April waited while he finished talking to the Parkers. Aaron turned to smile at her.

"Happy Birthday," she said warmly, reaching out to take his hand.

He folded her hand in both of his, glancing briefly at Noah.

"This one—he said to come look at the latest construction. And then he talked and talked—a man who usually is laconic—I should have known he was up to something! Have you seen his saloon, Miss April?"

"No. Not inside, of course."

"I know, ladies don't go to saloons, but early in the morning when there are few customers, McCloud, you should show Miss April what you've done."

Noah didn't know whether to laugh or frown. Aaron should mind his own business. But on the other hand, the chance to show his handiwork to April was what he had wanted for months now. "I'll take you tomorrow morning, April."

"Fine," she answered. "Mrs. Yishay has planned this party for weeks," she said to Aaron.

"Ahh, Mama. This makes her happy, so it makes me happy. We had letters this week from the boys. The next-best thing to having them here. Noah reminds me of our older one."

"Thanks, Aaron. I take that as a compliment," Noah said.

"You should go to San Antonio and live with your

family, my dear,'' Aaron said to April. ''You have nothing to hold you here.''

''Only a little independence,'' she replied, aware Noah was watching her.

''Happy Birthday, Doc!'' Jason Sutter boomed. They all said hello to Jason, and in minutes Noah took April's arm to move away.

''Would you like some punch?''

''Yes, please,'' she said, greeting people as they passed. Noah held her arm, having no intention of leaving her alone while he fetched the punch. He saw Mott Ferguson constantly glancing at her. He moved her to a quiet corner of the dining room while they sipped cool claret punch. Noah leaned one shoulder against the wall, slouching down slightly to be closer to her.

''You could go to San Antonio and be with your family. You'd be better off, April. You wouldn't have to work in a saloon.''

She gazed beyond him. ''I know. I'm considering it. That's what everyone wants, and the reason I stayed is gone now. I always thought I'd find Hattie here. It's funny, I was right. Of course, I'd heard she visited here on occasion, so I guessed she lived somewhere in this general area.''

''She left Javier over what he did.''

''Yes, and I hate that. I don't think Luke should have made an issue of it.''

''I have to agree with Luke. The man had it coming.''

''From what Tigre said, they've been sublimely happy all these years until she learned the truth about me.''

''Maybe they'll patch things up.''

''I don't know. I suspect my mother is a woman of strong beliefs.''

''You're probably right. She'd have to be to survive out here after being captured in an ambush.''

''How's Fanchette?''

''I suppose she's fine,'' he said, finding it difficult to think of Fanchette when he was gazing into April's wide ash-colored eyes. "We don't write. She's not much for reading or writing."

"Are you?'"

He shrugged. "I read when I was growing up, but I don't much anymore. Life changes."

"I hope Melissa is happy with her changes. No one knows where they've gone or what they're doing. I hope they moved away as Patrick once told her they would. She'd have a difficult time here."

'I think you worry more abut your friend's reputation than you do about your own," he said dryly.

"I don't hope to have a good marriage someday, or have parents who plan to see me married to a good man."

"Why the hell not? Because of someone you loved when you were twelve years old?"

"That's enough reason," she answered evenly, lifting her chin defiantly, wondering how the conversation had jumped so swiftly from Melissa to her.

"You were a child, April," he said frowning, disturbed that she still clung to memories of Emilio. "That's ridiculous. It was a young girl's first love. Like any first love, it grows out of proportion. If you would give these men half a chance—"

She forced a smile and tried to make her voice light. "I suppose you're absolutely right. I should go out with Lieutenant Ferguson who's obviously interested, or maybe some of the others who ask me."

Wondering how he had let the conversation take such a turn, Noah frowned. "I think you should," he said, but he sounded gruff, as if he wasn't completely convinced.

"I'll consider it."

He ached to touch her, but he moved a step away, holding the punch cup with both hands as if it were the most fragile crystal in the world. "Your family ought to pop with pride over you, April. You've managed well and you're beautiful."

"Why thank you!" she exclaimed, pleased and surprised.

"I don't know any other woman who could have done what you have," he said solemnly.

"Thank you," she answered. Her tone was as somber as his, yet her heart beat wildly with pleasure over his compliments. They gazed into each other's eyes, and there was an intentness in his that was breathtaking. Her cheeks warmed, and with an effort she looked away, glancing at the other guests milling around the rosewood dining table. It was set with shining silver, sparkling crystal, and laden with steaming bowls of sausages and biscuits, a platter piled high with golden chicken, a thick wedge of pale yellow cheese—a mixture of different types of food to please everyone.

"I've been thinking about that maybe Ralph hid a note somewhere," April said. "I've searched for it everywhere I can think to look."

"Want me to come help you hunt for it?"

The question seemed to float in the air like leaves caught in the wind. "If you'd like," she said cautiously, and he nodded.

"When would be convenient?"

How polite they were. So stiff and formal. She wondered what he thought and felt. He loved another woman. He couldn't feel anything more than he would if he were talking to Selma Hatfield, Vesta Dodworth, or Gerta Yishay! And she shouldn't want him to. When she looked at the situation logically, she realized that she didn't want to come between him and Fanchette. But in her heart, April couldn't even remember Fanchette Craddock very well. And anytime Noah came near her, all her scruples and kind feelings for Fanchette vanished.

He couldn't feel anything for her and love Fanchette at the same time, but he looked as if he felt something. Yet there was nothing in his actions to indicate he cared. Far from it. She hadn't talked to him, or even seen him for days.

"Anytime is fine," she answered, and hoped she sounded casual.

"I'll be by in the morning then. Maybe I can stay

awhile then, and we'll look for a note—if that suits you, of course.''

Suddenly she laughed. ''My goodness, you're getting polite!''

He grinned and rubbed the back of his neck. ''Sorry if I've been a little cavalier in the past.''

''A little cavalier! You've looked as if you wanted to beat me!''

''I wasn't *that* angry,'' he said, a teasing note back in his voice.

She felt giddy and happy as they smiled into each other's eyes. When he was with her, the threat of his approaching marriage diminished a fraction.

''I recall being frightened senseless.''

''I hoped you would forget that!''

''It was just once, that first morning when you came to call. After that, I didn't think you'd resort to violence, even though you looked as if you wanted to.''

''Don't remind me. It's one of the big mistakes of my life,'' he said, sounding so contrite that she laughed.

''Noah, forget it! I understand, and we won't talk about it. I forgive you. I hope we can find the note and you can get your gold and go home.''

''Don't send me off so eagerly.''

''I'll miss you,'' she said, surprising him. She sounded honest, impassive.

''You've had her to yourself long enough, McCloud,'' Mott Ferguson said, joining them. Noah mentally cursed the interruption at that specific moment. He had wanted to follow the drift of their conversation, and he certainly didn't want to share her with Ferguson.

''Soldiering must be easing up a little, Lieutenant,'' Noah said, sipping his punch. ''You seem to be spending more time on the 'whittlin' bench' in front of the general store than you do on duty.''

''I'm on duty when I'm sitting in front of the store. Special assignment,'' he replied. Ferguson's eyes never left April, making Noah want to step between them. He barely heard Ferguson's answer and didn't give it any thought. *Leave them alone. You've urged her to go out with others. Let her go.* He couldn't budge, and he couldn't get rid of the urge to push Mott Ferguson out of the way.

"The crowd has grown since our arrival," Ferguson said.

He talked as if he were alone with her, completely ignoring Noah, who looked as relaxed as ever until April glanced into his eyes and noticed the annoyance in his expression. Yet she found it difficult to think the reason for his glare was Mott's attention to her, and she decided there might be something about Mott Ferguson sitting in front of the general store that was stirring Noah's fury.

Noah fought to control his temper as he listened. Mott Ferguson had brought her tonight and would escort her home. He hated the thought, and he knew his reactions were unreasonable. He was marrying Fanchette. Why shouldn't April be escorted home by Ferguson? Noah simply didn't like the man; and that seemed sufficient reason, he argued with himself, amazed at the depth of his dislike of Mott Ferguson.

"Hello, April," Octavia Littleton said, standing expectantly close to them, gazing at Noah.

April introduced her, and in seconds Octavia was standing talking to Noah, flirting outrageously and openly with him while Mott Ferguson moved between them and April, his back to Noah.

"Have you eaten anything?"

"No, thanks."

"None of that. Mrs. Yishay is the best cook in the county and she knows how to cook hot potato salad and baklava and fricasseed rabbits, chopped liver, something besides tamales. Come on. Your friends won't even notice we're gone." He took her arm and they moved to the table, and for the next hour she was separated from Noah.

Noah tried to stay away, to keep from constantly watching April. He even tried to flirt with Octavia to take his mind off April, but he found it a dull business. His attention wandered, his gaze following April, the pink of her dress a soft color that made her look more innocent and younger than her dance-hall dresses ever could.

Tom Branigan, a young man who had recently started a law practice, stood talking to April. Only inches taller than April, Tom was darkly handsome, pleasant, and until this moment Noah had liked him. As he watched Tom laugh with April, though, he wished Tom Branigan lived in Texas, or anywhere else but Albuquerque.

He had never felt that way over Fanchette, but until her announcement of marriage to Samuel Craddock, she had never given Noah cause to worry. Maybe he worried more about April because she seemed so alone and unprotected.

He knew he was trying to fool himself. Tired of watching April with other men, he set down his plate and extricated himself from a cluster of guests, including Octavia. He started across the room toward April, but before he had taken six steps, Gerta Yishay gathered them all in a circle to watch Aaron open his gifts. Smiling happily, he sat in a wing chair, and friends piled his presents around him. To Noah's annoyance, Mott Ferguson slipped his arm around April as they watched Aaron open each present, thank the giver, and comment on it. Some were lighthearted pranks. There were home remedies with careful directions: a jar of chicken gizzards to cure his patients of stuttering, goose grease and camphor for colds, and black threads tied with nine knots for sore throats. Aaron unwrapped a toy derringer "for your next fight." Another gift that brought laughs and rowdy suggestions was a silver star for the "Honorary Marshal who whipped the town bully."

Finally, as Aaron finished the last present, the guests parted while servants brought in an apricot layer cake burning with candles. Aaron blew them out swiftly, his eyes twinkling while everyone cheered. The cake was carried to the center of the dining-room table, where it was cut and served, and Noah found Octavia at his side once again.

It was almost an hour later when Gerta Yishay clapped her hands. "Everyone gather round. Tom is going to play the piano, and we can all sing. Come on, Papa."

April had finally slipped away from Mott Ferguson. She stood beside the piano while Tom Branigan sat down to play. She knew before she turned and looked up that Noah had come to stand beside her. All the guests joined in the singing, but to April's surprise, Noah's clear, deep baritone carried above the others. He had a good strong voice.

As she sang, she glanced over at Aaron. He was gazing at Noah, and April realized she wasn't the only one who had noticed how well Noah sang. His voice mingled with hers, both rising above the others, even though April sang softly.

At the finish, everyone applauded, and Tom launched into another, a Mexican folk song. They sang three more and then Aaron waved his hands. "Now, for my birthday, I have a request. Miss April, will you and Noah sing something for me?"

"I can't sing, Doc," Noah protested, his cheeks turning bright red.

Amazed, April couldn't believe he would be embarrassed over something as simple as singing. This tough, hard man was blushing to the roots of his hair. His voice was good, and it was absurd for him to refuse.

"Noah," she coaxed.

"I can't sing with you. You're good."

"Of course you can," April said, trying to hide her amusement. She reached out to take his hand as Tom rippled over a chord. "Sing with me," she urged, her fingers wrapping around Noah's.

His gaze shifted to hers, his hands moving, lacing through her fingers, the touch sending a special warmth back to her. And then he was singing with her, never taking his gaze from her.

The song was for Aaron, but all April saw was Noah gazing into her eyes; all she heard was his rich, deep voice that was resonant and masculine, a perfect foil for hers.

Noah's embarrassment over singing with someone as good as April vanished as he looked at her. Lost in her wide-eyed gaze that could always hold his attention, he sang to her. Her hand was small and warm in his, her voice clear and lovely. He forgot the party and the place, singing to April, enjoying himself beyond measure.

To April's delight, he knew all the song's verses, and they continued, wrapped in their own tiny world of music and silent longing. As they reached the last verse, his fingers tightened imperceptibly while he watched her with an unwavering gaze.

Aaron slipped his arm around Gerta's ample waist. He glanced at her, and she smiled as she gazed back at him. He kissed her cheek lightly and returned to watching Noah and April.

When they finished, Noah was startled by everyone's applause. Instantly Aaron requested "Drink to Me Only." Tom played a chord, and then they were singing again, April's hand still resting in Noah's. As before, the words seemed to hold a special meaning when Noah sang to her, "Drink to me only with thine eyes—and I will pledge with mine—or leave a kiss within the cup, and I'll not ask for wine."

Dear Noah. She sang with all her heart. She hadn't intended to fall in love with him, and it was going to be as disastrous as Emilio. But she loved him deeply, and allowed her feelings into her song, hearing his strong voice while his hand squeezed hers lightly: "But might I of Jove's nectar sip—I would not change for thine."

Finally, after the third duet, Noah turned and motioned to everyone to join them in a lively old tune, and they all sang together through the next two songs. When they stopped and Tom left the piano, the crowd dispersed. Noah saw Mott watching them, and he turned April toward the hall, moving across the room to Aaron's closed, darkened office.

He pulled her inside and closed the door, gazing down at the pale oval of her face.

"Noah, we should stay with the others."

He knew they should, but as if he didn't have control over his hands and feet, he had brought her in here against his good judgment. "I just wanted to ask you if Mott Ferguson has already asked to see you home."

"No, he hasn't. We didn't come together—well, he rode up when I was about a block from here, so we came together from there." She should remind Noah of his engagement, but she couldn't get out the words.

"Are you ready to leave the party now?" he asked in a husky voice. He was acutely aware of their complete privacy. In the darkness with April, he was drawn to her, knowing all the time that Fanchette was waiting hundreds of miles away. But April was here, only inches away, her hands still resting in his.

"I suppose we might as well," she said. "It's getting late, and most of these folks go to bed so early."

"What time do you go to bed, April?" he asked, and the words made her tingle. His voice was as mellow as when he had sung, the inflection taking away all impersonal curiosity and making it a very personal question.

"I think you know the answer to that one, you've watched my house so many times. I go to bed much later than this."

"So do I."

The words were ordinary; their effect was not. She knew she shouldn't go home with him, shouldn't be standing in Aaron's darkened office with him, but she didn't have the power to do what she should. Silence stretched between them, neither able to break it, neither able to go back to the party.

In the darkness, he could see her large eyes, her upturned face, her parted lips. They should rejoin the other guests, but he didn't want to, and as seconds ticked past, he realized April didn't want to either. And knowing she didn't made his pulse race.

She was the first to move. "I'll get my cape."

All he had to do was reach out and take her in his

arms. She would respond instantly. It took all the strength and willpower he had to let her walk past him and leave the room. Clenching his fists, fighting an overwhelming urge to reach for her, he watched her go.

I am an engaged man. April's here. Fanchette is far away. That's all it is. Nothing more. April was right here in town when I asked Fanchette to marry me. And Fanchette asked me to wed her when she first stepped into my arms, again when she lay naked in my bed.

His arguments were stormy. He left the room, blinking in the light, staring at Aaron, who was in the parlor doorway talking to April. Gerta stood beside them, and Noah joined them to thank Gerta.

"Happy Birthday again, Doc," he said, shaking Aaron's hand.

"Thank you for the nice bottle. We'll open it together to celebrate some very special occasion," Aaron said. If Aaron wondered what Noah had been doing alone in the dark in his office, he gave no indication. He took April's and Noah's hands, holding them together in his. "You both made my birthday very special with your singing. Noah, I didn't know what a voice you have."

"So nice," Gerta added while Noah blushed to his curls.

"Thank you again, Miss April, for the jam. I'll treasure every bite."

April smiled, her eyes sparkling, and Noah couldn't resist slipping his arm around her waist. He glanced beyond her and saw Mott Ferguson looking around the room.

"Night, Doc, Mrs. Yishay. Come on, April." He led her outside, where the air was chilly, the stars as bright as the candles on Doc's cake.

Noah draped his arm across her shoulders, thinking that if Mott Ferguson came out, there was no way he was going to let the lieutenant escort April home.

The door opened, and light spilled out. Noah drew a breath, his arm tightening around April.

"Miss April," Aaron said.

"Yes?"

"Tonight—is this the one?" he asked in a bland voice.

Her cheeks flooded with embarrassment, and she cut a quick glance at Noah, who was staring blankly at Aaron. It was a meddlesome question asked through the years, yet beneath the light teasing, April sensed the Yishays' love and care.

"Yes, Doc," she answered solemnly. "You knew that before you asked," she added hoping Noah wasn't interested enough to figure out Aaron's question and her answer.

"Good night, you two," Aaron said, and closed the door.

"Where's your buggy?" Noah asked, as if he had already put Aaron's question out of mind.

"It's in the next block. Mrs. Yishay didn't want Doc to see the horses and buggies, so we had to park far away."

"And Ferguson walked with you to the party?"

"Yes, so that should please you," she said merrily.

"Why in blazes would you think I'd be pleased over that?"

Startled, she glanced up. "You're always urging me to go out with someone." She stared at him and wondered if he were blushing. He looked as if his skin had darkened, but in the night it was impossible to tell.

"Yeah, I guess I did."

"So that should make you happy. As a matter of fact, he'll see me home if you'd rather," she added, holding her breath.

"No, he won't. I enjoy being with you, April. You make more sense than most folks."

"Why, Noah, thank you!" she exclaimed, pleased, wondering at the gruffness in his voice. There were moments when she was so drawn to him she thought she could curl up and faint, suffering as much as she had over Emilio. And there were moments she had a strong feeling Noah McCloud was as drawn to her as she was to him. The experience back in Doc's house had been peculiar. She couldn't fathom Noah, suspecting he missed Fanchette and was simply hungry for female company. It didn't matter what he felt or thought about her, he was going home to Fanchette Craddock, and April knew she had better not forget it.

"We sang pretty well together, didn't we?" he asked, suddenly turning to walk backward and face her, laughing in the darkness.

She laughed with him. "You have a wonderful voice!"

"The hell I do. I can carry a tune. I didn't want to sing with someone of your caliber.

"That's ridiculous! You sing as well as I do! It was fun."

"Doc can get me into more things I don't want to be in."

"What has he ever gotten you into?"

"Conversations," he said abruptly. "You've never seen my house. Come look at it. I brought a new bed and chair from Santa Fe."

"Noah!"

He walked backward into a berry bush in a neighboring yard. April grabbed his arm as he stepped into the bush and lost his balance. He clutched her shoulders, and both of them started to fall.

With a quick step Noah caught her to him and regained his balance, holding her against him. Both of them laughed. Her hands had slipped beneath his coat; his chest was warm through his shirt, his arms tight around her waist.

Breathlessly she wiggled away and laughed. "You better face front."

He grinned at her and turned again to walk backward. "That might happen again," he retorted playfully. "I think I'll keep this up."

She wanted to laugh and let it happen again, but she couldn't. "Noah, don't run into any more bushes," she said quietly, thinking of Fanchette.

He blinked, nodded, and turned to walk beside her. Silence stretched between them.

In a few minutes she asked, "Why are you busy

furnishing a house and rebuilding a saloon when you plan to leave at any time?''

"I don't like an empty house and sleeping on the floor while I'm here," he answered, and the lightness had gone from his tone. "I'll take my furniture to Alabama with me. The saloon is already earning good money, and I like running it. Besides, I'm toying with the idea of bringing Fanchette here. I like it here in Albuquerque. Sometimes, when I think of going back, the memories overwhelm me. It's easier just to stay here and hold all the good memories in my heart than to go back and face the losses and emptiness. This land is good, filled with opportunity.''

"Will Mrs. Craddock like it here?''

"I don't know. I don't think she'll want to move away from her parents and Alabama. If she wants to marry me, she'll come out here,' he declared, but his words had a hollow ring. He didn't tell April how many times he had started to write to Fanchette that he wanted her to come west, only to think of April and destroy the letter. He suspected Fanchette would never want to leave Alabama, and he knew if he wanted to marry her, he would have to go home. He lifted his chin, gazing at stars. "Maybe it won't be as difficult to go back as I think. Once I'm there, it'll be all right.''

There were moments when his toughness fell away and he sounded young and vulnerable. The moments were rare and they were gone almost as swiftly as they came, but at those times April's sympathy was stirred, and she wished she could console him some way.

They moved among the buggies and horses, and he helped her into her buggy. "Will you let me show you my house?''

She nodded, knowing she shouldn't, but all his talk about Fanchette and Alabama made her more keenly aware of how soon he would be gone out of her life, just as Emilio Piedra was.

The starry night was chilly, the air clear, the moon gleaming with the milky luster of alabaster. As Noah drove, he began to hum. "Sing with me, April," he said, and they sang together softly, their voices mingling above the creak of the buggy and the steady clop of the horses.

He slowed in front of a long adobe house, a portal with hand-hewn columns across the front, the dark vigas protruding, and *canales* to drain the roof. Pedimented lintels topped the windows and doors, and April knew that at one time it had been a grand house. An iron gate, broken and hanging by one hinge, stood open at the entrance from the street, an adobe wall covered with vines surrounding the yard. Wisps of gray smoke spiraled up from two of the chimneys. Noah helped her down out of the buggy, his boots crunching pebbles beneath his feet in a yard bare except for yucca.

He waved his hand, "I'll have to plant something if I stay." He unlocked a thick wooden door and it creaked as it swung open on a dark hallway, the faint gleam of a fire coming through an open door down the hall.

"It's so big, Noah," she said, looking around while he took her cape, his fingers brushing across her neck. He hung it on a hook next to his coat.

"I like a big house. I grew up in one. Some family named Morelos built this. It's old, as I understand it. It was a hacienda way back in time. Like some of the other houses around here, the walls are four feet thick." He grinned. "I can stand off an Apache attack here."

They entered the front parlor, where a dying fire still glowed in a mammoth fireplace. Thick vigas braced the ceiling, and she gazed down the length of the spacious room as Noah moved to the fire.

"Noah, this is so *big,*" she repeated in awe. "Don't you feel lost?"

'No, I like it and feel comfortable with it. When it's furnished, it should be nice."

"You must hate my little house," she said, looking at the wide beams overhead. In one of those surprising ways he had of suddenly focusing intently on her, he turned to face her.

"No, April, I don't hate anything you own. Your house is very pretty. I feel welcome in it."

"I'm glad," she said, forgetting all about houses.

"I want you to feel welcome here," he said, his voice dropping a notch lower while he touched her cheek.

"It takes a little getting accustomed to. I've never lived with a lot of space around me like this," she said, aware of his casual touch and aware her voice had become breathless.

"I'll get the fire going." She followed him to the mantel where he had two polished brass candlesticks with tall candles, a wood carving of a horse, and the little chunk of brick from Bel Arbre. "So you have your little piece of home here."

"Such as it is."

He knelt to throw more piñon logs on the fire, their aroma filling the room as the wood crackled and popped, orange sparks dancing up the chimney. There were a leather settee, a leather wing chair, one small table, and a glass-fronted bookcase along one wall. She looked at his few books, less than a half-dozen, seeing some of the same titles she owned among them.

Noah knelt at the fireplace, his black trousers pulled tautly over his lean legs and hard muscles. He had placed the lamp on the table and along with the fire-light, it shed a soft glow in the room. He stood up and faced her, his gaze catching hers. It seemed so natural and right to be with him; his house was an extension of himself, part of him she had never seen before.

Longing filled her as she stared back at him, wanting to feel his arms around her. As his eyes narrowed, her cheeks warmed. She wondered if he had seen something in her expression that revealed her thoughts.

"You like to read. You never mentioned that," she said, wondering what she was doing in his house, barely knowing what she was saying to him.

Noah watched her while she turned her profile to him. Her breasts were rising and falling with the short, quick breaths that revealed her excitement. Her neck was slender, graceful, like the rest of her, her hands moving over his books. He was drawn by a power he didn't want to resist. April was the woman present in his parlor; April was here to be kissed and held in his arms. He moved toward her while she studied his books, taking one out to turn it in her hands, returning it to the shelf, talking without looking at him. He didn't pay any heed to what she said, and he wondered if she did either.

He paused inches behind her, inhaling deeply, his broad chest expanding as he caught the scent of violets from her. He reached out to tug loose the ribbon that held her hair. She wouldn't so much as glance his way, but kept talking and looking at his books while he withdrew the ribbon and watched the cascade of golden hair fall free over her shoulders.

He dropped the ribbon and let his hands rest on her shoulders. "April," he said in a husky voice.

Instantly her words stopped, and the only sound in the room was the crackle of the fire.

Time stopped, and April felt as if her heart had stopped with it. His hands were feather light on her shoulders, otherwise he wasn't touching her, but she couldn't get her breath. She closed her eyes, fighting for control, trying to resist turning to face him. She knew if she looked into his indigo eyes she would lose her will.

"April," he repeated in a husky voice. He bent his head, nuzzling her hair out of his way to let his lips brush so lightly across her nape.

Sweet agony followed his kiss. She moaned, winding her fingers on the folds of her skirt. "No, please." She whispered the words so softly, Noah couldn't possibly have heard them.

"Turn around and look at me, April," he commanded, and she thought she would melt from the heat that fanned up in waves to consume her. She shouldn't yield to his request, though she wanted to more than anything she had ever wanted in her life. With a deep breath she turned around slowly.

Meeting his gaze was as jolting as a caress. His blue eyes seemed to seek answers to unspoken questions, answers she was sure he could get so quickly. He stroked her cheek; she couldn't look away or step aside or close her eyes. She was compelled to watch him, to let him touch her. He stroked her shoulder, his hand sliding to her throat, fingers splayed out beneath her jaw. He tilted her face up slightly, and his gaze lowered to her lips.

At the look in his eyes a tremor swept over her. He wanted her. He leaned closer. She watched him through narrowed eyes until he was inches away, and her eyes closed.

His warm lips played on hers, tingles radiating from each slight contact. She felt as if she were a bowstring pulled tighter and tighter. His arm slipped around her waist, his mouth moving on hers while she stood completely still.

"Put your arms around me, April," he commanded in his deep voice. "April, *honey* . . ."

The word was the final tug in a gentle war of wills. With a soft moan she yielded. She slipped her arms around his neck and her lips parted beneath his.

When he felt her response, Noah's arms tightened and his heart's hammerblows became more violent and erratic. He burned with desire and he fought to keep his own control, wanting to kiss her, to touch her, to pleasure her in every way.

He groaned as his arms tightened, and he spread his feet, fitting her close to his body, bending over her, molding her to him. She was sweet and fiery, innocent and sensual. April. He had no illusions. This was April in his arms, and he had never been more shaken with longing. He had kissed her long ago, never-forgotten kisses, and memory had not exaggerated them with time. April's kisses were all he had remembered.

When she finally yielded, she gave to him completely, with all the warmth of a loving, caring woman. She returned his kisses with a tempestuous abandon that made his blood heat. She was so slender; his hands played over her waist. His tongue thrust deeply into her mouth, and he felt her instant response, the tremor that ran through her. Her tongue playing over and

against his, her hands running across his shoulders,
her fingers winding in his curls.

He picked her up, moving to the settee to sit down
and settle April on his lap. He pulled her down against
his shoulder as he bent over her, kissing her passionately. With April in his arms, tomorrow didn't exist.
His body throbbed with desire, and he ached to run
his hands over her sweet curves, to discover everything
about her. Cradling her head against his shoulder, he
shifted, letting his hand drift down her side, feeling
the flare of her hips, her long legs beneath the yards
of fleecy alpaca.

April thought she would faint with ecstasy and longing. "Noah," she whispered between kisses that
seared to her soul. She had never been loved passionately by an experienced man until now, and her senses
spun in giddy pleasure that was heightened a hundred
times simply because of the man who was loving her.

Noah was pouring his love out in his caresses, trying to please her in every way possible. His hand caressed her throat, then moved lower, slipping down so
lightly, so languorously to drift over her breasts. She
twisted against him, her kisses becoming deeper, more
passionate. He caressed and fondled her, wanting the
material out of his way, wanting to feel her soft flesh,
to hear her moan and call his name. He set her up on
his lap, gazing into her eyes. He could see the questions and desire warring in her. She was wide-eyed,
gasping for breath, her mouth red from his kisses, her
cheeks pink, and he wanted her desperately.

He reached out with deliberation to unfasten the
clasp to Emilio's locket. The locket fell in his fingers
and he pulled it away from her neck, holding it in his
hand. The ends of the golden chain swung loosely in
the air. "Tonight you won't belong to Emilio," Noah
said in a husky, deep voice. "I want you, April."

She gazed into his blue eyes that had darkened to
the color of the stormiest skies. This was Noah, whom
she loved with all her heart. He wanted her. He hadn't
said he loved her, he merely wanted her. Sadness filled
her, longing, and a faint, growing terror that this might

be the only time in her life she would hear those words
or be able to kiss him and hold him. If she had his
baby from this night, her life might be lonelier than
ever; she might be even more of an outcast.

While she weighed the consequences, her heart warring with her mind, Noah reached up to unfasten the
buttons at her throat. He bent his head, his tongue
flicking out to touch her beneath her ear, to kiss her
throat, to push away her dress as he unfastened more
buttons. His tongue trailed across her flesh down to
her chemise.

April closed her eyes, winding her fingers in his hair,
yielding to him, for once taking joy where she could
find it, knowing what the consequences might be.

As he kissed her, Noah thought his heart would
pound out of his rib cage. His fingers shook when he
unfastened her dress. He felt as if it were the first time
in his life he had touched a woman, and the feelings
April stirred in him confused him. His blood heated,
roaring in his ears as she pushed her dress to her waist.
Her breasts were high and full, the pink nipples straining at her delicate chemise that he wanted to rip away.
He bent and kissed her through the material, taking a
nipple in his mouth, feeling the hard peak. He slid her
off his lap and pulled her to her feet before him to
push the dress down over her hips. It fell with a billowing of material while he unfastened his belt, pulling it free of his pants, watching her.

Her cheeks were deep pink. Blushes fanned over
them as he undressed her, and then himself. He tried
to go slowly, to arouse her as much as possible. He
hurt, he wanted her so badly, kissing her lightly, and
then passionately while he peeled away the last of their
clothing. "Touch me, April," he whispered, thinking
he would lose control when she did.

He picked her up to place her on the settee, kneeling
beside her. He kissed her deeply while his hands
roamed over her, touching her intimately, listening to
her soft moans, feeling her passion reach a frenzy.

She was lost to his caresses, wanting him, trying to
please him, yet stormed by the passion he aroused.

His hands were flames, his mouth driving her beyond
the brink of reason. "Noah, love . . ." she whispered,
giving herself completely, not holding back her love
or her body. Her hands tangled in his thick black curls,
silky to the touch. She kissed his broad, hard chest,
whose mat of black curls tapered to a thin dark line
down to his navel.

She made him shake with eagerness, and finally he
knew he couldn't wait. He moved between her thighs,
lowering himself, showering her with kisses, and
pausing for just an instant as she looked up at him
through lethargic, sensual eyes. "Noah, my love," she
whispered, her gaze running down his body.

He came down, thrusting slowly into her warmth.
April tried to keep from crying out; then his mouth
covered hers, his kiss deep as he thrust again.

"Move, April," he whispered. "Oh, love, move!"

She knew the words were said in passion, but they
made her tremble as she raised her hips to thrust
against him. Another sharp pain came, and her cry
was lost in his throat. She moved, and other feelings
began to override the hurt. She found herself caught
in a need that was more urgent than she had ever
known, moving with him, passion building until she
felt a burst of release and heard his cry again.

"April, love . . . oh, love!"

Rapture enveloped her. Her arms were around Noah.
He was one with her, her body and his united. She
loved him totally, and this love was stronger than her
young girl's love for Emilio that had never been carried to fulfillment. She had just given more than her
body to Noah in their union. She clung to him, moving
with him, lost in ecstasy, showering his shoulder with
kisses.

They were drenched with perspiration, Noah's
weight coming down on top of her while their heartbeats slowed to regular, steady beats. Noah kissed her
lightly on the shoulders and neck, shifting her, rolling
on his side and turning her to face him. He still held
her close against him, but now he could look into her
eyes while he lay beside her.

"You're wonderful, April," he whispered. "I didn't want to hurt you."

"The pain was gone quickly," she said, knowing the next time he hurt her it wouldn't be physical or go quickly.

He stared at her, and suddenly he pulled her against him in a crushing hug. She clung to him, kissing him lightly, tasting his salty flesh. He stroked her hair, his hand drifting over her back. When he released her, he was solemn, staring into her eyes. He traced her lips with his finger.

"You're beautiful." Something like pain flickered in his eyes, and he groaned. She ran her hand along his thigh, feeling textures and shapes, memorizing every detail about him she could, aware that guilt was filling him now.

"Noah, don't worry. I did what I wanted."

"April, if you don't stop touching me like that," he murmured against her throat, "I can't be responsible for my actions."

She laughed softly, feeling suddenly lighthearted and giddy, wanting him to laugh. He raised his head to gaze into her eyes. "I've wanted you since that night you fell out of the tree into my arms."

"When you thought I was a soiled dove earning my night's wages."

"What else would a man think! I wanted you just as badly every time I helped you with your wash."

"I don't believe you, but it's nice that you found me even a little desirable with soapsuds all over me."

"You didn't have soapsuds all over you. You didn't have them here or here or here," he said, touching her playfully, yet he was solemn. They looked into each other's eyes, and his heart turned over.

'Oh, April, you're named well," he whispered, kissing her throat. "You're springtime to me every time I'm with you."

She played with his curls, her big eyes seeming to devour him. "Noah, I love you."

"Oh, God." He leaned down to kiss her, his heart

pounding, and he was lost again, desire bursting into flames.

This time she was eager, raising her hips to meet him. Noah tried to go slowly, to tease her, but he lost control.

April cried out in unison with his deep voice as he said her name over and over until finally they sank down again in exhaustion.

When they stirred, they talked softly, Noah shifting to his side, his leg thrown across her. She had no modesty now, and she lay relaxed with him as if she were fully clothed and sipping tea in her parlor. She was a marvel to him, and he wanted to yank the hands off the face of the clock in the hall and make time stop. The fire burned low while they talked, and he made love to her once more, but finally she pushed him away.

"I must go home, Noah," she said solemnly. Their stolen moment of magic ended as reality crowded in too fast. He nodded and handed her a lantern.

"My bedroom's down the hall if you want to dress there."

She gathered her things, leaving him alone. As she walked along the wide hall, she passed dark doorways open on empty rooms. Finally she looked in one room and saw a bed. She stepped inside, closing the door behind her. Moving across the room, she gazed at Noah's bed. It was carved rosewood, as elaborate as the bed he had probably grown up with, and she wondered where he had found it. There were a table and washstand, another bookcase, braided rugs on the floor, and the last orange embers of a dying fire in the hearth. The bedroom was huge, and she couldn't imagine staying alone in such a house. Her tiny house would fit in either the parlor or the bedroom.

She ran her fingers across the bed. "Noah," she whispered, filled with love for him. She moved to the washstand, shivering now as her body cooled.

While she was gone, Noah went outside to pump some water, hurrying in the chilly night, coming back to sponge off and dry hastily, before pulling on his clothes. Worries plagued him. He didn't want to take April home. He wanted her in his bed, in his arms.

When she appeared in the doorway, she stopped, watching him tuck his shirttail into his tight pants, remembering how he had looked. A tremor shook her, desire flaring. His hair was tangled over his forehead, the sleeves turned back on his shirt.

"Noah."

He turned to face her. April looked so lovely, his breath caught in his throat. Her face was flushed from lovemaking, her mouth still rosy, and it took an effort to keep from crossing the room to her and pulling her into his arms.

"I'm ready to go home."

"April—"

"Noah, please. I'm a grown woman and I made the decision I wanted to. Don't say any more. I know you're engaged."

In an easy stride he joined her, getting her cape to hold it. She slipped into it, wondering how she had gotten through her speech. She wanted to throw herself into his arms and cling to him, and tell him how much she loved him and always would.

He was quiet on the drive home, going inside to light her lamps and start a fire. He paused at the back door to kiss her lightly. Releasing her, he started to step away, his eyes dark and stormy as he looked down at her.

"Oh, hell," he said, reaching back to yank her to him and band his arms around her like steel while he kissed her long and hard, making her heart pound wildly. She clung to him, returning his kisses, wanting him so badly. And then he was gone.

She locked the door and finally let the tears come. She loved him heart, soul, and body, as much as she could love a man. He would never be hers. No more nights in his arms, no lives to share. She sank down in the kitchen chair, placing her head in her arms on the table to cry, wondering why she selected so badly when she loved. In reality though, she hadn't picked either time.

* * *

Noah rode home, his emotions seething like a boiling caldron. Twice he stopped and looked back at April's house, torn with the urge to ride back, gather her up, and take her home with him. Fanchette. He was engaged to one woman and in love with another. He swore out loud. Was he really in love with April, or was she simply the woman in town and Fanchette was far away? He relived the past hours, and all thoughts of Fanchette and Alabama vanished.

In the morning he was going to show April his saloon. About six more hours and he would be with her again. Something moved up ahead. Noah peered through the darkness while his thoughts returned to April, and he forgot about drifting shadows.

When he entered his house, he returned to the parlor, where the ashes smoldered, the last glowing embers lighting the room. He gazed at the settee, seeing April there in his arms, wanting her back. Something glittered and caught his eye, and he crossed the room to pick up the locket, Emilio Piedra's gift to her. Noah held it in his palm, the golden heart catching glints reflected from the firelight. He closed his palm over the necklace and stared into the twinkling embers.

April deserved more than he had given her tonight. She should have courtship and a wedding. He swore savagely, thinking about Fanchette. Was he really going home to Alabama to marry Fanchette? For the first time he considered packing, going back, and forgetting the gold. He gazed around his parlor, inhaling the piñon scent, his thoughts drifting to Alabama and home. He moved to the settee, gazing down at the dark leather, seeing April there. The memories were so vivid it hurt.

He recalled Doc Yishay talking to him about marriage. He remembered a hundred different moments with April, a hundred other times with Fanchette. He thought about going to Alabama. He considered staying in Albuquerque. Each decision was wrenching and tough in its own ways. One single decision was impossible.

24

April's spirits rose with the sun. She bathed, washed her hair, parting it in the center and pinning it back behind her ears on either side of her head. She changed her dresses twice, as she got ready to meet Noah, her excitement mounting as time passed. She saw him riding up to the house, and it was all she could do to keep from running outside and throwing herself into his arms.

"Don't act foolish," she told herself over and over. But when he knocked at the door and she opened it to face him, she couldn't resist.

Noah stood frowning in the sunshine. April was dressed in her pink gingham, a smile breaking across her face as she threw herself at him.

He stood still for an instant, stunned by April's reaction, and then he moved. Catching her in his arms, he stepped inside and kicked the door closed while he kissed her, his set speech evaporating like windblown smoke.

When he released her, he gazed down tenderly for a moment, all his concerns and worries vanishing, his intentions forgotten.

"Good morning," he said in a husky voice. Her eyes sparkled and her cheeks were flushed. He wished he had shown more control last night, because she deserved better. His arms tightened a fraction around her.

April ran her hands over his shoulders, wanting him to pick her up and carry her to the bedroom and love her just as he had last night. This morning he looked marvelous, and she gazed into his deep blue eyes with wonder. She touched him lightly on the arm, on his clean-shaven jaw, his throat, dazzled by him.

"April, I can't show you the saloon now," he said solemnly; and for the first time she saw the somberness in his expression.

Like a fragile bit of crystal shattering beneath a crushing weight, her joy crumbled. She had simply assumed he would feel the same way she did—and she should have known better. No matter how much she had given to him—Noah was in love with another woman.

She moved out of his arms. He scowled and caught her, pulling her back. "Wait a minute," he said, his voice becoming gentle. "I think you just made the wrong assumption." He wrapped his arms around her again, gazing at her warmly.

Now uncertainty assailed her. For the first time since yesterday evening, she was beginning to face reality.

"April, I'm going to write to Fanchette."

"No!" She touched his mouth. "You've told me time and again how much you love her. Don't make a decision in haste, Noah, I won't let you."

He saw the stubborn lift to her chin, the color that rose in her cheeks. Haste had nothing to do with it, and he would have to convince her, no matter how she resisted the idea now. His mind was made up, and it was only a matter of time before April must realize the depth and sureness of his feelings. Keeping one arm banded around her waist, he touched her constantly, brushing his fingers over her arm, along her throat. "I know what I want to do," he said in a husky voice.

She looked away from him. "In fairness to all of us, you have to give it time."

He smiled and brushed the corner of her mouth with a kiss that tingled and made her draw a deep breath. "We'll give it time, but I know what I want."

"You thought you knew what you wanted when you asked her to marry you."

He continued to smile at her, listening to her foolish arguments. He would prove his feeling to her. He knew April loved him in return.

"As much as I hate to change our plans," he finally

broke in, "I don't have a choice unless I shut down the saloon. Duero's sick, Hosea has to go home early, and I'm going to have to work the bar. I'll show you the saloon another time, as soon as everything returns to normal."

"That's fine, Noah."

"April, look at me."

She raised her head. The sparkle in her eyes had been replaced by worry. He gazed down at her, wishing with all his heart he hadn't been so dammed hasty in agreeing to wed Fanchette. Suddenly his arms tightened and he leaned over April, his mouth coming down on hers hard, his tongue thrusting deep into her mouth. He kissed her until he felt her arms wind tightly around him, her hips move against him.

He swung her up, both of them breathless as he gazed down at her and saw desire in her eyes. "That's better," he said. "Let me worry about Fanchette." He wanted time to do things right for April. "I have to get back to the saloon. I just came to tell you what's happened," he said, wanting to pull her into his arms and carry her to bed.

"Of course, you go on. We'll talk when you're not busy."

He leaned forward to brush her lips with a kiss. Then he was gone. Dazed, she waved and went inside to close the door. He had always talked about his deep love for Fanchette that had blossomed years ago when he was a boy. April knew she couldn't let him do something hasty he might regret, but she wasn't going to be able to argue too long or hard.

Last night she had simply closed her mind to the future, but now she had to face it. While he wanted to break his engagement, April knew the moment Fanchette Craddock received word, she would come back to the territory. She thought about Fanchette's beauty, her ties to his home. She had been his first love. If Noah went back to Alabama, April would sell her house and move to San Antonio. Memories here would soon be worse than the faded ones there.

She moved restlessly, convincing herself that Noah

would not write to Fanchette. He would go home to
Alabama, where his origins were.

In the meantime, she intended to keep busy. She
moved around the house, idly looking at things, knowing she should search for a note from Ralph McCloud.
She tried to concentrate on the problem of the missing
gold and not think about the man it belonged to.

An hour later she was still wandering aimlessly, unable
to get her thoughts off Noah long enough to think about a
lost letter. Finally she sat down, closing her eyes and trying to remember everything she had done that night. She
tried to think of Ralph McCloud and forget Noah.

Lost in thought, she went back over her memories.
She stood up to go to the back door, determined to
repeat everything she had done that night.

Dimly she remembered the cold, the falling snow,
her fear for the Rebel's safety as she helped him into
the house. She went to the rocker in the parlor. If
memory served her correctly, he had sat there and she
had gone to the bedroom to turn down the bed. Trying
to imagine what he could have done in her absence,
she sat down in the rocker. If he had gone to another
part of the house, he would have left a trail of blood,
and there hadn't been one. Concentrating with her eyes
closed, she rocked, letting memories drift through her
mind. She had gone to the bedroom to turn down the
bed, and recalled dropping her cape on a chair. There
had been a crash from the parlor, and she had thought
Ralph had fallen, but he was still in the rocker. What
had caused the crash?

For the next hour she searched around the rocker.
During the break-in the cushions had been slashed, so
if Ralph had hidden a note inside a cushion, it would
be gone now. Returning to the bedroom, April couldn't
find anything to indicate a hidden letter. She had
helped him into her bed. She paused a moment, remembered him lying in her bed. She ran her hand over
the pillow, recalling how he had asked if he could
touch her. Noah's little brother—he had been brave
and handsome, as golden and fair as Noah was dark.
She tried to imagine them together, riding on a pros-

perous southern plantation, a life of gentle ease, so different from their future.

For over half an hour she sat there lost in thought. Her memories to recent times . . . to Noah last night . . . and a fresh spurt of worries came.

Her thoughts were interrupted by a knock on the door. She didn't have any appetite for dinner, but the Dodworths wanted her to come have a roast with them, so April went.

It was after one when she returned home and re-sumed her search. She tried to guess what Ralph McCloud could have done while she was running er-rands to get clothing for him. There was little that had been missed in the break-in, and she wondered if pos-sibly the intruder had found the note and her search was in vain. She refused to think there might never have been a note. She went to the armoire, shuffling through clothing to remove the long heavy cape she had worn. She studied it, feeling in the empty pockets.

Discouraged, she sank down in the chair, letting the cape fall across her knees as her mind wandered. *"I'm going to write to Fanchette . . . "*

As much as she wanted him to, April couldn't let Noah do something hasty. If Fanchette were here, last night would never have happened. It hurt to face the truth, but April had to. She wouldn't want to marry Noah if he truly loved another woman.

She leaned her head back, closing her eyes and re-membering every detail of the evening before. Long-ing filled her until it hurt, she loved him so. In her mind she went over his every feature, his thick lashes and powerful muscles. She remembered how it felt to touch him, to be pressed against him. In the solitude of her own bedroom, she blushed when she recalled all they had done. Struggling to get her mind off Noah, she returned to the search.

Soon it would be time to leave for the saloon. When she was busy, she could forget Noah for long periods of time, but in her quiet, empty house, thoughts of him plagued her. She shifted, noticed a thread dan-gling from her cape, and pulled it tight to break it off.

She looked down at her cape and smoothed it, her gaze falling on the wide hem. The stitches were uneven and crooked. Melissa and Mrs. Hatfield had helped her make the cape several years ago, and her own sewing wasn't very good then. She ran her hands over the hem eagerly, and sat back in disappointment. She thought Ralph might have hidden a note in the hem. By three she gave up her search and heated water for a bath.

She dresed in her blue gingham, getting ready to ride to the Brown Owl to work. She smoothed the cape. It was chilly enough to wear it today, and by the time she came home, it would be cold. The nights were longer now, and cooler, with fall slowly changing, winter approaching.

As she swung the cape around her shoulders, she glanced at the bed and remembered she had given the Rebel one of her old capes that had hung in her dressing room. She glanced at the clock and saw it was time to go, but her curiosity was stirred now.

She hurried to the armoire to rummage through it. The cape wasn't there. For a few minutes she wondered if the intruder who had broken into her house had taken the cape. She glanced at the high cabinets where she stored her blankets. Pulling a chair over to them, she stood on one and gazed at the shelf. The cape was neatly folded near a blanket, and April pulled it down, feeling in the empty pockets, disappointed again.

She spread it wrong-side-up on the bed, running her gaze over the hem. The stitches were smooth and even along the hem to the center of the cape, but there they became uneven and crooked. They doubled back and forward, and then once again they became straight. She ran her hand over the hem and heard a crackle as she pressed her hand on the double layer of wool.

Her pulse jumped and she glanced around the empty room as if afraid she might be watched. She sat down and pulled the cape to her knees, taking the scissors from her sewing basket to cut loose the poorly sewn threads.

25

Her pulse raced as she worked her finger beneath a thread and pulled. She broke the thread, and a crumpled, yellowed piece of paper fell to the floor. She smoothed it out on her knee. The handwriting was shaky, smeared with blood, and it saddened April to remember Noah's dying brother.

Noah:
   Gold buried in gulch thirty miles north of San Felipe Cathedral . . . road to Santa Fe . . . pile of stones beside trail west to river. When you reach gulch another pile of stones. Fourteen steps. Two flat rocks a stick on top of cache buried by river. Give April D. my share. Saved me from hanging. Bluebellies searching . . . killed officer and took stolen gold.

April looked up from the paper. *Give April D. my share.* That made her even sadder. How Ralph had buried a cache of gold with his wounds, she couldn't imagine. The hiding spot wasn't far from Albuquerque. Now Noah could go get it, sell his house and saloon, and go home to Alabama. And she didn't think he would hesitate for a second to do so. She smoothed the note again, knowing it was her farewell to Noah. The gold had held him here.

She glanced at the clock. She wanted to get the note to him, but it was past time to leave for the saloon. She folded the note, tucked it into her cape, and locked up her house. Then she drove straight to McCloud's Place.

Even though she worked in a saloon, she had never entered one except to go to work. She went around to the back door, where she found a man hammering boards into place for a floor. She knocked loudly at the open door, and he paused.

"Evening, ma'am."

"Would you please get Mr. McCloud for me? Tell him it's Miss Danby and it's urgent."

"Yes, ma'am. Right away." While he hurried into the front of the saloon, she looked at the new addition. It would be the biggest, most splendid saloon in town, no doubt of that. She heard steps and looked around to see Noah.

"April? Come into my office," he said warmly, curiosity in his gaze. He took her hand. "See the new addition?" he asked, watching her.

"It's going to be grand."

As if he knew she had something important to tell him, he led her into his office and closed the door behind them. "Today's been a hell of a day. One thing happening right after another. What's wrong?" His voice softened as he looked down at her, a tone that made her feel special.

"I found it." She pulled out the paper.

"Found what?" he asked, tucking a stray curl behind her ear. Noah knew it had to be something important to bring her to the saloon, but all he could think about was that she was here and he wanted her to stay. "Are you going to work now?"

"Noah, are you listening to me? I found Ralph's note." She frowned at him, but her annoyance melted as she saw the warmth in the way he was looking at her. "Noah," she repeated slowly, "I *found* Ralph's note."

"Jesus," he said, finally hearing her. "Where?"

A knock came and she put the note behind her back as Noah turned, scowling at the door. "Yes?"

The door opened and a man stood there "Boss, we need someone at the bar. Who should take over?"

"Go get Juan. I'll be there shortly." He closed the door and she held out the note. He moved beside her to read it with her, scanning it quickly. "That's not far at all!"

He took it from her and looked down at her, suddenly giving her a squeeze. "Where did you find this?"

"In the hem of a cape I gave him to wear. It's an old cape that I never wore very much, and it was hanging in my dressing room. At home I stuffed it on the shelf and forgot about it."

"It's a wonder the intruder didn't tear it to pieces."

"It didn't seem any different from the rest of the clothes. The paper was folded up and tucked into the hem."

Noah looked at the note, running his finger over it, and she knew he was thinking about his brother. He swore quietly.

"What's wrong?"

"This," he answered, shaking the letter at her. "I know one thing, my brother was honorable, April, no matter how bad this sounds. Strange things happen in war, but he didn't kill this Union soldier for his gold. He wouldn't have killed him without provocation."

She nodded. "I understand. Look at Tigre."

Noah smoothed out the letter and bent his head over it. He leaned so close to April that their faces were almost touching. She could smell the fresh soapy scent of his skin, the faint trace of tobacco on his breath, and longing swamped her. She yearned to touch him, to have him turn his head the last few inches and kiss her.

"Now you'll go get your gold," she said softly.

He looked directly into her eyes, and she ached to close her eyes, to feel his arms slip around her.

Instead, he gave her a somber, fiery look. "April, I'm sorry for all the times I accused you of taking his gold."

"Forget it, please. That no longer matters, Noah. I'm late for work. I have to go." She couldn't resist one last sweeping glance at him as she tried to embed the image of his blue eyes and handsome features in her memory.

"Ralph wanted you to have his share."

"I don't need a share," she said quietly, touched by Ralph's generosity. "I didn't do much for your brother—I've always felt I should have done more, but he was adamant about not seeing a doctor."

"I know you did what he wanted, and he didn't die on a scaffold or in prison. That's a consolation to me." Noah's voice was tender. "I'll go after this as soon as Duero gets back to work and I can get ready."

She nodded. "I'm late."

He didn't move out of her way, and she looked up at him. He slipped his arms around her, and her heart seemed to stop beating.

"April," he said softly, tilting his head, his mouth coming down on hers. His kiss was passionate, and he leaned over her, pressing her against him, squeezing the breath from her lungs as his tongue played over hers. Her heart pounded violently, and she kissed him in return. Finally he swung her up and released her.

"April, be careful. Does anyone but us know about this?"

"No."

"Don't tell anyone. The way news travels in this town . . . I wish you'd stay with someone until—"

"Noah, I'm terribly late," she said, knowing she couldn't go stay with anyone.

"We'll talk later. Thanks, honey."

She nodded and left, the word "honey" echoing in her thoughts. She climbed into her buggy and drove across the street to the Brown Owl, unaware of men on the street or of eyes that had followed her progress from McCloud's Place to the Brown Owl.

Duero Corinto was ill with a fever when Noah rode out to see him the next morning. By noon Noah had found a woman to take care of Duero, but he knew it would be several days before he could get away to look for the gold. Impatience made him irritable at work, and he tried to curb his temper. He had sent a telegram to Fanchette. It would take time to reach her, but was far quicker than a letter.

Shorthanded, Noah had to tend bar, but he made time to see April, if only for a few minutes when she passed on her way to work. Days passed and Noah sent Doc Yishay out twice to look at Duero. After the second visit, Doc said he was on the mend and would be back at work in another three days, so Noah made plans to spend some time with April.

On Tuesday, the sixth of November, Noah received a message from Fanchette. It had been sent from New Orleans, which lay between Baldwin County and New Mexico Territory, and he guessed what he would read.

Pulling his coat collar higher beneath his chin, he strode outside to read the message:

Noah:
    Papa and I are on our way to Albuquerque. You are so far from me and home, and I know this decision is because you are lonesome. Our love runs deep and far into our pasts. Please give me a chance to talk to you. *Chéri,* you owe me that. I send all my love.

Fanchette.

He swore, gazing at the street, seeing nothing. He didn't want to wait and talk. He knew what he wanted. And he didn't think he owed Fanchette the wait. She hadn't waited to let him talk to her. He sighed, knowing full well he would wait, even though his mind was made up. He wanted April. He couldn't bear to think of a future without her, and he wanted to stay in the West, in Albuquerque. The town was growing, and there were no bleak, sad memories here. If April preferred San Antonio, he would go there. He didn't care. It was April he loved and April he needed. He glanced down the road in the direction of her house. He wanted her to have a wedding and a fancy weeding dress, and a wedding trip. She had spent too many years alone, without things that she should have had. He wanted to spoil her and love her and shower her with things, to be with her and to keep her with him. And she should have her own children to love. He had to get back to work, but he wanted to go see her and tell her what he felt for her.

"Trouble, son?"

He looked up to see Aaron standing a few feet away. "Oh, sorry, Doc. I didn't see you."

"I know you didn't. Or hear me either. Anything wrong?"

People milled past, saying hello to both of them. It was a poor place to discuss one's private business. Noah tilted his head in the direction of his saloon. "Going that way?"

"I am, for a fact. I have to get some cabbage for Mama. Little nip in the air this morning. I might have a toddy to take the chill off."

As they walked along, Noah spoke quietly. "I got a telegram from Fanchette. Doc, I wrote to her, breaking our engagement."

"Is that a fact?" He paused to look up at Noah. "Sure you know what you're doing?"

"Come inside. With Duero gone, I have to tend bar. Hosea's kids are sick and he's at home. I'm short of help all over the place. And yes, I know damn well what I'm doing."

"I thought Mrs. Craddock was your old childhood sweetheart."

"Are you playing devil's advocate?" Noah asked as they entered the saloon. The pot bellied stove glowed warmly. A game of faro was going at one table, and another card game was being played at a table in the corner, but otherwise the place was empty. Juan was behind the bar, but as soon as Noah came, he left to go to the back to replenish the liquor supply.

When they were alone, Doc Yishay shook his head. "I wasn't playing devil's advocate. I just want to make sure you know what you're doing. Don't want you to turn around and break an engagement to Miss April."

"Don't worry. I want April for my wife," Noah said firmly, gazing into Aaron's curious eyes. Aaron stared at him, and Noah stared right back. Then a slow smile spread across Aaron's face and he nodded.

"I think that's nice. Mama is going to be very happy to hear this, son."

"And someone is damned happy to hear it besides Mama," Noah said dryly. "C'mon, admit it, Doc. You've been after me to do this since I don't know when," he added with amusement. "Here's your toddy."

"Thank you. I suppose I've been hoping ever since I first thought you and Miss April were in love with each other," Aaron said smugly.

"Aw, to hell with that. She wasn't and I wasn't . . ."

"Is that a fact?"

"C'mon, Doc, I haven't been in love with April since . . ." He paused and thought back over moments with her, memories making him forget Aaron's presence. He remembered that first night when April dropped into his arms, that first Saturday when she had done her wash and had soapsuds up to her elbows, her hair tangled around her face. "I guess a man can be blind to a lot of things right in front of him," he said softly, wanting to leave and go the few blocks out to April's house now.

"When it comes to love, I think a man can be blind as a post."

Worries over April returned, and Noah distractedly polished the bar. "Doc, walk back out in the street with me, where no one can hear us and I'll tell you something."

They went back outside, where the day was gray and overcast, a stillness to it that hinted of snow. They moved to the middle of the street and studied the saloon, Noah pointing at the roof, but he wasn't talking about the saloon. "I don't want to take a chance on anyone overhearing me. April finally found a note my brother had hidden in her house. It tells where he hid our gold. I'm going to go get it as soon as Duero gets back."

"I hope as soon as you return and put the gold in a safe place, you'll let everyone in town know you found it."

"I intend to treat the whole town to drinks. I wish April would stay with someone until then."

Aaron frowned and tugged at his beard, nodding. "You're right. And of course, she won't."

"No. Won't even discuss it. Working the hours I have been, I haven't had much chance to see her lately. I'll be damned glad when Duero gets back."

"I'll try to get Mama to call on her every day. Do you have to be gone long to get it?"

"I hope not. We can go back inside now. It's cold out here today. Fanchette is coming to talk to me. She asked me to wait until we have a chance to talk." Back behind the bar, he looked into Doc's bright, dark eyes.

"And you're sure?" Aaron asked.

"I'm as sure about my love for April as you were about Mrs. Yishay. I don't want to live without her."

Aaron smiled and patted Noah's arm. "I'll drink to that."

Noah smiled, but his thoughts were on April.

That afternoon, Noah told April there was going to be a horse race south of town the next day. He asked her if she would attend with him, and after she was finished singing at the saloon that night, he would take her to dinner. At exactly ten minutes before eleven he went to get her in his buggy, anticipation mounting as he approached her house. The day was cold and cloudy, snow threatening again. He'd packed his buggy with a light dinner, a bottle of his best brandy, and blankets. He'd had Maria make divinity, which he carefully wrapped in a crystal candy dish he had bought at the Hatfield store. He held it clutched tightly in his hand, ready if April flung herself into his arms as she had the last time he had come to call.

April opened the door and smiled at him. This time she was far more restrained than she had been on that other morning, and Noah wanted to see the eagerness and sparkle in her again. Each time he saw her, she seemed more lovely than the time before, and the deep blue she wore today brought out the blue flecks in her eyes.

"Hello, Noah," she said softly, so happy to see him. He smiled, his teeth white and even, and produced a package from behind his back.

"I brought you something," he said, and she realized he looked happier and more relaxed than he had since the first night she had met him.

"For me?" She stared blankly at the box a moment. "Come in, Noah," she urged, taking the box from his hand. She ran her fingers over a lopsided red bow tied on brown paper, but in her opinion it was the most beautiful present she'd ever received. He followed her into the parlor, where a fire burned.

Noah shed his fleece-lined sheepskin coat and watched her fiddle with the bow. "Go ahead and open it," he said. He wanted to pull her into his arms, but was determined he would try to do what he should have been doing since Aaron's birthday party—courting April in a manner she deserved.

She looked up at him. He wore a pale blue woolen shirt. It was a flattering color on him, and as much as she wanted to look at her present, she couldn't take her gaze off Noah. He realized it, but if he took her in his arms now, all his plans for the day would go up like smoke in the chimney.

"Shall I open this for you?" he asked, moving close to grasp the end of the bow.

"Noah," she whispered, unable to resist. She set the present on a table and slipped her arms around his neck, standing on tiptoe.

Instantly his arms banded her waist, and he pulled her close, slanting his head to kiss her long and passionately. Abruptly he pulled way. "Hey, what's this— tears? April—"

"I'm happy," she lied, wiping them away swiftly and smiling at him. She moved out of his arms to pick up the present. She sat down in a chair and removed the ribbon carefully, trying to slide it off the box so she could preserve the bow just the way Noah had tied it. He had told her he had wired Fanchette that he was breaking the engagement, but April still didn't believe

it would work that way, and all of Noah's arguments
to the contrary were unconvincing.

"April, the last race will be over by the time you
get that open," he said dryly, leaning against the man-
telpiece while he watched her.

She smiled at him. It was wonderful to have him
here. Eagerly she lifted the lid of the box and gazed
down at the crystal dish, raising the lid to find the
divinity. "Why, Noah, thank you!" she said, pleased
and thrilled that he would give her candy. She stood
up to walk to him and hold out the box. "Have a
piece."

"No, it's all for you."

"C'mon," she said, taking a piece and holding it
out. Noah leaned forward, slipping his arm around her
waist. "You look sweeter," he said in a husky voice,
bending down to kiss her again. The candy was forgotten until he moved.

"I think my backside is on fire," he said, smiling
at her and stepping away from the fireplace. "Get your
wrap and we'll go, or we'll miss the races."

"We'll take some candy. Let me wrap it up."

In minutes he helped her into a long woolen cape
and she pulled on her bonnet to tie it beneath her chin.
Noah stepped up to take the ribbons and tie the bow,
his fingers brushing her throat. "There. Maybe you
should tie it, April. I'm not good with bows."

She laughed and picked up her muff. "I'd rather
have you tie it. It's fine."

He helped her into the buggy and turned north out
of town onto the Sawmill Road, crossing the Albuquerque drain.

"Ned Hatfield's got two horses he's racing and
Duero has a horse."

"I'm sure Lean Henry has one. Noah, I'll probably
be the only woman there."

"Who cares? You're the only proper woman in the
whole country who sings in a saloon."

"I might not be," she answered, her eyes developing
a twinkle as her mood matched his. "And I don't
think I'm so 'proper' anymore."

His head snapped around and then he saw the sparkle in her eyes, and he laughed, hugging her against him. "Damned marvelous, if you ask me!"

She laughed and tilted her face up and he kissed her. He shifted back to his driving. "There'll be some women present. Mrs. Hatfield won't miss a race. She loves her horses too much. She missed one right after Melissa left, but she was at the last one."

"I hope Melissa writes to her mother, but she probably can't because of Mr. Hatfield."

"He can't do anything to Patrick now that he's out of the territory. Maybe that's what I should do today, just keep riding north right over the line and not let you go home."

"Don't be ridiculous," she said, laughing.

He kept his face solemn. He enjoyed teasing her. "We could get to Raton before tomorrow morning."

"Noah, we can't run away! You have responsibilities and I have my job."

He turned his head, speculation in his eyes. "I was teasing, but the more I think about it, the more appeal the idea holds."

"No! I'd rather have sleepless nights—"

"You've been having sleepless nights?"

She bit her lip, wishing she could take back the words. "A few," she admitted.

"Why, April?" The tone of his voice had changed, lowering to a husky depth that always made her tingle.

She stared ahead as wind whipped tumbling weeds across the flat ground, and her cheeks became hot. "I guess . . . I don't know."

"You don't know why?"

"Noah, you're teasing me again!" she accused, and saw the dancing twinkle in his eyes.

"I'm going to get you to admit why you can't sleep," he drawled. "C'mon, April, tell me why."

"You know why! How are *you* sleeping?"

"Naked," he said, and chuckled when her cheeks became a deeper pink.

"Noah, you're scandalous!"

''You're trying to avoid an answer. Why can't you sleep?''

Exasperated and embarrassed, she twisted around to face him. ''Because I keep thinking about you.!''

''And that keeps you from sleeping?''

''Yes, and you know full well why. I think it looks as if it's going to snow.''

''When you don't like to discuss something, you always change the subject. That's interesting, April,'' he declared happily. ''What do you think about me?''

Her cheeks flamed and she sat primly ignoring him, her hands folded in her lap.

''April,'' he coaxed in a mellow voice, ''tell me what you think about me that keeps you awake nights.''

''Noah McCloud, you're the biggest tease on earth!''

He dropped his arm across her shoulders and pulled her close against him to hug her, laughing as he kissed her temple. ''You can't sleep,'' he said, sobering, his voice getting husky again, ''because you're remembering the same things I am. And I'm glad, April.''

She gazed up into his eyes and hugged him, pressing her cheek against his soft coat. ''Noah, you embarrass me, and you know it!''

''I'm only teasing. I love you. There's Duero's brother, Miguel. He came in place of Duero, since Duero's been sick. He'll ride Duero's horse.'' Noah raised his arm to return a wave, and April pulled out of his embrace as they drew closer to the crowd.

''Damn, there's Tom Branigan and Mott Ferguson. So help me—

''You don't like Tom?''

''No, I don't like Tom when he talks to you or looks at you.''

''Noah!'' she said, staring at him in shock. It had never occurred to her that she could stir a shred of jealousy in any man, and she was amazed to learn she had done so.

''Don't look so damned suprised. April, sometimes you act more like you were raised in a convent than a sporting house!''

Her cheeks flushed again, and she looked at him shyly. "Well, you can set your mind at rest. I never think about Tom Branigan the way I do you."

"You looked like you were having a hell of a good time with him at Doc's party. I've never had a shred of jealousy in my body before, but I'll have to admit I don't enjoy seeing you laughing with some good-looking man."

She laughed, trying to bite it back, but Noah saw and frowned. "What's funny about that?"

"You're the one who has been urging me to go out with those men, Noah! How do you explain that?"

"You'd have to understand southern boys, April. Or at least Baldwin County boys. We're raised with standards and rules drummed into us. You respect and revere ladies. You keep promises. I was engaged and thought I should honor that promise, but I couldn't stand the lonely life you led. I urged you to go out, but I know I would have hated it beyond measure if you had taken my advice."

"Well, do tell!" she said, pleased. "I thought you really wanted me to go. How far back did you *not* mean it?"

"Never once," he stated flatly, and shock buffeted April. She had thought it was an indication of his deep love for Fanchette when he had urged her to go out so many times.

"Howdy, Noah, Miss Danby," Will Carter said, riding past and tipping his hat as they returned his greeting. Ahead, buggies, wagons, and horses lined both sides of the wide track that was marked off with a rope at the starting line and a rope at the finish line. April had never attended the races and was amazed at the crowd. Most of the men from Albuquerque were present. Some of the dancing girls were there, as well as some of the married ladies.

"Lean Henry is taking the bets. I'll park and be right back," Noah said, pulling up near the finish line next to a buggy with Will Brinks and Hannah Spears, one of Lean Henry's dancers. The starting line was far to her right, but they would see the winners with no difficulty at all.

"April, I've never seen you at a race before," Hannah called.

"This is my first," April replied, adding a hello to Will. Noah jumped down out of the buggy, striding along in front of the line of spectators, and April watched him. His legs were long, his hat sat squarely on his head, and the woolly coat made his shoulders seem even broader. Her heart filled with love for him.

"This is a first. And with McCloud. Any special reason?" She turned around to find Mott Ferguson on his horse beside the buggy.

"Hello, Lieutenant. I've never seen a race before. Mr. McCloud thought I might enjoy it."

"How soon before Mrs. Craddock arrives in town?"

"I didn't know she was coming," April said stiffly, the words reminding her of Noah's engagement.

"Sorry. Maybe McCloud hadn't intended you to know. We'll see some good racing today. Hatfield's got the horse to watch. Billy Boy. He'll beat them all."

"I'll watch for him."

"I'll be back," Ferguson said, nodding and riding on. She glanced around as Noah came striding back toward the buggy. He climbed in beside her.

"I saw Mott Ferguson."

"He stopped to say hello. Stop scowling, Noah," she said lightly, touching his gloved hand. "I don't enjoy Lieutenant Ferguson any more than you do."

Noah's features softened. "I'm sorry, April. I just want you all to myself. Maybe I'm scared some other man will entice you away from me."

"No, Noah, That won't ever happen," she said solemnly, and Noah heard the strength of the promise in her words.

"Now I wish we were out here alone."

"Mr. McCloud," someone called.

Noah turned around and a man approached, stopping near Noah's side of the buggy. "How's Duero?"

"He's better. April, meet Miguel Corinto. Miguel, this is Miss Danby. Miguel's going to ride the winner."

He grinned, his white teeth showing. "*Sí. Positivo.* Azahar will leave them all behind." He waved and left them. Two more men April didn't know stopped to talk. Noah introduced her, and while they discussed the horses, she glanced around at the spectators and spotted the Hatfield buggy across from them. Selma Hatfield was seated inside. Ned was gone, so she was alone. April wanted to go speak to her, but she didn't think she would be welcome. Selma Hatfield seemed to look her way, so April waved. Mrs Hatfield waved back, and April felt a little better.

Fanchette was coming to Santa Fe. April had known all along she would. And Noah would be caught between the two of them. And always, April came back to the same conclusion: he could be bound to stronger, older ties. And Fanchette Craddock was stunningly beautiful.

April studied him as he was half-turned away from her. He cupped his hands to light a cheroot, exhaling the smoke and listening to one of the men talk about Duero's Azahar versus Ned Hatfield's Billy Boy. Lean Henry also had a horse, Bonnie Jean, named for a dancer. The talk about horses meant little to April, because she was busy studying Noah. His hat was pushed back, his black curls tangled over his forehead, the cheroot clenched in his white teeth. He had unfastened his coat and pushed it open, taken off his gloves, and his hand rested on his thigh. She wanted to touch him, to be alone with him. But it was still grand to get to spend the afternoon in his company, even if they were with at least fifty other people.

The men finally moved on, and Tom Branigan, riding a roan, stopped on April's side of the buggy. "Afternoon, Miss Danby, Noah. We ought to see some good races today. This is your first time, isn't it, Miss Danby?"

"Yes, it is. I'm looking forward to seeing the horses race."

"You'll find it exciting. Watch them line up, and you can tell which ones are eager. For my money, I'm betting on Golden Hay. That horse can outrun anything that moves. I've heard talk Azahar is a comer, but I haven't seen him race before. I hear I'm going to accompany you when you sing at the Misses Dodworths' musicale next week. I wouldn't have consented to play for a bunch of ladies if you hadn't been the singer."

"That's nice, Mr. Branigan."

"They said you live across the road. I'll come early and escort you to their house. I just moved into my new office. I hear your brother is a lawyer too."

"Yes, he is."

"Wish I'd met him while he was visiting. He's got a reputation in Texas and the territory for being a mighty fine lawyer. Well, see you folks later." He tipped his hat and turned away, and April twisted around to look at Noah, who sat back in the corner on his side of the buggy, smoking his cheroot, his eyes narrowed as he stared back at her.

She laughed and touched his hand. "Noah, don't scowl!"

He grinned. "And you don't think of him the way you do me?"

"Not one little bit."

"Well, Miss Danby, he sure takes a shine to you. He didn't even know I was in this buggy."

"Of course he did!" They both laughed and Noah squeezed her hand. It was on the tip of her tongue to ask him when Fanchette would arrive, and why he hadn't told her, but she was having fun and Fanchette would intrude far too soon anyway.

Noah folded back the top to his buggy and sat down again. "We'll have four races and then stop for a time. That's when I'll get out the dinner I brought, but until then . . . " He leaned around, his long body stretching out while he reached into the back and picked up the bottle of brandy and two pewter mugs.

"Noah, I don't drink brandy."

"I'll be your downfall, April. It'll warm your insides. Try some."

She sighed and nodded. "I can't keep my reason when I'm with you anyway, brandy or not, so I suppose I will."

He grinned, holding the cheroot in the corner of his mouth while he poured their drinks and corked up the brandy again. He lifted out the blanket and spread it over both their laps, and April welcomed its warmth because she was getting chilled.

"Cold?"

"A little."

He pulled her close against him. "Noah, you shouldn't! Everyone in town knows you're engaged to Mrs. Craddock."

"They're going to find out differently. And I'll bet everyone down to the last little three-year-old kid knows I sent her a telegram breaking our engagement. This is not a town for secrets."

"That's because everyone is friends with everyone else."

She took a sip of brandy and coughed as it burned going down her throat. "Noah, I don't know about this."

"Best brandy made. The next sip will be better. And you'll warm up. Ahh, we're going to start."

Horses lined up far down the track. Noah leaned forward, and when the gun fired signaling the start, he stood up, watching them pound along the track.

"Come on, Azahar! Come watch, April." He pulled her up, almost spilling the brandy as he leaned forward. He yelled again, waving his fist, jamming the cheroot back between his teeth as he watched and April watched him. He was exuberant, happy, enjoying himself as she had seldom seen him do, and she was happy to be with him. He was full of vitality and energy, and she wished her future were bound with his.

"Come on!" he shouted. Everyone around them was shouting now, the horses pounding closer, their legs stretched out in long strides. They headed toward the finish line with four in the front of the pack, and a small lead between a black and a bay.

"The bay is Azahar, the black is Billy Boy," Noah said, dropping his arm around her shoulders and shouting again, his voice deafening in her ear. In the next buggy Hannah was screaming, calling another horse's name, and across from them, standing in front of his buggy, was Net Hatfield, shouting and jumping up and down.

The black and bay pulled ahead and Noah shouted. Miguel leaned over his horse's neck, and they charged across the finish line, Azahar ahead by a nose. Noah whooped with joy, sweeping April up in his arms, the brandy tumbling out of the buggy to the ground. "I knew it! I knew he could win!"

"Noah!" she yelped, laughing and embarrassed at the same time, her hands resting on his shoulders.

He laughed and set her down, jumping out to retrieve the pewter mug. "I'm going to collect my bet. I'll be right back, honey."

How easily he said "honey." How marvelous it sounded. She dabbed at a bit of brandy that had splashed on the blanket, and in minutes Noah came striding back, carrying a leather pouch.

"Paid in gold dust," he said, sitting down beside her. "I'll get more brandy."

"No! You'll just spill it again."

"No, I won't. We'll celebrate. I just won a hundred dollars."

"Noah, you bet that much!" she asked, horrified at the extravagance.

"No. I *won* that much! My bet wasn't big. Not many expected Billy Boy to lose. He was the favorite. Don't worry. My gambling has limits."

His horse won the next race, the following one he lost, and he won the fourth one. When they unpacked the basket of food, he was in good spirits, spreading the red woolen blanket on the seat between them to set out wedges of cheese, a jar of jam, cornbread, cold slices of roast prairie chicken, coleslaw, and small squares of spice cake.

While they ate, he watched her. "April, why don't you stop singing at the saloon? Luke said he sends enough that you don't have to do that to get along," he said casually.

She paused and lowered a bit of cornbread back to her plate. "That's an old argument, Noah. I don't want to be dependent on Luke. He has a family, and now he has Hattie to take care of. I've asked him not to send me so much. He won't listen, so I put it in a bank, because I intend to send it back to his children someday."

"Well, now, I don't think that's what he wants at all."

"You discussed this with him?"

His face flushed. "Yes, I did. I don't like the idea of your singing there."

"I can't believe you discussed that with my brother! You were engaged! What difference did it make to you?"

"It made a difference."

Amusement came as she gazed at him. "Well, Noah, that's the best way I know to earn a living."

His jaw rose in a stubborn manner, "It's just doesn't seem necessary."

"It is. Noah, when does Fanchette arrive?"

He blinked, a scowl coming to his features. "I don't know. Who told you she was coming? Aaron?"

"No. Actually Lieutenant Ferguson did today."

"Oh, damn. See? How in blue blazes did Ferguson know that Fanchette is coming to Albuquerque?"

"I didn't ask."

"Well, I had a telegram from her. She and her father were in New Orleans, and they're on their way here. I figure if they get the right connections and get a train part of the way, they should be here sometime next week. It doesn't take as long now as it used to. They'll probably come up from the south this time. But, April, it won't matter. I won't change my mind."

She took a sip of brandy. "What horses run next?"

He took her hand in his, raising it to his lips to kiss. His voice lowered. "I promise you, I won't marry Fanchette."

Oh, how April wished she believed him, but she didn't. She nodded, hoping to drop the subject. For today, Fanchette Craddock was a long way from Albuquerque.

The races commenced again, Ned Hatfield's Golden Hay winning. Azahar won another race, Noah won his bets, and finally they started back home before the last race. Noah wanted to have her to himself, and not find himself riding back accompanied by Tom Branigan or Mott Ferguson or someone else who had taken a shine to April.

By the time they reached town, it was time for April to change and go to work. Noah drove her home and went in while she changed to a brown calico.

"I'm ready to go."

"Sure you want to go to work?"

She laughed. "Yes, of course, I do!"

"Damn, I hate to think about you up on that stage with all those men looking at you!"

Amazed and pleased, she crossed the room to him. "No one has ever looked at me the way you do."

He grinned and slipped his arms around her. "I hope not."

"Are you coming tonight?"

A strange mixture of expressions crossed his features. "I hate to see you up there with all those men watching you," he said so gruffly, that her amusement vanished, "but I want to be with you." She gazed into his eyes and she saw desire flare to life. He pulled her closer, bending over to kiss her until she finally pushed him away.

"Noah, I'll be late!"

"Come on." He let her out at the back door of the Brown Owl, helping her down from the buggy. He told her he would be waiting when she finished, and they would go eat.

Noah sat in front of the saloon, leaning back, one foot propped on one knee, watching her constantly and she sang only to him, trying to ignore all the others. She was aware now that Noah didn't approve, yet she was happy about his reasons. The day had been special, unique in her life, and the thought of meeting him after work was exciting.

It was after twelve when she met him again and they crossed the road to have two steak dinners. Candlelight burned in the center of the table. The room was empty at that hour, but even so, they talked in hushed tones, Noah leaning close over the table.

"April, I'm going to leave the day after tomorrow to try to find the gold. Any day now it could start snowing, and when it does, I'll have to wait until spring."

"Should you go alone?"

"Yes. I'll be all right. This is one secret everyone in town doesn't know about."

"How can you be sure?"

"If nothing else, Aaron would have told me if he

had heard any gossip. I'm worried about your staying alone, though, particularly if I'm not here in town."

"I can't spend my life hiding."

He took her hand in his. "It won't be forever."

"Noah, you're always so positive."

Their steaks came, and he changed to lighter topics, talking about the races, the furniture he was having made, what kind of curtains he should have, finally becoming silent while he watched her enjoy the steak as much as she had the first one. It reminded him of her passion for everything, for singing, for work and in bed.

He drove her home and went up to the door. April unlocked it and pulled him inside, stepping into his arms instantly. As he kissed her, Noah shed his coat. Then he unfastened her cape and let it fall on the floor, moving her close to a chair by the fire. He pulled her down on his lap and kissed her softly until she lay still in his arms.

He suddenly shifted, pulling away from her. April ran her hands over his shoulders and up through his silky, thick curls.

"Noah, what are you doing?"

"I'm waiting. I should have courted you, April."

"Noah, I love you," she whispered as she hugged him and kissed the corners of his mouth. "That's absurd."

"No. It's not. I'll not have the whole damned town gossiping about you or a baby born too early."

When she heard the earnestness in his voice, she sat up and stared at him. "You mean it."

"Yes, I do."

"You're being true to Fanchette."

"April, that's crazy," he said gruffly, anger flaring in his dark eyes. "Oh hell," he said. He crushed her in his arms and kissed her wildly. Finally he stopped and once again pulled away from her.

"I hope that answers your last argument. I should have courted you, April, and done things the right way."

"Oh, Noah, how can you be so old-fashioned!"

"I'm anything but old-fashioned, honey. But I want this for you, and it's right."

He stood her up, pulling his clothes back together, picking up his coat. He patted her cheek and kissed her lightly. "This won't go on long, so enjoy my restraint while you can."

"Enjoy?"

He smiled. "It'll make our wedding night very special."

April was stunned. It was the first he had talked about a wedding, and she stared at him as he walked to the door. She followed, gazing up at him, feeling befuddled.

"I don't want my wife gossiped about. I want our wedding night to be special, April."

It would be special, she thought. But she was still unable to fathom that it would ever actually happen. "You never worried about gossip before!"

"I wasn't concerned about gossip when I met you," he said with a maddening calm.

"Noah, I can't sleep. I might not have you long, because Fanchette—"

He kissed her, stopping her words. When he finally straightened up, his lashes raised slowly and he appeared dazed, as if he had just heard what she had been saying. "You'll have me a long time, God willing, love."

"Tonight was fun, Noah. The most fun I've had except for the night of Aaron's party."

"Good. I'm glad. I wanted you to have fun. Good night, honey." He left, climbing into his buggy to drive down the lane. She locked up, smiling, remembering every minute of the day, taking her present to the bedroom where she could see it constantly. Noah was leaving to get the gold. She shivered in the warmth of her bedroom. Everything about the gold had been tainted. Ralph had died and her house had been broken into. She wondered if she would have been better off if she had burned the letter and never said anything, but she knew she couldn't have done that. It was Noah's gold, but she'd be thankful when he had found it and put it away safely.

26

Noah was taking a pack mule in case he needed an extra animal, and he carried provisions for several days' travel. It was a misty, cold morning when he left town, and Noah made certain that he remained alert throughout the ride. He couldn't forget that someone else was after the gold, and on several occasions he was certain he was being followed.

He rode due east, then took a circuitous route—he had learned from the war to use caution.

He twisted in the saddle, turning to look back at the mist swirling behind him. It fell over the town and only a few feet away the trail became lost from sight. Every few yards he would halt and look back, ears straining for any sound. Then, satisfied that he was alone, he would proceed.

By noon the mists had lifted, and a glorious sun came out with the chill of winter in the air. He could see for miles now, but remained cautious, watching to make sure he was alone.

He tried not to think about Ralph making this same trek, mortally wounded, struggling to keep the family gold safe. How thankful Noah was that Ralph had found April. When he had ridden about thirty miles north of Albuquerque, Noah began to look for the pile of rocks.

When he spotted a small pile of stones, some scattered beside the pile, he couldn't decide if that was the sign left by Ralph or not. So he rode past if for an hour and then doubled back, turning west to ride toward the river. An inner excitement mounted. More than for the monetary value, he wanted his gold be-

cause he felt it was a tie to his family and home, a
legacy given to him by his father, preserved by his
brother.

It took two hours of walking back and forth to find
the next pile of stones, and then he moved close to the
riverbank. He found a tall cottonwood and climbed it,
going up to the top to gaze all around. Land stretched
away in all directions, mountains rose in the distance
and the tumbling river flowed below. Hawks circled,
gliding with wide-spread wings on warm air currents.

He sat quietly for an hour. Two coyotes ran across
the open ground in the distance, later some deer
bounded into sight and then were gone, but there were
no riders. Satisfied that no one had followed him, Noah
climbed back down. He thought of April and all he
wanted to do for her; he wanted to give her everything,
and make her happy.

He went back to the stones and looked around.
Fourteen steps wasn't far. He searched for the two flat
rocks and a stick, knowing that by now the stick would
be gone. He spotted a flat rock and walked over to it.
It lay on top of another one. Once again he looked all
around to make certain he was alone. He knelt and
shoved the rocks out of the way. He took a shovel from
his pack and began to dig, rolling up his sleeves in
minutes as he began to sweat from the effort. A foot
of dirt had been displaced when the shovel clanged
against something metallic.

Noah worked quickly, uncovering a box. He dug
next to it and in seconds had unearthed another box.
He continued to dig until he had a large hole and four
boxes. He tossed down the shovel and pulled out his
knife to cut the cords around one box. As he pried
open the lid, he became lost in concentration over what
he was doing. His pulse raced in anticipation, while
all he could think about was his family and April. He
wanted to share this with her, and how he wished his
parents had known her. His mother would have loved
her in a way she had never loved Fanchette.

The lid flew back and sunlight glinted off ingots that
were as golden as buttercups. Noah felt as if he had

come to the end of a long road. "You go home to April," he said softly, running his finger along a smooth bar.

April cleaned house that morning, mists swirling outside, hiding everything. Gerta Yishay had been coming to call every day, and April couldn't figure out why. It wasn't like her to call so often. She would sit smiling and talking, her eyes twinkling, trying to get April to come stay with them at night for a while, but April didn't see the point in staying a few nights away from home. Eventaully she would just have to return to staying alone.

To her delight, that afternoon when she was in Hatfield's store, which also served as the post office, she had a letter waiting. At first she thought it was from Luke, but as she left the store and stood outside, she realized it wasn't from San Antonio. It was from Colorado Territory. Moving away from the general store, afraid that Ned Hatfield might step outside and take the letter from her hands, she paused in front of the shoe shop and opened the letter.

Dear April:

We are married now, as you know, and have settled in Colorado Territory. I won't write where yet, so if my parents question you, you can answer honestly that you don't know. I want you to know I am truly happy. I am sorry if I caused Tigre any hurt, but he will get over what we felt for each other. I love Patrick deeply, and he is good to me beyond imagination. April, I hope you marry happily. It is wonderful. I love Patrick with all my heart. Thank you for everything you did for us.

Our love,
M.

She folded the letter as a mixture of emotions stirred within her. She was thankful Melissa was happy in her choice, relieved they had settled out of the territory and away from her father. But it made her miss Noah even more.

When she finished work that night she rode home through a cold, clear night. Gazing at twinkling stars overhead, she thought about Noah traveling under the same stars, and she wondered if he had found his gold and was safely on his way back yet. She went inside, locking the house, feeling more lonely than ever when she climbed into bed. She lay in the darkness remembering her night with Noah, until finally she groaned and sat up, rubbing her temples.

"Noah, I love you," she whispered. She stretched out again, closing her eyes. She tried to think of Melissa, to get her mind off Noah, who made sleep impossible.

She drifted to sleep, waking as if coming up out of the depths of a well. She stared into the darkness, wondering what had awakened her, when she heard a scrape in the next room. Thinking it might be Ta-nehaddle, she sat up, but then she remembered he was in San Antonio. Another scrape came, and April felt chilled to the bone. She held her breath, her mind racing.

The six-shooter Noah had give her was in a drawer in her chiffonier, alongside the little derringer. As the days had passed, she had grown careless until she finally stopped carrying either one.

Someone was in her house, moving through her parlor. With a pounding heart she pushed back the covers and stepped out of bed. A board creaked and she froze, standing terrified and straining to see or hear. Her white nightgown would be easy to see in the darkness. Something moved, and suddenly the bulk of a man's dark silhouette filled her doorway.

27

Loneliness was something April had experienced many times, but never sheer terror. She ran for a window, yanking on it.

Boots clumped as someone ran toward her. Arms banded around her, pulling her away, and a hand slammed the window down, then clamped over her mouth. She was pushed to the bed, shoved down on her face. A knee pressed in the small of her back while her hands were lashed behind her.

It happened so fast she was in shock. She couldn't get her breath, and her back hurt. Spots danced before her eyes and she thought she would faint, but then the pressure of the knee was gone, and she was rolled over. As she gasped for breath, a handkerchief was knotted tightly over her mouth. She was turned over again while her captor tied the handkerchief behind her head.

Once more hands rolled her over roughly, and she gazed up in the darkness at a man whose black hat was pulled low, a bandana covering the lower part of his face. She had no idea who he was.

"Be quiet and cooperate and you won't get hurt."

She recognized the voice. Mott Ferguson. He moved away from her to light a lamp and pull the curtains, glancing at her. He selected clothes, throwing them into a bag, finally slipping on her shoes and sitting her up to put her cape around her.

He paused, his face inches from hers. "I won't hurt you. I'm going to use you to bargain with and I won't hurt one little hair on your head as long as McCloud hands over his gold. He went after it yesterday and he should return today. I've already sent him a message, and when he returns, we'll make the trade.''

She couldn't make a sound. The handkerchief around her mouth hurt, and talking was impossible. But she couldn't imagine Noah trading his gold for her, and she didn't want him to give it up for her. He had spent over a year searching for it, riding hundreds of miles. His whole purpose in life was to get it back.

Ferguson picked her up easily, gathered up the bag, and carried her outside, closing the door quietly behind them. He mounted, settling her in the saddle against him, holding her tightly. ''Don't struggle or try anything or I'll tie you up like a sack of flour and you can ride on your belly across a mules' back.''

She sat stiffly in front of him, worried about Noah, frightened of Mott Ferguson, and stunned by everything that had happened in the past few minutes. He rode across the back of her yard, heading east toward the Sandias, and she wondered if she would ever return to Albuquerque alive.

Skirting town, he went south first before heading east. As they reached the foothills and began to climb, she grew colder. The air was still clear, the temperature dropping. The bindings on her wrists hurt, the handkerchief cut into her mouth, and it was uncomfortable to sit in one position. She shivered against him as they climbed higher into the mountains, dawn breaking while they rode. When they finally stopped, they were high on a mountain slope, tall white trunks of aspen behind them. They were on a rocky promontory that jutted out, wind rising and whistling across it. Albuquerque spread in the distance below to the west.

He pulled her down off the horse and left her, ground-reining his horse, removing the saddle, and beginning to make camp. She knew if she ran, Ferguson would catch her easily. She couldn't get away from him, and with her hands tied, there was little she could do.

He built a fire and opened cans of food. She stood shivering, buffeted by the wind until finally she moved closer to him, staring at him. He glanced up and stood, going around behind her to untie the handkerchief.

"Now, Miss Danby, don't try to scream for help. There's no one around for miles," he warned.

"Here's some grub. You'll have to eat out of the plate off the ground like a dog if you want any." He set a plate down with slices of ham and eggs cooked together, beans steaming beside them. The food smelled tempting and hunger assailed her, but she hated to eat like an animal, so she sat back and glared at him. He shrugged. "You'll get hungry enough to eat off the ground."

"He won't give you the gold in exchange for me."

"The hell you say," he said good-naturedly, drinking a cup of steaming coffee. "The man's in love with you."

"He's engaged to a woman in Alabama."

"He sent her a wire. You're no virgin now, Miss Danby. You're Noah McCloud's woman as of the night of Aaron Yishay's birthday party."

April blushed hotly. "How . . . ?"

"How do I know? I followed you. I've followed him for weeks. And I've watched you. During Fiesta Miss Hatfield told me you hadn't found the gold. I arranged my duties so I could sit in front of the store to watch the street and McCloud's saloon. I knew the minute you found a map or letter, you'd head straight for Noah McCloud to let him know. And I was right. You didn't even look around. You went to his saloon and took a map to him, and then went to work at the Brown Owl."

She stared at him in consternation, realizing how careless she had been. "You're the one who tore up my house."

"Yes. We knew the Rebel was carrying Union gold. At that time we didn't know he also had his family's gold. A Union soldier stole that gold from a Confederate. It's a hell of a lot of money. We knew the Rebel had it. I thought it was gone until McCloud showed up. Then I knew it was still around somewhere and he thought you had it. It was just a matter of biding my time."

"You can't do this. You're in the army."

He laughed. "How long do you think I'll stay in the army with a million dollars in gold?"

"That's not how—" She bit off the words.

"Not how much there is? There may not be that much of the McCloud gold, but put that with the stolen amount, and I think it'll come out to a sweet million," he said, chewing a mouthful of beans. "The United States Cavalry can go hang for all I care. I intend to start a new life far, far away. I'll live in luxury. McCloud, for his part, will get you. We'll all be happy."

"He'll hunt you down."

"No, he won't. I'm not scared of Noah McCloud. He's settled in Albuquerque. He's in love with you. He'll give it up."

She didn't think he would, but she didn't care to argue the point. She had to find a way to escape.

"In the meantime, you might as well be nice. We're going to be together for quite a little while."

"How long?"

"I'm not telling my plans to anyone. I'll let you know when the time comes."

The next hours passed in silence. The cold food began to look good to her as hunger grew. She worried about Noah, wondering where he was and what would happen when he found Ferguson's message.

Mott Ferguson stood up and got his rope, coming over to tie her up. "I'm getting sleepy. You're going to stay right here," he said, tying her ankles and looping the rope through the one tied around her wrists. She could sit or lie down, but that was all. He walked away, unfolded a bedroll, and stretched out to sleep.

April was cold, hungry, frightened, and miserable. She couldn't do anything to get free, so finally, she curled up. She had decided to sleep when Mott Ferguson did, because whatever happened, she knew she would need her strength.

Wind swept across the land, flinging sprays of dust into the air while low clouds scudded overhead. Noah rode into town at night and went straight to the back of the saloon to his office. While music mingled with the howl of the wind, he unloaded the boxes from the mule, carrying them into his office to put them in his safe. He left one box to take home with him so all of the gold wouldn't be in one place. He opened the cabinet and removed brandy and a glass to pour a drink, throwing it down and letting the brandy warm him.

Someone knocked on the door and Noah turned. "Come in."

Music became loud, the chatter of customers and laughter of a woman carrying clearly as the door opened. Duero entered, a white apron tied around his waist. "I'm supposed to give you this note the first time I see you. He said it was urgent."

"Who?"

"That lieutenant. Ferguson."

Noah took the note and Duero left, closing the door behind him. Noah unfolded the paper sitting down in his chair and propping his feet on the table as he read:

McCloud.

You are to follow my directions and no one will get hurt. I have April Danby.

Noah's feet hit the floor, and he sat up, his eyes narrowing as a shock went through him with the swift violence of a bolt of lightning.

We'll make a deal. You get her back alive and unharmed. I get the gold. All of it. If you ever want to see April Danby again, do not tell another person. Do not contact Sheriff Pacheco or the military. Miss Danby will be killed in a slow, unpleasant manner if you do. If you'll deal, put a white flag on top of your house. I can see it from where I am. I'll contact you.

Experiencing fear such as he hadn't known before, Noah swore in a steady stream of expletives, standing up and jamming his hat on his head. He shoved the note into his pocket and stormed outside, mounting

up and swinging the horse around to ride straight to
April's. He opened the back door, stepped into the
empty house, and his spirits plummeted. He hadn't
doubted the note, but he had held out a tiny shred of
hope until he entered her silent house.

He lit a lamp and looked around. No signs of a
struggle in the kitchen or parlor. At the door of the
bedroom he felt as if someone had slugged him. The
bedcovers lay half on the floor, rumpled and tossed
aside. A faint smell of violets sweetened the air and
he could imagine April struggling with Ferguson.

Noah shook with a chill, swearing violently, his fists
clenched. Why had he left her alone? He slammed his
fist into a wall, rubbing his knuckles, wanting her so
badly he hurt all over.

Hunching his shoulders and turning his collar up to
protect him from the wind, he rode toward his house.
The town was dark and quiet, his thoughts seething
with fear and rage. Where was Ferguson holding her?
Lighting a lamp, Noah headed to his room in long
steps. He flung back the coverlet to yank up a sheet,
carrying it outside, where he tied it to a pole. He
scrambled to his flat roof to rig the flag up as high as
possible. Wind buffeted him and he had to secure the
pole with wires.

Chilled to the bone, he worked until the sheet rippled in the wind. He knew Ferguson probably wouldn't
look for the flag until daylight, but he couldn't stand
inactivity, doing nothing except worrying about her.

"There, you son of a bitch," he snapped. He
climbed down and stood in his yard staring up at the
flag, his only tenuous tie to April. He swore again and
went inside, moving restlessly, trying to think. Ferguson would watch for the white flag and then he would
have to get a message to Noah some way. He would
have to come into town or send someone. Noah swore
and kicked a piece of furniture, knotting his fists at
the thought of April in Ferguson's hands. He knew
how the man had tried to kiss her and how he had
wanted to take her out. Noah ran his hand over his
pistol, wishing he could do something besides wait.

* * *

Dawn came, a filtering of rosy light slanting through the tall, bare aspens, and a hush fell over the mountain. April was chilled and cramped, staring at Ferguson as he rolled over and blinked, coming awake and on his feet immediately, something, she assumed, he had developed through years of soldiering. After eating and allowing her to move around, he tied her to a tree again, her wrists behind her. "I'm leaving you. McCloud should have my message by now, and I need to leave the next set of instructions with him."

"You're leaving me here tied like this?" she asked, panic seizing her. "Wild animals or Indians could come—"

"Nope. Chances of that are slim. I've planned this a long time. I sent my men up here, one or two at a time, to sit as sentries." He chuckled. "Not a damned thing to watch for, but I wanted to see how safe it was. They've never been bothered by anything."

"There's always a first time. Suppose something happens to you?"

He paused to gaze into her eyes. "You better pray that nothing happens to me. Then you'll starve to death up here, but that's a chance we'll take."

"Please." He didn't answer, merely making her bonds secure. "You'll be gone all day," she said.

"Maybe, maybe not, but this is the way it's going to be." He stepped back to look at her. "I'll leave a plate of cold beans and a cup of water, and I'll be back as soon as possible. Don't worry. I want this over and done as badly as you do."

"He won't give you the gold."

He grinned. "I know men like McCloud. He'll hand it over. I think he'd give it to me even if he didn't love you. But as it is, there's no doubt what he'll do."

"If you're wrong and he doesn't, you can't go back to the cavalry now."

"I cut my traces behind me, but he'll give me the gold. I can promise you that much."

He mounted and turned his horse, riding out of sight down the slope. She leaned back against the rock, hurting, worried. She didn't think Noah would give up his gold without a fight, and one of them would be killed. She turned, looking at the rope, searching for the end where Ferguson had tied it. The knot was on the other side of the tree. Frustrated, she leaned back against the trunk, trying to work her fingers around to where she could reach the knots at her wrist, but all she succeeded in doing was hurting her wrists. She tried to think of some way to get free. There were no weapons; with her hands behind her back, though, she couldn't use a weapon if she had it.

Waiting was agony, worrying and wondering if the two men would have a confrontation. The wind died during the day, and the sun came out, warming her. It was almost dark when she heard the approach of hoof-beats, and she stiffened.

"April Danby."

Mott Ferguson rode up and dismounted. She waited, wishing there was something she could do. He stood over her and grinned. "He put up the white flag on his roof like I told him. That was a message to me that he'll deal. I left a message for him. He's to ride out here tomorrow and we'll talk, so he'll know you're all right."

"Please untie me. I can't escape with you here."

He moved around, and in a few minutes set her free. "Don't try anything. All you'll do is get hurt."

The sun was slanting behind the horizon, and after he let her walk around and stretch her legs, he handed her a plate of more cold beans, bread, and beef jerky. By now she was famished, and it tasted good to her. She drank several cups of water, eating every bite of food, worrying about Noah. "How'd you give him a message?"

White teeth flashed as Mott grinned. "I just watched and waited. When he went to the saloon, I slipped into his house. His servant didn't even hear me. I left a note right on his pillow; that'll make him madder than hell. He's to ride out here tomorrow and talk to us."

"Suppose he brings the cavalry?"

"He won't. I keep telling you, I know McCloud. I've ridden and fought with men like him. He can keep his mouth shut. He'll want you back in one piece."

* * *

Her nerves were stretched raw the next day when Mott Ferguson pulled her to her feet. "I'm going to tie you up again. Look there. What did I tell you. See that dust rising?"

Her heart thudded as she spotted the column of dust. Noah. While time passed, she stared until she could make out the lone rider approaching. The simple knowledge that Noah was near made her feel safer.

"I told you," Ferguson reminded her smugly. "He's all alone. He'll play my game, because I have what he wants. C'mon, sugar. First, you get dressed. I brought your things. And comb your hair. I want you looking good. Don't argue with me, or I'll dress you."

She gathered her things, moving behind a rock, dressing swiftly. She expected Mott Ferguson to appear at any moment, but he stayed where he was, and when she was ready, he glanced at her appreciatively. "That's the way, sugar. You cooperate, he cooperates, and we'll be through with this in no time. Then all of us will be happy."

"He won't let the gold go without a fight."

"He'll have to. And when he does, I'm gone. To hell and gone forever."

"He's a stubborn man, and that gold means the world to him."

"You're selling yourself short. You mean the world to him."

She turned away. She didn't want Noah to give up his gold for her. He would do it, but he would hate doing it.

"Tell me when he gets a little closer," he instructed her.

She watched the rider approach, and in another quarter of an hour Mott Ferguson stood up, jammed his hat on his head, and took her arm. "Come on. Cooperate now, do exactly as I tell you, or he's a dead man, do you understand?"

She nodded stiffly, hating what was about to happen. Winding through the trees, he led her down the mountain until they reached a grassy expanse, where he

paused behind a boulder. "He's to ride through the
foothills to the base of this slope. I left a trail for him.
He's to fire his pistol once. Keep quiet and do exactly
as I say. I can pick him off before you know what
happens. Understand?"

She nodded again and waited until they heard the
approach of hoofbeats. A gun blast echoed off the
mountain, reverberating in her ears.

"McCloud!" Ferguson yelled. "I'm coming out
with a six-shooter at her temple. You do one thing and
she's dead."

He pulled her in front of him, holding her tightly
against him with the muzzle of his pistol pressed cold
and hard against her head. They stepped into sight.

Noah sat on his horse, his hat squarely on his head,
his expression grim. He gazed straight at her. "Dammit, Ferguson—April, has he hurt you?"

"No. Noah, you don't—"

The arm around her waist jerked hard against her. "Shut
up," Ferguson whispered. "Drop the reins to the ground,
McCloud. Put your hands in the air while we talk."

Noah raised both hands. Wind blew strands of
April's hair across her cheek, fluttering the ends of the
bandanna around Noah's neck. His sheepskin coat
hung open, his six-shooter in his holster.

"She's not hurt, as you can see. I'll trade her for
your gold."

"No!" she cried, and received another tight squeeze
across the middle.

"Shut your mouth or it's over."

"Has he hurt you, April?" Noah asked again.

"No, he hasn't." How she ached to be in Noah's
arms! He looked like safety and security.

"She's telling the truth, McCloud. Not so much as
one little harmless kiss. She's been tied up, that's all.
Now, you follow directions, and you'll get her back
tomorrow. Have we got a deal?"

"Yes."

"Don't hold out on me. That Union soldier your
brother killed lived just long enough to talk. I know
exactly how much gold the man had."

"I understand."

"I hope you do. Your instructions are behind the bookshelf in your parlor. Just do as the note says. Now, get out of here. Ride away fast. One little squeeze of my finger and she's a very dead lady."

"Ferguson, I want her before I hand over the gold. I don't want you riding off with my gold and my woman."

"You don't hold the aces here, McCloud. You do it my way or you'll have a dead woman. I get the gold and you'll get instructions where to find her. Take it or leave it."

"Don't hurt her, and you'll have what you want." Noah gazed into her eyes again and winked. She gave him a smile that took all the strength she had. She didn't think Ferguson would give her up unharmed. He did hold all the aces. And in the past he had often been angry with her for rejecting him. She watched Noah ride away around a slope out of sight, and she wanted to cry out to him.

"Move quickly." Ferguson pulled her with him as they scrambled into the trees and up the side of the mountain. He kept his pistol drawn, turning constantly to look over his shoulder.

When they reached their campsite, she asked, "Please, untie my wrists again. They're beginning to hurt."

"For a time." He untied the bonds, working silently, glancing up once into her eyes. "I don't even want to kiss you. You're the coldest woman I've ever known. Give me a woman who'll try to please me. I'll bet you're an icicle in bed. Takes all kinds, I guess. Maybe he likes a cold woman. Maybe he doesn't give a damn. Maybe he's a little rough with you, huh?"

April clamped her lips closed and twisted her head away from him. He laughed.

"Colder'n a January pond. He can have you, April Danby. And you better pray he delivers." Ferguson walked around, straining to see through the trees to make sure Noah hadn't followed them back to their campsite. April looked around desperately for anything to use as a weapon. He had taken their eating utensils with him, and his horse was too far away to reach. A coffeepot was set on cold ashes, and two tin plates were on the ground. Then she saw the jagged lid of a can sticking up. She yanked up the can, trying to twist the lid free, working frantically. With a snap, the top broke off, cutting her finger. She jammed the jagged bit of tin into her cloak pocket, wrapping her hands in the end of her cloak to soak up the blood from the cut.

He reappeared, saw her, and frowned. "What the hell you got there?"

"Nothing. My hands are cold."

"Move over here. I'll build a fire."

She prayed the blood was gone, scooting closer and glancing at her hands. More than one cut showed, blood oozing from them, but Ferguson was bending down, stacking wood. She lowered her hand to wipe away the blood again, placing her hand on the ground and leaning on it.

"Ouch!"

He paused to look at her, and she held up her hand. "I cut my hand on a rock."

"How in thunder did you do that?"

"I don't know."

He came over, took her hand to look at it, picked up a canteen of water, and poured a little over her fingers. He pulled out his white handkerchief and tied up her hand.

"There. If he asks, you tell him the truth. I didn't do that to you."

"I know."

"I don't now how you did it. Must have tender skin," he said with a sly smile. He poured two cups of coffee and moved back away from her. "Go ahead. Have some coffee."

She drank, leaning back against a hard boulder, thinking about Noah.

At dawn Ferguson shook her awake. "C'mon. We're going to ride."

He picked her up, placing her before him on his horse. In the dusky light of the new day, she glanced back and saw that all signs of a campsite had been obliterated. No one would know anyone had stopped there. In the distance she looked at Albuquerque in the hazy light of early morning. Somewhere down there, Noah was getting ready to do something, either attack Mott Ferguson or hand over all his gold.

Streaks of ivory, yellow, and pink rays alternated in the sky, playing out above the mesa like a giant fan unfurled. If the circumstances had been different when she viewed it, she would have thought the sunrise beautiful. She shivered constantly, whether from cold or fright, she didn't know.

"Where are we going?"

"North. Where he can find you. I'll double back to get my gold."

"Please don't hurt him."

He laughed. "So there is a little bit of feeling in your icy heart! He's a cold man. Maybe the two of you belong together."

They wound down the foothills in silence and headed north while the sunrise splashed bright rays across the flat land. It was noon when they stopped on a rocky stretch of ground near a sloping hogback.

"Here's where we part ways, April Danby. He should find you about sundown." He dismounted, pulling her down. "Put your hands behind you."

"Oh, please, what can I do out here?"

"You can run away and get lost, get into trouble, get back to him. Hands out."

She stuck them in front of her. "At least tie them in front so it doesn't hurt so badly. There's no way I can get free."

He shrugged. "I suppose that's true." He worked swiftly, then paused. "Sit down."

"Please don't tie my feet."

"Sit down," he ordered gruffly, and she did as he asked. He bound her ankles, then tied the wrist and ankle bindings together. He stood up. "This is farewell. If he does what I've asked, you'll be back in Albuquerque by evening." He mounted up and rode away. While dust still rose in the air from his horse crossing the land, she struggled to get to her pocket and fish out the can lid.

Her fingers closed on the jagged piece of tin, and she felt a sharp prick as she cut herself on the lid again. She clung to the metal doggedly, though, praying she could get free and stop Noah before he handed over all his gold.

She drew out the lid, finally freeing it from her cloak, only to drop it. She grabbed it again and began to saw away at the rope binding her ankles. Clouds swept past overhead, the sun climbing. She was thirsty, and grew cold in spite of the cape. Wind howled across the hogback, swirling eddies of dust, a bird circling high overhead.

The sun was slanting toward the west when she finally worked her ankles free. Instantly she stood up, searching for Mott's tracks, and she began to hurry after them. Her wrists were still tied, but she didn't think she could cut them free. If she could just get back to where the men would meet, if she could get to Noah, he wouldn't have to give up his gold.

Following Ferguson's directions, Noah rode grimly toward the mountains. His mule followed, the boxes clattering together as the mule moved. He wore his knife, a six-shooter in his belt, and another in his holster. His Henry was tucked in the boot on his saddle. He hated how careless he had been. Mott Ferguson had been in his house to leave the note of instructions, was the culprit who had ripped April's house to shreds, and no doubt was the man who had followed Noah on occasion.

Noah condemned himself for not taking more precautions. He had been so lost in thought about the women in his life, he hadn't seen to April's protection. He prayed she was all right, and he wouldn't consider that she might not be.

The sun was high and warm when he reached the rendezvous. He unloaded the mule according to instructions, setting the boxes on the ground and opening them

so the gold glittered in the sunlight, plainly evident. He
stood and fired his pistol once.

"McCloud!"

Mott Ferguson's head appeared high above him on
the mountain, a rifle aimed squarely at Noah. "Don't
shoot if you want her. Go ten steps to your left."

Noah did as Ferguson said, pausing to look up.
"McCloud. Look down the slope to your right. See the
boulder beyond you?" Ferguson called.

"Yes," Noah yelled back, a faint echo sounding.

"Directions are behind it where you can find her. She's
safe and unharmed, but you better not waste time or she'll
spend the night out there alone and hog-tied. Don't come
after me. Get your directions and ride north."

Noah swore and did as instructed. He walked around
the boulder to pick up a piece of paper weighted by a
rock, but in plain sight. He was still in sight of Mott
Ferguson, who peered down, holding his rifle steadily.
It occurred to Noah how easy it would be for Ferguson
to pick him off and then take the gold and April. He
was ready to jump at the slightest provocation, his skin
tingling with wariness.

He looked at the map and saw he had a hard ride
north. He ran to his mount. "There's your gold."
Suddenly he drew and fired repeatedly. He didn't want
a shot in the back as he rode north, and he intended
to keep Mott Ferguson pinned down out of sight.

He fired again twice and then wheeled his horse,
galloping away, turning where the slopes would give
him cover.

Another shot rang out, dirt kicking up only inches
from his horse, and Noah leaned over his mount, urging it on faster.

In minutes there were no more shots, a haze of dust
marking the trail where he had ridden. It was an hour
later when he spotted someone walking, and he turned
in that direction, urging his horse to a canter. In minutes he saw it was a woman, and he urged the horse
to a gallop, catching up to her as she stopped.

28

Noah flung himself down, running to April to wrap her in his arms while she cried against him.

"I heard shots," she gasped, unable to express the fears for his safety that had tormented her every second since she heard the echoes of gunfire.

"We're okay. Shh, April. It's over, and we're both okay." He moved, pulling out his knife to cut her wrist free, swearing as he looked at the jagged cuts on her hand.

"Your gold—"

"To hell with it. Are you all right?"

"Noah. I'm sorry you lost your gold," she said, suddenly sobbing.

"April, stop crying, It's only gold. Please, honey . . ." He tilted her face up to his, "You're all right? He didn't hurt you?"

"No. My wrists hurt from being tied up so much, but he didn't touch me otherwise. Noah, I'll pay you back as much as I can."

He grinned suddenly. "Will you, now?"

She nodded, still crying. "Yes. I know what it meant to you."

He scooped her up and set her on his horse, swinging into the saddle behind her to hold her pressed tightly against him. "Thank God you're okay. Let's get home." She twisted, wrapping her arms around him, clinging to him while she cried. He slowed and stroked her head and back.

"April, it's over. Don't cry."

"I feel so terrible. You've hunted for your gold so long—"

"Not all that long," he said, smiling.

"And you had plans for it. It belonged to your family—"

He tugged on the reins. "April, stop worrying about the damned gold. I'm not a poor man. I've got a thriving saloon."

"I know, and Mrs. Craddock inherited enough for both of you," she said, still sobbing, unable to control her emotions.

"April," Noah said solemnly, tilting her chin up to gaze down at her. "Look at me." He wiped away her tears with his fingers. "Mrs. Craddock and I are no longer engaged."

"Oh, Noah!" She burst into fresh sobs. "You did that just because of that night. You don't know what you're doing."

He pulled her face back up. "Will you stop bawling like a lost calf," he coaxed gently, knowing the ordeal had stretched her nerves raw. "I do know what I'm doing. I know very well what I'm doing. And I can get along without the gold. Forget it."

"You're not going after him?"

"He has a hell of a lead, and no, I'm not. I have other things to keep me in Albuquerque, so he can just take the gold and go."

She stared at him in amazement, and he gazed back at her warmly. He didn't look like a man who had just lost a fortune. Far from it. He looked happier than he had most of the time she had known him.

"I don't understand you. You wanted that gold more than anything else on earth. You wouldn't go home with Fanchette because of it, you wouldn't give up your search, you bought a saloon because of it, yet now you hand it to Mott Ferguson with all but a pat on the back and good wishes."

"Not quite that, April, but I'm not going after him. And I got what I wanted out of the deal," he said warmly, leaning closer. "Can't you understand that?"

"You wanted me more than your gold?" she asked in a whisper, astounded that he might actually feel that way.

He laughed. "Damn, have I been that hard-hearted?"

"You love me that much?"

"A whole lot more than 'that much'!" His eyes danced with merriment, and she suddenly felt warmth stealing through her from her toes to her head.

"You do?"

His smile vanished and he stroked her cheek. "I'm going to see to it that you don't have to ask that question."

"You really do?"

"I just told you, I intend to court you, April, so you know you're loved."

"I want to hear you say it," she said stubbornly.

"I love you, April."

She searched his expression, her eyes gazing into his, and he met her squarely. She threw her arms around his neck and clung to him, bursting into sobs again. "Noah! Oh, Noah! I didn't know."

"Now you know, and you'll know better tomorrow and the day after that. I'm going to court you and propose to you in a proper manner, and I'll ask Luke and Ta-ne-haddle for your hand."

"Noah!" She leaned back, and her eyes were wide with wonder.

"How could you doubt after our night together?" he asked gently.

"You were in love with Fanchette then."

"Did I act in love with Fanchette?"

"Noah, are you sure?" She was still dazzled by the prospects.

"Would I have given away my gold if I weren't?" He was deliriously happy to have her in his arms, not caring how many times she questioned him. "I think the past few days of exposure to the sun have done something to your mind. I'm sure, April. Positive, absolutely certain. I have no doubts, no qualms. Forever, I know with all my heart, you are the woman for me."

"Noah!" She almost unseated him, she threw herself at him so violently. He caught her and held her as her lips covered his and her tongue thrust into his mouth. For just an instant he was taken by surprise; then his arms surrounded her, crushing the breath from her lungs. All his pent-up fears and worries for her safety drove him to bend over her, cupping her head with his hand while he kissed her fervently, as if he couldn't believe she was real.

Finally he released her, and she gazed up at him happily, snuggling closer. "This is nice," he remarked, "but I'd just as soon get back to town before dark sets in. Turn around so I can see where we're going."

"Your horse will keep moving. I want some answers to some questions. What about Fanchette?"

"She should arrive in Albuquerque any day now. And you let me worry about Fanchette. I imagine Fanchette will have no trouble finding suitors. And from what she's written to me, her father was a Union sympathizer, so there should be plenty of northern men who will be more than happy to meet Fanchette, and probably several she wouldn't mind marrying."

"You're sure about this?" she said, unable to believe him.

"I told you, I intend to convince you. Before long, you won't have to ask."

She tried to twist around to look at him better, "If you're sure, let's discuss your plans. You don't have to court me."

"Is that so?"

"Noah, be serious."

He pulled a long face. "Of course. Now, my dear, as I see it, I'm madly in love with you."

She laughed, and he joined her, giving her another squeeze. "I want to marry you."

"Ahh, at last, a proposal," she said warmly, thrilling over his words. "Say it again, Noah."

"I want to marry you."

"Oh, Noah! Yes!"

"I should ask Luke and Ta-ne-haddle."

"No, no, and no! You don't have to ask them. I can do what I want."

"I'm going to do this right," he said with a stubborn lift of his jaw..

"I hope that doesn't mean months of waiting."

"No," he said tenderly, stroking her neck. "It doesn't. Now where shall we go for a wedding trip? Name any place you want."

"After you just gave your gold away?"

"Stop worrying about the gold. Where would you like to go?"

"I'll think about it."

It was dusk when they reached her house. All the lights blazed from the windows, and a wisp of smoke curled up from the chimney. April rode behind him, her legs dangling down as she sat astride, her hands locked around his narrow waist. She clung to him for warmth. "Noah, my house—it looks as if I have company."

"No. I sent Maria, the woman who works for me, over to clean your house and get it ready for your homecoming."

He helped her down from the horse and carried her inside. She clung to his neck, smiling up at him. "I can walk."

"I like this better." Inside, he stood her on her feet, gazing down at her. He pulled her into his arms to kiss her again, as if to reassure himself she was all right.

"Noah, let me get cleaned up and change clothes."

"And then I'm taking you to the hotel for one of those steak dinners."

"We can eat here."

He shook his head. "Definitely a steak dinner. And first, before the steak dinner, we go tell Sheriff Pacheco so he can notify the cavalry. They'll go after Ferguson, but he's got a hell of a head start. I underestimated our opponent, and I was careless, April."

"Don't blame yourself. You told me not to stay here alone."

"Where was the six-shooter?"

"Tucked away in the drawer."

"We both underestimated him, and I should have known better."

"Noah, I meant it when I said I would try to pay you back."

He leaned down so his eyes were level with hers. "Didn't you hear what I said about a proposal?"

She drew a deep breath. He wanted to kiss her and kiss her and never stop. He had been badly frightened, worrying about her safety. He had been terrified about what Mott Ferguson might do to her, but now all he could do was grin and try to exercise control, because more than anything, he wanted to scoop her up and carry her off to bed and love her all night long.

"Yes, I heard, but I feel I owe you something."

"I'll think of some way for you to pay me back," he said in a husky voice, he eyes sparkling with love. "Now, hurry up and change so we can get the law after Ferguson. I'll heat water for a bath."

"I thought you wanted me to hurry."

"Would you like a bath?"

"Oh, yes! Why don't you go to see the sheriff—"

His change was so swift it startled her. "No! I'm not leaving you alone again, April. When I'm not here, Maria will be. I'm paying her to stay."

She laughed. "Noah, you can't afford to pay someone to stay."

"Of course I can." He placed his hand against the teakettle on the stove. "Ah, Maria did a good job. This is still warm. I'll fill the tub."

April followed him to the bedroom, where the tub was in the center of the floor. She laid out clean clothes while Noah filled the tub for her and closed the door, pausing before he shut it completely to thrust his head back inside. "Hurry."

Snow fell, swirling and tumbling down, blanketing the town and sending everyone scurrying inside. It was over two hours later before they were finished talking to the sheriff, who notified the calvary. Finally they went to the hotel, where Noah sat across from her and ordered two steaks. The darkened window was frosty, and the lights from the saloon across the street were fuzzy yellow rectangles while flakes spun against the glass, melted, and ran down to form ice at the bottom of the window.

Across the table Noah gazed at her tenderly. She was dressed in her pink alpaca, her hair tied behind her head the way he liked it.

He fished in his pocket and withdrew a box, opening it to remove something. "You left this at my house that night," he said, holding out Emilio's locket.

Her hand flew to her throat, a guilty look crossing her features. "I didn't know it was gone. I forgot."

He handed her the box. "I know you'll always have a special place in your heart for Emilio, but I'd like to replace his necklace with this."

She raised the top of the box to lift out a sterling rose. "Oh, Noah, it's gorgeous!"

"I wrote Ta-ne-haddle what I wanted, and he made it for me. I wanted something like springtime, because that's what you are to me," he said softly. Moving slowly, he took it from her fingers, leaning across the table while she bowed her head as he fastened the silver chain around her neck. When she looked up, he kissed her.

"Noah, we're out in public!"

"I don't care. I want the whole town to know I love you."

He removed another box from his pocket. "Here's something else. Will you marry me, April?"

"Yes. Oh, yes!" she exclaimed, her eyes dancing with happiness.

He removed a glittering diamond from the box and slipped it on her slender finger and leaned forward to kiss her again. April thought she would faint with happiness.

"April, when we marry, I'd like you to have my mother's wedding band."

"I'd love that."

"Now, bride-to-be, the first thing you do is give notice at the saloon."

"If I worked a little longer, I could earn something to pay back what you lost."

"April, forget the gold." He grinned. "Besides, I didn't give him all of it."

Her jawed dropped. "You didn't? He said he would know!"

"Ferguson was lying. No way in sweet hell could he or anyone else know how much was there except the men who had it in their hands. I gave him the stolen gold and a couple of bars of ours."

"How'd you know the difference?"

"We had ours in gold bars in boxes made at Bel Arbre. The other was in metal boxes marked with Mexican words. God knows who the gold really belonged to." He shrugged. "It doesn't matter. And you quit the saloon as of yesterday," he added.

"Yes, sir," she answered demurely and he laughed.

"And where would you like to go for a wedding trip?"

She lifted her shoulders. "I don't know. You've been more places. You pick something. We have to wait until Fanchette comes."

"How about a wedding about three weeks from now, December first?"

"I can't make a dress that quickly!"

"I've already thought about your dress. Maria's mother and sister are sewing every day, and you can go see them tomorrow and see if it's suitable."

"Noah, how long have you planned this?"

"How long do you think?" he asked, becoming solemn, desire flaring in his eyes so hotly it made her breath catch.

"Since that night?"

"Yes." For an instant they gazed at each other and longing flared, making them both breathless. He reached across the table and took her hand.

"Do you like my house?" he asked. "Is it too big?"

"Yes, I like it because it's yours. And no, it's not too big."

"Good. Do you like Albuquerque?"

She nodded and he smiled. "You're easy to please, April Danby."

"No, I'm terribly in love."

He blinked and drew a deep breath, his chest expanding. "Back to the wedding. Again, how about December first?"

Dazed, knowing only that she wanted Noah and wanted to be his wife as soon as possible, she nodded.

"We'll stay home for our first night, and then I thought you might like to go to San Antonio to see your family." He watched her eyes shine, her cheeks flush, and he wanted her more than ever before. "And then I'd like to take you to New Orleans."

"Oh, Noah, I'd love it!"

They paused while the waiter placed steaming steaks in front of them. Noah watched her eat, remembering that first dinner with her. All his appetite was gone, but he suspected she had had little to eat when she was with Ferguson. She had looked alarmingly pale and thin, but the color was back in her face now, and she enjoyed the steak to the fullest, finally putting down her fork.

"You haven't eaten."

"I'll eat in New Orleans. Right now I'm hungry for only one thing," he said in a husky voice, and she blushed. She turned her hand to look at her ring sparkling in the candlelight.

"Let's go, April."

Outside, as he sat down beside her in the buggy, he said, "I'd like Aaron Yishay to be my best man."

"Melissa isn't here, and she was my very best friend. I can ask Octavia to be in my wedding, although the last time she was around you, she couldn't stop flirting with you."

"I never noticed."

"Noah, you must be joking."

He laughed and gave her a squeeze. At her house he helped her down. "Maria didn't know to stay tonight. I'll be right outside, April."

"Noah, it's snowing. Come inside?"

"No. It's time I started doing this right. I'll say good night here."

She laughed softly, catching his wrist. "Come here, Noah. You don't have to start getting so proper now. It's a little late for that."

"I should have been all along," he said gruffly.

"Yes, you should have. Come on."

"April, I'm trying to do the right thing. I saw the Dodworths peek out the window."

"Did you really?" she asked playfully, opening the door and pulling him inside. He caught her shoulders, gazing down at her hungrily before he drew her to him to slip his arms around her and kiss her. She clung to him until he released her and stepped away. "Good night, April. I'm going to do what I said."

"Well, wait a minute before you go. I have something to show you." She left him, hurrying through the house, drawing the curtains quickly, and moving to the bedroom, where one small lamp still burned. She stepped out of her dress, letting it fall around her feet, then slipped on her wrapper, but left it open. She climbed onto her high bed and called to him.

"Noah, come here, please."

Noah frowned and crossed the parlor. "April, I should go home—" He paused in the doorway. She sat on her bed in her chemise, the wrapper falling open around her, her long legs tucked under her. She had untied her hair and it cascaded softly across her shoulders. His heart leapt into his throat.

He couldn't leave. "April, I'm trying to do what I should have done before. You should have a wedding, and everything should be right," he said gruffly.

"Everything *is* right," she replied in a quiet voice, gazing up at him, love making her eyes shine. "You love me, and we're going to get married. Come here, Noah."

His heart thudded violently as he crossed the room. Shedding his coat, he lowered himself to the bed to take her in his arms.

While snow tumbled down, covering the already white ground, lights glowed in the church windows that were steamed over inside, frosty outside. Music carried in the stillness of the snowfall.

Wearing a white peau de soie gown with a high neck, trimmed in Valenciennes lace, a white veil falling behind her, April came down the aisle of the church. Reverend Nokes stood at the altar, Winnie Dalrimple played the piano, Octavia Littleton stood to one side of the center aisle, close friends sat in the pews, but all April could see was Noah, smiling at her, looking so handsome in his black suit. She couldn't stop smiling.

Walking beside her, Aaron Yishay held April's arm firmly as they moved down the aisle. The white dress Noah had given her was a dream, and she felt as if she had never looked as pretty before in her life. Her eyes didn't leave Noah's, and when Aaron placed her hand in Noah's and stepped beside Noah to do his duties as best man, her heart beat with joy.

They said their vows, Noah gazing down at her, thinking he had everything in the world he wanted now. April was beautiful, her eyes shone with love, and he wanted to do everything in his power to make her happy.

He kissed her and they strode back up the aisle, laughing with joy. A party was held at the Yishay's house where Aaron happily opened the bottle Noah had given him on his birthday. While the festivities were in full swing, Noah took April's hand and they slipped out the back door to his horse. He put April

before him, holding her close. Even though she wore
her heaviest woolen wrap, Noah pulled a blanket
around both of their shoulders to shield them from the
snow.

Snowflakes sparkled on his thick lashes and he
smiled at her continually as she kept twisting around
to look up at him. April couldn't feel any cold, not
even from flakes falling on her cheeks, because she
was with Noah and that warmed her completely.

At last they were alone in Noah's big bedroom, a
fire roaring in the grate as Noah unfastened her cape
and tossed it aside. His warm fingers worked at the
buttons of her dress while she pushed away his coat,
reaching up to touch damp black curls.

He kissed her throat, the corners of her mouth, his
hands drifting lower. Framing his face with her hands,
April gazed up at him.

"Noah, how I love you!"

"Not even half as much as I love you, and I intend
to take years to prove it to you," he said as his fingers
tugged at buttons. "Years and years."

"Noah, we've never talked about it—do you want
children?"

He kissed her throat. "As soon as possible," he
whispered.

She smiled and stood on tiptoe to wind her arms
around his neck and cling to him, sliding her body
against his. "So do I. When I was a little girl, I used
to dream of my own family, and then after Emilio, I
thought I'd never have children. I'd like to name one
Aaron."

Noah smiled at her, nodding, looking into her ash-
colored eyes. His smile faded as longing came, and he
bent his head to kiss her.

April's hear pounded with a joy that was complete,
returning her husband's kiss, her new name running
through her mind: *Mrs. McCloud. Forever, Mrs. Noah
McCloud.*

About the Author

Sara Orwig is a native Oklahoman who has had many novels published in more than a dozen languages. She is married to the man she met at Oklahoma State University and is the mother of three children. Except for a few unforgettable years as an English teacher, she has been writing full-time. An avid reader, Sara Orwig loves history, acrylic painting, swimming, and traveling with her husband.